WE HAVE MET THE ENEMY . . .
AND THEY SURE AIN'T US!

Tomorrow the men and women of FAC would storm ashore at beaches called Redondo, Santa Monica, Huntington, and Newport. They would, I knew, be in for the fight of their lives.

Those beaches would be a living hell of pillboxes, dragon's teeth, tank trenches, land mines, sinkholes, and mutated creatures that would defy all imagination. A soldier could handle laser blasts and machine-gun nests, but try dealing with a six-year-old human child with the head of a bat coming at you carrying a satchel charge, or maybe a bulldozer chugging after you with fully functional human arms and legs grafted to the controls. I knew what the RIHMs were capable of and I shuddered to think what some fuzz-faced corporal would do when confronted by an enemy with the body of a woman and the head of a Labrador retriever. Personally, I'd sh$#@!

BLOOD AND BONE

Volume 3 of Eagleheart

C. T. WESTCOTT

A DELL BOOK

Published by
Dell Publishing
a division of
Bantam Doubleday Dell Publishing Group, Inc.
666 Fifth Avenue
New York, New York 10103

ISBN: 0-440-20241-8

Printed in the United States of America

Published simultaneously in Canada

April 1989

10 9 8 7 6 5 4 3 2 1

KRI

PART ONE
Across the River

1

Their bonfires lit up the night sky for as far as we could see, and the throb of their ceremonial drums echoed across the water through the empty canyons of the city. I decided either the armies of the Great Northern Horde were psyching themselves up for battle or it was the biggest goddamn weenie roast in the history of contaminated meat products.

"Cold night, Bucko," I heard the general mutter. "I'd sure as hell hate to be in your shoes."

That made two of us.

"Damn, Cy," I answered with my usual bravado, "if you think my shoes are bad, try slipping into a wet suit that's four sizes too small for ya. Feels like my gonads are blocking my sinuses."

"Sorry about that," General Skoff said, lowering his night binos and glancing (with some disgust, I noticed) at the unsightly bulges in my Plas-tex wet suit. "We got your measurements from your FAC-COMP file. How were we suppose to know you'd turned into a slug?"

I didn't bother to answer the old pile of bark. January 25th, 2045, was fast becoming the worst day of my life. Not only was I about to put life and limb in jeopardy against overwhelming odds, but I had just passed my forty-first birthday and had discovered what so many veterans of my demographic already knew —ten years of beans, burritos, and booze can't be worked off with a few weeks of low-impact aerobics. Trying to hold in my blubber gut and breathe at the same time, I lifted my own night-sight binoculars and quickly changed the subject.

"Judging by those fires, there must be a couple hundred thousand of the bastards over there, General," I said. "What are they waiting for?"

"A hard freeze, my boy," General Skoff answered. "A hard freeze. Soon as the river is frozen over, they'll be coming across with everything they've got. That's why your mission is so important."

Major General Cyrus "Mad Dog" Skoff was a delicate-looking little man with wire-rimmed glasses and a smooth pink complexion that always made you think he belonged behind a computer terminal in a financial institution rather than leading the Central Field Forces of the Federal Air Command. Yet his credentials were impeccable: he had fought against the RIHMs* for more than thirty years and had won four Distinguished Service Crosses to go along with six Purple Hearts and the Order of Lenin. He'd earned his nickname and the Green Star of Gallantry at the Battle of Mount Hood, when, as a captain, he and his company had single-handedly accounted for six thousand RIHM dead.

He was also one of the few flag-ranked officers in FAC who had never flown a high-performance jet aircraft or been advised to seek help from Smokers Anonymous.

"What's going to happen if they've already killed her?" I asked, not for the first time regretting that I'd allowed myself to get talked into volunteering for this fiasco.

"I thought I made that quite clear in the briefing," Skoff said impatiently. "Without Lieutenant Colonel Lane providing us with the RIHM order of battle and their crossing points, our forces are spread so thin that they'll cut through us like a laser through brain tissue. And if that happens, we lose Motown. And if we lose Motown, well, I don't have to tell you what that'll mean."

No, he didn't. While new defense plants and factories were opening every day in places like Saint Louis, Memphis, and Plantar's Wart, Arkansas, Detroit was still responsible for the production of nearly all new combat aircraft in the United States. Since our clear-cut domination of the skies was one of the few advantages we humans had over the RIHMs, it was easy to figure out that if Detroit fell, the entire country would be in a world of hurt; not only would FAC be crippled, but the whole vital midsection of the country would be laid open to invasion.

"Sure, Cy," I quipped facetiously, "it'll mean no more Diana Ross look-alike contests or wildcat UAW† strikes."

General Skoff looked at me like I was something caught between his teeth. Rather than do battle with those icy eyes, I turned back and once again trained my glasses on the enemy lines.

* Radioactivity-Induced Human Mutations.
† United Aircraft Workers Union.

The general and I were standing in the observation bunker on the roof of the old RenCen Complex down at the waterfront. From seventy-two stories up we had a pretty clear look at the Great Northern Horde of RIHMs that had been gathering on the Canadian side of the Detroit River for more than three months. Despite a daily bombardment from our artillery and SS missile batteries, Aerial Recon estimated the enemy currently numbered in the neighborhood of a quarter million, fully half that figure being warriors.

In the moonlight the river below looked like a thin ribbon of black velvet coiling through a flat empty whiteness. For the last twenty days or so every available combat aircraft in the area had been used to keep the ice from forming a solid bridge across the border. Thermal bombs, incendiaries, even napalm had been dropped all along the length of the river on an almost continuous basis. Still, even FAC could not compete with Mother-Humping-Nature. The thermometer had been hovering in the subzero range for a week, and the distance between banks had gradually decreased until only a few hundred feet of open water were still visible.

Despite the fact that we were warm and cozy in the Plexiglas shelter of the bunker, I shivered.

From the streets below, the low rumble of our H&I (Harassment and Interdiction) fire rolled through the night. Refocusing the night-sight binoculars, I could see the points of impact across the river as the artillery rounds turned the rubble of what had been the Canadian city of Windsor into more rubble. We all knew that any RIHM that close to our lines was far below ground in reinforced bunkers, which only a direct hit could penetrate. The H&I was no more than a wake-up call. Nevertheless, there was something reassuring about hearing our own guns in action, a man-made thunder rolling through the freezing Michigan night like a men's bowling league in full swing.

General Skoff checked his watch. "Right on time," he said. "Better saddle up, Bucko. Won't be long now."

"Christ, you can say that again, Cy," I said, clutching the crotch of my suit as though it was full of ice cubes. "Damn thing has shriveled up and hidden from the cold."

Those chilly eyes of his swept over me like active radar locking onto a target. "You, sir," he said flatly, "are an idiot."

Before I could form a suitable retort, an urgent-sounding male voice called from the hatch below us. "General Skoff, sir. Slipped Disk Leader reports B-1s at station Charlie. Requests permission to commence Operation Hammered Dork."

Mad Dog let his hands drop to the scrimshaw-handled 9mm handguns he wore crossdraw on his skinny hips. He gave me a very long and hard look before finally speaking.

"Permission granted," he gruffly called out.

"Aye, sir," came the reply.

"Well, Bucko," Skoff continued, suddenly unwilling to make any eye contact with me, "I guess this is where we part company. Can't say as I'm all choked up over the prospect of getting you out of my craw, but I never send a man out on a suicide mission without wishing him good luck first, so consider yourself duly wished the same. And remember, our science boys say even with constant thermal bombing, we can't keep the river open much more than six more days. You've got to locate Colonel Lane and either get her or her report back here before then or you might as well forget the whole thing. If those bastards come across unchecked, we won't have another decent line to defend until they get to the Ohio River."

"Damn, Cy"—I tried to laugh—"will you quit trying to cheer me up? Tell me the truth—I bet your old lady really looks forward to you coming home after a hard day's work, right? Where does she hide? Under the sink? In the bathtub? Out in the trout pond?"

"You're trying my patience, Bucko," the general warned.

"Aw, come on, Mad Dog," I teased, "face reality. Without a damn battle of survival looming around every bend, your life would be a drag, and you know it. So loosen up. Try to enjoy yourself. I'll be back soon enough, then we can bop till we drop. Just make sure none of your trigger-happy troops cuts me down when I come through wire, that's all. What's the goddamn password again?"

"Titty-whistle," the general mumbled.

I could've sworn Mad Dog blushed.

Along with a Major Bronstein from G-2, I took the inside elevator down to the basement of the RenCen Complex and got the rest of my gear. While we trudged on down to the mouth of the tunnel, he briefed me one more time on the limited amount of firm intelligence the Two-Shop had been able to compile.

"Our last contact with the MapleLeaf Underground indicates that if Lieutenant Colonel Lane is still alive she more than likely has been subject to some pretty intense grilling . . . not to mention panfrying and broiling as well as—"

I silenced the man with a slap across his face. He looked startled, but unhurt.

"Pardon me, Colonel Bucko," the major apologized as soon as the bleeding stopped and he'd regained his composure. "Your file indicated a certain bizarre sense of humor, and I was only trying to—"

"Stuff it, Bronstein," I said. "No joke is funny when it's that goddamn obvious. Besides, this is the love of my life we're talking about. You don't have to remind me what the RIHMs are capable of when interrogating spies. I've been there, pal."

"Yes sir, I understand. Can I help you carry some of that gear?"

I was humping about four times my body weight in equipment, and I guess he misinterpreted the wheeze in my voice as fatigue. "Major," I lectured, "no commando worth his salt lets another man carry his parachute for him. Just isn't done. Call it superstition if you must, but—"

"Begging the colonel's pardon," Bronstein interrupted, a confused look on his face. "I don't recall anything in the OP order about a jump. I thought the plan called for you to cross the border underwater."

He was right. I nonchalantly let the main chute and its backup slip out of my arms to the deck while mumbling some excuse about not having had time to argue with an overzealous supply sergeant.

By the time we got to the tunnel, I'd also conveniently "lost" a PRC-25 radio, three cases of MRE rations, a five-gallon can of grape Kool-Aid, and an assortment of knives, flares, and antitank mines, which I had decided would only tend to weigh me down once in the water. For about the five-hundredth time since being recalled to active duty, I reminded myself that I was out of practice for this sort of thing and wished there was some way to haul Melodie's chestnuts out of the fire without risking my own out-of-shape butt.

"Sorry about the wet suit, Colonel," I heard Bronstein say as we picked our way through the concertina barbed wire and bristling steel hedgehogs set up around the tunnel's entrance. "If we'd had a little more time, we might've been able to find a larger size for you. I hope that one isn't too uncomfortable."

The ultrathin Plas-tex wet suit hugged my body like a ribbed condom that had met its match. Unsightly bulges of flesh around my midriff looked like puff-pastry batter under high pressure, and a good three inches of pale skin showed at both ankles and wrists. Most embarrassing, however, was that each time I took a step my thighs rubbed together and made a sound like hands sliding across the surface of an overinflated party balloon.

Major Bronstein wasn't the only one who had noticed the tight fit of my wet suit. As we passed one of the gun emplacements, I heard a female voice speaking in a loud whisper.

"Holy shit, Dinks! Check out the fuckin porker down there. Looks like a link of kielbasa, don't he. Mean ta tell me the hopes of the free world are hanging on that? Hell, do me a favor and cut my throat."

What could I say? True, I had been breveted a lieutenant colonel for this mission and had every right to climb up into that gun pit and chew ass. But what good would it have done? I'd still be thirty pounds overweight.

The major and I entered the tunnel and moved forward until we reached the water's edge. It was at that point that I slipped into my flippers and began going through a final predive check. The lightweight oxygen canisters would give me three hours of air as well as enough compression to operate the Remington 20mm on my forearm. The arc light in my helmet was fully charged, and the infrared aiming device for the Remington had been calibrated for my height. The breathing regulator seemed to be working fine, and my wrist compass/chronometer/video recorder was functioning perfectly.

There was only one thing left to do. I reached into my ditty bag and pulled out an eight-ounce olive-drab plastic can, then broke the seal.

"Good Godfrey, man!" the major exclaimed, immediately squeezing his nostrils with his fingers. "What in the name of all that's holy is that?"

"Rendered RIHM fat, Major." I chuckled, reaching into the

can with my fingers and digging out a large dollop of the sickly yellow gunk. "Not only will it keep those bastards from picking up my scent when I get over to the other side, but it's also the best insulator in the world."

"But . . . but how can you stand the smell?" The poor man gagged as I smeared the stuff over the wet suit as well as my exposed flesh.

"You get used to it. Hell, you think this is bad, you oughta get a whiff of a Calcutta whorehouse on a hot morning after payday. Geez, one sniff and your tongue turns black and your eyebrows fall off. Or is it the other way around?"

Major Bronstein didn't remain to answer my ruminations. Last I saw of him, he was staggering back out of the tunnel, coughing and retching as he went. The joke was on him: I'd never been to Calcutta in my life.

The first shock wave from Operation Hammered Dork shook me out of my revelry. A little more than two miles away an island in the river called Belle Isle was about to be pulverized by two squadrons of BICS (B-1C bombers). FAC and the RIHMs had been battling over the island for weeks; our troops would take it by day, the mutants would then slip in at night and steal it back. While its strategic value was apparently almost nill, it was still a hotly contested piece of real estate, simply because both sides wanted it. Tonight, however, the bombing served a dual purpose. Not only were RIHMs being evaporated, but a diversion was being provided to cover the midnight swim of yours truly.

As the shock waves of exploding five thousand pounders shook the sand out of my joints, I took one long last look into the darkness in front of me, then crawled into the frigid black water and began to swim.

Once again, I realized, the fate of the nation—nay, the entire free world—rested squarely on my shoulders.

2

Thirty feet under the mud of the river bottom, I swam through the relics of Motown's past. The tunnel had once been a conduit for ground traffic and commerce between two friendly nations. Now, in the fourth decade after the Big Blast, the Detroit-Windsor Tunnel was only a decaying reminder of what had once been the glory of twentieth-century technology.

Yet even in its old age, the tunnel had served its purpose long and well, right up until the moment the lead elements of the Great Northern Horde approached its mouth on the Canadian side. At the same time, in accordance with the joint executive order previously issued by the President and the Canadian Prime Minister, tracs, Land Rovers, hover buses, and a few hundred other means of land transport were driven into the tube and left there in place. Then, as the last human refugees stumbled up into the sunlight on the American side of the border, the Federal Corps of Environmental Engineers (FECEES) pulled the plug on the old girl, opening a hundred preplaced valves, which allowed the river to pour in. The tunnel was soon as clogged as an old man's arteries.

Along with the blowing of the Ambassador Bridge further down river, this tactic successfully stopped the RIHM invasion in its slimy tracks . . . for the time being.

Swimming through an underwater junkyard in the dark is not my idea of a good use of quality time, but I was doing it anyway, and paying the price. I estimated I was only halfway through when the warning light on my first air canister started blinking at me.

Great. The going had been slower than I'd anticipated because the turbulence of the river had thrown some of the vehicles on top of each other. I'd been forced to swim through a number of vehicles rather than around or over them. This took time, more time than I would have liked. I was trying to recalculate my point of no return when I came face-to-face with what I took to be my predecessor.

Actually, "face-to-face" isn't a very apt description. Tell you the truth, in the glow of my helmet's arc light the guy had very little left in the way of facial features. True, there were two empty eye sockets and a little nub of gelatinous flesh that might've been a nose, but it appeared that something (or someone?) had gnawed off most of his lower jaw and both his ears. The only real evidence that he was from FAC was a few tatters of wet suit still clinging to what remained of his torso, and the FAC identity decal hot-stamped on the left shoulder.

"Well, Perry," I said into the underwater voice enhancer as I quickly videotaped the decal, "your folks will be glad to know you didn't go over the hill after all. Means they can collect on your FAC life insurance without going to a court of inquiry. Ha ha. Only kidding, pal. Listen, Per, nod if you understand what I'm saying, okay, buddy? . . . On second thought, don't."

The banter was, of course, for my benefit only. By the looks of it, Perry had told his last sea story several weeks before. My chatter was designed to calm my own nerves. Quite frankly, I didn't like the way things were going at all.

Major Bronstein and the other intelligence poags on the General Staff had briefed me on FAC's previous attempts to rescue Melodie Lane. Five different times one of our boys had tried to slip across the border on the surface of the river, and five times they were seen being captured and sucked dry by RIHM sentries. What with enemy "sniffer" radar, starlight video, heat sensors, and the fact that the river offered no cover to conceal movement, it seemed our boys were doomed from the start.

My new pal Perry had been the latest guinea pig of G-2's experimentation. They'd figured a lone diver might be able to sneak through the tunnel and be out into the open before anyone at RIHM Command was the wiser. Captain Perry Chillers, Blood type O, Religion Protestant, FAC #A339-65D-7, had volunteered. When good ol' Per hadn't shown up back in CONUS two weeks after slipping over the side, the staff boys had figured he'd gotten waxed farther inland. So much for bad dope. Perry had lost his life and his face right there in the tunnel, and he wasn't even Oriental.

I had a couple of yuks over that thought until I realized that I still didn't have any idea what Captain Chillers had encountered down there in the dark besides derelict vehicles and water as cold as snowballs in your armpit. Northern RIHMs? I doubted it. Unlike the Island RIHMs down in the Caribbean, the Northern Horde were not swimmers. In fact, one of the reasons they'd delayed their invasion so long was their general aversion to water. Obviously, whatever had delayed Captain Chillers had not been a patrol of Northern RIHM grunts doing the breaststroke.

Time to return to the RenCen, I decided, and let the computer hackers figure out who or what had chewed off Chiller's face. I think it was von Clausewitz (or maybe it was Al Capone) who said: "Never attack nothin' ya don't know how ta kill." Words to live by, I say. Besides, I couldn't leave poor Perry like that, his left leg wrapped around the sideview display screen of a '97 Plymouth Zarc, his right gone at the hip. He deserved a decent burial with full military honors, and if that meant cutting short my mission, well, so be it.

After disengaging Captain Chillers, I was about to begin the long swim back to our lines when a loudspeaker went off in my brain just nanoseconds after something feeling like a writhing section of hawser cable covered with wet felt had slid by my calf. The loudspeaker loudly suggested that I GET THE FUCK OUT OF HERE!

"Sorry, Per," I said to my fellow officer, "but I'm going to have to leave you behind. Don't worry—someone from Graves and Registration will be along eventually. Isn't as if you've got a hot date or anything."

I let the carcass slide out of my grasp. As it floated off into the darkness above me, I resumed my voyage back to Motown, this time smartly and by the numbers. And I was doing just fine, thank you, until I came across an old electric Blunder Bus blocking the passage and was forced to crawl through the back window. I was halfway down the aisle, heading in the direction of the front windshield, when I saw the nest.

At first I thought they were eels, all bundled together like a big ball of gray-green tubing. If it hadn't been for the fact that the squirming mass completely blocked my route, I would've probably just swam on by and been about my business. Thing was, though, this great living tumor of wriggling, twisting, undulating bodies filled the entire front of the bus.

In the throw of my helmet light, I could see that some of those eel-like creatures were as long as my arm and as thick as optic-fiber cable. The safest (and sanest) thing to do, I determined, was to back out and find some other way down the tunnel. After all, I hadn't come through this particular bus on my way in; logic dictated there were other routes I could take on the long road home. There was absolutely no reason I could think of to attempt to dig through what looked to be several thousand river eels with my bare hands.

The joke was, they weren't eels. This I discovered when one of the creatures—a particularly large sonuvabitch—untangled itself from the undulating pile and began swimming towards my faceplate.

Give me a fucking break.

Its body reminded me of one of those poisonous sea snakes that the jet-jock veterans of the Battle of the East China Sea* had always talked about in drunken stupors towards the end of Happy Hour out in the "O" Club at Twenty-nine Palms.

"Sharks are one thing, Will," I remember my Dad slobbering in his beer when I showed up to cart him home to quarters, "but the idea of punching out into a nest of those sea snakes . . . hell, most of us took a silent vow that we'd stay with our birds right into the deck rather than go that route."

The creature coiling its way through the water at me there in the tunnel was almost what I'd imagined those serpents would look like. But only almost. Its fat gray-green body resembled a snake's all right, but the thing's head was something straight out of two zillion B.C. As big as a grown man's fist, it had huge yellow catlike eyes that glowed with some phosphorescent weirdness, and its jaws were full of a pale ridged plate that reminded me of pictures of the mouth of a baleen whale. The thing seemed to have no fear of me, and as it approached, I saw two long antennalike appendages unfold from along the first third of its body. Unless I was mistaken (and I kind of hoped to God I was), each antenna had an additional eyeball attached to the end of it.

Very cute.

The standard procedure for snake encounters, I recalled from

* See Arthur P. Dimwitty's *Air War for the Philippines: Aces High* (London: Gilletin Press, 2019).

some long ago FAC survival course,* was to remain calm and still, making no sudden movements that the snake would interpret as threatening. While I never had much confidence in such advice, I decided to give it a try, the alternative being to quite possibly stir up the rest of the family.

Which partially explains why I remained in a paralyzed state right up until the moment when it was fairly clear that the creature meant to rip my head off with or without a perceived threat on my part. This goal seemed obvious when, about three feet in front of my face, the ungodly serpent unhinged its jaw, rolled back the ridged plate, and revealed a mouthful of jagged needle-sharp fangs each as long as my middle finger.

I yelled involuntarily, partly out of surprise, partly out of disgust, but mostly out of sheer sphincter-loosening terror. This creature meant to have a chunk of me, no doubt about it, and I quickly determined that unless I wanted to end up like Captain Chillers, I'd better take my act on the road. Swallowing my soldier's pride, I kicked out as hard as I could with my flippers and started retreating off that goddamn bus as fast as was humanly possible.

The mutant creature from the pages of a *Time-Life* book on prehistoric marine life didn't waste a second. With a couple of quick flicks of its undulating body it doubled its speed and was at once on me like warm slobber on a sow's tit. That mouth full of viper fangs seemed to open even wider, and for an instant I caught a good glimpse of hell down at the very bottom of the creature's gullet.

A lesser man, I believe, would've shat his drawers.

But Will Bucko hadn't survived forty-odd years on his good-to-average looks alone. At the last possible instant I brought the wrist-mounted Remington Pneumatic into play and blew that slimy schmuck's head off with a 20mm compression round at point-blank range. There was a flash, a lot of bubbles, then what looked like a six-foot section of garden hose leaking mud was

* The course was undoubtedly taught by a short, wall-eyed, demented-looking corporal from Mississippi who took great delight in executing a bunny rabbit with one judo chop to the neck, and then hacking the poor thing to pieces, all to show how ruthless one must be to survive in the wilds.

floating down in front of my faceplate. I figured Captain Chillers's had been avenged.

Just as I had feared, however, the concussion from the explosion woke up the rest of the neighborhood. I was nearly out the back of the bus when on the periphery of my helmet's arc light I caught sight of one wriggling body, then another, then another, all coming out of the gloom directly at me. Given the fact that my Remington was a single-shot weapon and that the extra ammo for it was zipped up in my fanny pack along with my civilian clothes and a handy nostril hair trimmer, I surmised that I was a dead man.

No question about it—I definitely would've been goners had it not been for an innate sense of reason and logical deduction that I believe the good Lord has given me in compensation for a bad overbite. For as I watched more and more of the snakelike creatures come out of the darkness, I spotted out of the corner of my faceplate one of the yellow phosphorescent eyeballs that had only seconds before been attached to the head of the first attacker. It was suspended in the water, floating gently.

Suddenly, three of the mutations veered towards this eyeball and then tore at it in a frenzy, biting not only the eye but ripping each other to shreds as well. Could it be, I wondered, could it be that they'd been attracted to the eyeball because of the light reflecting from it? The light coming from my—

With nothing to lose, I reached down and unplugged my helmet's arc light from its power source.

What followed was probably the longest thirty seconds of my life. Motionless, barely able to breathe, surrounded by darkness and death, I waited for the tear of fangs. Yet the attack did not come. As my heart skipped, I became aware that I was still in one piece long after the first snake should have struck. For the moment it seemed as though I was safe.

Life, unfortunately, is a series of trade-offs. What I got instead of ripped flesh was, in some respects, a lot worse. Suddenly the creatures—dozens of them—were all around me, brushing my body, coiling themselves around my arms and legs, pulling and pushing and slithering, PULSATING FOR CHRIST'S SAKES, like what you'd imagine a giant earthworm would be doing if it was wrapped around your thigh.

Being torn to shreds would've been painful, but at least it

would've been quick. When it became obvious that the goddamn things meant to make a new nest with Will Bucko at the center (perhaps I was just some warm body that the "young" could feed off of when hatched, just as is depicted on those endless goddamn nature videos on public TV about wasps or spiders or large African spit beetles), it would've been quite easy for my mind to snap.

Maybe it did. How else can I explain what prompted me to begin humming an old Gregorian chant called "Stairway to Heaven" as I gently went about removing those writhing, revolting, mung-coated things from my body. It certainly wasn't the action of a sane man, a man in control. No, a man in control would have quickly figured out that if the creatures were attracted by light, then the only way out of the predicament was to somehow—

Slowly and precisely, I reached up, removed one of the snakes that had entwined itself around my mouthpiece and broke the airtight neck seal between my wet suit and the helmet.

The sudden exposure of bare skin to the freezing cold river water was excruciating, and for a long moment I could not breathe, the air sucked from my lungs by the shock. Too late I wondered if the respirator would freeze up on me. And what if the rest of the wet suit leaked? And what if the world really was flat, as my pa always claimed?

I was losing it; no shit. Luckily, the chemical heating elements on my air canisters automatically kicked in, and I was able to grab a gulp of warm air. My face would probably develop acute frostbite, but I wasn't going to drown. Not yet, anyway.

Still clinging to the electrical cable, which had connected the helmet with the battery pack at my belt, I sent the helmet apparatus spinning away from me. When it reached the end of the cord, I unfastened the battery pack from my waist, plugged in the cord, and then watched in blurry fascination as the helmet's light drew the snakes away from me and into a feeding frenzy.

With one last shudder of revulsion, I turned tail and hauled ass . . .

Safe for the moment, I was still not out of the woods . . . or the tunnel. The mutations on the bus had pretty well established that I must continue on my mission (being as they were still between me and our lines), so I made for Canada, groping through the darkness, praying that I would discover no more nests of undocumented life forms.

The traffic was terrible. Even when I'd had the aid of the arc light, movement through the vehicles jammed in the tube had been slow and ponderous. In the dark, it was just about impossible. I hadn't progressed more than a few hundred feet when the warning light on my second air canister began to blink.

I reckon that the average guy—swimming in freezing, mutant-infested waters inside a flooded tunnel, in the dark, low on air, suffering from claustrophobia and the makings of a humongous head cold—would have quit right then and there. But I'd discovered over the years that even if one aspired to be a comic book hero, it didn't hurt to use one's brain every once in a while.

Recalling some old theory from high school science about cream rising to the top, I hit the buckle on my weight belt and let my body float towards the ceiling of the tunnel.

Sure enough, when I got there, I discovered a cramped but generally clear passage above the vehicles, leading, I hoped, all the way to the Windsor side. Using the tiled ceiling as a guide, I began swimming along this passage—slowly and gently—stretching whatever air I had left in the third canister for as long as I could . . .

About half an hour later, the water level began to recede and I was forced once again to pick my way through the traffic jam. This time, however, there was no problem: first, because I now had plenty of fresh air to breath (putrid and acrid to be sure) and so didn't have to worry about overexerting myself; second, because I knew I was very nearly at the end of the first leg of my journey; and third, because at long last I could see daylight at the end of the tunnel.

Unfortunately, as I staggered out of the scum and filth floating on the last few inches of river, I realized it was still the dead of night. Unless I was suffering from some sort of bizarro jet lag caused by a little too much nitrogen in my air mix, the light at the end of the tunnel was not daylight at all, but a RIHM high-intensity illumination beam focused on the center of my chest.

There was nothing left for me to do except raise my hands slowly over my head and pray that the bastards didn't have orders to shoot on sight . . .

3

"Got anything to declare?"

It was a human voice; part rumble, part squeaky reed, but nonetheless human. A sense of relief swept over me as I realized that I had apparently been snatched from the edge of the abyss for the second time that night.

"No," I said, "nothing to declare."

"Business or pleasure?" the cracking voice asked.

"Business," I responded truthfully, raising a hand to shade my eyes from the glaring spotlight. Back in the tunnel I had taken the precaution of reloading the Remington Pneumatic on my wrist. One false move and whoever was behind the spotlight would be dog grease.

"How long will you be staying in Canada?" the voice asked one more time.

"How long is a Chinaman," I answered, complying with the last of the silly-ass code I'd been briefed on back at G-2. "You wanna lower that light a little, pal? You're frying my eyeballs."

"Advance and be recognized."

Spastically, I flopped the last few feet out of the water and up the gentle incline of pavement towards my contact with the MapleLeaf Underground. Twice I staggered and almost fell. The beam of the spotlight dropped and played around my feet.

"You can take the flippers off now, old Grace," the voice behind the light said in an extremely sarcastic tone. "Swim period's over."

I was too tired to argue. The flippers were stripped away, and I was soon face-to-face with my tour guide. He was, to put it bluntly, nothing to write home about. Western civilization was hanging in the balance, and the Canadians had sent me a teenage boy. He looked no more than fifteen despite the body armor and an over-and-under sawed-off bufgun that he kept loosely trained in my direction as he played the spotlight beam over my body.

"Jeez-oh," he finally said, his upper lip curling back in a sneer, "yer a fat one. Hope ta blue-fire you can keep up. We got a long hump ahead of us."

He was wearing his hair in a longknot—the fad that year among teenagers—and I could see the ubiquitous strobe pin-light through the left nostril that all the boys had started wearing.* There was a dark shadow of a mustache on his upper lip, but his cheeks and chin were only sprouting peach fuzz, and he had that skinny gangly look of a kid whose growth hormones were raging day and night. He was, therefore, not completely responsible for his actions or his mouth.

Consequently, I decided not to kill him.

"Don't worry about me, kid," I said, sucking in my stomach. "I'll march you into the ground then shit on your grave. Now let's get outta here before the RIHM sentries show up and suck us dry."

The kid laughed, a facetious-sounding laugh that held about as much real humor as a thumbtack through the eardrum. "Hold the perspiration, old jock," he said. "No RIHMs coming down here. They hate the H-two-O. That's why they planted the jelly snakes to guard the tunnel for 'em."

"Jelly snakes?"

"Yeah," he giggled, "that's what I call 'em, mainly cause when you hit 'em with a hammer their guts turn to jelly. Chief says the Island RIHMs invented 'em for religious purposes and sent a batch up here as a gesture of solidarity with the Northern Horde." As he got more excited, the boy's voice began breaking up and down like stressed sheet metal. "Sure wouldn't mind havin one for a pet," he continued. "Mutherin fierce they are, a real species!"

I could feel the anger building in my gizzard. "Oh, shit yes!" I said. "Mutherin fierce! Tell me, how long have the jelly snakes been in the tunnel here, son?"

The boy paused to rub at a mass of messy-looking zits on his forehead. "Creeze, can't say for real certain, guy. Never was too good at dates. Been in the tube about a month I would guess."

My hands had the youngster secured by the stacking swivel before he knew what hit him. I lifted him off the deck and brought his face right into mine, so he could read my lips and see my rage just before I strangled the life out of him.

---

* The strobe light in the nostril had been *de rigueur* since the Prince of Wales had appeared with one during his famous gig on MTV in 2042.

"A month!" I screamed. "A month? You've known about those fucking mutated snakes from hell for a month? Why in the name of Christ didn't you tell us about them?"

"We did! We did!" the boy croaked back at me. He was trying to maintain his cool, but I could see that my behavior had him worried. "I seen the chief send the message to FAC myself! The day they was implanted in the tube! I promise, mister, I promise!"

It only took a moment, then I knew he was telling the truth. Would I—would any sane man—have gone into that tunnel knowing I might run into those snakes? Bet your ass no. General Skoff and his staff must've realized that fact and so had kept the information from me. Which meant I had a score to settle with that beady-eyed old bugger and his cronies the second I got back.

The sound of someone strangling returned me to the here and now. The boy's face was turning purple, and his eyes bulged like the legendary PeeWee Herman with a fireplace poker up his ass. I immediately loosened my grip and let the kid slip back down to his feet. Wasn't his fault I'd been lied to.

"What's your name, stud?" I asked as I began peeling out of my wet suit.

"Johnny Doone," he answered meekly, all the teen spirit squeezed out of him. "Creeze, guy, you coulda killed me."

"Let that be a lesson to you, Johnny. Never be the barer of bad tidings. Lie if you have to or get somebody else to relay your message. Hand me that fanny pack, will ya? I'm freezing my balls off."

Buck-ass naked and shivering, I pointed to my gear. Doone did what I asked then stood back and quietly watched as I got dressed. While I struggled with a pair of trousers with a waistband three sizes too small, the boy slowly regained some of his composure.

"You sure do stink, old dog," he eventually offered, "like the bottom of a fish tank ain't been cleaned in a deuce."

"That's rendered RIHM fat, kid," I answered. "You oughta try it. Keeps the bastards from sniffing out your meat."

"Fractured thinking, old dude. You got a can of the wrong juice."

"What're you talking about?" I asked. He was using the latest teen slang, and understanding him, I suspected, was going to be about as easy as reading Arabic.

"That fragrance you're wearin. That's the whiff of a female RIHM in heat. Unless you clean up real good and real quick, we gonna have a few hundred of the suckers with hard-ons keepin us company."

Luckily, I had packed a quantity of steel wool soap pads in my kit. Although the process was painful (particularly around the nether regions and the face), I quickly rid myself of the offending material while the kid stood by and snickered.

"How'd ya come to bring them soap pads with ya, guy?" he asked as I once again struggled to get the trousers Velcroed shut. "Me, I woulda loaded up on ammo and smokes."

It was hard not to laugh. These Canadian provincials were tough fighters, but they lacked a certain *savoir-faire* when it came to the intricacies of clandestine operations.

"Lesson number two, Johnny," I said, holding up one of the steel wool pads. "Always give yourself a means of communicating with your people. This is an S-O-S pad. Anybody following my trail finds one of these, they know I'm in trouble."

"Dorky, duder! Massively dorky!" The boy's face lit up, and although I wasn't sure what he'd said, the tone was full of admiration.

"Right, kid." I chuckled at his enthusiasm. "But we'd better mount up. Night isn't going to last forever. You got any iron for me? Damn Remington there needs compressed air and I'm all out."

Doone nodded and produced a modified British Scorpion A-3 Assault Rifle much like the weapon the Brits had used to eradicate the Highland RIHMs in the war of '32.* The Scorpion worked on the same basic principle as a microwave oven, and although ineffective at ranges over fifty meters, it could do a number in close.

From his rucksack the kid pulled out the Scorpion's energy pack, which he handed over to me along with a translation helmet with a built-in starlight scope. Without too much more fart-

---

* See *My Heart's in the Highland, My Gut's in the Sea: The Story of the Royal Marines in the War of 2032* by Brigadier Seth-Thomas MacCaroon (Cornhole-on-Avon, England: Ego Press, 2039).

ing around, we moved off, Johnny in the lead, Will Bucko following in trace.

The devastation around the city was total and complete. Windsor had not been leveled as much as it had been pulverized. I was reminded of old holograms of Los Angeles and San Francisco and other California cities after the Mad Russian sub driver had loosened his megatons on them back around the turn of the century. Here and there the skeletons of a building might rise out of the rubble, but on the whole the city was one giant slag heap.

To do such damage without nuclear weapons, I knew, must have taken a huge chunk out of the Northern Horde's ordnance supplies, another reason why they had put off their invasion of the U.S.A. We Americans owed a great debt of gratitude to our Canadian brothers and sisters who had fought so hard and gallantly; they had stopped the RIHMs in their tracks and had held them in check longer than anyone had a right to expect.

Thanks to Johnny Doone, we slipped past at least a half a dozen RIHM sentries on our way inland from the river. I had to hand it to him, the kid was a veritable barnyard of animal sounds. Anytime a RIHM sentry got too inquisitive, Johnny would do his impression of an alligator or a flying bat or an armadillo, and the damn idiot mutant would return to his bonfire and the friendly camaraderie of soldiers in bivouac. Begrudgingly, I had to give Johnny his due—he was a street-savvy little dude who might make it to his next birthday if only he could learn to control his mouth.

"You're too damn fat, jock," he whispered back at me once when I asked him to slow down. "I gotta wonder if you've got the sap to pull this caper off."

"Don't worry," I wheezed, "I'll run your ass into the ground, then—"

"I know, I know. Shit on my grave. Think you could breathe just a *little* harder? There's probably a few RIHMs over in Russia who ain't heard ya yet."

We were soon in a network of trenches that had been used by the Canadian army in their long stand against the Northern Horde. It was from these interconnecting trenches, some of which extended for miles, that a few courageous battalions had held off the final enemy assault long enough for the bulk of the army and 2 million civilian refugees to get across the river to safety.

All along the sections of the trench we passed through, I found sad little reminders of those brave soldiers. Yes, there was the usual flotsam and Jetsons (sic) of battle—the broken weapons, the spent cartridge casings, the occasional empty boot or dented helmet or torn piece of body armor. But there was more, the personal things that told me that flesh and bone had fought here, real people, not machines or computers.

Here was a hologram of someone's wife or sweetheart, dressed in a flimsy garter belt, black stockings, and a push-up bra. "To Bill, Thanks for the good time"—it read on the back—"Love, Cheetah."

Here was an empty case of Elk's Breath Beer, one of the finest artificial brews ever invented in the lab. It was heartening to know that in their final moments before the big battle, the troopers in this sector had had the chance for one last taste of home.

At one spot I discovered a hastily scrawled letter to an Ontario bank asking for more time in paying off a loan for rain. At another, a broken commemorative plate of the last Honda built in North America. At another, a brochure for videotapes including something called *Great Moments in Curling* and a two-hour CBC documentary on buckwheat. I felt a lump grow in my throat when I found a tattered and torn satin team jacket with the words "Mike's Meats" embroidered on the back.

When I came across the GI Joe doll, however, jammed in the mud at the top of a parapet, all decked out in cammies, blue beret, and miniature AK-47, I could look no more. My eyes were too full of tears. I saluted the little fuck and was about to break into a rendition of the GI-Joe video theme song when Johnny whispered loudly from about twenty yards up the trench.

"Hang on, old dog," I heard him say. "We're near there. Hot grub and a warm douche'll fix ya right up."

I gestured frantically to him to shut up. It was too late. Doone had meant well, but his nearly constant cajoling had at last been heard by the enemy. Shifting shafts of light danced over the lip of the trench about fifty meters up the line. As Johnny dove for cover, I risked a peek.

Chemical torches held high, the pale blobby shapes of two Northern RIHM sentries appeared out of the gloom. They were unquestionably headed our way. I put my Scorpion on the Fry setting, then attempted to tune the translation helmet to whatever frequency the RIHMs were on. Maybe, just maybe, they hadn't heard Johnny at all. Maybe they were out looking for loose change or a missing contact lens.

At first all I got over the translator's earpiece were the usual gurgles and drips and grunts associated with all RIHMs. Then, although it was difficult to fully understand, I began picking up bits of the conversation.

"I tell thee, Excedrin, I heard something out here."

"Only an animal protoplasm, I betcha."

"I sense not. There is, in the air, the stink of human meat."

"Funny," the other one said, "I kinda thought I detected quiff on the hoof. Tell ya, Contac, my sacs haven't been emptied in two weeks. I sure would like to meet some hot-to-trot dolly right about now. This I say all in truth."

Damn, I thought, some of that rendered RIHM fat must've gotten under my fingernails.

"It is not female glandular secretions thee smell, Excedrin," the first RIHM said. "It is the reek of—" Here he used a word that I can't even begin to pronounce, much less spell. It translates into something like *those-that-would-devour-our-children's-organs,* or words to that effect.

The two sentries had by this time approached to within a few feet of where Johnny Doone was crouched. I could not see them since by then I'd also scrambled for cover, but I heard what happened next very clearly.

"There! Did you hear that?" the one called Contac gurgled. "It came from down there in the trench."

"Ha!" the other one taunted. "Only the cry of a Bavarian titmouse, you load. Told ya it was animal protoplasm. I warn thee, Contac, if you've dragged me all the way out here just—"

"Threaten not," Contac warned. "Remember who is senior here. And answer me this, O wise one. How do you suppose a Bavarian titmouse got all the way over here to the land of white lakes?"

"Oh," Excedrin answered rather meekly. "Lights out then, eh?"

Suddenly the flickering glow of the chemical torches ceased and the trench was returned to darkness. I realized that unless I acted, and acted quickly, Johnny Doone had produced his last pimple. They had already picked up his scent. His only choice was to blast them both with his bufgun, in which case we were both doomed because the sound would bring every RIHM within a mile right down our throats.

Without any real heavy thinking about the matter, I slipped my K-17 fighting knife out of its ankle sheath, quietly dumped the cumbersome helmet and assault rifle, then rolled up over the lip of the trench. I took a moment to establish my bearings, spotted the pale shapes of the RIHMs down the trench line facing away from me, then began low crawling in their direction.

Without the translation helmet, I couldn't tell what the sentries were saying. All I heard was their coughing grunts. They still hadn't located the boy's exact position.

A light snow had been falling most of the night; an inch or two had accumulated on the plundered and torn ground. Approaching to within a few yards of the nearest RIHM, I eased to a crouch and slipped up on the creature, the snow muffling my footsteps.

As per standard kill procedure, I closed a hand around the thing's communication pod and then pulled down and backwards. At the same time, I plunged the K-17 to the hilt just beside the base of the major spinal column, tearing up at the prescribed forty-five degree angle to the juncture of the secondary spine and the first heart. A quick twist of the blade and I was through the tangle of gristle and ligaments that were attached to the ball and socket joint of the neck. With one last heave, I brought the knife down sharply, severing the third and final spinal cord and leaving my enemy twitching silently in its death throes.*

The second sentry was about ten yards away, its back still to me. By the way it continued to spit and gurgle, I knew it hadn't

* Space does not allow a full clinical description of a typical Northern RIHM. Almost devoid of pigmentation, their pale skin and shell tone produced an excellent chameleonlike ability to blend in with natural surroundings. Each model came equipped with a long, trunklike proboscis which it used both for eating and for reproduction. Suffice it to say that they generally smelled like old goat goobers and in good light had the transparent, membranous look of a string of stuffed bowel.

heard a thing. I was halfway to its funeral when my good luck
finally turned sour; my foot broke through a thin crust of ice into
a pothole. My full weight came down on the twisted ankle and I
must have screamed. Next thing I knew, I was on my duff looking down the business end of an old SPIKE III.

"Excuse me," I blustered, "but can you tell me where the nearest currency exchange office is located? I've got a bunch of funny-
looking Canadian money I'd like to change into greenbacks."

The RIHM obviously didn't have the slightest idea what I was
talking about, and even if it had, I doubt very seriously that it
would've bought my "lost American tourist" routine. With a
couple angry-sounding grunts and a unmistakable gesture with
the barrel of the rifle, the creature indicated I should raise my
hands.

Well, I recall thinking, thank Buddha for small favors. The
RIHM apparently had orders to take prisoners, which was perfectly all right with me. Unfortunately, I had no more than gin-
gerly hauled myself to my feet, when the thing spotted the steam
rising from the gutted carcass of its pal.

Talk about your basic overreaction! Good golly, Miss Molly!
Son of a bitch started trumpeting like a bull elephant with a belly
full of ground glass. It was a sound full of fury and anger, but
something else too, something hidden underneath that I couldn't
quite identify. Was it grief? Sadness? Heartbreak?

Impossible. This was a RIHM after all, not some soap opera
star or quiz show host. As the old joke goes: RIHMs didn't laugh
or cry, they just sucked.

The creature paused in its bellowing rage and turned on me.
Judging from the black color of its sight receptacles, I concluded
I was personally being blamed for the demise of its chum. It
looked as though my days as a prisoner of war were over.

Rather than be sucked dry, I reached the decision that if I had
to die I would prefer a burst of automatic rifle fire any day, so I
gritted my teeth and charged the fiend, moving as fast as my
damaged ankle would allow, the stained and still dripping K-17
clutched in my hand.

The muzzle of the SPIKE III was level with my face when it
exploded. There was no pain, only a bright flash and then the
warm gooey feel of wet tissue and blood showering my body. I'd
been shot before (five or six times at this point in my career) and

therefore knew from experience that this was a mortal wound. There would be no miracle surgery on this one, I concluded as I fell to my knees. Will Bucko had definitely watched his last *Different Strokes* rerun. (Oh, were only that true!)

A second explosion, followed a split second later by another shower of tripe and warm fluid, rocked me to my boot heels. I felt myself plunging into the void on the great elevator ride to oblivion. I was on the roller coaster to nowhere, the midnight bus to Barstow, the last train to Clarksville. My ticket had been punched, my name scratched off the list, the bucket had been kicked, the farm bought. It was all over now, except for—

Someone slapped me across the face and knocked the silly clichés right out of me. I opened my eyes and saw Johnny Doone standing beside me, a smoking bufgun in one hand, a length of what appeared to be two-inch canvas fire hose in the other.

"Come on, old dog," he said as he flopped the battle trophy over one shoulder, then broke the buf at the breach and inserted two flat-nosed anti-RIHM rounds. "Things is gonna get brisk around here in a minute. Best we shag ass."

Over to our left I spotted what was left of the second sentry. Judging by the two ragged basketball-size holes in its chest, I presumed that Johnny had come up behind the creature while I was distracting it, and had dropped it with two bufgun shots from point-blank range. I also noticed that the RIHM's trunk was missing and wondered if the Hudson's Bay Company was still offering twenty credits apiece for them.

"Thanks, kid," I muttered. "Thought I was history. Help me up."

Doone gave me a hand, and I managed to stagger to my feet. Despite the pain in the ankle and the gore splattered all over my body, it felt good to be alive.

"How far?" I asked.

"Maybe a klic," Johnny answered, looking over my shoulder with a nervous, cornered animal cast to his eyes. "We're gonna have to run for it."

"No way, kid," I said, staggering a bit to emphasize my point. "I won't be going anywhere very fast with this foot. Tell you what. You slip on back to your base and bring back a few corpsmen with a stretcher. Be a lot quicker that way."

"Suit yourself," the lad said. "You think you can hold off that many RIHMs single-handed, that's beasty fortitude. Me, I got my orders. See ya next year at the Grey Cup, eh?"*

Johnny had turned and was three steps away before I thought to question him.

"What are you talking about, Doone?" I hollered.

He didn't bother to look back. Instead, he gestured with a thumb to something over my shoulder and continued to walk away. Awkwardly, I pivoted on my good foot.

Judging by the number of chemical torches, there was something in the neighborhood of a battalion of RIHMs formed on-line about a quarter mile away and moving in my general direction. They probably hadn't gotten a visual on me yet, otherwise I would've already been taking hostile fire, but their sensors had undoubtedly picked up the discharge of the bufgun and they had worked out the cross bearings well enough to pinpoint my position. I looked down at the knife still in my hand and decided that the odds were overwhelmingly against me.

"Hey, Johnny," I shouted. "Wait for me!"

Funny how fast a fat guy on one leg can move when he's got the right motivation. By the time we got to the vicinity of MapleLeaf headquarters, it was the kid who was huffing and puffing to stay up with me.

---

* In pre-RIHM days the Grey Cup was awarded annually to Canadian pro football's championship team, a championship determined by the outcome of the Grey Cup game. After the invasion and conquest of their country, free Canadians everywhere used the term "See ya next year at the Grey Cup, eh?" as a patriotic farewell.

4

About a mile and a half later Johnny Doone grabbed my arm and pointed out what first appeared to be no more than a crack in the rubble.

"We're there, jock," the boy said.

Two huge cement slabs had collapsed on each other in such a manner as to form a small A-shaped hole, a hole big enough for varmints perhaps, but certainly not a man.

"You'd better be kidding," I grumbled.

It had been a long night and I was getting cranky. We'd been running over and around huge piles of loose debris and frozen ground since leaving the trench line, and the going had been slow and painful, especially for a guy hobbling on one leg. The RIHM mortar rounds walking their way down to us didn't help morale much either.

"Wouldn't kid you, old dorker," Doone chuckled as he fell to his knees in front of the crack. "Where'd you think HQ was gonna be? Top of the Hilton?"

I could see he was serious. "Listen, kid," I said, my breath still coming like an Italian soccer player (i.e., in short little pants), "there's no damn way I can fit in there. It's not even big enough for a good-sized rat."

" 'Zactly what all the RIHM patrols think, too," the boy answered, "though I have often wondered what a 'good' size is for a rat. Come on, old duff. It ain't bad once ya get past the black widders."

In disgust I watched as he flopped down on his washboard belly and with a good bit of contortion, began squirming his way into the hole. A moment later and he was gone.

Good-bye to bad rubbish I thought. After my swim through the Windsor tunnel there was absolutely no way I was going to enter another black hole filled with God only knew what, not tonight or any other night in the near future. If the MapleLeaf Underground wanted to take themselves so goddamn literally, the hell with 'em; I'd find Melodie Lane on my own, and be all the safer for it.

I began to reconsider when a RIHM four-deuce round impacted less than fifty meters away. Luckily, it landed behind a great mound of brick and splintered timber, so all I got out of it was a mild concussion from the blast and a harmless shower of debris. If, however, the bastards decided to fire for effect, I knew my chances of survival were rather shitty.

"Come on, old tit," I heard Doone say, "I was only doing a sitcom on ya. There ain't no black widders in here."

His head was sticking out of the crack between the slabs, his grin a reminder of Halloween jack-o'-lanterns and covers of *Mad* magazine and other symbols of satanic worship so dear to my childhood. I probably would've drop-kicked the lad into the next decade had it not occurred to me as I raised a nine EE combat boot that he had last been seen entering the hole headfirst. Somehow, he was now turned completely around, leering out at me with his gapped-tooth moronic smile that recalled old tintypes of Billy the Kid.

It didn't take much deep thought or mathematical extrapolation to figure out that there was more room to maneuver inside the hole than outside appearances had heretofore indicated. My alternatives, I quickly decided, were simple: Either attempt to dodge a battalion of RIHMs and a mortar barrage on a gimpy foot with absolutely no idea where I was going, or follow Johnny into the hole. Consequently, I found myself dropping to my belly and crawling towards the opening.

With visions of jelly snakes and black widow spiders and any number of other creepy-crawly vermin waiting for me in the darkness, I took a deep breath and plunged ahead.

Needless to say, I was pleasantly surprised when, once I'd squeezed myself through the hole in the rubble, I found myself following Doone down a cluttered but passable stairwell leading deep into the frozen ground.

Headquarters for the MapleLeaf Underground was located six stories beneath the outskirts of Windsor in a subbasement of a demolished parking structure. There, I soon discovered, a beehive of squat low-ceiling little rooms, offices, and storage areas had been hewn out of the broken concrete and heavy clay, all connected by a labyrinth of timber-reinforced shafts so low and

constricting that even the likes of Alfredo the Hunchbacked
Dwarf would've had plenty of room to bitch.

As Johnny led me through this maze, he filled me in on some
of the amenities of the joint, and although he continued to use the
jargon of his kind (teenage punk), I managed to understand at
least a portion of what he was saying.

There was no electricity; illumination was provided by candlelight and a few syngas Coleman lanterns. The vital radio equipment—the Underground's only link with the outside world—was
run on rechargeable batteries and a hand-cranked generator inge-
niously hooked up to an old exercise bike. The only bathroom for
the sixty or so volunteers who lived there in HQ was a
honeybucket that got dumped once a week up on the surface.
Fresh water was in critical supply—the one antique recycling
unit could produce no more than twenty or thirty gallons a day,
depending on how much urine could be collected—but there was
plenty of canned food, particularly if you liked crackers and
meatless pimento loaf.

I hoped to hell no banquet had been planned for my arrival.

Despite its drawbacks, however, the Headquarters of the
MapleLeaf Underground looked like the Garden of Eden to me,
for as Doone led me past the various offices and living spaces, I
soon noticed in the flickering candlelight that a good number of
the female resistance fighters were some of the most beautiful
young women I had ever seen. And lest I be misunderstood, I
don't mean your nice, sweet, girl-next-door, blush of the rose,
sorority sweetheart-type beautiful. What I saw down there in the
damp frigid bunker complex was the most amazing collection of
git-down-and-boogie talent ever assembled on the North American continent. We're talking nasty nymphs here, the kind that
cavort through a young man's dreams and a porno writer's
manuscript, the kind that bring new meaning to the words *lust,
perverse,* and *engorged,* the kind of girl who could arouse a
ninety-year-old eunuch to reinforced concrete simply by batting
an eye.

To put it another way: even though they were bundled up in a
ragtag assortment of ill-fitting military surplus work uniforms
and field jackets, I detected more round, firm, well-muscled T&A
in five minutes than the original editor of *Penthouse* had probably
seen in a lifetime.

So although MapleLeaf HQ was as cold as death's breath, and smelled like a locker room full of damp old socks and suppurating crotch rot, it was the place where I wanted to spend the rest of my natural life, and I made no bones about it when Doone led me into a dank twelve-by-twelve hovel and introduced me to his boss, a pug-nosed barrel-chested ex-Canadian Mountie by the name of Major Tyrone Fangbone.

With his thinning gray curly hair and jug ears, I thought for a moment I'd once seen his photograph long ago on the dust jacket of the commemorative edition of *The Naked and the Dead* but dismissed the notion as speculative fiction.

"Nice place you've got here, Fangbone," I said, shaking his hand. "Reminds me of my days slaving in a Colorado zircon pit, only there, quite frankly, I didn't feel quite so overwhelmed by upturned breasts, thrusting buttocks, and quality haunch. Damn it, man, what you've got here is downright criminal!"

Fangbone looked at me with his droopy hound-dog eyes as though I had just stomped his grandmother. "My God," he muttered, "were you the best they could do?"

"Oh, he's a No-kay right duder, Chief," Doone said in my defense as he slathered some of the ersatz pimento loaf onto a Ritz. "Slashed a Mute, got through the jelly snakes, can't be all shit."

"Thanks, kid," I said, "but I can speak for myself." It was time, I knew from experience, to lay down the rules. "Listen, Fangbone," I said, more frustrated than angry, "and listen good. Three weeks ago I was soaking rays on a warm Mexican beach with a dozen señoritas waiting on me hand and foot. Then an old pal of mine in FAC shows up and talks me into coming up here to the wild north and risking my ass to save mankind, my country, and an old girlfriend I haven't seen in ten years. Well, so far it's been a bitch. What I really need now is some food and some rest and whatever else might be available to soothe the savage beast. What I don't need is a ragging, from you or anybody else in this lash-up. And I'll tell you what I've told every other asshole in the chain of command for the past twenty days—I will eventually lose the weight!"

For a moment Fangbone seemed stunned by my outburst. He finally looked over to Johnny, then back at me. "Please accept my apology, Colonel. We're all under a great deal of strain down here, and sometimes its difficult to maintain decorum. I'm very touchy about the girls, you understand, and I'll tell you why. Most of them worked in Windsor's fashionable strip clubs right up until the time the evacuation order came down. Reluctant to leave our gallant boys alone in the trenches, these girls—thoroughbreds all, as you have apparently already noticed—stayed on, to entertain and encourage and stiffen morale. By God, sir! There is nothing more rewarding to a soldier about to face the test of battle than to have a twenty-year-old with exquisite curves dance naked upon his table, powdered and perfumed pudendum not twelve inches from his nose! Our boys went to their deaths knowing exactly what they were fighting for, sir! Of that you can be sure! What more could a warrior ask?"

By this time Major Fangbone was shouting into my face, and his eyes had gone a little glassy. For a moment I was worried that he'd totally flipped out.

"When the final days arrived," he continued, suddenly sounding very sad (but a whole lot less insane), "and these patriotic young ladies discovered they were cut off from escape, rather than surrender and throw themselves on the mercy of the hated enemy, they joined the Underground to continue the fight for Canadian freedom . . . as did we all."

"Well spoken, Major," I said after a long pause. "My apologies for jumping to conclusions. By the way, did we miss our last lithium shot by any chance?"

Fangbone grimaced, but remained composed. "Colonel," he sighed, "General Skoff warned me about you. He said you were a brilliant field officer but a bit of a pig in garrison. Appreciating the fact that you've had a fairly tiring time of it so far this evening, I think the most prudent thing we can do is to delay any discussion of strategies until you've had a chance to rest. Johnny, please show our guest to his quarters."

"Just a minute now, Major," I argued. "I've got a few questions I'd like to have answered first."

"Make it quick."

"Is Colonel Lane still alive?"

Fangbone softened. "We've been working under that assumption, yes."

"And do you know where she is?"

"Generally speaking, yes."

I wasn't sure I liked his answer. "What's that suppose to mean?"

"She's still somewhere in Canada."

"Oh, great."

"We think."

I suddenly felt very, very tired.

"Sorry to be so blunt," Fangbone said. "Things are not quite as bleak as you might think, however. We've got scout patrols out right now working on a few leads. Once we have their reports, we may be able to formulate a plan. Until then, better you have that ankle attended to, then get some hot food and shut-eye. Believe me, as soon as I know anything I'll have you rousted out. Fair enough?"

"Yeah, sure, Major," I said disgustedly (although, truth be known, I was totally whacked-out by this time and wouldn't have gone after Melodie right away if she was two doors down the block hanging by her thumbs over a vat of boiling peanut oil). "Whatever you say."

"Very good. Johnny boy, show Colonel Bucko here the mess hall, eh? Then make sure he gets a cot and a blanket."

"Yes, sir," the boy answered, wiping a gob of the sandwich spread off his chin. He made a move as though to leave, then hesitated. "Oh, almost forgot, Maj. Got a secret message for yourself from some of the lads on the pad."

Fangbone scowled. "And what would that be?"

Doone grinned, flexed his backside in our direction, then let loose a terribly long and loud fart.

Fangbone was apparently amused. "Sweet, very sweet. You did a good job tonight, Johnny." The major chuckled, tenderly grabbing the boy by the longknot hanging down his back and using it to draw him closer. "Your dad would've been proud, eh? Whoever or whatever he was."

Most likely a goat, I thought. But I kept the comment to myself. After all, the kid had saved my life.

Sixteen hours later and I was beginning to feel human again. Hot grub, some sleep, and a wet-wipe body bath had rejuvenated both mind and muscle. A medical team made up of a pharmacist from Toronto and a local vet's assistant had done a nice job of taping up my ankle, and while it was still swollen pretty badly, I discovered I could get around on it without too much trouble or pain. The crutches were actually more of a sympathy-inducing prop than a necessity.

Although I was not too pleased with the acidic aftertaste of my coffee (or its yellowish tint for that matter), all in all things weren't too bad, and by the time I'd spent fifteen minutes with the group gathered in the comm center for the major's daily four o'clock briefing, I was pretty near back to my old self.

". . . And so there I was," I said, approaching the climax of my sea story, "on hover, fifty feet above the waves, cannons blasting, a bullet through the thigh and another in the chest, my G-suit filling with blood, my bird riddled with holes. And so help me, here comes that damn pseudo-Indian and his submarine, right down my throat."

Using the cherished hand gestures passed down through time immemorial by jet-jock storyteller to jet-jock storyteller, I had the assembled members of Fangbone's staff mesmerized with my tale of the big shoot-out between myself and the infamous Carlos Membranous, chief cook and bottle washer for the long defunct pirate gang known as the Shrimpers.*

I was just about to fire the first of two Sea Skua missiles into the ill-fated U-235 when Fangbone came piling into the room and impolitely distracted everyone except a luscious little number in tight cammies, who had introduced herself earlier as "Tawny." Judging from her slack jaw, glazed eyes, and noticeable facial tic, Tawny was hanging on my every word.

"Attention to orders, everyone," the major announced excitedly. "Raven Patrol has just reported in. It seems they've had a bit of success, up in the northeast sector. They are in the pipeline right now and will be with us shortly."

Good, I thought, still some time to kill. "So you see, Tawny," I continued, "there I was with—"

"And while we wait," the major loudly interrupted, sounding almost giddy with enthusiasm, "let's all sing something bilingually, shall we? In true Canadian spirit! This side of the room in French, the other in English. What will it be then?"

"Que Sera!" someone shouted out.

And just like that, what I had come to think of as a fairly

* See Volume 2 of this series, *Broadsides and Brass.*

professional group of fighting people turned into a disappointing imitation of the Mitch Miller Singers.*

Blessedly, their caterwauling didn't last long. Just about the time I had successfully broken into the ammo locker and found some linked 7.62 ball, the babbling abomination came to a halt thanks to the arrival of the leader of the Raven Patrol.

Her name was Chandelier.

That's what Fangbone called her when he greeted her. Chandelier. Never has a name so matched a vision.

From the moment this black-haired beauty sashayed her way through those singing idiots and came to a stop next to Major Fangbone, I was ruined for any other woman. I can still see her now as she was that day in the bunker, reflecting the harsh yellow glare of the syngas lanterns, her features at first painfully pale and bright, then, in an instant, hidden in shadow, much like the woman herself (as I would later learn)—part secret and mystery, part brutal honesty and straightforward bluntness. Like a chandelier she was French. And like a chandelier she both produced and reflected the warm illumination of her beauty in a hundred dazzling shards of light.

Unlike a chandelier, however, she did not hang from the ceiling.

From where I sat in the very back of the room, she appeared to be at least ten years older than Tawny and the other nymphets inhabiting our underground warren. And, quite honestly, despite the radiant beauty of her face, she didn't look the part of a nude table dancer. She was a tiny little thing, dressed in a baggy set of dark blue coveralls and a pair of broken-down department store work boots. Her hair was cut in a sensible but severe commando curl, and I could see the faint traces of cammy grease still on her face and hands, exquisitely small hands—fragile almost, like a china doll's.

Yet there was nothing fragile-looking in those amber eyes of hers as she glared out at the staff after Fangbone had given her

* *Editor's Note:* No amount of research has been able to unearth the meaning of this particular reference. Even under deep hypnosis, Colonel Bucko could not recall what it meant either. It remains here, however, because of the author's almost pathological desire to quote—keep the facts straight, as I saw 'em—end quote.

the floor. Even from where I lounged it was easy to see intensity and dedication striking sparks like steel off flint. She wore, I noticed for the first time, a shoulder holster full of blue-black magnum steel and a bandolier of bufgun fléchette rounds draped down across her chest. A soot-blackened double-edged Gurkha fighting knife hung from her belt. I got the distinct impression that she took her resistance fighting seriously.

"I believe," she said triumphantly, "that we've found Colonel Lane. . . . At least we've found what's left of her."

While Fangbone and the rest of his mixed chorus cheered the news, my bowels suddenly felt as though they'd come in contact with the bottom of a metal ice tray just out of the freezer. As much as I'd tried not to think the worse, chances were good that Melodie Lane was dead.

A few minutes later, in the privacy the filthy twelve-by-twelve dugout that Fangbone called his office, the three of us—Tyrone, Chandelier, and myself—were seated on ammo boxes surrounding a rough-hewn camp table. Spread out in front of us was a map of the province of Ontario, its markings barely legible in the dull candlelight. Chandelier had just finished a detailed debriefing of her patrol, and if she was correct, things looked dark indeed for the Mudville Nine.

"I'm having a hard time believing this, honey," I said, the shock of her report still weighing heavy on my mind. "Perhaps what you found was not Colonel Lane at all but simply a butchered hog carcass carelessly left out on a busy highway. Or maybe, just maybe, this is all some story you've cooked up to gain some personal recognition. Whatever the reason, I can only ask—where's your proof?"

Chandelier was the first to speak. "Who the hell are you again?" she asked.

Fangbone came to her rescue. "I thought I made that clear when I introduced him, my dear," he said softly. "This is Bucko. The American."

"Funny," the woman responded, those gold-flecked eyes of hers locked on me like hot rivets, "I thought we were all Americans here."

"From FAC," the Major said uneasily. "Across the river."

"A FACer, eh?" she asked rhetorically. *"Sacrebleu!* I guess we should all get down on our knees and kiss his great big derriere!"

"Chandelier," the maj warned, "enough. Colonel Bucko is here because he is one of the few who can identify Colonel Lane—"

"Thank you, Fang," I murmured.

"—or at least identify her remains. Without his help we might—"

"God damn it!" I roared. "Both of you, listen up. We go with the idea that she's still alive, got that? Until there's irrefutable proof otherwise!"

While the major hemmed and hawed, Chandelier defiantly unzipped the top of her coveralls and pulled out a sheet of what appeared to be contact film. With a muscular dexterity I have seldom seen in a member of her subspecies, she proceeded to slam the film down in front of me and pin it to the table with her Gurkha knife, all in one incredibly quick motion.

"Here's your proof, you *tête-de-merde,*" she snarled. "I took it myself, three days ago."

It was an infrared hologram, one of the new "instant" kind that did not require a laboratory laser to process. While it was not as sharp as a lab hollie, the final product was passable enough for intelligence work.

But it was not the technique or quality that caught my eye, rather the content, for it showed a badly decomposing body of a human female.

My throat went dry. The contents of my belly lurched, and I could feel a cold sweat break on my forehead. A thick wave of nausea rolled up from my gullet, and for a second I was sure I was going to puke all over Fangbone's table. Yet for all that, I could not tear my sight from that hollie.

The figure was lying half-buried in a smoldering pile of rubble. It had been sucked dry, decapitated, and otherwise mutilated in the Northern RIHM manner: both kneecaps were missing, the abdomen had been opened and eviscerated, the breasts cut away. Horrible, inhuman, and fairly typical of the savages. For more years than I cared to count, I had seen similar evidence of RIHM destruction and barbarity, but it was something you never got used to, not if you had an ounce of humanity in your soul.

"It's not Melodie Lane," I finally croaked.

"I'm sorry, Colonel Bunko, but I think it is," Chandelier answered. Despite badly mispronouncing my name, her tone had softened, as though she understood somehow that there was more between Melodie Lane and me than just a common profession and enemy. "Look over here."

She pointed to an item in a corner of the hologram about ten feet to the rear of the body, an item nearly obscured by the remains of a refrigerator and a section of roofing tile. I hadn't seen it before, but with her bringing it to my attention, it seemed to jump out at me. Charred and battered but still recognizable was the unmistakable form of a FAC flight helmet. The name LANE was printed above the visor.

"It's not Melodie Lane, damn it!" I barked, banging my fist on the table.

"But who else could it be?" Fangbone asked gently. "No, Colonel, I think we must face facts, as disagreeable to our cause as they might be. Mankind's last hope lies in this hologram, feeding the maggots."

"How delicately put," I answered.

"Doomed," Fangbone moaned, ignoring my sarcasm. "We're all doomed."

"Mon Dieu, Tyrone," Chandelier scolded, "you are such a *bébé.* Doomed? *Oui.* But we are not dead. We can still fight. While there is still blood flowing in our veins, we shall never give up!"

I couldn't help laughing out loud. "Come on folks, this is getting a little thick, wouldn't you say? Fact of the matter is, no matter how much you whine and carry on, the poor bitch in this hollie is *not* Melodie Lane!"

"But Colonel Bucko," Fangbone bawled, "how else can you explain—"

"First off," I cut in, "Lane was flying an A-69 StudBuzzard when she was shot down. The A-69 is a two-seater. Lane's copilot on that mission, as I recall from the file, was a Captain Patty P. Potts—female type. I believe the poor creature in this hollie is none other than the unfortunate Miss P. Potts."

"But Colonel Bunko," Chandelier questioned, "how can you be so sure of this? Odds are still fifty-fifty that this is Lane."

"The name is Bucko, lady. And to answer your question, come around here and take a look at something you missed."

Both Fangbone and Chandelier got up and moved around behind me. While they watched over my shoulder, I tilted the hologram at an angle. One of the benefits of a three-dimensional photograph, especially in the fields of both military intelligence and forensic science, is the ability to look over, around, and under objects on the film. By manipulating the sheet in front of me, I was able to show both Fangbone and Chandelier what I had already discovered.

"Do you see the right arm and hand now?" I asked. "The body blocks it in the frontal view, but if I get the angle just right here you can—"

"Yes, I see it," Fangbone said unenthusiastically. "As far as I can tell, though, mankind is still doomed."

"You may be right, Tyrone," I chuckled, "but I'll tell you one thing—this ain't Melodie Lane."

"*Tout alors!*" Chandelier exclaimed. "You are playing with us!"

"No, ma'am," I said. "For as you can see, this poor gal's hand has a full deck of digits. Count 'em—one, two, three, four, five. I happen to know, from personal experience, that Melodie Lane only has three."

"Three what?" Fangbone asked.

"Fingers," I answered. "The other two were bitten off by an old boyfriend."

"Sicko," Chandelier chimed in.

"Well, that might be so, lady, but as far as—OUCH!"

I had turned my head to address her face-to-face and had been rewarded with a rock-hard nipple in the eye. It hurt like hell.

"Oh, *pardon, monsieur!*" she cried. "Are you all right?"

"I'll be okay," I grumbled. There was a lot more to this woman than met the eye, I decided, at least that's the way it had felt. "What we have to decide now is what our next course of action's gonna be."

"I'll just have to order more patrols," Fangbone pouted.

"Not enough time. Hell, Major, it's not getting any warmer up there, ya know," I said, pointing at the ceiling. "And once the river freezes, we can all kiss it good-bye."

"Then what do you suggest?"

"It's a long shot," I said, "but I think it's worth the gamble. Chandelier's hollie here is not completely worthless. At least it tells us the general location of where Melodie's aircraft went down. I propose taking a patrol back to this spot. Maybe we can pick up her trail from there. Worth a try anyway. We know the RIHMs have her. The question is where."

"Makes sense," Fangbone agreed. "Can you lead Colonel Bucko back there, Chandelier?"

"Mais oui," she said.

"Fine," I said, "but if you're coming with me, honey, you gonna have to knock off that French shit, okay? I mean, it's fine in the bedroom and a fancy restaurant, but if we get into a firefight, I don't want to be worrying about what the sam-fuck you're saying. Agreed?"

This time when I turned I wisely tilted my head so as to avoid those marvelous metal-tipped boobies of hers. Instead, I looked up into her eyes and found two coke-burning furnaces about ready to dump molten iron down my pants.

"Canada is a bilingual nation, buster," she growled, "and I'll thank you to remember that. You're on *our* turf now, and that means Canadian laws apply. If you cannot understand me so hot, then I suggest you find yourself a French-English dictionary and get cracking!"

With that, Chandelier pivoted around sharply and stormed through the burlap curtain hanging in the dugout's door. In silence, Fangbone returned to the upright ammo box he'd been sitting on and slumped back into place.

"I'm afraid she has a point, Colonel," he finally said. "It's our law."

"Could be worse," I said, using only the sign language of the hearing-impaired to convey the thought.

Fangbone didn't have the faintest idea what I meant.

"Forget it," I finally grumbled out loud. "How many men can you give me?"

"Five, not counting Chandelier or your scout."

"My scout?"

"Johnny Doone. If anybody can trail Colonel Lane and the RIHMs, it is that lad. The boy is a natural tracker."

"Shit, Fang!" I yelled. "With a juvenile delinquent stirred in it's going to be like the goddamn League of Nations out there! How many foreign languages do you think I can handle for God's sakes? Next thing you're going to tell me is that my radio

man is a Romanian beet farmer and the guy on point only understands Hebrew! Give me a break, pal. I've got a friend to rescue
and a war to fight."

"Hmmmmm," Fangbone ruminated, "I think I understand
what you're saying."

"Thank Christ."

"Okay. Boris and Chaim don't go with you, eh? But it's going
to leave you short-handed I'm afraid."

Thankfully, the major's own personal bottle of Canadian Club
whisky was only a heartbeat away. It was all I could do to keep
my hands from shaking as I reached for the only sane thing left in
a world of buffoons and brain-damaged hootchy-kootchy dancers
with boobs like stainless steel sno-cones . . .

5

We shoved off early the next morning well before dawn; Chandelier on point followed in trace by myself, three of Fangbone's volunteers, and Johnny Doone. Our mission was a simple one: return to the crash site, find the trail of Melodie Lane and her captors, follow it, rescue her, then get her back to Detroit and FAC OPS before the river froze over and the RIHMs launched their invasion. Piece of cake.

We were traveling light—no body armor or crew-serves or sophisticated radio gear to weigh us down. Instead, we had opted for stealth and speed. Fangbone's supply people had managed to rustle up some goose-down winter camouflage snowsuits for us, and we were bristling with small arms including a brace of bufguns, automatic rifles, and grenades, as well as gas-smoke-illum canisters, throwing knives, poison darts, battle prods, decoding rings, tide charts, astrological forecasts, and a Ouiji board. Added to this prescribed load was chow for three days, citizen-band walkie-talkies, and of course the usual first-aid gear, vitamin pills, diet supplements, extra ammo, two changes of underwear, four of socks, a CD player with a collection of Johnny Cash discs, Tabasco sauce, mosquito repellent, a videotape of the '84 Olympics, a Coleman stove and three gallons of syngas, and an assortment of glass beads and iron ax heads in case we ran into any friendly Indians.

About twenty minutes out of the wire I unceremoniously dumped my ninety-pound field pack, deciding I would make do with the bare essentials as the others were doing—bufgun, knife, ammo, grenades, and a sock full of dried corn—nothing more.

We did not move on the surface. Instead, we were in what Fangbone had referred to as "the pipeline," and what I soon came to call (only half in jest) "the Windsor sewer system."

Fortunately, with the total devastation of the city above us and lack of any noticeable human population, our route was generally unimpeded. It stunk like hell, of course, and there was a slimy slippery gunk all over the deck and walls, but at least we didn't have to wade through neck-deep shit.

Apparently the RIHMs had overlooked this obvious communication network right under their feet (?), maybe because they had no such system in their own society (their excrement, instead of going down the drain, usually grew to adult RIHMhood in about three years) and therefore were ignorant of its existence, or maybe they were so convinced of their invulnerability that they just did not give a loud goddamn that a few human mice were scurrying around under the rubble-filled streets.

If so, they'd made one heck of a big mistake.

Chandelier knew the system like the back of her fragile china-doll-like hand. Even so, for the first few kilometers I was not only cold but edgy and tight, figuring that any creature that would put mutated sea serpents in a traffic tunnel would just as likely have dropped equally disturbing creations into a city's sewers, if only for the sheer perverted fun of it. As we continued on the trek, however, and as I noticed that no one else seemed to be showing too much concern, I was able to relax a little, even managed to whistle a few bars of "Strangers in the Night" before I was shushed.

"Brown out, old duff!" an excited Johnny Doone whispered in my ear. "You wanna rouse the blood beasts?"

Blood beasts? Sweet fuck on a Popsicle stick.

We traveled in almost total darkness, the only light coming from a battery-powered penlight Chandelier carried at her side with its cast pointed down at her feet. Every few hundred yards or so we would stop for a minute and in complete silence would listen for any sounds of approaching trouble. Then, with a wave from the penlight, we would move off again, slowly but deliberately eating up the miles—sorry—kilometers.

Dawn arrived as per usual. Topside a storm had moved in, so only a pasty gray light filtered down to us through the grates in the storm drains and the places where heavy shelling and bombing had ripped holes in the street above. It was enough.

We paused for a break about 10:00 A.M. While the others chewed some corn or smoked, Chandelier came back to see how I was doing.

"*Comment ça va,* Colonel Bunko?" she asked.

"That's Bucko, sweetroll, how many times I gotta tell ya."

"Ha! And I told you that you would never make it with all that gear you packed last night, *n'est pas?* And I was right."

In the gray haze I could see she was smiling at me with those scrumptious edible-looking lips of hers pulled back over brilliantly white teeth.

"Yeah, you were right, baby," I said, "but I thought you knew —I'm a jet-jock, not a grunt. This commandos-strike-at-dawn jazz is all new to me. By the way, if this little conversation wakes up the 'blood beasts,' I'm personally going to blow you away."

"Relax, Colonel," she laughed, "we passed the last nest in this sector several kilometers back. And yes, I know that you are a fly-boy. Major Fangbone showed me your FAC printout. Two Congressional Medals of Honor! *Très bien, monsieur!* Little did I suspect when I was a schoolgirl in Montreal that someday I would be on a mission with the Hero of Yaki Point and the Containment Bridge. You are a legend, *mon* Colonel, even in my country!"

"Yeah, right," I grumbled, even though I was pleased that such a neat chick was impressed with my rap sheet. "If you know that much, then you also know I got the second one in the mail . . . with postage due no less. Medals are for chumps, honey. Only thing they're good for is impressing boots and green shavetails. Give me a cash stipend anytime, I always say."

"Oh, you can't be serious. Is it not a patriot's highest duty to die gloriously for his or her country?"

"No way. Highest duty anybody's got is to save his own butt. Let the other guy's patriots try to win one for the Gripper [sic]. Me, I personally want to be there when they wheel out my ninetieth birthday cake."

Chandelier studied me for a few long moments, her expression giving away nothing. Then a very faint smile twitched at the corners of that lovely mouth.

"What?" I asked.

"I think, *mon* Colonel," she said slowly, "that you talk a good game."

"Think what you like," I answered curtly. "If you read my profile, then you know I've been an outlaw for the past ten years. That's hardly what you'd call heroic or patriotic."

"Oui," she said, knitting her eyebrows together as though unable to put a finger on something. "I understand you killed a high government official in a duel of some sort?"

"Actually, I dropped him from the belly of my Harrier jet off the coast of Georgia, but you're partially right. Technically speaking, I murdered his ass. His name was Kyle Befeeter and he deserved to die, but his people had connections in DC and I became a wanted man."

"And yet, you are here. How can that be if you are such a rogue?"

"Simple," I said. "Melodie Lane is a friend."

Chandelier nodded. "More than a friend, I think," she said softly.

"Once upon a time—yeah. Now? I don't know. Somewhere along the line she changed from being a cuddly love-toy into a hard-nosed FAC Cutter-jock.* But I guarantee, if the situation was reversed, she'd be risking her big bottom for me."

"So, it is for friendship you are here." Chandelier's dark eyes widened in awe. *"Quel beau geste!"*

"Sure, babe," I chuckled, "whatever you say."

I didn't have the heart to tell her about the ten thousand gold credits and total amnesty McBride had offered me as part of the deal. But what the hay. The guy who first said "Honesty is the best policy" obviously never tried to score in a singles' bar.

The patrol shoved off again, and we began to make better time, partially because of the daylight (dim as it was), but mostly because it was so damn cold that the only way to keep warm was to move along at a fairly brisk pace. Chandelier seemed to know exactly where she was going, so I did little more than follow her footprints in the greenish black slime.

The day passed without incident. At about 1600 we stopped again. This time Chandelier seemed just a little bit more spooked.

"We are near the spot where I found the body of P. Potts," she whispered, as she stood at the base of a steel rod ladder leading up to a closed manhole in the street. *"Beaucoup* RIHMs in this area. We will wait here until dark."

"Good," I muttered. "I need to take a leak."

"Then you've come to the right place." She managed to laugh. I was glad to see that the lady had a sense of humor, tiny and undeveloped as it might have been. "Roget!" she hissed to a

---

* The F/A 1020 Cutter, for more than thirty years the hottest aircraft in the American arsenal.

member of the patrol. "Go take point security. Be careful, *mon ami.*"

"Hey, Roget," I quipped as the young man brushed past me. "What's another word for 'sacrificial lamb'?"

The fair-haired youth just looked at me with an expression of total and complete ignorance. Another wasted joke, I thought, as I waved him away. Poor chucklehead. It was the last time I would ever see him alive.

We ate standing up. Gaulois—another member of the patrol—showed me how to mix my dried corn with some canteen water and turn it into a thick gruel. Although it had the color and consistency of vomit, I was too hungry to be picky.

As we slurped down the awful stuff I learned that my messmate had been an apprentice chef in Quebec before the Northern Horde had descended on his country. Thoughtlessly, I pointed out that if our current meal was any indication of his talent, the world owed the RIHMs a debt of gratitude. In a fit of pique, Gaulois stomped off back down the sewer, all the while making obscene hand and arm gestures in my direction.

Hell of an attitude for a comrade in arms, if you ask me, but that's what you get when you're involved with rank amateurs.

The third volunteer was a friendly chap from Alberta named Cliff. Cliff, I learned, had made a living pressing pants before the war started and was also active in the Canadian gay rights movement. I beat a hasty retreat from that conversation and was actually thinking about shooting-the-shit with Johnny Doone when we heard human screams coming from up the tube where poor Roget had been dispatched by Chandelier.

And *dispatched* is the correct word here, for as we would soon discover, the poor lad would never again have the chance to be rooked by a used amtrac salesman or fall for some phony telephone pitch offering a free vacation to Hawaii.

"Cliff!" Chandelier ordered. "Stay here and watch our rear! The rest of you with me!"

"My pleasure!" I heard Cliff answer as we began running through the slime in the direction of Roget's cries.

It was only about fifty meters, but it seemed a lot longer. By the time we reached the spot where footprints indicated Roget had stationed himself, his screams had stopped. All I could hear was the sound of something like a huge plastic garbage bag being dragged away through the sludge. This sound was accompanied by a repetitive clicking as though a blind man was tapping his way through the tunnel with his white cane.

"Blood beast!" I heard Doone exclaim in that cracking high-low pitch of his.

The boy immediately broke the breach of his bufgun and replaced his RIHM-fires with a couple of fléchettes. With a snap of the wrist, he closed the buf with the satisfying hollow thonk, which to a trained ear said the weapon was on-line. Before I could ask him what kind of powder load he was using—and, oh, by the way, what the exact specific fucking hell was a blood beast —he brushed past me, headed farther up the sewer.

And he would've probably gone up there and gotten us all killed if Chandelier hadn't reached out and grabbed him by the collar, halting his progress.

"Don't be a fool, Jean," she said, her words edged with sadness and fatigue. "It is too late."

"No, it ain't," Doone growled. "I can hear the fracker! It ain't got that far yet. Roget was a no-kay duder. That frackin' crawly is gonna pay!"

"Non, it will not, *mon petit,"* Chandelier said, still holding his collar. "Roget is gone. Killing the blood beast will only attract the attention of our enemies."

She waited for a moment. When she saw that Doone was no longer pulling against her, she gently released him. Johnny took another step in the direction of the fast-fading clicking sounds, stopped, then turned his head towards Chandelier. Surprisingly, I detected a glint of a tear in the boy's eyes. The woman must have seen it, too, for she took his face in her hands and kissed him full on the lips, apparently *à la français.*

Erotic as hell if you want to know the God's honest truth, and I was seriously considering stepping up for my own share of bilingual cultural exchange when my eye caught movement far up the sewer. It was a spot where a large artillery shell or bomb had opened a large hole in the street. The hour was late, and it was January, and the storm topside was getting worse, but there was still enough gray muted light being thrown through that hole for me to get my first glimpse of a blood beast. Even today, my guts run cold just remembering that moment.

At first I thought I was seeing a badly scuffed medicine ball about the size of a classic 1994 Chrysler bubble van. Then, as my sight adjusted to the distant light, I knew I was watching some monstrous living thing with a body that was more tear-drop-shaped than round, covered in something closer to grayish-brown vinyl than scuffed leather.

The beast's movements were awkward and slow, as though it was dragging a tremendous body weight with its woefully inadequate spidery legs. It was these legs, each tapering to a point, that were causing the clicking sound as they pulled that massive shape away from us through the sewer.

The blood beast, I finally realized, was a tick the size of a pickup truck, bloated beyond reason with the vital body fluids of poor Roget.

Visions of my childhood—when I would pluck miniature versions of this same insect from the ears of my dear and faithful dog, Tripod—suddenly infested my brain.*

"I thought you said we'd already passed through their nests?" I inquired of Chandelier once the monster moved out of the light.

"I guess I was wrong," she admitted. "Usually you don't see them this far from the river."

"Well, listen," I said, turning around smartly and heading back to where the faithful Cliff guarded our rear, "it's been swell, but I've had my fill of below-ground surprises for this lifetime. See you topside, okay?"

"But, Colonel," Chandelier called, the tension heavy in her voice, "you can't go up there now! You will reveal our position to the RIHMs! Poor Roget will have died for nothing, and your Melodie Lane will certainly be condemned!"

"Tough tits!" I retorted. "At least I'll die in battle and not from some damn giant insect bite! Besides, from what I can see,

---

* I vividly recalled one particular fucker that I'd allow to feed on that poor three-legged creature long after I'd discovered the thing lodged on the back of Tri's neck. When the bastard was as big as a golf ball, I'd taken great delight in excising it from my pet and pinning it to my English teacher's desk blotter where she was sure to see it during first period. Her screams, they tell me, still echo in the hallowed halls of Twenty-nine Palms High. The blood beast in the sewer was about a thousand times bigger.

there's a blue-norther blowing up out there right now. The RIHMs might be mutants, but they're not stupid enough to be caught exposed and unprotected in such a storm."

"And you are?"

"I've got no choice, lady. And neither do you. This storm means the river might freeze over sooner than we thought. Besides, it'll be perfect cover."

I'd taken another dozen steps before she spoke again. "Colonel," she called.

"What?" I slowed but didn't stop.

"You are right. It is a time for boldness. We shall go up. Come, Johnny! Gaulois! Not a moment to lose. We shall avenge Roget and save all of humankind. Arise, *mes amis!* Destiny awaits us!"

For all our melodramatics, both Chandelier and I forgot one important point: Not only would the storm keep the RIHMs from spotting us, but it would also wipe out any trail—however cold—Melodie might have left when she was captured.

Little wonder then, when we pushed through the manhole cover leading out of the sewer and found six inches of new snow on the ground, as well as a forty-knot wind blowing it into frozen drifts, Johnny Doone articulated the feelings of the whole patrol.

"Butt rape," he fumed.

"I'll second that emotion," Cliff joined in.

"Johnny," Chandelier asked a few minutes later, after we'd all piled out of the sewer, "can you find nothing?"

The words were literally whipped out of her mouth by the gale. Already snow was beginning to collect on our hats, shoulders, and gear.

"Hell, that ain't the prob," the boy called out as he staggered around through the mounds of snow-covered debris looking for some sign. "Any dickwick can find *nothing*. I'm tryin ta find *something!*"

"I thought you were suppose to be the world's greatest tracker, kid?" I hollered into the teeth of the shrieking wind.

"Memo this, old frack!" Doone called back, raising a middle finger in my direction, then turning away to resume his useless search.

By this time Cliff and Gaulois had crawled to the top of a high pile of rubble where they could keep a three-sixty lookout. While

Johnny continued to stomp around the area Chandelier claimed was the spot where she'd hollied the body of Melodie's copilot (the carcass of the unfortunate Ms. P. Potts was nowhere to be seen), I tried to keep warm by burying my hands in the beautiful woman's undergarments.

At least that's what I was contemplating when Doone rudely butted in.

"Bite this, old slug!" he shouted joyfully. He was pointing down at something in the new snow. "Come catch a glimpse!"

Chandelier and I staggered over to the side of the clearing where he was crouched. There, like the indentation your head might leave in last night's pillow, was a very faint impression of a bootprint.

"See what I have found, Fat Bear," Doone shouted into my face, doing his bad imitation of a Hollywood Indian. "Pony soldiers, many wagons, pass this way two moons ago. Ugh."

"Very humorous, John!" I yelled in his ear. "Where do you want the first bullet? Kneecap or groin?"

The boy gave out a laugh. "Only foolin, old duder. Check this." He got up and began moving around, pointing to other indentations in the snow. "Them there was made by FAC boots. Over here, RIHM. Six of 'em. They did their hikin when it was muddy. Footprints froze. Had to be end of November, last time ground was thawed round these parts. Snow's driftin in the prints but I can still follow 'em. Gotta burn rubber, though, or else the storm'll eat 'um up."

"You're full of it, kid!" I roared over the turbulence. "Those aren't tracks. Just marks from all the shelling."

I felt busy fingers tugging on my parka. "But, Colonel," Chandelier shouted into my ear as I bent down to hear her better, "what other choice do we have? We either follow the boy or go back into the sewer. Otherwise, we will sit here and freeze to death."

What she said made sense. And as much as I doubted the teenage boy's tracking ability, there was no way I was going to descend underground again, not with a rogue blood beast on the rampage.

"You're absolutely correct," I said. "Lead on, John."

* * *

We moved out in a modified wedge formation towards the southeast, Gaulois and Cliff on the flanks, Doone far out front, Chandelier at the top of the wedge, yours truly back in patrol command. Tactically, this choice of formation was sound. Practically, it sucked. Not only did the terrain not cooperate, but as the storm continued, and as the pale light melted into darkness, we began losing contact with each other. Rather than risk somebody getting lost, we finally banded together, linked ourselves with rope, and dutifully followed Doone single file through the brutalized landscape.

The cold was bone-numbing; my feet and hands soon lost most of their feeling. Ice formed on eyebrows and eyelashes, grew into icicles, then painfully broke off, only to be replaced shortly by more of the same. Nostril hairs froze, making breathing difficult, and the wind whipping on exposed flesh slashed like a thousand tiny razor blades. (I think it goes without saying that under such circumstances no one requested any stops for a head-call.)

It was about two in the morning when we finally came to a halt. After a very long wait, I heard Doone talking to Chandelier and moved up to see what was going on. The wind had died down a little, but the dense cloud cover continued to hide the moon, and it was still about as dark out there as the bottom of a tar pit. Which explains why I rammed right into Chandelier and promptly chipped a tooth on one of her breasts.

No, that isn't quite true. Actually, my mouth hit the muzzle of her bufgun. Whatever the source, however, the slap of cold metal against tooth enamel rammed a bicycle spoke deep into my brain and I'm afraid I cried out.

"Colonel, that must be you," Chandelier fumed. *"Mon Dieu!* Have you no patience?"

"Can the small talk, honey," I mumbled through my hand. "What's the hot poop?"

"Tracks lead to the airport, old jim," I heard Doone say, sniffling and snorting from a runny nose. "I was thinkin about goin in for a lookie. Wanna come along?"

"Anything to get warm," I answered.

"If you're not back in exactly sixty minutes, we will come in after you," Chandelier said.

"Roger that," I answered, unslinging my own buf and checking to see that the bore was clear of ice and snow. "Let's go, kid."

"And remember, Colonel," Chandelier cautioned as I made to follow Doone, "if your Melodie Lane is in there, she has been their captive for almost two months. She may not be the same woman you once knew, but she must live! For all our sakes!"

"I can dig it," I said, trying to put on a happy face. Then, realizing how dark it was, I gave up. "You be careful, hear? Keep an eye on your six . . . especially with Cliff behind you." I turned and whispered loudly, "Any port in a storm, right, Cliff?"

"That's right, asshole," a voice growled from the darkness.

Gross insubordination, of course, but there was no time to waste reprimanding anyone; there were bigger fish to buy (sic).

After I remembered to untie myself from our lifeline, Doone and I humped about five hundred meters until we hit the snow-covered Tarmac of one of the runways and followed it on in to the terminal area. I knew that any sensors or other forms of electronic surveillance would be rendered useless by the ice and wind of the storm, and if the RIHMs had assigned perimeter sentries, they were all obviously bagging it (probably scrunched up someplace trying to keep warm), because we saw nary a one and heard no challenge.

I was initially amazed to see in the dim glow of a few functioning standing lights that most of the airport's buildings were still intact, apparently unscathed by shot or shell. Then I realized that FAC had spared the area intentionally. If ever there was to be a counterinvasion by our forces, an intact airport would be of invaluable strategic importance. Since the RIHMs had no airpower at all, the airport was useless to them anyway, so there was no reason for us to reduce it.

Why the enemy hadn't been able to reach the same conclusion, and thus have safely demolished the entire Windsor airport, was not very clear. Once again, I think, they were way overconfident. Either that or they just liked having a place above ground that FAC would not likely bomb.

Not that the RIHMs hadn't installed defensive positions. As Johnny and I made our way carefully towards the main terminal we passed numerous looming shapes and shadows that I could identify as missile batteries and antiaircraft gun emplacements as well as mobile radar vans and communication gear. Perhaps they had left the airport intact as a trap, for there was nothing the RIHMs would like better than a chance to reduce our aircraft inventory.

As Doone and I neared the main terminal, I spotted the first of the enemy's troops. They were on guard up in the air-control tower, and it was pretty doggone obvious that they weren't too attentive to duty; otherwise the boy and I would've already been waxed, since they had a perfect view of all avenues of approach. From what little I could see, they were just kind of lounging around up there, probably BS-ing and drinking coffee and generally killing time till dawn. That's the way it is with most soldiers far from the front. Alertness, I have found, is directly proportional to the likelihood of getting shot—when one goes down, so too does the other.*

"You think she's in there, old scrum?" Doone whispered in my ear as we paused in the shadows of a nearby outbuilding.

"If she's still alive," I said. "Makes sense they'd keep her at the main building. Better security."

"Bet it's crawlin with RIHMs in there."

"Could be they're all crapped out," I answered.

"Crapped out?" the boy questioned. "You mean they can't have no more babies? What's that got ta do with—"

"Asleep," I cut in. "I mean maybe they're all asleep. Come on, let's look for a back entrance."

We found a door on the side of the main building that read Employees Only, Eh? It was locked, but with a quick flick of my K-17 knife, I popped it open. Doone went in first; I followed him a second later after checking to make sure the coast was clear.

Except for half a dozen well-armed RIHMs with their weapons pointed at our heads, and what was left of Frank Tibbs, the hallway was deserted.

"What's the matter, kid?" Tibbs gurgled almost indecipherably

---

* *Editor's Note:* According to Doctor James-Willy Chung's *Military Psychology For Beginners,* Colonel Bucko's theory is flawed. True, as the probability of getting shot decreases, alertness also declines. However, as alertness declines, the probability of getting shot increases. Therefore, the two are not directly proportional.

to Johnny as he pointed up at the sign on the door. "Can't you read?"

Then he turned to me. For an instant I thought I saw what could have been either a smile or a very badly infected sword wound crease his rotting face. "Hello, Will," I think he said. "We've been expecting you."

6

Frank Tibbs. Once upon a time, way back in the days of the old United States Marine Corps and later in FAC, Tibbs and my old man had been as close as two guys can get without committing an act of sodomy. Both were Cutter jocks, which automatically made them blood brothers of the soul, but added to that was the fact that Major Frank Tibbs flew Lieutenant Colonel Wolf Bucko's wing, a position that above all required absolute unshakeable mutual trust.

On the last combat sortie he would ever make, my dad had vectored into a nest of Western RIHMs holed up in San Jose, thinking, I'm sure, that Frank Tibbs was right there beside him as always, watching his six for SAMs. Imagine the Wolf's surprise then when he took a surface-to-air missile up the poop-shute and discovered that his bosom buddy had lit up afterburner and gone over to the enemy.

Even though his bird was mortally wounded, Pap had been able to hit the silk successfully, but the RIHMs had torched his chute on the way down, and by the time FAC Search and Rescue could get him back to the base hospital at Twenty-nine Palms, he was already a goner.

On his deathbed, Dad had made me swear that I would avenge the treachery perpetrated on him by Tibbs.

For the next twenty-plus years, Uncle Frank had loomed just over the next cloud bank or horizon, never quite close enough for me to lock on to with my gun sights, always just out of range of whatever ordnance I was carrying. No matter where I went or what I did, though, there remained the certain knowledge that someday I would track the bastard down and avenge Wolf Bucko.

Strangely enough, on the few occasions when he and I had butted heads in person, it seemed he somehow always ended up saving my ass. This macabre twist of irony didn't change my mind though; I still wanted him dead, still dreamed of the day I'd open his guts and rip out his heart with my own two hands . . .

* * *

So it had been for more than a score of years. During that time a lot of garbage scows had passed under the bridge, but I didn't realize just how many until I came face-to-face with Tibbs again there in the Windsor airport terminal building. Uncle Frank was in real bad shape.

Imagine, if you will, what a hundred and sixty pounds of cirrhosis of the liver might look like under an electron holoscope.

For those without any medical background, try to picture a severely worn and bent man in his late seventies with a bald crown and what little hair he had left around the edges braided and hanging far down his back. His fingernails, long and curled and yellow, looked as though they hadn't been cut in years, and his skin had the color and texture of tapioca pudding that hadn't set quite right. His toothless mouth reminded me of a broken fever blister, and his too-bright eyes were red-rimmed and leaking a reddish-brown gunk that smelled like brake fluid. All in all, from where I was standing, Frank Tibbs just didn't appear to be doing all that hot in his twilight years.

On the other hand, I really didn't have time to get a close look at him. After being waylaid at the door, Doone and I were disarmed, stripped naked, and marched inside the building.

Even though the shock of capture had not completely worn off, it quickly became apparent to me, judging by the number of battle totems hanging from the walls, that we were in nothing less than the headquarters of Supreme RIHM Command. Each totem represented an individual tribal cell (about a battalion's worth of troops), and I counted seventy-two of them before I lost track. Plainly, there was a shitpot full of individual RIHM commands being controlled from under that roof—a fact I salted away for future reference.

You had to hand it to the bastards: if nothing else, their science was ingenious. Unable to mass-manufacture those commodities required of sophisticated modern warfare, and unwilling to rely solely on the world's unscrupulous arms dealers for support, whenever possible the RIHMs had substituted gross mutations of living creatures to replace missing silicon and super conductor technology.

For instance, fully half of the communication gear I saw as I was rushed through their HQ was made up of insect parts grafted onto old transistor radios, televisions, and antique telephone equipment. Whiplike cockroach antennas a thousand times larger than normal sprouted out of plastic and fake wood console cabinets. One surveillance system was a whole bank of giant fly heads, their multiport omnidirectional eyes blinking a silky blue-green light through bundles of colorful electric cables connected to a wide-screen Sony hanging from the ceiling. Transmitters made up of what looked like huge cricket legs hooked into a field telephone switchboard sawed out a constant chirp, which I assumed could be picked up at the other end of the line and translated using the same technology as a translation helmet.

Oh hell, there were all kinds of other stuff that I couldn't even guess the function of: mandibles and pinchers and gossamer wings, all plugged in, attached to, wired up, or hooked into a lot of electronic gizmos and gadgets straight out of one of those old Radio Shack catalogs.

"Hey, Frank," I shouted without looking back at him, "I don't know if you realize it or not, but you guys have got one hell of a big bug problem here!"

Someone put a rifle butt between my shoulder blades and sent me tumbling down the corridor. By the time I came to a stop, two of the fungoid guards were jerking me to my feet. Frank gargled and gagged something to them, and I suddenly found myself being shoved through an open doorway into a small room, bare except for a table and a couple of chairs. I turned just in time to see Doone being dragged off down the hall.

"You speak their lingo pretty good, Frank," I snarled. "Where're they taking the boy?"

"He'll be examined, interrogated, then executed," I think Tibbs answered as he shut the door behind him. He sounded as though he had a mouthful of warm soapsuds.

"You hurt him and you'll answer to me, garbage face."

Frank made a sound that could've either been a laugh or a toilet flushing. He tossed me a translation helmet and squeezed one over his own gnarled old head.

"There," I heard him say clearly and distinctly through my earpieces, "now we can talk. Sorry, but I'm losing my English very quickly now. Voicebox, you know. Shot to hell."

"I asked you about the boy," I said as authoritatively as I

could, given the fact that I was standing in front of him buck naked.

"He's ground round," Frank shot back. He paused then, to give me a once-over. "I see you've gained some weight," he eventually commented. "Don't worry, though, we'll have that flab off you in no time."

"Bon appetit," I sneered. "I hope you fucking choke."

"Ninety-nine percent of the time, you'd be right. But there is absolutely no way we'd feed on the great Eagleheart.* No, the Grand Council has already ruled that you'll be stuffed and put on display in the Great Hall of Heroic Enemies. Course, by the looks of it, you've already done half our work for us. Stuffed, I mean. Hee hee hee."

"You're a rotting scab, Tibbs. And I mean that in the finest sense of the word. But you're making a big mistake with that kid. He's a scout with the MapleLeaf Underground. He led me here. You waste him, and you'll throw away a good chance to find out where their hideout is. I sure as hell couldn't tell ya."

"Well, thanks for the tip, Will. I appreciate it. You can relax though. Hadn't intended on doing him in until tomorrow at the earliest. Have to say in all honesty that I did not expect such excellent cooperation from you. Not *yet* anyway."

"Implying what?"

"There you go again," Tibbs chuckled, "going off half-cocked before you know what's going on. I just want to talk to you, that's all. Explain a few things."

"Before they stuff and mount me."

"We've all gotta go sometime. Ha! Just kidding. Actually, I think you're old enough now to grasp some facts that a younger Will Bucko couldn't."

"Where's Melodie Lane?"

"I wondered how long it would take you to get around to her. She was my bait, you see, to get you here. When I heard she'd been shot down and captured, I jumped. Leaked word to your side that we had her. I knew if FAC got desperate enough, they'd pull you in. And it worked."

* "Eagleheart" was the nickname given to Will by the Western RIHMs after his single-handed victory over them at the Battle of Yaki Point. See Volume 1 for details of that great fight.

I could've jumped him then and strangled the life out of him before any of his friends could arrive. He was old and frail and I imagined his neck would snap like a year-old wishbone. That's what I wanted to do, but something told me that if Melodie was still alive, my killing Tibbs would be like signing her death warrant.

"Can I see her, Frank?" I asked.

"In due time. First, let's you and me have a little chat. Maybe you won't have to be stuffed after all. Sit."

He motioned me to the table where we sat down across from each other in aluminum chairs. You wanna talk brass monkeys, let me tell ya—felt like I was sitting on a fifty-pound block of dry ice.

"Smoke 'em if ya got 'em," Frank said through the helmet.

"Screw you, Tibbs," I responded, delicately placing my hands under my buttocks. "And what's all this crap about you luring me here? What the hell would you want with me? Until a few weeks ago I was nothing but a FAC fugitive living at the Hacienda del Placenta Negro. If you're after U.S. intelligence, you're barking up the wrong alley [sic]."

Frank clasped his gloved hands in front of him on the table. "Let me ask you something, Will," he said after a moment or two during which he seemed to be gathering his thoughts. "Just how much do you know about the RIHMs? As a people, I mean."

"Come on, Frank, who gives a shit?"

"Do you know of their origins?"

"Common knowledge," I answered, already a little bored. "After the Big Blast various combinations of nuclear radiation, hydrocarbons, man-made chemicals, and microbe technology produced genetic mutations of the human form. Said mutations reproduced and grew at ten times the normal rate. Within a few years the RIHM Tribal Nations appeared and began their war of global domination against the human race. We could've wiped them out in an instant, but because any use of nuclear weapons results only in increasing their numbers, we've had to fight your friends on a conventional basis. At first, as a result of the huge loss of human life coming from even the very limited exchange of the Big Blast, we had some setbacks. But you bastards ain't been too successful lately, have ya, Frank? Little glitch in your plans. RIHMs can't sustain flight because of a hereditary inner ear imbalance. So FAC rules the air, and without the air you and the rest of these pustules cannot win. Stop me here if I start offending anyone."

"Spoken like a true bigot," Frank whispered. "My God, they've brainwashed you pretty damn well, haven't they?"

"Brainwashed? You're a little confused, aren't you, pal? *You're* the one who's spent the last twenty-three, twenty-four years fighting for these walking sores. Hell, Frank, not only was your brain washed, but it was hung out to dry!"

Tibbs made a horrible choking sound, like somebody with double pneumonia trying to clear a passage. "Damn you!" he at last said. "I told her it would be like talking to the sink!"

"Told who?"

"Your mother."

"Yeah, right." I laughed coldly. "You had me going, ya know, after you sent me that message at Boca Grande saying that my mother was still alive. When I had a chance to think about it, though, I knew you were lying. Except for jet jocks like Melodie, RIHMs don't keep woman prisoners."

"Who said she was a prisoner?"

Something inside of me snapped when he said that. The idea that my poor old mum, who never wanted anything more than to become a star on Broadway (or at least garner a supporting role on a daytime soap), had somehow survived the Cuban neutron attack on New York and then had freely joined the RIHMs was just too much to bear.

"You lying scum!" I roared as I launched myself across the table at him. My head hit him squarely in the chest, and he and his chair toppled over backwards with me on top. We rolled across the cold deck in each other's arms—me grappling for his throat, Frank making sounds like a rubber plunger sucking mud.

He was a helluva lot stronger than I had thought. Rather than snapping like a twig, he did a pretty good job of reversing the tables on me. Quicker than I like to admit, he had my shoulders pinned. Still, by the way he was gasping, I could tell that I'd given him a pretty fair go-around.

"Join us, Will," he croaked. His own translation helmet had come off during the melee, but mine was still on so I could understand what he was saying. "Join us before it's too late! Mankind is finished. WE ARE THE FUTURE! FOR YOUR MOTHER'S SAKE, I OFFER YOU SALVATION!"

At which point (and if you're eating anything, don't read any further) his eyes seemed to roll to the back of his head so only two brownish yellow blood shot orbs remained. Then horribly, the festering slash that was Frank Tibbs's mouth opened and an appendage that might once have been his tongue but now more closely resembled a squid tentacle shot out and wrapped itself around my neck. It began to squeeze as though determined to pop off the top of my head like a big infected pimple. With my shoulders pinned, there wasn't much I could do except beg for mercy.

"Pretty neat Halloween mask, Frank," I managed to sputter. "Okay. I give. You want me to join up? You got it. Where do I sign?"

He did not answer. Instead, his whole body began to quiver and shake as though there was some great conflict (good vs. evil? Ying vs. yang? Louis vs. Schmelling?) going on inside him. The part of him that had me by the throat started to spasm, first tightening then loosening its death grip on my brain's blood supply.

This goofy bout of indecision went on for about thirty seconds, with Tibbs and his tongue getting more and more violent until finally he most closely resembled my dad on the day so long ago when he'd received ten million jigavolts from the toilet seat I'd rigged to the base power station to get even with him for cutting my allowance. Much to my delight and relief, the spasms became so great that Tibbs was finally tossed off my body and thrown clear across the room where he smashed into the wall.

By this time, of course, I was three shades of purple and almost out cold. Somehow, however, I willed myself to my feet and closed in for the kill. Brandishing the only weapon I could find— one of the aluminum chairs we'd been sitting on—I approached the man-thing as he struggled to regain his composure. With all the strength I had left, I raised the chair over my head and brought it down on the back of his neck.

There was a sharp crack, a groan, then Frank went facedown. Gasping for breath, I dropped the now grotesquely bent chair, spread my arms, and cried to the heavens.

"Hear me, O father! Now have I avenged thee!"

I'd heard the lines many years before in some old late-show vid about Vikings. The words seemed appropriate, even though I was not all that sure Frank Tibbs was dead. From where I stood, huffing and puffing, it looked like his chest was moving up and down in a fairly regular pattern.

Yeah, you're right. I should've bashed his brains in right then and there and been done with the whole sordid deal. Sentimental old me, though, got to remembering that Uncle Frank had saved my life once after I'd been mortally wounded at Yaki Point. And ten years later, after rescuing me from the sinking Shrimper oil rig called Paradise Cove, he'd tried to warn me about the devious Carlos Membranous, which I guess counted for something, too.

"We're even, Frank," I said, sinking to my knees beside him. "If we ever fight again, though, it'll be to the death."

Even though I knew Tibbs couldn't hear me, I was just as certain that the Wolf could. "Hope you understand, Pop," I whispered.

Quickly, I stripped the unconscious man of his coveralls, which reminded me of the skin of a large reptile. Luck was finally with me; he was wearing insulated longjohns so the coveralls were technically uncontaminated even though they smelled like decomposing fishtails. Yes, I knew wearing RIHM clothing was dangerous, but I had no choice. A naked human would stick out like a sore dick if caught wandering around Supreme Headquarters.

I found a survival knife in one of Frank's boots and used it to complete my disguise. After all, no RIHM sentry was going to take me for Frank Tibbs unless I was wearing that long gray braid of hair. So I gave the bastard a field-expedient crew cut, tied one end of the braid inside my translation helmet, and went dee-dee boppin out the door like I owned the place.

Two RIHM sentries armed with stun guns were waiting for me. It was time to put up or get sucked up.

"HA!" I roared through my mouthpiece. "The once mighty Eagleheart has passed out in a quivering pool of fear! The interrogation is over for a while, I'm afraid."

Although neither sentry was wearing a translation helmet, I hoped my yelling would make up for this lack of retransmission capability on their part. *

---

* The old AN-604 translation helmet would transmit a translation of whatever language it had been preset for—in this case, RIHM. Optimum

"You there!" I ordered one of them. "Lock that door and see to it that nobody enters without my permission. And you," I shouted, turning on the second RIHM, "take me to where the female human is being kept. Immediately!"

"Yes, O great Hawkclaw," the RIHM sentry responded, as the other one slammed shut the door and threw the electronic bolts. "Yet the female human does remain where she has been these past weeks—in your quarters."

"Well, I knew that, you human drizzle! What do you take me for, a fool? I need someone to come with me, to, ah, you know, make sure the ah—"

"That the boy doesn't try anything funny?" the second RIHM sentry suggested hopefully.

"Exactly!" I bellowed back. "Now, let's go!"

The subservient idiot insisted on me taking the lead. Since I didn't have the slightest idea where I was going, there wasn't anything I could do except test my improvisational acting ability one more time.

"OW!" I howled, crumpling to the deck as if in extreme pain.

"Hawkclaw? What is it, my lord?" the cringing toady wanted to know, rushing to where I lay writhing in agony.

"Old football injury," I spat between gritted teeth. "Trick knee. Give me a hand, will ya?"

The monster helped me to my feet, and I used him as a crutch as we staggered off down the corridor.

"Do you want to go to sickbay, my lord?" the thing snorted.

"No," I answered, "just get me to my quarters. I'll be all right. It pops right back in. What's your name again, son?"

"Percodan, sire," the putrid mass responded.

"Where you from, Perc?"

"Originally, sire?"

"Whatever."

"Third Amphibian Fungus Colony. Although, when I was six weeks old, the whole family moved to the Guano Caves of the Rotary King. That's where I grew up, so technically speaking, I guess, I'd have to say that was home."

---

comm was achieved with two units, but in a pinch, a transmission from a single helmet could be understood up to ten meters away if sent loudly enough.

"Right. Fine. Ah, any brothers and sisters?"

"Oh, hell yes, sire. About six thousand before the petri dish broke."

This incredible banter went on for what seemed like a half an hour as the two of us limped to Frank's quarters. Finally, the RIHM called Percodan stopped in front of a door and indicated by a sudden interest in his weapon that we had arrived at our destination. I reached for the handle and pushed, but nothing happened.

"It's locked!" I said with some surprise.

"Correct, sire," Perc answered. "So the humans could not escape."

"Open it for me," I ordered.

"As you wish, sire."

Using his long elephantlike proboscis as a third arm, the sentry reached over and plucked a T-shaped piece of plastic from my belt, then inserted it into the door's scanner lock. When the door opened with a soft pop, I felt certain I was coming across to the sentry as the lad in the village who'd been dropped on his head at an early age.

"Thanks, son," I said. "The pressures and responsibilities of high command are apparently getting to me. Sometimes I don't even remember to shave."

"Shave, sire?"

"Forget it. Just a disgusting human trait. You can get back to duty. Appreciate your help, but I can handle it from here."

"Shall I have them send you some refreshment, sire? A fine fat Windsor burgher perhaps?"

"Some other time. Run along now, Percodan. You're dismissed."

After giving me some sort of bizarre salute with his long honker, the evil creature slogged off down the corridor. I waited until he was turning a corner, then slipped into Frank's quarters and closed the door behind me.

What I found there was enough to make me wonder again why I hadn't killed Tibbs when I'd had the chance.

7

If there were any doubts that Frank Tibbs had gone completely native, those thoughts were put to rest once and for all when I turned from the doorway of his quarters and took my first gander at the ghastly suite of rooms he called home. Place looked like the inside of a head cold.

Hanging from the ceiling were long dripping tendrils of a clear jellylike substance that reminded me of raw eggs minus the yolk. As I watched, a strand of the stuff broke away from the ceiling and fell to the deck where some sort of suction device located in the baseboards slurped it out of the room.

Where a bunk should have been there was a large cocoon made out of a milky translucent skin so delicate against the light as to display the shadows of veinlike vessels throbbing just beneath the outer membrane. Deep inside, I thought I could vaguely see the shape of a very large insect. Like some huge maggot, the creature was obviously using the space until it reached maturity and could hatch. (Probably, I surmised, into parts for a RIHM early warning radar or cellular car phone.)

The source of the room's light was remarkable in itself, being a clear lucite cylinder about the size of a trash can filled with some sort of lime-colored crap that produced chemical illumination as it broke up and then reformed in a constant slow churn.

The light revealed a separate living area, which included some furniture that looked like toadstools and a couch made out of clear plastic filled with a brownish sludge that you usually only see on the bottoms of toilet bowls that haven't been cleaned in several years.

Sitting on the couch, as oblivious to his surroundings as you please, was none other than my good friend Johnny Doone, dressed in his own clothes and thumbing through old copies of a magazine called *Boy's Life*, which I took to be Uncle Frank's last link with the human race.*

---

* For those less literately inclined, *Boy's Life* was a periodical published during a good chunk of the twentieth century, which, through its in-

"What say, whacker," Johnny uttered, obviously unable to recognize me in my RIHM garb. "What's a duder gotta do ta get some grub around here? And what've ya done with Colonel Bucko, ya heathen smug."

"If it's grub you want, Johnny," I said, lifting the helmet from my shoulders while gesturing back towards the throbbing cocoon, "there's enough meat in that baby over there to give you the backyard trots for a week."

His eyes widened in recognition, and he immediately got up and began pounding me on the back as though I was choking on a hunk of Kansas City strip. "Colonel Bucko!" he yelped. "Thought you was a dead-goner for sure! Plenty good to see ya, old bum! What's it been, two-three years?"

"About half an hour, you smartass punk." I laughed.

Despite the manly banter, I was glad to see the kid. Always assuming the worst, I'd already written him off to the horrors of RIHM torture and scientific mutilation. It was heartening to see him there, still in one piece, still generally human (or as human as a teenager can ever get). At once I suspected that Tibbs had delayed torturing the boy as another trump card to be used in his mad game to convert me to his cause. With both Melodie and Doone safely in his clutches—to torture and maim in front of me —he undoubtedly thought he was doubling his chances of breaking my spirit. Fat fucking chance.

"Nice seams, duder," Doone said, admiring my RIHM coveralls after I'd explained to him how I'd gotten away from Frank Tibbs. "Where'd ya find a K mart open this late?"

"Get hosed, kid. Then tell me where Colonel Lane is hiding. I don't know how long Tibbs will stay unconscious, but I'd like to shag ass before every mungball in this place starts looking for us."

"Colonel Lane?" Doone seemed surprised. "Didn't you see her when you came in?"

"No," I said, just before his meaning dawned on me. "Aw, Christ. Don't tell me she's—"

"Sleepin in that nifty body bag over by the door!"

sightful articles, cartoons, and essays, urged young boys to live a good, clean, celibate life, and to sell cans of white salve to their neighbors at Christmas time.

I might've known. The mission had been one ill-conceived shit hole after another since I'd left Motown, and frankly, I was getting tired of wading through the crap. For a split second I wondered if maybe Tibbs had been right, maybe humankind *would* be better off if it got wiped off the face of the earth. At least then I wouldn't get stuck with so many disgusting little jobs trying to save it.

"Did you want to wake her up, coach?" Doone asked, breaking my depressing chain of thought.

"Naw, we'll let her get her beauty sleep," I answered sarcastically. "She'll need it when the RIHMs get around to turning her into strained baby food." None too gently I reached over and gave the boy a nuggie. "Calling all cars, calling all cars," I hollered in his ear. "Be on the lookout for teenage shit-for-brains posing as Canadian freedom fighter. Suspect is armed and extremely dumb. Calling all cars."

Johnny jumped away from my lethal knuckle, rubbing the top of his head and looking at me with a painful expression. "Hey! What's the play, old slug? You tryin to bean me? She was in that thing when I got here, already snorin like a honker!"

I answered by reaching down and pulling Frank's knife out of my boot top. "Cry me a river, John," I said as I turned towards the cocoon. "Then give me a hand. Time for reveille."

Opening that cocoon was like gutting a rotten carp. The membrane was so putrid that once I'd punctured it, the knife did not cut it as much as it simply pulled it apart, releasing a flood of warm fluid very similar to the stuff dripping from the overhead. Once deflated, the walls of the cocoon peeled away like the skin on overripe fruit, and we soon had Melodie free of her prison.

Better she'd stayed in bed.

They had wrapped her body in lengths of two-inch linen, like some ancient Egyptian mummy. Only her head had been left unswathed, which was a bit of good luck; otherwise, I would never have imagined that this thing was Melodie Lane, my one and only true love.

And even then I couldn't be sure, for when Johnny and I had wiped away some of the mucilage she was packed in, there was still a certain amount of doubt in my mind that this was Melodie. Her beautiful blond hair had been hacked short and was artificially darkened by a thick layer of Cosmoline, which plastered it to her skull. Her face looked emaciated, as though she'd lost weight, all hollowed-eyed and sharp-boned and sunken-cheeked. Her lips were bloodless, her skin the color of congealed bacon grease, her smooth complexion pitted with angry sores and lesions. It was enough to make Helena Rubinstein turn over in her grave.

Melodie was either in a coma or sleeping very soundly. I slapped her face a few times to revive her and got nothing more for my trouble than a few bruised knuckles.

"Mel," I whispered in her ear after clearing it of the grease she'd been packed in like some goddamn crew-served machine gun in a mount-out box. "It's me, Will. Time to go home." There was no response whatsoever. "Come on," I said to Doone, "let's get her out of these bandages. I can feel her heart beating, but the pulse is slow and weak. She needs air!"

"Hell, cap," Johnny frowned, "what this lady needs is a priest. And I'll tell ya what, we ain't gonna get far trying to haul the body back to camp. Must weigh two hundred pounds."

"Don't give me that, kid," I snarled. "She's alive, and as long as she's alive she goes out of here with us, I don't care if we've got to carry her piggyback! Now you go keep a lookout at the door while I work on these bandages!"

Doone wandered off muttering something about looking for a forklift, but I was too worried to bother with him. I grabbed a section of Melodie's wrapping up near her neck and gave it a hard pull. It came away like wallpaper being torn from a wall, as though it had been glued on her body. I imagine it felt about the same as having a six-foot strip of adhesive tape pulled from a hairy part of your anatomy.

Painful as hell, but beneficial also, for a moment after I had pulled on the wrap, Melodie's eyes bulged open, a wad of orange waxy shit popped out of her mouth, and she sat up like someone who'd just gotten an unexpectedly swift kick in the can.

"WHAT THE FUCK!" she screamed in a very unladylike (but totally FAC jet-jock) fashion.

"Nice to see you, too, bitch goddess," I joked.

It took a moment for her eyes to uncross, then focus. "Will?" she asked, her uncertainty understandable. "Will Bucko, is that you?"

"Yes, ma'am, in the flesh."

"Will, O Will," she cried happily (albeit hoarsely), "I've just had the most depressing dream! I dreamed my bird got shot down and I was captured by the RIHMs while my copilot got splattered. And then Uncle Frank was there, but he looked real gross. He took me to lunch, then said he had some important things to wrap up before—"

This was Melodie Lane all right. She'd always been a bit of a gab. As gently as I could, I cut her off by placing my hand over her mouth.

"Yes, yes, Melodie. Time for that later. Right now, the important thing is to haul buns out of here. Can you walk? No, no, you don't have to say anything, just nod."

I wasn't going to risk getting caught listening to any more of Mel's dream. Not only did the subject matter give me the willies, but from past experience I knew such exposition could go on for a week. In answer to my question, she shook her head and pointed down at her legs, which were bound together by the wrappings. Realizing that she could never withstand the agony of having those bandages pulled off, I instead inserted my knife near the juncture of her thighs and slit downward.

Melodie gasped but didn't say anything, partly because my hand was still over her mouth, but primarily because she'd passed out again. I was savvy to the methodology by then, however, and merely had to tug on the bandage near her head to once more bring her back to consciousness.

"Bloody Christ, Will," Melodie groaned, "do you have to be so goddamn rough?"

This was Mel all right, no question about it. Ever since I'd known her she'd had a split personality, at once the excitable happy little girl, eager to tell you her dreams, while at the same time being the rough-edged, foul-mouthed, duty-God-and-country fighter pilot with more awards for gallantry in combat than half the FAC General Staff. Why I loved her so, I couldn't say—fast approaching forty, she sure as hell didn't *look* that good—but love her I did, ever since the day in high school when she'd given me a peek at her cookie jar as she bent over to pick up a one hundred dollar gold coupon I'd inadvertently left on the floor near her locker.

"It wasn't a dream, was it," she said as she got a good look at her surroundings.

"No, I'm afraid it wasn't," I said. "Can you walk?"

Melodie flexed the muscles in her legs. "I think so. Is Gunny Pugh with you?"

"No," I said. "Gunny Pugh is dead."

Melodie made a little squeaking sound as she sucked in her breath. "Oh, Will," she said, "I'm so sorry to hear that. He was a—"

"Doone!" I called, interrupting her. The subject was a painful one and we really didn't have time to dwell on it. "Come over here and help us."

As the boy meandered over from his post at the door, I hurriedly made the introductions. "Mel, meet Johnny Doone. He's a tracker for the MapleLeaf Underground. Johnny hails from right here in Windsor and likes to tie fish flies in his spare time. Doone, this is Colonel Melodie Lane. Although she doesn't look it at the moment, she was once voted 'sexiest cheerleader' by her high school class."

"She still looks pretty bold to me!" the boy gushed.

"Well, thanks, good-lookin!" Melodie answered. I didn't like the way she winked at him, but said nothing. Instead, I turned my attention to helping her to her feet. We still had many a mile to go, and promises to keep.

"Uh-oh," she said once Johnny and I had gotten her up, "I think I'm going to be sick." With that, she let go a great gout of black vomit that made me wonder for a second how long she'd been eating Tarmac. There wasn't time however to question what her diet had been there in that beastly bastion of RIHMdom.

"Are you going to be all right?" I asked when her stomach stopped heaving and she'd wiped away the last traces of the foul black bile from her lips.

"I hope so," she gasped as she looked at her fingers. "My God, what is this stuff?"

"Beats the hell out of me. Do you recall being fed any blacktop or soft coal, stuff like that?"

"Of course not," she answered in a huff. "Well, whatever it is, I've effectively purged it from my system. Let's get out of here. Where are your troops and what is their order of battle?"

Once again, typical Melodie. She had assumed right off the bat that I'd come with a division of FAC commandos to back me up.

"Now let me see," I pretended to ruminate as Johnny and I led her towards the door. "You've already met Doone. We've also got a naked table dancer named Chandelier—although she was wearing clothes the last time I looked. She's the titular honcho of this expedition. Backing her is a gay rights activist called Cliff, and a chef from Quebec ironically named after a French fag. We did have another trooper with us but he got eaten by a giant tick. Poor bastard never had a chance."

"You're joking, of course," Melodie said. It was a flat statement of fact.

"You wish," I answered.

"Johnny?" she asked, turning to the teenager for help. "Is this true?"

"Yes, ma'am. Blood beast slickered Roget before he knew what hit him."

For the first time since we'd revived her, a note of anger crept into Melodie's voice. "Just how the hell were you planning on getting me back to FAC then? If I recall correctly, I was more than five miles behind enemy lines when I was shot down."

"Easy, Mel," I said. "We go out the same way I came in."

"That's right, ma'am," Doone added. "We just gotta blast our way outta here, then slip back through the pipeline, past the blood-beast nests, on in to MapleLeaf HQ. Then all you got is a simple romp through the RIHM trench line and a little swim through the Windsor tunnel and you'll be home safe and sound. Smooth as latex, long as the jelly snakes don't get ya."

"Unless, of course, you can come up with a better idea," I hastily jumped in. Hearing the return route mapped out like that didn't exactly thrill my pants off.

"What's the date today?" Mel asked, her forehead creased in a frown.

I quickly calculated the days since leaving Detroit. "January 28th," I said.

At first she looked as though she didn't believe me, then an expression of deep concern crossed her face. "My God. That means I've been here almost two months."

"Doesn't time fly when you're having fun," I quipped.

She turned to Doone, which I thought was rather insulting. "How long will the return trip take?"

Johnny stuck a finger in his ear and thought for a moment. I knew if he used FAC's "How long is a Chinaman" joke with Melodie, he'd be dead meat. Kid surprised me though. "Maybe three days," he said. "Depends on how hungry the jelly snakes is."

"Trouble is," I quickly injected, "the river is just about completely frozen over. For all I know, it already is. We've got to get you back ASAP, if not sooner, since you're the only FAC recon pilot to get a look at the RIHM positions before they went underground. General Skoff figures you're the only person who could pinpoint likely enemy crossing points. Three days might be stretching our luck."

"Old squawl's right about that, ma'am," Doone said, "though I don't know what else we can do."

"Hmmmmmm. I think I might have an idea," Melodie said. "When I was being brought in by the RIHM patrol that captured me, I noticed one of the hangars over on the other side of the field with the doors open. Looked to me like there were a few private aircraft parked inside. Now, if we could get over there and grab a plane, we might be able to—"

"No way, Mel," I broke in. "This whole area has more air defenses than DC and Omaha combined."

"Yes," she answered cooly, "but you're forgetting one thing. The RIHMs are only watching for in-coming aircraft. They'll never be looking for an out-going bird."

She had a point, and I sure as hell liked the idea of flying home. Fact of the matter was, I would've done about anything to avoid confronting blood beasts and jelly snakes again.

"Let's do it," I said.

Posing once again as Frank Tibbs, I led Doone and Melodie off down the corridor. An immediate problem developed when it became apparent that Mel's mobility was greatly hampered by her wrappings. Even though her legs and arms were free, she was forced to walk in a strange, staggering gait, similar to the one Boris Karloff made famous in his famous Frankenstein role. We hadn't gone fifty feet before we had to stop and let Mel catch up.

"At this rate it'll take us a week just to get out of this building," I grumbled to myself. There was only one solution: I boosted her over my shoulder and set off in the fireman's carry, shuffling along as best I could under the load. For someone who'd been in a coma for two months she sure did weigh a lot.

We were in a section of the terminal that was obviously set aside as the living spaces, and at that time of night it was nearly deserted. The only RIHMs we ran into were either just coming off duty, or just going on. I guess they didn't think it unusual to see Frank Tibbs escorting a couple of humans through their headquarters, and thanks to the translation helmet I was able to pick up their comments.

"Looks like old Hawkclaw caught him some lunch," one big dark-hued chap said.

"Eat death, human crud!" another spat as we passed.

"Hey, Hawkclaw!" a third called out to me as we approached a door with an Exit sign over it. "Save some of that for me!"

I was glad Johnny couldn't understand them. If he had, I'm sure he'd have gotten into a pissing match that would've eventually exposed our disguise. As it was, he got the general idea.

"What'd that big slugger say, Colonel?" the boy whispered back at me. "I don't like the way he was gurglin'."

"Shut up, Doone," I answered, turning the helmet's voice selector to human mode. "Just open that door before somebody else shows up."

I should've anticipated that the door was wired to a security alarm. It didn't register, though, until Johnny bulled it open and every goddamn buzzer, bell, and siren on the entire North American continent began to sound. As soon as I stepped outside, I put Melodie down and looked around in the darkness. At least a foot of new snow had fallen while we'd been inside and the temperature felt as though it had dropped another twenty degrees.

"Which way, Melodie?" I asked, my teeth already beginning to chatter.

She staggered around for a second or two to get her bearings, then pointed off into the void. "Over there," she said. "Straight ahead."

"ON, KING!" Doone roared as he lit out through the snow. "MUSH, YOU HUSKIES!"

I had no choice except to swing Mel back over my shoulder and follow the trail being plowed through the snow by Sergeant

Preston of the Yukon. Our only hope was that Johnny knew where the hell he was going.

And the going was slow. Too slow. We had gotten only a few hundred yards away from the terminal when, over the howl of the wind, I heard the distinct growl of snowmobiles being cranked up and revved. The RIHM security force had been caught napping, but they were quickly making up for lost time. Once they cut our rather conspicuous trail through the snow, it would be all over except for the bloodletting.

Lugging a heftier than average woman through knee-deep snow with a band of killer mutants hot on your trail is not something that produces the most astute decisions. Maybe if I'd had a little more time to think about it—say, three or four days—I might've been able to come up with something better. In the heat of the moment, however, I could only muster one half-assed idea.

"Doone!" I shouted into the wind. "Come back here and take Colonel Lane! I'll stay here and try to hold 'em off till you get her to safety."

Brilliant. My only weapon was a knife. I'd be able to hold off a platoon of mechanized RIHM recon for about three quarters of a second before they cut me to pieces. Luckily, Doone immediately realized this and countermanded my order.

"Don't be a jerk-off, old mug," he yelled back at me. "Dump the broad right here. We'll bury her in the snow. Come back for her when the coast is clear!" The boy paused for dramatic effect before finishing his thought. "—In the spring mebbe."

"AH-HA!" I screamed absurdly. "Look who's calling the kettle black, dildo-breath! If we wait until spring, any intelligence she can provide FAC will probably be next to worthless!"

As we argued the ominous buzz of the snowmobiles grew closer and closer.* While neither of our ideas had been very good,

---

* SNM-3Cs, if my ears were any judge, the combat snowmobile of the Canadian army—1075 cc's of pure ass-kicking power. The SNM-3 Charlies came equipped with twin 5.22mm machine guns and a driver-aimed LANCET rocket pod, which carried four of the deadly wire-guided antiarmor missiles. Each LANCET was fully capable of penetrating even Johnny Doone's thick skull.

the alternative seemed to be that we stand there with our thumbs
up our ass and get blown away without a fight.

"Will you two quit bellyaching and get moving!" Melodie
butted in. I'd almost forgotten that she was anything more than a
two-hundred pound rucksack. "Our only chance is to get to the
hangar before RIHM security catches up. So run! Run like hell!"

"Easy for you to say," I said as quietly as I could.

"What's that supposed to mean?" she asked. From the insulted
tenor of her voice, there was no doubt that she already knew the
answer.

"Nothing, nothing," I muttered as I once again began lurching
through the snow headed in the general direction of a hangar I
could not see. "Get moving, Doone!" I hollered. "Colonel Lane is
right. Our only chance is the hangar."

We staggered ahead, the angry hornet's nest of SNM-3s buzz-
ing all around us. Amazingly, they still hadn't discovered our
trail, but it was only a matter of time. Somewhere far off to our
left, I heard the chatter of automatic weapons and knew the bastards were wasting ammo on swirling snow. Great. Maybe they'd
zap some of their own troops in the mad race to be the first to bag
us.

Suddenly the ground fell out from under me and I found myself rolling through frozen stuff down some sort of incline while
the curses of Melodie Lane rang in my ears. It was only when I at
last came to a stop, dinged and cut by the sharp shards of ice I'd
rolled through, that I heard Johnny Doone's warning.

"Watch your step back there, old sot!" he yelled. "We're
crossin the field's drainage ditch! Fulla sharp ice! Be careful!"

I knew that someday I would have to kill the boy, perhaps with
a dull utility cutting tool or a piece of broken glass. As it was, it
was all I could do to locate Melodie, lift her over my shoulder,
and try to scramble up the opposite side of the embankment.

As fate would have it, I'd no sooner pulled myself out of one
hole than I found myself in another, for waiting on the top of the
opposite side of the drainage ditch were two SNM-3s, their engines stilled, their crews training their weapons on Doone and
yours truly.

"Surrender or die," a RIHM with an amplified translation helmet ordered.

"Go ahead and shoot, ya filthy smugs!" Johnny challenged.

"Me and the colonels would rather eat lead than go back to yer groady warren of shit."

"He's just kidding, officer!" I cried. "Be quiet, Johnny. These guys are just trying to do their job."

"Speaking for myself, Will," I heard Melodie say from her perch over my shoulder, "the boy is right. I'd much rather be gunned down out here than have to go back to that horrid place."

Unless I'd badly miscounted, my life had just been outvoted by a fairly substantial two-to-one margin. As much as I love democracy, I figured this was one time when the majority was not going to rule.

"Okay," I said. "You two can commit suicide if that's what suits you. Me, I'll take my chances with—"

There was no opportunity to finish. In a spectacular explosion of machined metal and animal protein, the RIHM snowmobiles disintegrated in two great balls of fiery heat so fierce that it could only have come with the sympathetic detonation of each vehicle's onboard ordnance.

Although it was far too late to do any good, all three of us hit the deck as hunks of white-hot shrapnel whirred over our heads, and charred bits of RIHM tore up the ground around us. I guess I was too busy making yellow snow to realize that I was still in one piece. When my ears stopped ringing all I was conscious of was Melodie's ceaseless bitching. Then I heard approaching snowmobiles.

"Oh hell, look," Mel said, extremely disgusted, "here come two more. Will, please try to pull yourself together. A warrior's death is the most we ever expected or hoped for. Try to go out in good fashion, will you?"

"Melodie," I scolded as I rolled over and faced her, "you're so damn full of it that it makes my 'rhoids ache just to mention it. Dead is dead, doesn't matter if you go out with a bang or a whimper, so pardon the shit outta me if I don't stand up and give the bastards a stationary ten-ring to aim at."

"Must you always be the coward?" the girl of my dreams asked.

For a moment I contemplated giving her a good belt to the chops. Wouldn't have done a damn bit of good though. FAC had long ago numbed her brain to all but the most cursory outside stimulus. She could never understand the ancient art and philosophy of Yuwon-itsu.*

"We're all cowards, Melodie," I said softly. "Otherwise we'd have blown our own brains out the second our parents told us about the RIHMs. Me, I choose to go out screaming and scratching for every breath, but if you want to die like a wet tissue now, be my guest. Tell you the truth, if my complexion was as bad as yours, I'd do the same."

My trick worked. If there's one thing Melodie Lane had never let pass without a fight, it was an insult to her personal appearance. By the look that came into her eyes I could tell that the approaching RIHMs were going to get a hell of a lot more than they bargained for . . . too bad I wouldn't be alive to see it.

The two new SNM-3s, their headlights shimmering in the falling snow, came out of the gloom and ground to a halt only a few yards away. For some visceral reason—I'm not sure why except, goddamn it, IT SUITED ME—I shoved Melodie's head deep into the snow, leaped to my feet, and began hurling baseball-size snowballs at the enemy.

"Save your energy, *mon* Colonel!" a familiar laughing voice cried from the front seat of the nearest SNM.

"Holy tornadoes of beef!" Johnny Doone shouted from off to my left. "It's Chandelier and the boyos!"

"*Mais oui,* Jean," Chandelier sang out in that sexy French-Canadian lingo of hers. "Who did you expect—George Patton?"

Leaving Melodie to flounder in the ice, Doone and I raced forward and joyfully embraced our comrades in arms (although, speaking only for myself, Cliff had to make do with a friendly handshake). Through the laughter and the tears we learned that the bursts of automatic weapons fire we'd heard earlier had been the MapleLeaf patrol ambushing the crews of the two RIHM snow-choppers. Chandelier, Gaulois, and Cliff had then back-cut our trail and had almost caught up to us when their infrared target acquisition monitors had alerted them to the two SNMs that had waylaid us. It was our own guys then who had turned the enemy into RIHM soup.

---

* Yuwon-itsu, the code of the American samurai as taught to me by my mentor, Black Pugh. Literally translated, it meant "You won when it suited you."

Just as quickly, I gave a mini-encapsulated account of our own adventures inside RIHM Supreme Command and pointed out the bandaged bundle thrashing in the snow. With a growing concern for our safety, I described to Chandelier my plan to get Melodie Lane back to FAC via the commercial air route. She agreed, and minutes later we were all speeding across the tundra in the two snow-choppers, headed for the hangar.

The RIHMs had made a significant mistake. The hangar was locked but unguarded, and once we had blown the doors with a little shape charge that Cliff formed out of some C-4 and detcord, we were halfway home.

Unfortunately, the bitter reality of war then reared its ugly mug. Because of the ever-worsening weather conditions outside and the heavy amounts of snow already on the ground, the only aircraft available that could possibly get Melodie out of Canada and back to Motown was an antique single-engine four-seat Cessna mounted with skis instead of wheels. It didn't take Alberto Einstein to figure out that two of our number would have to remain behind and face the enraged RIHMs.

"I'll stay," Melodie Lane immediately volunteered.

I was busy checking out the Cessna's engine at the time and, in total frustration, could only begin banging my head off the carburetor. Doone was keeping a lookout for RIHM patrols, and since Cliff and Gaulois were off searching for some syngas and a hand pump, it was left to Chandelier to answer Mel's courageous but imbecilic statement.

"You poor, dear, silly slut," the dark-eyed beauty said, tightening the straps on her arctic mittens. "Your stay with the Northern Horde has reduced your brains to goat *fromage*. If anyone must go, it is you."

For just a moment I was sure I was in for that treat men look forward to with huge anticipation: A genuine, knock-down, drag-out, hair-pulling, tit-twisting, ass-biting, cat fight between two good-looking women. Regretfully, unlike a porn movie, life does not have its obligatory scenes. Instead of jumping in Chandelier's shit, Melodie just thought hard for a couple of seconds, then nodded her head.

"You're right, miss," she said. "Thanks for bringing it to my attention before I did something stupid."

"I am your servant, Mademoiselle Colonel," I heard Chandelier reply. "*Alors,* we are still faced with deciding who goes and who stays. Shall we draw lots?"

"Hmmmm. No, I don't think so," Melodie said, "I never could draw a lick." Female laughter, titters really, echoed in the hangar. Suddenly the two of them were acting like two old chums deciding the fate of their pet hamsters.

"Just as the battlefield surgeon during triage must make the decision of who lives and who dies based on hard fact," Melodie lectured, "so too must we pick our crew. I must go, of course—as you have already pointed out—since I'm the only one who knows where the RIHMs are planning to attack." She actually giggled. "And I'd be a fool to tell any of you, right?"

Ludicrously (to my mind) Chandelier giggled right back. "I'm beginning to see why you've survived so long, Colonel Lane. No, tell no one, not even Bunko."

"Right," Mel came right back. "Now, we'll have to take Will. He's the only pilot among us besides me and I'm in no condition to handle the controls. You'll have to come, because you're a girl. That leaves the other three, and unless you're dead set against it, I vote for the boy. He's young, attractive, and—if I'm any judge —a real stud under the sheets."

By this time I'd pretty much forgotten about the Cessna's engine (it looked fine to me) and was trailing the two women while eavesdropping on their incredible conversation.

"Basically, I agree," Chandelier said. "But, Colonel Lane, you must understand why I cannot go. I am in command of this patrol. It is my duty to stay behind and die."

Was there anything better she could have said, I wondered, to insure that Melodie would love her ass until the end of time?

"Yikes!" Mel exclaimed. "I hadn't thought of that. Maybe you're right."

"Hold it right there you two!" I finally butted in. "If the choice is to be among a French chef, a gay activist, or a nude table dancer with breasts like armored turrets, there just ain't no contest. You want me to fly this bird, you damn well better make sure this little exotic entertainer is sitting right next to me. That is all, over and out."

Without waiting for their reaction, I pivoted and went back to work over the aircraft's open cowling. I heard them murmuring between themselves for a few more minutes, then they were quiet.

When Cliff and Gaulois returned with the gas, it was Chandelier who gave them the bad news.

A few hours later, just as dawn's steel-gray blanket appeared, I gave the Cessna full throttle, eased back the yoke, added some trim, and began a long slow climb out of the Windsor airport.

As Melodie had predicted, the RIHM antiair missile batteries were caught with their power down, and I knew that as long as I maintained a max altitude of no more than fifty feet, their radar would never be able to lock on to us, even when it eventually came up on-line.

Behind us, mortar fire and heavy machine guns were reducing the hangar to aluminum Swiss cheese. The RIHMs had finally found our hiding place, but they were paying a heavy price for its destruction because Gaulois and Cliff were putting up one hell of a battle. Never again, I vowed, would I make fun of a sweetheart who was a little light in his Reeboks or send back a plate of nouvelle cuisine just because the duck was still half raw. I owe those two dudes my life . . . as do we all.

The rest of the passengers were quiet as the aircraft's engine strained through the frozen air. The snowstorm was over, but there was still the danger of ice. Melodie and Johnny Doone were in back, Chandelier sat by my side in the copilot's seat.

"What did you say to them?" I asked her once we were safely over the Detroit River and about to request clearance at Motown City Airport.

"Who?"

"Cliff and Gaulois. When you told them that they'd been chosen to stay behind."

Chandelier gazed out through the windshield at the cold white sky. "I told them the truth," she finally said, "that life is like a pulp adventure novel, that some of us are main characters while others are simply bit players, to be introduced, used, and then swept aside when the time comes to proceed with the main plot . . . whatever the hell that may be."

"And they bought that crap?" I asked incredulously as I reached for the radio handset.

Chandelier turned to face me then, and I saw a tear slide down her cheek. "But, Colonel Bucko," she said, ever so softly, "they had absolutely no choice. *You* should know that better than anyone."

She had a point.

8

I won't waste your time with a long discourse on the Battle of the
Detroit River. Historians and military experts have written just
about all there is to know about that big fight. Suffice it to say
that with the valuable information Melodie Lane was able to
provide, FAC kicked the living dog snot out of the armies of the
Northern Horde when they mounted their ill-advised invasion
only two days after our escape.

The three-pronged attack across the frozen river was blunted
and stopped in the north by the gallant Polack Brigade made up
of FACers and volunteers from old Hamtramck. In the south, the
River Rouge Boys, using Henry Ford's old manufacturing empire
as their base, suckered the RIHMs onto Zug Island where they
were literally deep-fried en masse with interlocking fire from
three hundred flame-throwing Billy Martin tanks. In the center,
where the main enemy thrust came, the famous Michigan Black
Hat Division held the RIHMs long enough for elements of FAC's
Central Wing to catch the bastards on the open ice. It was, for
our fighter and bomber pilots, like a training run. Of the thousand sorties run that day, we lost only six aircraft.*

The Battle of the Detroit River was an important and decisive
victory for the side of good and right, but a few details still
trouble me from that period.

First, I am unable to understand why the RIHMs mounted
their attack despite the escape of Melodie Lane. I can only con-
clude that either they believed she had been killed in the destruction of the hangar or the arrogance of their commanders lulled
them into believing they could defeat us even if we did know their
crossing points.

Second, Melodie has never been given the credit she deserves

---

* For more scholarly details of the battle see *A Mad Dog Speaks: The
Autobiography of Lieutenant General Cyrus Skoff, USFAC* (Grand Rapids,
MI: Vanity Publications, 2049), and Professor Cassius R. McPhee's
Grease on Ice: An Examination of the Battle of the Detroit River (Miami,
Florida: The University of Northern Ontario Press, 2054).

for the ultimate outcome of the battle, since all the information about her mission and subsequent report were immediately classified Ultra Top Secret by FAC Intelligence. Thus the story I have just related was not accessible to the various authors and researchers of the battle when most of the volumes of work on the subject were being written. I hope I have set the record straight.

Third and most distressing, when I personally vectored the flight of F/A-1020s over the Windsor Air Terminal (RIHM Supreme Command) from an airborne E-16 Birdseye and had them drop enough ordnance to create what is now Lake Cliff-Gaulois, I was positive I was ridding the world of Frank Tibbs. How he got away, I still don't know. I believe he turned yellow and bolted, just like he'd done so many times before.

A couple of days after the mop-up of RIHM stragglers was complete, and the Northern Horde was in a disorganized retreat back up past the Arctic Circle, I headed down to the Grand Boulevard field hospital set up in the basement of the old General Motors Building. I'd heard through the grapeline (sic) that Melodie had collapsed soon after her debriefing and had been placed in private UR.*

"She began vomiting some sort of black shit that we can't identify," the sawbones in charge of her case blurted out to me when I cornered him in the cafeteria. "It's in the lab for analysis now, but if you want my opinion, I think she's been poisoned with roofing tar. If that isn't bad enough, those bastards were fooling around in other areas. Those wrapping weren't glued to her body, you know."

"What do you mean?" I blurted. "Sure they were. When I tried to unwrap them it was like pulling tape off a bad scalp wound."

The doctor stared at me through his tinted contacts and chewed his lip as though trying to decide whether to go any further. "How close are you to Colonel Lane?" he finally asked.

"Well," I said, "she's about the only woman I've ever loved."

"I recommend that you start playing the field."

"That bad, huh? Spill it, doc."

* As in You Are sick. Goddamn FAC doctors and nurses have the sense of humor of asphalt.

"Fact of the matter is, Colonel Bucko, those wrapping weren't glued to her body. They were biologically a part of her. To be more blunt, they were growing out of her skin, and we had to surgically remove them."

I shuddered and tried to keep my voice from shaking. "How . . . how is she?"

"About as good as you could expect," the doctor said. "After all, technically she's been skinned alive. She won't be taking any hot showers for a while, I can tell you that."

"Can I go in and see her?"

"Sure. Only be advised. It's not pretty."

Boy, was he right! When I finally got into Melodie's UR I was shocked at what I found—yellow and green walls, for the love of mung, and a bright orange carpet, not to mention some real tacky before-and-after prints of famous twentieth-century EPA toxic waste clean-up sites hanging on the walls. Thankfully, all I could see of Mel was her head, since her body was under some sort of tent made out of olive-colored plastic sheets. She seemed genuinely glad to see me.

"Hello, Will," she said weakly, "I hear we kicked some butt."

"You got that right, Mel," I answered. If anything, her face looked even more pale and gaunt than it had in Frank's room. The doctors had dressed the wounds on her face; some were covered with bandages, others were bare stitches. Someone had washed the gunk out of her hair, but it was now wildly spiked and made her look like some bizarre battered blond porcupine. "And you'll be pleased to know the Windsor airfield terminal is now just a great big hole in the ground. I'm pretty sure that makes Frank Tibbs a bad dream." I tried to smile, but it was hard work. "How are you feeling?" I asked.

"Like, I've got the world's worst sunburn. Did the doctor tell you what they had to do?"

"Yeah. Sounded pretty gruesome."

"Oh, it wasn't so bad," she said, trying like hell to sound up. "Heck, it's only skin. The doctors say they're doing wondrous things with synthetic tissue these days—I can actually choose my own color!"

"FAC gray and blue I'll bet." I chuckled.

"Not a bad idea, come to think of it. How are the others?"

"Good. Chandelier finally managed to make contact with Major Fangbone, the leader of the MapleLeaf Underground. Most of his people survived. According to Fang, there are enough girls left to think about opening another club. He wants her to headline it for him."

"How very interesting."

By the tone of her voice I could tell Melodie did not approve of nude table dancing, but I knew if Windsor was ever to rise out of the ashes of war, it would only start with the resumption of its most famous attraction.

"Johnny Doone says hello," I continued. "He was able to help me pinpoint targets for our bombers, and now General Skoff has offered him a job as a FAC scout."

"Will he accept?"

I chuckled. "I doubt it. He says he wants to learn to fly the Harrier."

Melodie's eyes widened in amazement. "You mean you've still got that old TAV-8 your dad left you? The one we found in the desert that day?"

"Yup." I grinned. "Seems like only yesterday, doesn't it? She's held together with Krazy-Glu and bailing wire, but she still flies. Brought her north with me when I got this mission. Doone about fouled his shorts when I told him what she could do. Now he can't wait to take a spin."

Her eyes glanced over at a bedside chair. "Will, can you stay awhile? I really want to hear all about what you've been up to since Boca Grande, and about Gunny Pugh. But first, I've got something I want to tell you. It's kind of crazy, but . . . well, just hear me out, okay?"

"Sure, Mel," I said, both alarmed and intrigued at how serious she suddenly sounded.

I took a seat in the chair and pulled it closer to the bed. For a few long moments the only sounds in the room came from the machinery and monitors hooked up to Melodie's hidden body. Then she managed to turn her head and look at me.

"Do you remember after you woke me up in Frank's room that I told you everything I remembered about my capture was like a dream?" I nodded and she continued. "There was something I didn't tell you about that dream. It was very strange, and I'm still not sure what it meant or whether I was just hallucinating or what. But I think I owe it to you to tell you what I think I remember, as difficult and painful as that may be to you."

Good old Mel. When it came to dispensing bad-tasting medicine, she could care less if you were sick or not. Usually, by the time she got finished, you would be. Considering the shape she was in, though, I didn't see how I could refuse her.

"Go ahead," I said glumly.

"Do you recall ever meeting a RIHM named Darvon?" Melodie asked.

"That fruitcake?" I blurted out. "Good grief! How could I forget!"

"Then you do know her?"

"Her? Him? It? What's the difference? Yeah, your sister and I shared the brig aboard *Paradise Cove* with an Island RIHM named Darvon for a few days back in '34. A complete knucklehead. Couldn't keep its tentacles off me. Real bag of sludge."

"Oh, Will," Melodie admonished, "that's no way for a boy to speak about his mother."

I could see she wasn't kidding.

Suddenly I felt like some poor schmuck who'd gotten caught standing behind the huge brass gong during the opening of a J. Arthur Rank film. Everything was at once rattling and reverberating—my brain, my breathing, my dental fillings—and my vision went out of focus, as though someone had spread Vaseline over my eyes.

"I think she and I had some long talks," I heard Melodie prattling on, from somewhere far away, maybe from inside a conch shell. "She was really very nice, not at all what you would expect from a RIHM. She told me how sorry she was she hadn't brought you to New York with her when she left your father, and how she'd gone to Cuba just before the Big Blast to perform in a workers' musical. She was out chopping sugar cane when the bomb hit. That's when she was contaminated, only they refer to it as 'the change.'"

I rocked forward in my chair as if taking a sucker punch to the midsection and slapped my hands over my ears to block out what Melodie was saying. Untrue, it had to be untrue. MY MOTHER WAS A RIHM? HOW GODDAMN DEPRESSING CAN YOU GET!

"Stop telling me this crap, Mel," I said quietly, trying to maintain control. "I don't want to hear anymore. Please stop."

"Not until I'm finished," she answered. "I think I promised her that. She said it was time you knew, that you were old enough to handle it, or at least you should be. You know, Will, it's been very hard for her. She's one of the few surviving former humans among them. On the one hand, she's supposed to hate all of us and fight for our ultimate destruction. On the other hand, she's extremely proud of her human son—Eagleheart, the Killer of Legions. Quite a dilemma."

"I fucking-A bet," I mumbled. "Ya know, Mel, I thought reruns of *Dynasty* and *Dallas* were hard to take seriously, but your little dream sequence here gives new meaning to the word *ludicrous.*"

"Let me finish. Darvon was up here as part of an Island RIHM contingent, which brought some religious tokens to the Northern Horde to symbolize the—"

"Jelly snakes," I interrupted her.

"What?"

"Nothing."

"Anyway, Darvon found out from Frank Tibbs that you were due any day, so she tried to hang around and tell you all this herself. Unfortunately, she was scheduled for some function or other out in Southern California and couldn't stay. So she told me, hoping, I suppose, that you and I would have a chance to talk before they started experimenting on us."

I laughed out loud. It was impolite, I know, but I couldn't help it. "Come on, Mel," I joked, "hurry up and get to the part where I'm suppose to buy the Golden Gate Bridge from you. This is too much!"

Melodie almost looked amused. "Darvon said you might be a little skeptical. That's when she told me to remind you of the birthmark under your arm that looks like a profile of U.S. Grant."

U.S. Grant? I always thought it looked like a map of Puerto Rico, but I guess it's all a matter of interpretation and point of view. The very fact that Melodie knew about the birthmark in itself was enough to make me cry out.

"Damn! Nobody knows about that mark, Mel! Nobody. How did you find out?"

"Darvon told me. She also said to ask you if you remember that your father used to urinate into the bathtub instead of the john."

That did it. The RIHMs might have found out about the birthmark through their network of spies and computer hackers, but only my mother would have known about the family's deepest darkest secret, that Pop used to come home from Friday evening Happy Hours so drunk and disoriented that he'd relieve himself in the bathtub, then try to take a bath in the toilet.

"Oh, my God," I mumbled. "Oh, my God."

"She said to tell you that if you ever get the chance, come on out to California for a visit. She'd love to see you again, and try to talk you into taking 'the change.' And if you decide to visit, she said to tell you she'd be living in a retirement village that used to be called La Jolla."

Blessedly, Melodie shut up at that point, and I buried my face in my hands. My mind was on overload. I tried to remember what the RIHM named Darvon looked like and then compared that vision with the old hollies of Mom that Wolf had left me. The two did not superimpose. Ma a RIHM? Totally impossible. She had died in the Big Blast. Somehow, nevertheless, the enemy had gotten a hold of some very private and personal information and was using it against me. Hadn't Tibbs begged me to become one of them? If they were that all fired hot to get me on their side, they would evidently stop at nothing, and that included tricking a guy into believing his mother was—if slightly disfigured and not quite human—still hanging in there.*

"Remember, Will," I heard Melodie whisper, "I said it seemed like a dream. Maybe it was."

I dropped my hands and looked up into her eyes. They were sad eyes, full of pain and fatigue. Yet there was something else there, something I'd seen often when we were kids but which had not been there for many years since. Compassion.

"Now tell me about Black Pugh and Mexico," she said.

And so I did . . .

* *Editor's Note:* Will is being too kind. From all evidence, Darvon the RIHM resembled a cross between a squid and a giant hydra.

PART TWO
Down South

9

Puta Madre was just a sleepy little Mexican fishing village about twenty-five miles up the coast from the resort town of Mazatlán when Gunny Pugh and I first set eyes on it in that spring of '35; nothing like the monstrous tourist attraction for wealthy jet-setters it is now. And that was good because I had pretty well been shot-to-shit in my big showdown with Carlos Membranous and the U-235; the last thing in the world I needed at that particular point in my life was a crowded social calendar filled with cotillions and tea dances or blistering verbal encounters with surly bellhops and cab drivers with bad breath.

Luck brought us to Puta Madre, and luck, I have found, is a damn big part of staying alive.

As I recall, on the day we discovered the village we had been flying the tandem-seated TAV-8B Harrier for almost a week, stopping only to refuel or sleep, searching for a place where we would be safe from bounty hunters and reporters from the north, as well as inquisitive local officials curious as to why two gringos in a V/STOL (Vertical/Short Take-Off and Landing) jet aircraft hadn't stopped in to have their visas and passports checked.

Politicans and bureaucrats were not my favorite people right about then. Not only had the President of the United States found it politically expedient to renege on his promise of a full pardon for my alleged high crimes and misdemeanors, but some fucking federal judge named Mason-Madison had signed a shoot-on-sight order that gave me about as much chance of survival in the States as, say, a sixteen-point buck wandering into a gun shop on the opening day of hunting season. While I understood why the judge did what he did (his daughter, Bambi, had been my copilot when she got her ass handed to her by Island RIHMs), the President's little nocturnal sleepwalk really torked my lizard. I DON'T CARE IF THE CHUMP WAS UP FOR REELECTION!

To put it bluntly, after saving my country from the evil genius of the Shrimper King and his plan to rule the seas, I'd been shafted with a rusty railroad spike, and if it hadn't been for Black

Pugh, I would've probably ended up doing a long stretch in Portsmouth.*

My gunshot wounds—sustained in the final big shoot-out with Membranous—were not life-threatening but bad enough so I would never have been able to fly the Harrier away from Boca Grande by myself. Soon after he learned I was still a wanted man, however, and without a thought to his own culpability in the matter, Pugh jammed me into the backseat of the patched-up aircraft and took off into the sunset, his own future suddenly as dim as my own.

And so we'd made it safely to the central-west coast of Mexico and, after some searching, found Puta Madre. When we landed on its strip of pristine white beach—the Pacific Ocean crashing on one side, the dense jungle rotting on the other—we both knew we had found the perfect getaway spot. Weighed down with several hundred gold credit vouchers Pugh had lifted from a safe he'd found in Dick Squidlic's bombed-out office back in Boca Grande, we thought it would be wine, women, and song for a good long while, compliments of my traitorous ex-salvage partner.

Wrong. Puta Madre turned out to be about as exciting as changing light bulbs. Hell, there were only two public-access channels on the local cable (neither HBO nor SHOWTIME was available), and the sole radio station played nothing but Latin music. A mere half dozen fast-food franchises tried to service the entire town, and one of them was something called Bingo's Lunch, which advertised hamburgers made from char-broiled cabbage.

The primary form of employment in Puta Madre was rumored to be fishing and/or smuggling cigarettes and blank video cassettes from freighters far at sea, but a stroll through town suggested either sleeping or contracting infectious diseases was the main occupation. Fresh water, Coke, and Pepsi came in once a month by barge, and the only strong drink available was a local concoction made by mixing swine bile with old newspaper, seawater, and a few aged fishheads, and then fermenting the whole mess for about six days. Stuff packed one hell of a wallop but

---

* FAC's prison for serious felons . . . and maybe some who weren't so serious, HA HA, and tell 'em Groucho sent ya.

produced a hangover that made your brain feel as though someone had scrubbed it with coarse steel wool.*

Unfortunately, it did not take long to discover that in Puta Madre the women matched the wine—what there was of it would probably rot your socks off. It soon became evident that every girl between the ages of twelve and sixty without serious yeast infection or missing limbs was married to a cop or off studying for nundom in Mexico City. The town did have a couple ladies of the night, but their prices were outrageous, and after three or four restless days nursing an infected dork swollen to the size of hydroponic summer squash, I rammed home about a thousand cc's of ampicillin and became celibate.

This lack of female companionship did not bother Pugh as much as it did me, for I had visions of a bevy of high-breasted señoritas waiting on me hand and foot for the rest of my life, while he—being late in his seventh decade of life—only pined for someone to cook for him. We did eventually hire an old crone named Carmine to keep house for us, but she was in her mid-eighties and was anything but high-breasted. Give her credit, though, she kept the hacienda spotless, and I was never at a loss for clean underwear.

Which brings me to our home-sweet-home. Rudy, the local real-estate agent, showed it to us about our third day in town. After seeing nothing but broken-down hovels and corregated adobe shacks, we were quite pleased when he at last led us down a path through the outskirts of town and down the coast about a quarter of a mile where he somewhat hesitantly pointed the hacienda out to us.

The so-called Main House (for the hacienda was a collection of about six different edifices built in the traditional Spanish manner around a plaza and Olympic-size swimming pool) was a fairly large one-story building backing the ocean and designed as sort of a cross between Tahitian modern and peasant-chic. The floor of

* In the bottom of each bottle of this stuff the natives called Agua Pendejo, the moonshiners placed a dead sparrow. Although it was considered the ultimate in macho to eat this little pickled bird when killing a bottle of Agua Pendejo, I didn't get around to trying it until a few years later. Pugh always said the taste of the bird reminded him a little of rattlesnake meat.

its large single room was hard clay, the roof woven palm fronds, and the walls were sail canvas, which could be rolled up in the stifling heat that came every day between the hours of 6:00 A.M. and midnight, and rolled down the rest of the time when it rained. Except for a couple of hammocks strung between roof supports and a small brazier for those chilly nights that came once in a while, it was a rather spartan living space.

Upon further inspection of the grounds and other buildings, however, we discovered that things were not as bad as they had at first seemed in the Main House. There was a microwave oven and a refrigerator in the Kitchen House, and a large screen TV with a passable VCR system and tape library over in the Recreation House. We found a well-maintained electric generator that ran on syngas in the Power House, and an adequate bath and chemical toilet located in the (what else but) Shit House.

There was no guest in the Guest House except for a nest of scorpions, which Rudy killed with a canister of insecticide and six shots from a .38 revolver.

All in all, the place looked pretty good to us and we asked Rudy what it would take to move us in. The clever bastard said two hundred Bonus Credits (American) per month. We offered fifty. He accepted it without so much as a counter. We asked why. He claimed it was the off-season.

I suppose it is quite sobering to have an angry-looking six-foot nine-inch black man shove a gun in your face. I suppose it would loosen the tongue of even the most reluctant real-estate agent. With the barrel of Pugh's .45 automatic jammed into his left nostril, Rudy told us the true story of our new home . . .

The hacienda had once belonged to a highborn gentleman named Don Carlo Estrada Estaban, one of the richest men in that part of old Mexico. According to Rudy, the family had made a fortune producing little hand-painted plaster-of-paris saints for tourists and the local Indians.

Tragically, soon after coming to Puta Madre and presenting her husband with a baby girl—their only child—the Don's wife had been killed by a broadside from a Portuguese man-of-war while taking a morning dip in the nearby ocean.

Don Carlo had taken the loss hard, but over the years had managed to forget his grief as he watched the child grow into an enchanting beauty. By the time she was a nubile eighteen-year-old she had made his life a joy. During those years the Hacienda D'Estaban (as it was then called) had echoed with the laughter of friends and the jaunty brass and gut-string phrases of a mariachi band, which played morning, noon, and evening at Don Carlo's pleasure.

Little wonder then that the Hacienda D'Estaban had grown to be known up and down the coast as a real party place, sort of like the famous Playboy Mansion of early American mythology. Carlotta (for that was the daughter's name) and her equally nubile eighteen-year-old friends, clad only in skimpy costumes made of see-through material, would make even the oldest male guest feel young again as they played games like Swimming Pool Volleyball, Pocket Pool, and Pin the Thing on the Donkey. All perfectly harmless, of course, since the girls were virgins and meant to stay that way until Mr. Right happened by with a good line and plenty of long green. And while some of the guests occasionally bitched about Carlotta being one big tease, her father cherished the very ground she walked on.

Then one night, the Comancheros came.

Seldom if ever, Rudy said, had a Comanchero hunting party ventured so far south, even though the buildup of Western RIHMs had forced many of the outlaw tribes out of Southern California and into the vast northern deserts of old Mexico. Little had been heard from these disciples of Ramases II for several years. And then, like a plague of hungry locusts, they had swooped down out of the north and rained havoc on the major cities of central Mexico. At the same time, most of the major resort towns on the west coast were raped and ransacked.

Alas, when the country's armed forces finally regrouped from the shock of the attack and sent out punitive expeditions, they found the Comancheros had melted back into the scorching deserts, safe from all but tactical nukes. And since the last thing in the world the Mexican government wanted was to start a RIHM colony in their own land, the Comancheros were left unpunished.

Having discovered a good thing, Ramases II would periodically send out hunting parties from his desert strongholds. But why such a hunting party would have picked the poor town of Puta Madre as their target, no one could figure. Maybe the

Comanchero spies had heard the stories of the brilliant and fashionable parties thrown at Hacienda D'Estaban or maybe they just took a wrong turn off Route 15. Whatever the reason, one night when the mariachi band was in full flower, and the giggles and laughter of young women playing Who's Got the Button tinkled across the estate like little silver bells, the Hacienda D'Estaban was attacked by a Comanchero hunting party.

Real real messy.

Don Carlo, who was in Mexico City getting a hair-plug implant at the time, came home to find that his guests had all been strung up by their toes from the rafters of the Main House and slaughtered like so many Christmas geese. His daughter, while spared the fate of her friends, had been raped, sodomized, and generally made to feel unlikely to be selected to play the Virgin Mary at the local mission's next Christmas pageant.

But that was not the worst of it, oh no! After the coroner and the delivery trucks and the doctor had left, and while Carlotta lay in a deep sangria-induced sleep, Don Carlo had also discovered that the Hacienda D'Estaban itself had been pretty much gutted by the bad guys and that the family's most prized possession—a complete collection of twentieth-century Elvis Presley velvet portraits—had been stolen.

This horrific discovery couldn't have come at a more inopportune time. The plaster-of-paris saint business was just then hitting the skids thanks to an influx of Plas-tex dolls (which stuck to the walls where you threw them) pouring in from Formosa. Without the priceless Presley Collection as collateral, Don Carlo could secure no loans to see him through the bad times and was forced to declare bankruptcy. Then the families of the wealthy landowners and businessmen who had attended the last fateful party at the hacienda filed numerous lawsuits against the Don for his failure to adequately protect his guests. His insurance company then informed him they were not responsible for an "Act of God."

The very worst news came, however, when Don Carlo learned that his beloved daughter Carlotta was pregnant.

Oh, that poor man! Being a strict Catholic (and not being pregnant himself) there was nothing Don Carlo could do except see the thing through to term. Carlotta was not particularly pleased with this news, but she had little choice. The alternative—to be disowned and thrown into the streets of Puta Madre on her own —was totally unacceptable.

And so, nine months after the attack, on a night filled with the thunder and lightning and pelting rain of a tropical storm found mostly in trashy romance novels, a child was born in the Kitchen House at the Hacienda D'Estaban.

Don Carlo suspected something was wrong when the old woman he'd hired as a midwife ran screaming from the Kitchen House and threw herself off the cliff overlooking the ocean.

He got even more anxious when the town's doctor ran screaming from the Kitchen House. The doctor, a well-educated man who should've known better, also threw himself off the cliff into the raging dark water below.

Finally, when Carlotta herself ran screaming from the Kitchen House and made a perfect swan dive off the cliff into the jagged spum-covered rocks (because she had failed to time her dive with the rush of the incoming waves as had so often been preached by the TV commentary team covering the cliff-divers of Acapulco), Don Carlo could contain neither himself nor his curiosity any longer. He rushed into the Kitchen House where—to his everlasting shock and revulsion—he found a man-child with horns and yellow eyes lying next to a still steaming black placenta.

Holy Mother of God, Rudy screamed (our real-estate agent was really into his storytelling role by this time), the Black Placenta! The sign of RIHM infection! With no more thought than he would've given to ripping up a parking ticket, Don Carlo picked up the child and all too predictably ran screaming to the edge of the cliff where he threw both himself and the baby into the seething cauldron of the angry sea.

And ever since that night, the Hacienda D'Estaban had been called Hacienda del Placenta Negro. According to Rudy, the place was cursed. No one had lived there in the almost seven years since the unfortunate incident.

"And you expect fifty bucks American a month for this joint?" I cried at Rudy after he'd finished his tale. "You should be payin us, pal!"

"We'll take it," Pugh joined right in, his usual contrary self. "One-year lease, paid in advance, with an option to buy in the second year. Have the contract on my desk in the morning and you've got yourself a deal."

"Gunny," I said, trying to mask my displeasure, "could I speak to you in private?"

We left Rudy near the empty swimming pool and strolled to the edge of the compound where I proceeded to let Pugh have it.

"Have you lost your senses?" I snarled at him. "First of all, you don't have a desk. Second, and probably more important, do you really think we can have any fun living in a house named after RIHM afterbirth for shit's sakes?"

The Gunny grinned. "Calm down, Will," he said in his special oily tone reserved for getting his own way, "this place is perfect."

"Oh shit, yes!" I growled, "I can see the Christmas card lists now. Will Bucko, in care of the House of the Black Placenta, Puta Madre, Mexico."

"Come off it, son," Pugh scoffed. "Since when you been on anybody's Christmas card list? Listen to me, this curse rap is perfect. Means nobody in town is going to be bothering us down here. With the ocean so close, and that big empty lawn to build a ramp for the Harrier, we can set up shop as pretty as you please."

On our journey out of Boca Grande, Pugh had bored me to tears talking about starting up his arms and munitions business again in Mexico. I hadn't thought too much about it because, quite frankly, running guns wasn't something you just jumped into like the stock market or women's riding apparel. It took a lot of time, money, and contacts to become a Merchant of Death, and Pugh was getting old.

"Aw, Gunny," I chided, "you're just talking pipe dreams. Even if you had an inventory—which you don't—who the hell you gonna sell to? Your neighbors in Puta Madre?"

Pugh grinned his big shit-eating grin. "Hey, Rudy!" he bellowed. "Know anybody wants to buy a dozen Stingers?"

Our real-estate agent looked dumbfounded for a minute, then answered. "Certainly, Senor Pugh. Four or five that I can think of offhand. Would you need some assistance contacting them?"

"Later, *compadre,*" the Gunny answered with a wave of his hand, "later." He turned back to me. "Hell, Will, this is Latin America! Bandits, revolutionaries, counterrevolutionaries, right-wing factions, left-wing factions, separatists, republicans, socialists, capitalists, and commies—all the good things the RIHM-infected world is missing right now. This is a gunrunner's paradise, boy! Always somebody wanting to shoot at somebody else down here; been that way for three-four hundred years or more! Damn, didn't you learn any history in school?"

"Do you mean stuff like most American Blacks came across the frozen Bearing [sic] Strait in Cadillacs and settled in Newark in 1219 A.D.?"

"Watch your lip, son. You ain't too old to get whupped."

"But you are. Right?"

"Always gotta be the comedian, don't ya?" Pugh sighed. "Seems to me, you're getting a might long-in-the-tusks for this kind of sophomoric banter."

"Hey," I retorted, "if it was good enough for Mel, it's good enough for me."*

"Yeah, yeah, yeah. I'm just saying if there's one place a man can get rich selling guns, it's right here."

"But Gunny," I whispered, "we're already rich."

My giant Negro friend and mentor took a step backwards and arched his graying eyebrows. "You mean to tell me," he grumbled, "that you fully intend to kick-back and become a lazy good-fer-nothin gringo ex-patriot living off his ill-gotten gains till you croak of clogged arteries or something?"

"That was the general idea, yes."

"Will, believe me, it gets old real quick." Pugh paused and looked out to sea where the water was at a dead turquoise calm. "Life without adventure is like a piece of fruit with all the juice squeezed out of it. It's like making love to a whore or stealin Monopoly money or fryin up bacon made of soybean—no matter how much you tell yourself you're enjoying it, deep down inside you know it ain't the real thing. Besides, rich is relative. Stick with me, boy, and we'll turn ol' Dick Squidlic's vouchers into millions!"

Well, I'd be lying if I didn't admit that the old duffer's line of bullshit got to me. I think it was the term *millions* that did the trick. There was little left to do except go along with his crazy plans and hope we didn't end up in one of those infamous Mexican jails.

* Mel Brooks, an American comedic genius of the mid through late twentieth century never honored by the French.

Although, come to think of it, might have been better if we had.

Within two years P&B Arms and Munitions was an operational concern. The overhead was extremely high, what with bribes, payoffs, and putting the town's fishing fleet on a permanent retainer to ferry the stock from merchant vessels clandestinely anchored off the cliffs, but we still managed to make a decent profit, and all our graphs, printouts, and sales charts indicated a steady upward trend.

Personally, I was having the time of my life. Funny, as soon as word leaked out (via Rudy) that we had a few bucks and weren't just a couple of beach bums, some of the village girls gave up life in the convent and appeared on our doorstep, apparently none too concerned with the curse of the Black Placenta. Soon, Pugh and I were having our backs scrubbed in all the right places on a fairly regular basis.

The cooking improved, too, once the old crone the Gunny had hired threw herself off the cliff one night in a raging storm. The only explanation I could come up with for this bizarre act was that she had caught a glimpse of Pugh in the nude moving between the Main House and the Shit House, and had incorrectly concluded that the curse had manifested itself in human form. So she'd ended it all. I reckon I would've done the same.

As the Gunny had correctly foreseen, there was no lack of clientele for our business. Whether it was a group of starving peasants angry with a wealthy landowner, or a disgruntled civil servant eager to change the form of his local government, or even a few boney-fide (sic) outlaws in need of armor-piercing weaponry, P&B was there to provide the supplies and expertise. By the end of our second year, we were doing okay and the future looked bright.

Both Pugh and I fell easily into our roles. While he dickered via telex with a Persian middleman on securing a heavy-lift chopper to deliver our goods to those clients residing outside the reach of Mexico's fabulous highway network, I became the corporation's air express expert. "If it doesn't get there overnight, it probably never will" was the motto I liked to start my sales presentation with when meeting new clients. And while this motto seemed to puzzle many of them initially, they quickly understood the gist of it when I took them out to the hacienda's front lawn and gave them a demonstration.

Using the sweat equity of the schoolchildren of Puta Madre, P&B had constructed a nifty jump-ramp for my Harrier out of scrap lumber and several million flattened aluminum cans. The ramp looked something like a ski jump that had been stretched out and flattened a bit; approximately fifty yards of thirty degree incline was terminated with a slightly upturned lip, which effectively catapulted the taxiing Harrier into the air. Admittedly, it looked a little strange out there in our front yard, but it was a proven battlefield design, which allowed the TAV-8B to make takeoffs and landings in a space too small for a regular jet aircraft to operate.

My Harrier, of course, had vertical takeoff and landing capabilities, but this "short takeoff and landing" system (STOL) allowed the aircraft to carry a bigger payload since fuel economy was greatly enhanced over that of the vertical mode. Bigger payloads meant fewer trips to deliver an order, which meant more bucks. The STOL was also less stressful on the aircraft, which meant maintenance downtime was generally cut in half. More bucks. Most of all, though, using the ramp was more fun than a carnival ride. No bucks, but what the hell, you gotta get some enjoyment out of your work or why bother.

Quite honestly, using the Harrier delivery system did have its limitations. If one of our customers, say, wanted a tank, well, he'd just have to figure out how to get it home on his own. But for most small arms, crew-serves, and attendant ammo, pyrotechnics, and maintenance gear, the jump-jet worked just fine. On a good day, the aircraft was capable of carrying an external load of nearly four tons; all Pugh and I did was rehab the drop tanks so they could hold weapons and ammo instead of synfuel. Even with max load, our effective combat radius was still a little over two hundred miles, which was about as far from home as we wanted to get in the beginning anyway. If our clients wanted delivery outside that radius, we simply added more fuel, subtracted from the ordnance load, and upped our freight charges exponentially.

Although my father and Pugh had built the aircraft piece by piece in the second decade of the century, it had originally been manufactured for the old U.S. Marine Corps by McDonnell

Douglas way back in the late 1980s. Needless to say, with equipment that old there were some mechanical failures and metal fatigue along the way. Without a corporate or military supply system, such failures could have brought our whole operation to an abrupt halt. What saved us was the fact that Gunny Pugh had once been a FAC crew chief and was adept at the art of jury rigging as well as being able to fashion replacement parts from scratch.

This talent to improvise was demonstrated time and time again with Pugh manning an old drill press and metal lathe he'd found in Don Carlo's private study. (The Don, we later discovered, had been experimenting with a new line of religious artifacts made out of used coffee cans and door handles from '58 Chevies.) Wasn't nuthin for the Gunny to whip out a turbine blade or a new hydraulic line or even manufacture from scratch a doolywacker for the thingamajig attached to the whatjamacallit. The guy was truly an artist.

And so, with Pugh to handle the procurement, inventory, and maintenance sides of the business (a business he'd been in for many years, I might add), the delivery, public relations, and advertising arms of P&B were left in my hands. And although I was new to the game, it did not take long for me to realize that my areas of expertise sometimes overlapped and complemented one another, usually to the betterment of our enterprise.

Usually, I say, but not always.

10

Along about the middle of P&B's third year of operation, I got a call out at the hacienda that indirectly lead to the end of our life of leisure. The call came from the producer of a local cable production called *The Gringo Hour,* a bimonthly show hosted by an ex-swimming pool contractor from Phoenix named Harry Riviero.

For some arcane reason buried in the slopshoot of his brain, Harry insisted he be addressed as "Haroldo" at all nonprivate functions. Whether he was just trying to exploit his Hispanic heritage or simply wanted a name which might eventually lead to the endorsing of local products, I just couldn't tell you, for although he and his wife were the only other *norteamericanos* in town we didn't socialize with them much, due primarily to the bitch's politics, which were just a tad left of Uncle Joe Stalin.

Despite pretensions to the contrary, Harry's *Gringo Hour* (at least the little of it I'd seen) was pretty much limited to Harry bitching in English about what had happened to him over the past two weeks. Things like clogged bathroom pipes or a dull carving knife or burnt toast, or an attack of diarrhea, or any of a myriad of other mundane day-to-day setbacks were all fodder for Harry's script, a script he delivered in a monotone so sleep-inducing that Pugh and I watched the show solely when suffering from severe bouts of insomnia. Harry was guaranteed zonk-zone within the first five minutes or your money back.

Given the format and the fact that only Rudy, Pugh, and I, and maybe a half a dozen other residents of Puta Madre understood Anglo, little wonder that you needed a microscope to find the show's ratings. Add to it the limited technical quality and amateurish production techniques found on any small-town public access channel, and there was some question as to whether anybody except Harry's wife ever watched the show, and she only because she was his cameraperson.

"We're gonna try somethin kinda different," the producer of *The Gringo Hour* (not surprisingly, Harry himself) said to me over the phone that day. "Kinda like an interview kinda thing. Know what I mean?"

"Kinda," I answered, wondering what it would be like trying to talk with the guy for a full hour. Harry's years of working in cement ponds up north had (I'd already discovered at a couple of cocktail parties thrown by Rudy) rusted the reinforcing rods in his brain. That, or he'd gotten down to one too many pickled sparrows. Either way, chatting with Harry Riviero was like trying to converse with an empty grain silo.

"I was figurin," he continued in that flat sleep-inducing drawl of his, "that you could come on the show and you and me could, you know, kinda have a dialogue of some kind. Like Troy Donahue."*

"Sounds like fun," I answered, lying through my teeth. "What would you like to talk about?"

There was a long pause, as though Harry hadn't really gotten that far in his head yet. Nevertheless, after he'd cleared his throat for about five minutes, he managed to hit the jackpot as far as I was concerned.

"Well," he said, "I was thinking, maybe we could talk about your business."

"That would be swell," I answered, suspecting that a little free publicity was better than no publicity at all, even if it meant the self-flagellation of listening to Harry for an hour.

"Oh, good. Lotta area people would kinda be interested in how a big outfit like A&P works."

"P&B, Harry. Listen, have you cleared this with Sandinista? She doesn't seem to have much use for gunrunners."

"Gunrunners?"

"Yeah, Harry, that's what we do here at P&B. Didn't you know that?"

"Not really. Always had the impression you guys were in the grocery business."

"No, Harry, we sell guns."

"Oh." There followed another long pause. I could almost hear

_____

* A relatively obscure but masterful talk show host who made television history when, in front of a live studio audience, he cold-cocked a multiple-personality transvestite textbook author for calling him a white-haired old prick.

the gears clicking. "That's okay," he finally said, "you come on the show anyway. A guy gets lonely down here, ya know?"

The plaintive tone got to me. I realized that poor Harry just wanted somebody—besides the bitch—to talk to in his own native tongue. Like a fool, I agree to the interview.

The fella who let me into the tiny Puta Madre cable studio a couple of afternoons later looked more like a pro wrestler gone to seed than somebody who aspired to be Mexico's numero uno talk show host. Harry was four hundred pounds of Hispanic-heritage on the hoof with a face that was a cross between Cochise and a British bulldog. With a shock of black hair falling across his forehead, sideburns down to his jaw, and a "Wayne Newton" growing above his upper lip, Harry could've easily passed as the guy in *Sierra Madre* who "didn't need no stinkin badges," if only his Spanish was a little better.

He was dressed in an ill-fitting wine-colored polyester suit the likes of which I had seen only a few times before, mostly on the backs of old math profs at the Service Academy. A lime-hued ruffled shirt, opened to mid-chest, served to highlight a dazzling array of gold chain including enough religious medallions to qualify for sainthood. The whole ensemble was set off by a pair of gold alligator shoes and rose-tinted wrap-around sunglasses. For the first time I realized that Harry was a member of the Vegas Cult.*

"Glad you could make it, Mister Bucko," Haroldo—don't call me Harry on the air—Riviero said with a nervous laugh as he led me to a dais where two folding chairs had been arranged facing each other over a plastic coffee table. On the table was a telephone and a pitcher of water. No glasses, just a pitcher of water.

"We're on the air in just a couple," Harry said as he slapped some talcum powder on my face and darkened my eyebrows with a makeup pencil. "Live TV. Can't beat it for spondinuity [sic] but it's a pain in the ass to set up."

We hooked on our mikes and sat down. "You met the little woman before, haven't ya?" Harry asked. "Come on out, honey, say hello to today's guest."

---

* A group dedicated to preserving the style and fashion of a small Nevada city where bad taste was legally practiced twenty-four hours a day.

Harry's wife stepped out from behind the tripod mounted minicam and glared at me through heavy horn-rimmed glasses. She was a tall skinny woman in her mid-thirties with a boney pelvis, long dark hair, and a face like a starved moose. As I recalled from a previous brief conversation with the woman, she had been a liberal arts major back in the States studying pre–Big Blast Central American history when she'd had her name legally changed from Thelma Groot to Sandinista in memory of the ill-fated Nicaraguan army caught by Uncle Sam's 82nd Airborne Division trying to "liberate" the Panama Canal. How Ms. Farinahead and Harry had subsequently gotten together and migrated down to Puta Madre, I couldn't have given less of a shit, but I enjoyed pulling her chain every opportunity I got.

"Hi, Sandy," I said. "Read any good commie manifestos lately? Or is it just a touch of constipation that has you looking so full of it?"

True to those of her political ilk, her scowl got scowlier and she awkwardly flipped me the finger before stepping back behind the minicam. Meanwhile, under the intense heat of the studio's 100-watt light bulb, Harry was beginning to sweat like he was wearing rubber underwear; large dark stains were already spreading out from under his arms and his groin area. I tried to loosen him up with some light banter, but the guy was really too uptight for any meaningful conversation. For a "personality" in his line of work this seemed like a bad omen, but who was I to judge?

Thirty seconds before air, Sandinista cued Harry who produced a cassette player from under his chair and placed it on the table in front of him. At exactly three o'clock, the red light on the camera came on and Harry punched up his theme music—a badly recorded version of Herb Alpert's classic "Tijuana Taxi."

The cassette player must've been low on batteries because the music slowed noticeably, then faded out completely of its own accord only a few minutes into the broadcast. During that entire time, Harry just stared at the tabletop while I watched the monitor set up on the opposite side of the room. It was about as boring as television can get.

"Bueno," Harry said, using up virtually a quarter of his entire Spanish vocabulary as he reached over and shut off the machine. It was only then that he looked into the camera's lens. "Hello, everybody, and welcome to *The Gringo Hour*. This is your host,

Haroldo Riviero, and today we're gonna investigate the whole stinkin corrupt world of gunrunnin with my very special guest, William T. Bucko, who has asked for anominity [sic]. I gotta warn you that we aren't gonna pull no punches this afternoon, and you might hear some pretty gruesome stuff, but the story's gotta be told." Still dripping sweat, Harry glanced over at me. "Am I right or what?" he asked.

"Well, Haroldo," I responded cheerfully, "it's not quite as bad as all that. Sure, there are some rotten apples in my line of work, but you get that in all professions."

"I guess you're right," Harry answered after some interior head scratching, "but what I'd really like to know—and what I think our audience would really like to know—is where in the world can a guy go in Puta Madre to get a decent haircut?"

Damn right I was flabbergasted, but that was Harry for ya. For the next fifteen minutes he bitched and moaned about his last haircut while I sat there and nodded my head and watched on the monitor as Sandinista got even with me for being so impolite.

Or maybe she was just grossly incompetent. Hard to say, since, as I've previously mentioned, I'd never watched *The Gringo Hour* except those times I'd desperately needed some sleep. All I know is that every time she put me on camera there was a serious fuckup attached. Once, as her husband droned on into infinity, she caught me dozing off. Another time I looked up to see my crotch filling the monitor's screen. Invariably in close-up shots the top or bottom of my head was missing and other times the picture was so out of focus that it looked as though it had been shot through ten pounds of phlegm. Once she shot such an extreme close-up that the only thing on the screen was my ear, and later she pulled the same stunt zooming in and out on the jagged fishhook scar on my lip so that instead of it being a manly reminder of my long ago encounter with the evil Donny Smiles, it looked more like I was dribbling tobacco juice.

The more bizarre her camera work, the more I steamed. It was bad enough that I had to sit there and listen to Harry; to be abused by the cameraperson seemed just a hair too much to bear, especially since I knew Gunny Pugh was watching and would undoubtedly rag me unmercifully when I got home.

And the bitch knew she was getting to me because every once

in a while, after she'd pulled one of her little tricks, she'd step out from behind the camera and stare at me, the studio light reflecting off her beer-bottle glasses, a sly smile on her face. Then, as soon as she was sure she had my attention, she would begin making almost imperceptible thrusting motions at me with her jutting hips.

Real embarrassing shit. Gross, too. Of course, I tried to give as good as I took by making obscene gestures with my tongue and hands in her direction. Unfortunately, she quickly discovered she could bring this assault to a halt simply by putting me on camera. I had enough business sense to know that no matter how small the audience, it wouldn't do for a partner of P&B to be seen on TV acting like a pervert.

At some point, I'm not sure exactly when, I gave up in defeat and just sat there in my uncomfortable chair while trying to think about what I wanted for my birthday. Eventually, I knew, Harry would run out of things to say about his barber. I wanted to be awake when he did . . .

"And so, William T. Bucko, my special guest on today's program," I heard a voice say through the coastal fog, "let's take some telephone calls!"

I awoke just in time to find Harry staring down at the telephone on the table between us. Momentarily unsure of where I was and what was expected of me, I too just stared at the phone.

We must've sat there for five minutes of absolute silence before the damn thing began to ring . . . and ring . . . and ring. Harry didn't seem to mind, but I started to squirm.

"Hey, Haroldo," I blurted on the seventh ring, "you want me to get it?"

"Naw," he said, still staring at Mr. Bell's infernal machine, "let it go. Makes the caller think there is other people callin in; that he is lucky to get through. Not so many goofball questions that way."

Round about the tenth head-splitting tooth-jarring ring Harry reached out a hand the size of Connecticut and lifted the receiver to his ear. *"The Gringo Hour,"* he said, "an' you're on the air with Haroldo and his very special guest. Talk to me."

The phone had been rigged up to one of those speakers that

allows everyone in the room to hear the conversation. The only problem was that it hadn't been rigged very well. Along with the muffled garbled sound of a voice came enough feedback howl and squeal to get the local Humane Society involved.

Out of the corner of my eye I saw Sandinista scurry across the room and rip the wires out of the remote telephone speaker. Not only did this silence the horrible feedback, but it also shorted out the studio light. Harry and I became a couple of silhouettes on the monitor's screen.

"It's for you," the host of *The Gringo Hour* said, holding the receiver out to me in the dark.

"Hello," I said, "Will Bucko of P&B Arms and Munitions. You buy; we fly."

I heard a not entirely unfamiliar laugh on the other end of the line, a laugh full of cruelty and contempt. Try as I might, however, I couldn't place it.

"Still taking abuse up the caramel-coated love canal I see, Bucko," the voice said after the laughter had stopped. "I'll have to hand it to you, though, you always had stones. Hey, but come on, *The Gringo Hour,* for heaven's sakes? Have you no pride?"

"*You're* watching, aren't you, pal?" I growled. "Think about that . . . then tell me which one of us qualifies as the village idiot."

"What's he sayin?" the shadow that was Harry Riviero whispered loudly. "I'm sure our studio audience would like ta know."

"Tell him it's an old acquaintance," the voice said.

"I'll tell him its a pound of used fuck if I choose to," I nearly shouted into the mouthpiece, still unable to put a name and face to the voice.

"Bear with us, folks," Harry cautioned. "This is live TV."

"Who is this?" I demanded angrily.

That strange laughter echoed again, followed by what sounded like a sneer. "Can't tell you over the phone, Bucko. That would all but ruin my little surprise. When can we meet?"

"When? When *M*A*S*H* is no longer being shown in syndication," I said, "which probably means never. Besides, my daddy always told me not to make dates with bunghole bandits."

From the otherside of the dais I could hear Harry addressing the audience(?). "Advice I think we can all appreciate," he nervously commented. "As I always like ta say—this is *live* TV, folks. What you see is what you get."

"I didn't expect you to come see me without a little incentive," the mystery man on the telephone continued. "Fact of the matter is, I'd like to put in an order to your company for a few things."

"Like what?"

"Oh, shall we say your entire inventory?"

"You're dreamin, pal," I scoffed. "You have any idea what kind of BonusBucks you're talkin here?"

"You name a price, Bucko . . . I'll double it."

"HA! Very funny, Gunny!" I roared, at last recognizing the put-on. "You had me going there, I gotta admit. Listen, now that I've got you—how about taking the chicken out of the freezer to thaw. I thought maybe one of the girls could—"

I was cut off by the voice, which suddenly was spitting pure venom. "You miserable churl! This is not your negroid live-in companion! And this is very definitely not a joke! No, not a joke, by any means! Are you listening, Bucko?"

"A quarter mil, in gold credits," I grunted, figuring to call the bluff. "No bullion and no credit cards."

"Half a million," came the answer.

"Talk is cheap."

"Two days," the voice said, suddenly back to a calmer tone, "El Paso de Diablo. You'll find it on the map, about one hundred and forty miles northeast of Puta Madre, in the La Bamba Mountains. Bring a list of your current inventory and samples of any man-portable ground-to-air missiles and launchers you've got. Half the gold credits when we make the deal, the other half on delivery."

"What if I say two million?"

"Then I say four million."

"You're shitting me. Eight million then."

"Don't be ridiculous. Four million. Take it or leave it. El Paso de Diablo. Two days. Look for the panels. Deal?"

"Deal. Just tell me who this—"

The line went dead in my hand. For a moment I sat there in stunned silence, unable to grasp the ramifications of what had been said. All I could think was that if this guy was on the level, Pugh and I would be rich beyond our wildest dreams. The peckerhead had to be crazy, of course, but business was business.

"So that's about all the time we got left," Harry said as he punched on his cassette player again, this time to the legendary Frankie Valli and the Four Seasons singing their all-time bonanza hit, "Sherri." "I wanna thank our special guest, William T. Bucko," Harry continued over the music, "for stoppin by today. Also wanna remind everybody that video cassettes of our big Christmas show are still available upon request. For the whole gang here at *The Gringo Hour,* this is you friend Haroldo sayin so long till next time."

Miraculously, the studio light bulb flickered on, and the dais was once again bathed in light. Feeling euphoric and a little giddy, I began madly waving my arms and making all the obscene gestures I could come up with in the direction of *The Gringo Hour*'s cameraperson. Just as I hoped, Sandinista turned her camera in my direction and zoomed in for a tight close-up.

Well now . . .

Revenge is sweetest, I've found, when you're in a good mood already. The phone call had lifted my spirits, especially considering the fact that if all went well I might never have to work again as long as I lived. No longer concerned with what the great unwashed public of Puta Madre and environs might think of P&B enterprises, I did what any red-blooded American would do when confronted by an ugly and humorless commie chick: I dropped trou, spread cheeks, and shat on the coffee table—all accomplished before a confused and befuddled cameraperson could react and turn away the lens from what I believe was a milestone in the history of live television.

Sandinista ran screaming from the studio.

A convenient cliff overlooking the ocean, however, was too much to hope for.

I was feeling pretty cocky until I got back to the hacienda and proceeded to get my head handed to me by my partner.

"You ignorant cow teat!" he bellowed after I'd explained the deal I'd made over the phone. "You imbecilic booger hound! You pus-gushin wound, you! That guy could be anybody!"

"No shit, Gunny," I laughed. "Brilliant deduction, even for you."

"Now don't get smart with me," the big lug warned. "You

know damn well what I mean. Guy could be a FUC'er for all we know!* Maybe even a RIHM sympathizer!"

"Easy, big fella." I yawned, falling into my hammock there in the Rec House. "I guess I wasn't too clear: we're talking FOUR MILLION IN GOLD HERE! I don't care if the guy is the Beast from the Burning Pit; for four mil in gold I'll risk it! Hell, he's even talking half up front. I've got absolutely nothing to lose."

"Except your ass."

"Aw, come on. You mean you think this might be some kind of elaborate trap designed just to nail li'l ol' me?"

"Could be," Pugh said, calming down noticeably. "You've made a few enemies over the years, Will, not to mention the fact that there's still a price on your head back in the States. Hell, every once in a while I wanna kill you myself."

I looked for a telltale smirk, but the Gunny was a master at disguising his true emotions. "Give me credit for having a few brain cells, old friend," I said. "I'm going into this with every bullet, rocket, and missile the Harrier can carry. Any sign of funny stuff, I'll turn El Paso de Diablo into a site for a drive-in theater. I'll be fine."

The Gunny glared over at me from the bar stool where he'd taken refuge.† "Ain't *you* I'm concerned with," he said. "It's my own butt I'm talking about here, that self-same butt that'll be hanging out, sure as shit, if I've got to go in and play your fuggin sidekick again. Boy, I am too damn old for this silly Saturday matinee bullshit! Why do you have to be so gaw-damned greedy?"

"Greedy?" I bristled. "Excuse the hell out of me! Maybe I'm just tired of working my tail off for pinto beans, tortillas, and wrought-iron furniture! Look at the books, for shit's sakes! This is a cash-depleted operation. Most of our savings are tied up in inventory. And as for profits, what have we got to show for the last two and a half years?"

Without waiting for an answer, I rolled out of the hammock and walked over to the sailcloth-covered window.

"I'll tell ya what we've got to show for it!" I shouted at my partner. "A goddamn flea market, that's what!"

---

* An unflattering reference to a member of FAC's Undercover Investigation Agency, the secret police of the uniformed service.
† *Editor's Note:* Taken refuge?????

With a flourish, I pulled open the canvas to reveal a plaza full of animals—pigs, geese, goats, armadillos, a donkey—as well as an incredible amount and assortment of junk. Our yard looked like somebody was getting ready for a gigantic garage sale. There were old clothes on hangars, used kitchen appliances, stacks of books and old magazines, ratty deck furniture, gallon jugs of Agua Pendejo, bald tires, strings of dried fish, a piece of modern sculpture made of driftwood, a case of empty pop bottles, and somebody's embalmed grandmother.

Demand for our goods had been pretty brisk throughout P&B's years of operation you see, but except for a wealthy fascist landowner or two, most of our customers were cash-poor and paid us instead using the barter system. (It was not an easy system to work with. Have you ever tried to figure how many pairs of sandals a TOW-2 antitank missile was worth? How about how many chickens equals an AN/TPQ-36 Firefinder weapon-locating radar? And how many pounds of rancid goat butter do you charge for an M-249 Squad Automatic Weapon?)

"I'm tired of doing business this way, Gunny," I said, gesturing out at our piles of wealth. "I want to make some *money* for a change."

Pugh poured himself a glass of imported water, then spoke. "I smell a trap, Will," he said quietly.

"No, Gunny, what you smell is that damn parrot you traded sixteen bullet trap rifle grenades for last month. Thing shits like some kind of poop machine."

"Well, it talks too, ya know," Pugh said defensively.

"Yeah. But who around here understands Mandarin Chinese?"

Black Pugh gulped down his drink, slammed the glass down on the bar, then pushed off his stool. "All right. Have it your way," he sighed. "But if I get killed, I hope you'll feel real guilty."

"You've got my word on it."

"Then break out the maps and let's make some plans."

Two days later, with the Gunny riding shotgun in the backseat of the Harrier, and with my wings heavy with full cannon and SNEB rockets, we jumped off and vectored to the vicinity of El Paso de Diablo.

Wish to hell we'd stayed at home.

11

We reached the Devil's Pass around noon. While the Gunny kept an eye out for any telltale signs of SAM launches or small arms fire aimed in our direction, I made a few easy passes over the rendezvous area at about a thousand feet. All either of us spotted was a badly rusted TRAC-4 vehicle and three figures standing on the edge of a wide scrub-rimmed clearing.

Whoever they were, they were expecting us. A set of fluorescent pink ground panels had been laid out in the LZ, and, as I made my second pass, one of the men popped a lavender smoke to give me a general idea of wind speed and direction.

On the whole, the set-up looked pretty unsuspicious. Just to be on the safe side, however, I verticaled down to a nearby ridge line and dropped off Black Pugh along with a sixty mike-mike mortar tube and fifty rounds of ammunition.

The Gunny did not need any coaxing. For all his previous bitching and moaning, I could see the fire of excitement in his eyes as he dropped down from the wing and gave me a thumbs-up. Even in his seventies the old warrior was getting a hard-on thinking about a fight, and at the first sign of trouble I knew he'd turn the clearing into a bad place to be caught taking a leak. I saluted him and took off again, this time banking sharply as I came around to the clearing one more time and brought the Harrier in for a landing.

By the time the aircraft settled to a stop and I cut the engine, two of the men had approached from the TRAC and were waiting for me to climb down. From where I sat they looked like ordinary pseudomercs; one was an Oriental with piercing blue eyes, and the other was a Cauc badly in need of a shave and a skin graft. Both men were decked out in mail-order military geedunk like cammie sweatbands (for forehead and wrists), big bulky "survival" knifes (complete with built-in compass, map case, AM-FM radio, a bag of peanuts), and huge brass belt buckles inscribed with such witty sayings as "I served my time in Hell one Saturday night in Des Moines."

Neither one of these two chumps struck me as possibly being

the guy on the phone. Number one because neither looked nasty enough and number two because I didn't recognize either one of them. I was still as positive as I could be that I'd heard the voice on the phone before and was equally as sure I'd recognize the face as soon as I saw it.

The two soldiers were grinning up at me and motioning for me to join them. As soon as I caught a glint of metal reflecting from the ridge line—Pugh's signal that he had sighted his tube and was ready to drop in a few rounds at a moment's notice—I unbuckled myself from my harness and popped the canopy.

"Afternoon, boys," I hollered down to my welcoming party as I pulled off my helmet. "Which one of you wants to run back and tell your boss that I'm carrying a pressure-release detonator in my flight suit that'll blow this aircraft and about twelve square miles of surrounding landscape into the Bay of Baja if anybody so much as twitches wrong. How about you, Charlie Chan? Come on, what do you say, double time."

Without a word, the Oriental pivoted and began an easy jog back towards the TRAC. Quite frankly I didn't like his reaction one bit. My deliberate use of the ethnic slur had been intended to determine if these two were as they had at first seemed—a couple of rooks playing soldier. The disciplined reaction of the man to my order, when by all rights he should've tried to blow my head off, put me on my guard. For all their silly accoutrements, I had the feeling that these guys were the real thing.

"Whaddaya know about that," I said out loud to the second hellion, "a blue-eyed chink. Hell of a lot better than being as ugly as a dutch oven though." I glanced down at the other man and stared him straight in the eyes. "What happened to you? Accident with a piece of farm machinery? Shouldn't get your face so close to a thresher while it's in operation, pal. But I guess it's a little late for that kind of advice, right?"

Not a peep. The guy didn't even flinch, just stood there with his thumbs hooked in his web belt. I thought I saw a muscle in his cheek jump, but that was it. No doubt about it, somebody was playing games with me; these two were definitely not the green tinhorns they were pretending to be.

"You can come on over, Bucko," someone boomed over the TRAC's PA system. "We're all businessmen here." I recognized the voice as being the same one I'd heard over Harry's phone.

Leery, but curious as hell, I chambered a round in my .45 automatic, put it on safe, slipped it back into by shoulder holster, then eased over the lip of the aircraft's fuselage and dropped lightly to the ground.

"Lead the way, slick," I said to the second soldier. "And don't forget—one false move and we all become volcanic ash."

"Sure, buddy," the guy said, not one iota of fear in his voice, "I'll keep that in mind."

The ramp at the back of the TRAC was down when he arrived. The ugly soldier motioned me inside while he went over to squat next to a campfire with the blue-eyed Oriental and another guy who looked like he might've worked once as a wall. They were roasting weenies skewered on long sticks, but the Norman Rockwell scene didn't fool me a bit. I felt for the butt of my holstered .45 and walked into the darkness of the TRAC.

"Up here in the command bubble, Bucko," a voice from the gloom announced. "Watch your head. Low ceiling."

I carefully moved up the ladder through a connecting safety hatch into the command bubble. The frag screens were up, and the small confined area was lighted in red as though during night combat operations, so it took a few moments for my eyes to adjust. When they did, I gradually was able to make out a huge bloated shape sitting in the TRAC commander's chair. Not the face mind you, just the shape, because my host was wearing some sort of heavy complicated-looking vision contraption over the top half of his face, a polished metallic device with dials and number settings and control knobs that reminded me of those machines you look through when you go in to get a prescription for glasses.

"Ah, Bucko," that same unidentified voice said, "even after all these years I'd still recognize that face of yours anywhere. Oh, but please forgive the lighting. My eyes are very sensitive. In college, you see, I had an accident with some fire-retardant chemicals. Over the years, the residue of those chemicals—which the doctors could never completely flush away—ate away the membrane inside my eyelids, then the eyelids themselves. Now, unfortunately, I must wear this silly and cumbersome thing over face, as well as remain in near total darkness, for without the lubrication and blinking capabilities of my eyelids, I'm afraid my eyeballs would fry if I exposed them to the rays of the sun, or even the small amount of radiation produced by a white light bulb. I'm sure you'll understand."

"Sure, pard," I said, "we've all got our little crosses to bare. Me, I can't chew gum or eat popcorn anymore. Bad bridge work." I opened my mouth wide and pointed to a couple of phony molars way in the back. Hell, I was just trying to make conversation.

"I think you're mocking me," the voice said, almost with a trace of humor, "but that's all right, all right, indeed. So, did you bring the inventory list?"

"In my pocket," I said, tapping the chest of my flight suit, "right in there with my detonator."

"Yes, so you've already warned. Really, *Mister* Bucko, I don't know how to make you feel more comfortable and less suspicious. Any suggestions?"

"Yeah, now that you mention it. How about telling me who you are for starters, and how you came to know me."

"Oh my, I would've thought you'd already guessed." The fat stranger laughed. "My goodness gracious, Bucko, even after sixteen years can't you recognize an old shipmate when you see him? I'm hurt, really hurt."

With that, the guy reached over and fiddled with a knob on the command console next to him. There followed a whir of hydraulics and the contraption over his face smoothly lifted away on some sort of jointed arm. Even in the dim red glow of the battle light, I had no trouble whatsoever in finally identifying the mystery man.

"My God," I heard myself whisper, "Jerry Roast."

Jerry Roast. By Christ, I had once hated him more than anything on earth, and that included two-minute magazine-subscription commercials that started with a switchboard operator named Nancy or Judy or Betty. Years before, during my plebe (and only) year at the Academy, Roast and his roommate had nearly killed me with their insane hazing. One night, in retaliation for their cruelty, I had bombed their room with a specially prepared device packed with chemicals taken from an Academy fire extinguisher. As fine as talcum powder, these chemicals had, upon detonation, found there way into every nook and cranny of their bodies. The burning pain, as I had hoped, had been excruciating.

In fact, as I recall, the scuttlebutt was that the two of them did not stop screaming for a week. I wouldn't know for sure, since they were in a soundproof isolation ward in the hospital all during that time.

The two had eventually found me out, and I had paid dearly for my revenge. I had weathered the ensuing storm bravely, however, and would've made it through even the bouts with the leeches and broom-handle buggering had not the cruel sadists decided to turn their evil on my fellow plebe, Melodie Lane. In trying to defend her sexuality from their insanity, I had brought about my own expulsion from the school on Beaver Dam Run.

"Yes, that's right—Jerry Roast," my old adversary said, "how very perceptive of you."

Quickly, the hydraulic arm lowered the vision device back over his face, but not until I'd gotten a good look at his lidless eyes, a good enough look to know that Jerry would never be the first to blink in a stare-down. In that quick little moment when his facial features had been uncovered, I'd seen two nearly perfectly round eyeballs—wild and muddy-looking—both bulging from his doughy face, both rimmed with raw exposed flesh, which looked as though it was being eaten away by acid.

"Jeez, Jer," I exclaimed, unable to resist the obvious, "are *you* a sight for sore eyes!"

Obvious, yes. Smart, no. Roast made no actual move in response to my pun, but I was sure I heard a little gasp coming from his bulky shape, almost as though he could not believe I would be so bold as to poke fun at his lidless peepers. Futilely, I tried to regroup.

"Seriously though," I said with my best hale-fellow-well-met voice, "it's good to see you, Jer. And I mean that sincerely." A pack of lies, actually. Roast's overall general appearance had changed, but my hatred for him hadn't. Still, business is business. I decided to hear ol' Jer out before I cut his fucking throat.

"Sixteen years, Bucko," Roast rasped. "Sixteen long years."

"Has it been that long? Lordy, how time flies. Tell me, Jer, what've you been doing with yourself?" I didn't like the sound of his voice. It was full of anger and bitterness as if he blamed *me* for his poor eyesight.

"Oh, a little of this and a little of this," Jerry answered in a more normal-sounding voice. "You knew of course that FAC surveyed me a year after graduation; said my eye problem was not conducive to good morale, especially in the field of Public Relations. Had to go to work for my father's firm back in Grosse Pointe until even he had to give me the pink slip. Said his clients were beginning to complain; said they felt as though I was always staring at them. Well, I ask you, Bucko, was that fair, given the nature of my disability?"

"No, I don't suppose it was," I answered. "But that's the breaks, I guess."

Yes, he'd changed quite a bit physically, but the sound of his voice was exactly as I remembered it on those wet cold January mornings at the Academy when he'd use my shivering naked body for his experiments in torture; it had given me goose pimples then and did so now.

"Then my mother asked me to leave the house," he continued. "She claimed my appearance was upsetting the hired help." Roast paused and heaved an obviously exaggerated sigh. "Dear, dear Mumsie," he went on, "I wonder if she'll ever forget that last bite of steak tartar. I'd rigged it with a spring-loaded piece of sharpened plastic, you see. A couple or three chews and dear Mumsie was no more, her throat pierced from the inside out in front of two hundred of her closest friends at the Fuel Injectors Ball."

"Shoot," I said, "I bet that was an eyeful."

"Needless to say," Roast said, all but ignoring me, "I was elsewhere at the time. On my way to Greenland actually. Greenland, where the sun only shines six months out of the year [?]. Lived with the Eskimos. Became their king. They called me *Ishlatuk,* which means 'He who has eyes like a snow frog.' I ruled with an iron hand. Only way. Many died on my order, impaled on their own barbed lances. You must *crush* a rebellion, Bucko, *crush* it in its infancy. Otherwise . . ."

His thought trailed off and I felt obligated to complete it. "Otherwise," I said, "the men in white coats will soon be knocking on your igloo. Say listen, Jer, it's been great seeing you again, but I gotta go. Couple of land-hungry peasants want to barter for some RPGs. If you ever get to Puta Madre, feel free to drop—"

"Alas," Jerry rambled, "the traitors behind the revolution finally drove me from my throne, and I was driven deep into the Arctic, much like Mary Shelley's famous monster."*

"You mean like Russ?" I asked.

"Say what?" For the first time, Roast actually sounded surprised at something I'd said.

After a prolonged period of silence, he got back to his story. "It was while in the frozen wastes of that far-off northern land that I met the brilliant Doctor Fizz, an ophthalmologist from Baltimore who had been run out of town by an angry mob when several hundred lying and deceitful children claimed Doctor Fizz had groped them during eye examinations. When Doctor Fizz saw my problem, he fashioned this machine for me. It protects and lubricates my eyes and covers them when it is time to sleep. Without it, I would most certainly have gone blind years ago."

"And a very fashionable device it is," I said, eager to get the hell on the road. My hate for Roast was quickly turning to pity and, yeah, maybe even a little fear; the guy was apparently crazier than hammered turtle eggs. "You almost don't even notice it. Damn, Jer, I'm glad to hear everything turned out okay for you. Me, I've got the rent to pay. Why don't I give you my address and you could—"

"With the funds I'd managed to embezzle from my father's business, I was able to purchase and rehab this vehicle to my own specifications," he continued without (fairly predictably) batting an eyelash. "After careful consideration of the viable areas of the world where my expertise could be utilized, I had this TRAC airlifted down here, oh, I guess about six years ago. I then placed an ad in several journals and periodicals soliciting the services of professional fighting men. As you can see by the hard-chargers outside, I was able to pick and choose the most hearty from a large number of responses."

"I assume then," I tried to joke, "that you're now in the food-catering business."

A sound not totally unlike a laugh came from the hulking dark shape sitting across the bubble from me. "Har har har," Roast responded, "not quite. No, Bucko, much like your own opera-

---

* As any school child could tell you, the reference here is made to Baron Ludwig Von Frankenstein's horrible creation, whom he named "Russ."

tion, we provide a service to those in need. You are familiar with PMS?"

"Not personally," I blurted, somewhat offended by his question. "Has something to do with women being bitchy and irritable at certain times of the month, right?"

"Professional Military Service, you dullard. Which brings me to why I got in contact with you. We need a resupply. The group I usually do business with made the mistake of trying to gouge us with their prices. Neither they nor any of their offspring will ever sell weapons again. But perhaps you can already see my predicament. It appears I cut off my nose to spite my face. Luckily, I'm a regular viewer of *The Gringo Hour*. Image my surprise and pleasure when I discovered that my dear old plebe, Will Bucko, was dealing in the very commodity that I'm in fairly desperate need of."

"Well," I said, "it's true. I can get you a real decent price on a case of sunglasses. Polaroids. UV tested. Perfect for your, ah, situation."

"Come come, Bucko," the sack of blubber said. "Let's not play games."

"Then let's play ball!" I chuckled. "You can be the umpire."

It was, I quickly determined, the last straw. Roast made a low guttural sound like a RIHM ready to charge. I saw him reach for something behind his chair, then, all at once, the hydraulic arm was lifting the vision device from his face again, and I found myself looking straight into those horrible bulging eyes. At the same time a leather satchel was being thrown at my feet.

"Count it!" Jerry screamed. "Count it you miserable punster! Two million U.S. government gold credits! I want your entire inventory of weapons and ammunition! Do I make myself clear? Or would you rather talk it over with my bloodthirsty boys?"

"Easy Jer," I soothed, trying not to look at those hideous eyeballs and the chewed-up meat around them. "Let's not forget the detonator."

"GO AHEAD!" he screamed even louder. "It would be worth it to know you'd finally be dead. Go ahead, do it. Do it, OR JUST SHUT UP!"

Just as I'd thought all along, he was blaming me for his little eye problem and the subsequent disasters in his life.

"Okay, Roast," I said, making a concerted effort to sound unconcerned with his outburst, "since we finally seem to be laying our cards on the table . . . Number one: I doubt very seriously if those Hollywood bad guys out there cooking hotdogs and marshmallows are going to risk getting reduced to molecular debris just because you want me roughed up. In the second place: Even if you have grown into an obese gob of slop, and have been reduced to living like a goddamn fruit bat, you're still alive and apparently have a nice moderate little business enterprise going here. No sense screwing up the works just to get even with me. Which brings me to the third place: Despite the fact that I hate your guts as much now as I did back when you were attaching electrodes to my *cajones,* business is business. You got the funds, I got the guns. 'Nuff said?"

With that weak little chin of his quivering, Roast stared at me for a very long while. (I'm only guessing here, of course, since the word *staring* seems redundant given Jer's condition. On the other hand, it was easy to see why his father had seen fit to fire him.) Then, with another soft whir, he manipulated the eye contraption back down over his face. I deduced the crisis had passed.

"Very glibly put, Bucko," he croaked. "Perhaps you're right. Perhaps I am allowing my personal feelings to interfere with business. All right. You have the two million gold credits. Upon delivery of your inventory, another two million will be turned over to you. Agreed?"

"Agreed. You understand, though, we're talking quite a load of stuff. I've got to haul it all out here by Harrier. It's gonna take some time."

"I understand. When can you start?"

"Give me a week to get everything squared away."

"A week? That long? I had hoped that—"

"Jer, Jer," I interrupted, "trust me. Not only do we have to rig things for max load, but the aircraft is going to need some downtime for preventive maintenance. You don't want me augering into the side of a mountain carrying your merchandise just because the oil filter needed changing, right?"

"Very well, Bucko. One week. I'll contact you for exact time and place of delivery."

"You mean delivery won't be here?"

"No, certainly not." Roast made a little harumping sound, as though he was losing his patience again. "I may be—as you so eloquently put it—living like a fruit bat, but I'm not completely brain dead. I wasn't about to reveal my secret base of operations to you for the first meeting. I'll send you coordinates of the drop point later."

"Don't make it too much later," I said. "Where you're located has a lot to do with how much ordnance I can carry and how much fuel I'll need. Better give me at least two days leeway."

"I'll take that under advisement. Until then, get out of my sight."

"Easier said than done, Jer," I quipped as I picked up the satchel full of gold credits. "But I'll give it a try." With that, I flipped him a little two-finger salute and then slid down the ladder back into the TRAC's main hold.

The boy scouts were still squatting around the campfire when I stumbled off the ramp, my eyes painfully aware that there was still plenty of daylight left. All three gave me their best psychopathic glares but said not a word. The blue-eyed Oriental blew on a bubbling blackened marshmallow, then lasciviously sucked the thing off his stick. I assumed it was some ancient Chinese gesture of contempt but paid it no mind. After all, I was carrying two million in gold credits—if the guy wanted to risk scalding off half his taste buds with such a macho move, that was his prerogative. Me, I just headed back to my bird without sayin nuthin.

The Harrier's engine started on the third crank thanks to the ingenious self-starter unit Pugh had installed many years before. While I let her warm up, I checked my gauges and calculated that there was more than enough synfuel to get us back to Puta Madre; but not enough, unfortunately, for me to wait around and perhaps trail Roast and his TRAC back to his home base. Consequently, as I lifted out of the clearing, there was no way for me to know when or where our next meeting would be; I would just have to trust Jerry.

The Gunny was waiting patiently on the ridge line as I guided the Harrier in for a pickup. He looked a little disappointed (probably because he hadn't been allowed to fire for effect) but perked right up when I held up the satchel in one hand, a fistful of gold credits in the other.*

We didn't waste any time reloading the mortar or 60mm ammunition back aboard the bird. Being in the business, we were up to our armpits in such weapons, so Pugh simply booby-trapped the whole shebang and left it for the vultures. By the time he'd settled into his seat and strapped in, I was already at Angels-5 and vectored for home. After he reamed me out for nearly decapitating him with my no-hands landing, I related to him the deal I had struck with the myopic Mister Roast. When I'd finished, Pugh seemed pleased as hell.

"You crafty sonuvabuck!" He laughed heartily over the intercom. "Why, I guess that's just about the easiest two million we ever made!"

"And the second two won't be much harder." I laughed along with him. It was good seeing the old buzzard so happy.

Pugh's amusement seemed to fad a bit. "Second two what?" he asked.

"The second two million, you old woolly mammoth! What the hell do you think?" I was still feeling pretty euphoric.

"Hold on now, Will," the Gunny growled from the backseat. "You don't mean ta tell me you're thinkin about going through with the deal?"

"Sure!" I answered happily. "Why the hell not?"

"Why not?" Pugh sputtered. "Why not? I'll tell ya why not, you fuggin lamebrain! Because based on what you've told me, we are dealin with some extremely weird asshole who's got a damn good reason to want you dead, that's why not. Because this whole thing smells like a setup. Because the two million gold credits we've already got is more money than we'll ever need! Because, like I thought I'd already taught you, the second great tenet of Yuwon-itsu is that you quit while you're ahead."

"Come on," I said, "you're beginning to sound like an old fart."

"Don't disappoint me, son. Listen to Pugh. We get back to

---

* A word to the nuts out there who collect and fly antique aircraft. . . . Never ever try to land the TAV-8B Harrier, or any other jet aircraft for that matter, with no hands. Only a superbly trained professional can pull the trick off, and even then it's a dicey situation.

Puta Madre, we pack our bags, fill up this bird's drop tanks, and deedee our butts down to Rio where we will live like fuggin kings for the rest of our natural lives!"

"Try to relax, Gunny," I answered as calmly as I could. "You're getting all worked up over nothing. I've got this thing figured. Sure Roast has reason to want to see me dead, but unless I'm a real poor judge of character, he wants our inventory a lot more."

"Only means he'll try to grease your ass on the last shipment instead of the first," Pugh grumbled.

"And that's why the last shipment will be wired with enough HE to remove old Mexico from the world map. I'll tell him going in that he'll only get defusing instructions when me and the second two million are safely on our way."

"It ain't worth it," Pugh snapped.

"Sure it is. Listen, four million divided by two is better than two divided by two. If we can live like kings off of what I've got here, think what it'll be like if we double it!"

"Will," my partner said gloomily, "there's just so much tail and T-bone a man can handle, then it becomes nothin but pure greed. Take my word for it, son. My knees tell me it's time to cut loose."

His badgering and cajoling were beginning to wear on my nerves. I'd made up my mind to follow through on the deal with Roast, and that was enough. I didn't need old Pugh spouting tenets of East Coast mysticism at me to tell me things could get dangerous, but that was the chance I was willing to take. It was my own life I would be laying on the line, not his.

Knowing that my partner's cranky old-biddy routine would change nothing, I reached over and turned off the intercom. If Pugh wanted to rant and rave all the way back to Puta Madre, he could do so in private. All I wanted to do was kickback and dream about what I was going to do with my share of four million in gold.

12

The Gunny gave me the silent treatment for the next three days or so, but gradually changed his tune as he came to realize that I would not be swayed in my crusade to become a wealthy man. When my old friend began to mumble under his breath about his nightmares and a strong sense of impending doom, I knew he was returning to his old self. Soon he was back working on the Harrier, getting her ready for the task to come.

We heard nothing from Roast, however, and as the days went by I grew restless. Had I imagined the whole encounter? No, the two million in gold credits sitting on the table in the Rec House said otherwise. The meeting had been real, so why hadn't we heard anything from our client? Had Roast gotten cold feet? Was he so well off that he could afford to eat the two million? I didn't think so.

Without a specific set of coordinates for delivery, there was little I could do in the way of load-lift planning, so while Pugh kept himself busy tinkering with the aircraft, I was left to rot. Take it from me, there's just so many videos you can watch in a row before your body and brain begin to sprout like an Idaho tuber. Therefore, it was for personal health reasons—both physical and mental—as well as a desire to break the boredom, that after four days of inactivity (and twelve straight hours of *Webster* reruns) I decided to wander into town and see what was shaking.

Since the local cantina didn't open until noon, I decided to take a leisurely stroll through Puta Madre's bustling open market, a scene of free enterprise as old as Mexico herself. Here were the colorful stalls full of produce fresh from the countryside with, like as not, the proud farmer or his wife standing by to bargain in the traditional fashion.

"How much for this onion?" I ask in the native tongue.

"Forty pesos" comes the reply.

"Forty? Are you crazy? This onion is worth no more than twenty!"

"Thirty-five then!" cries the farmer, his smile displaying several dozen missing teeth framed against cracked skin the shade of soy sauce.

"Fifteen! And not a peso more!" I counter.

"Robbery!" shouts the farmer's wife, her large nipples visibly hardening under her simple peasant smock. "Thirty pesos!"

"Twelve!" I cry. "And even then you are swindling me!"

Now both the farmer and his wife are grinning, both enjoying the fun of bargaining. The woman brings out a machete hidden under her colorful skirt and points it at my nose.

"You piece of dung!" she shouts. "You could not have this onion now if you offered your first born! You bargain like some ignoramus from the boondocks. Get out of here before I am forced to cut off your face!"

"Ten!" I bellow. "And I promise it is my last offer!"

"You are correct about that, father of wild dogs!" the woman screams in a shrill falsetto. Only a well-rehearsed blocking blow by her husband prevents the flashing machete from decapitating me.

"There are other stalls in the market, my friends." I laugh. "And other onions at half your price. Good day to you."

I turn and begin to walk away as though the bargaining is over. It is the signal for the final offer and the farmer knows it. He lets me take ten more steps before he gives in.

"Wait, gringo," I hear him say.

I stop and turn, feigning surprise. The farmer's wife is on her knees weeping, the long knife no longer in her hand. The farmer himself looks as though he has just had his head kicked in. He holds the onion loosely in one hand at his side.

"The onion is yours for ten pesos," he whimpers. "Take it and go."

"Not until your wife disrobes and squats on a cactus," I respond.

Like many Mexican farmers, this one obviously plays on a semi-pro baseball team in his spare time because the onion is going about ninety-five miles an hour when it passes my ear and explodes on a nearby adobe wall.

I laugh, wave, and resume my saunter through the market, wishing every day in my life could be this exciting and eventful. But what the hell, it's a way to kill time.

There were many other stalls in the plaza; I stopped and bargained at most of them, enjoying myself for a while, then growing weary and moving on to the next.

Here was the small business that sold peyote buttons and sacred mushrooms and holograms of famous matadors caught in the nude. Nothing there for me, of course, but I enjoyed watching the town's teenagers pretend to be of age.

Next was the man displaying at least one hubcap from every make of car ever assembled. I looked for something in a BMW that I could hang on the Harrier, but his prices were way too steep.

The aroma of something succulent drew me to the taco wagon further down the line. The same aroma, I quickly saw, has also attracted every fly in Puta Madre, but the cook has prudently hired three small children whose sole job it was to kill as many of the pesky insects as they could with rolled-up newspapers. After much haggling, I settled on a meatball burrito and a bottle of nasty-looking grape drink. Hoping that my shot card was up to date, I sat down next to the town fountain and ate my lunch.

Later, when I had at last completed my tour of the plaza, I was about to head on over to the cantina for some liquid refreshment when, out of pure chance, I happened to notice another stall set away from all the others, one that I had not seen before. The sign hanging from the gaily decorated facade intrigued me: Fortunes Told—RIHM Parts Sold, it read. Thinking that I might find a pelvis Pugh could make into a lamp, I wandered on over.

There was, I soon discovered, no one minding the store. The stall was empty of customers as well as a proprietor, and I simply assumed they were all off taking a fiesta (sic). Unfortunately, the only RIHM parts I saw on display were the usual pieces of tourist bullshit—fingerjoints, kneecaps, earhorns, lower incisors—the kind of stuff you could find for sale almost anywhere. Disappointed, I turned to leave. Only then did I discover that the proprietor was in.

"May I help you, señor?" I heard an ancient quaking voice ask.

He'd been sitting in the shade far in back of the stall, which explains why I'd missed seeing him when I'd come in. As he emerged from the shadows I saw him to be a fragile, frail-looking man of Indian descent with skin the color of dried blood and a face as old as a mountain top. His hair, long and white, was decorated with an array of his wares—small RIHM bones and teeth—as well as bits of colored feather and pieces of red yarn and strung popcorn. He wore a baggy peasant blouse far too large for his body; the cuffs on the sleeves almost covered his hands and the oversized opening at the neck only tended to emphasize his wizenedness. Less than five feet tall, he immediately reminded me of a character you might find described in a child's fairy tale —a character usually living inside a hollow tree or under a bridge. Kind of disconcerting to see one in the flesh, if you want the gospel truth.

"Ah, just looking for RIHM parts," I gulped in response to his query, trying not to stare.

"Well," he said, gesturing spastically at his wares, "you've come to the right spot. Was there something in particular?"

"Naw. It's for my partner. He's a bit of a collector. Got most of this stuff already."

"Aha! A collector! In that case, perhaps you would like to see what I have in back. It is truly a marvel, señor. The kind of thing one does not put out for public display. There are things, after all, that women and small children should never have to see."

"Like liposuction on a fat lady's thighs."

"Come again, señor?"

"Forget it. Let's see what you've got."

The tiny old man led me out an opening at the rear of his stall and into a tent made from stitched together RIHM skins. The place smelled like the inside of a rotting molar, and I was nearly knocked to my knees by the fumes but managed to stay standing long enough to see the old Indian's prized possession. Hanging by thongs of rawhide attached to the tent's centerpole was the mummified head of a large male Western RIHM.

"Very nice," I gagged. "What are you asking for it?"

"Two million in gold, señor."

The way he said it, the way it came out sounding as though there was nothing unusual at all about him knowing of the gold credits, sort of threw me for a loop. I tried to respond casually, but it was difficult.

"Get real, old one," I stammered. "Would I be living in this dump if I had two mil to throw away on RIHM heads?"

The old gizzer smiled a toothless grin. "The bones never lie, señor," he scolded. "They told me that you have two million in gold."

"Sure, sure," I answered, realizing I was being conned, "the bones never lie." I quickly figured one of the hired help out at the hacienda had spotted our haul and had blabbed it all over town. (Hell, no wonder the farmer with the onion had tried to rip me off!) This old hombre had also gotten wind of it and was using the information to mess up my mind. "Tell you what," I continued, "I don't want to dicker with you. I'll give you ten bucks for this head if you can have it wrapped and delivered this afternoon. Take it or leave it."

The old dude's resulting laughter sounded like the airbrakes on a crosstown hoverbus. "Sí, sí," he finally managed to choke, "the bones said you had quite the sense of humor, señor, as well as being a fine judge of head. Forget this poor excuse for a curio. You are right—it is already infested with worms and beginning to stink. But if you will permit me, I will show you something much grander. I will roll the bones and show you your future."

It was my turn to yuk. "Nice try, pal," I chuckled as I made a motion to leave. "I'd like to stay and help you put your kids through college, but I've got better things to do with my hard earned loot than waste it on a Mexican fortune cookie, so I'll pass. Asta la vista, and via con carne."

I was nearly out the tent flap when he called out to me and turned my blood to liquid Freon.

"The hombre with metal eyes wants you dead, señor," the old man said in a voice from the grave. "He has made a pact with the devil that not even the big hummingbird or the black giant with the plastic pinochle can break."

Okay. The "big hummingbird" was a gimme—everybody in town knew about the Harrier—and I suspected there were more than a few señoritas who could confirm that Black Pugh's fully functional johnson was made of reinforced Plas-tex. But how the hell this old RIHM-parts dealer had found out about Jerry Roast's eye problem was something I could not explain. Maybe it would be worth a few centavos to find out.

"And how much do the bones want in order to tell me more?" I asked as I stepped back inside the tent.

The old man's toothless gums were exposed through a big up-turned ear-to-ear crack in his face. "Why, two million in gold of course," he sang to me.

"You're unreal, pal."

"The bones say you are due to collect two million more, señor. Why quibble? Will not the knowledge of the future be worth such a sum?"

I contemplated that for a moment, and then a thought struck me. "Come to think of it," I said, "no, it wouldn't, not for half that, not for one one-hundredth of that. Tell you the truth, old man, I suspect I'll be a lot better off letting the future surprise me just like it always does. Where and when I'm gonna buy the farm is not something I want to know just yet. Roll your bones for the women and old men. A warrior will know soon enough when his time has come."

"Spoken like a jibbering idiot!" the old Indian howled. "Consider this: By knowing your future, dummy, you may change that future."

"The future cannot be changed, no more than the winds can be made to crack or the seas made to wave. No, old man," I said quietly as I ducked under the tent flap, "the future must be left to fate."

"At least you will know if you should make out your will!" the shaman screeched, following me out of the tent and through the stall, trying furiously to regain lost ground. "And what about the women in your life? Wouldn't you like to get a jump on that? The bones don't have to talk about life and death, they can get real mundane if you like. I can give you the answers to *Jeopardy* in advance!"

"Give it a rest, old one," I muttered. "Besides, I'd need the questions to *Jeopardy,* not the answers."

"Whatever!" he howled. "How about a good reliable weather report? Lottery numbers! I got lottery numbers! How about your child's SAT scores?"

"Forget it," I laughed. "Might've had a deal if you hadn't gotten so greedy. Here, get yourself a cup of jose on me." I flipped the old guy a peso and continued to walk across the crowded plaza in the direction of the cantina.

"Beware, señor!" I heard him say from far away as I approached the swinging doors of the bar. "Beware!"

I pivoted and shouted back to him although all I could see through the throng of shoppers was his distinctively decorated white head. "Beware of what, old-timer?" I hollered through cupped hands.

"Beware of the dog!" he answered.

He stood there in front of his business and stared at me for a few long seconds, then turned and got out of the sun. Shakespeare was only half right: not only are we all actors, but a few too many of us—old Indian shamans included—think we're stand-up comedians as well.

Without any more thought to the warning issued by the man who sold RIHM parts, I went into the cantina and got blithering drunk.

The message from Roast came just as I was beginning to recover from a hangover as horrible as anything I have ever experienced. As the locals liked to say, I had "eaten the sparrow" and would probably not be able to see clearly or hold down solid food for another twenty-four hours. No wonder then that Pugh had a big smile on his face when he came in with the telex in his hand— the old shit was experiencing something akin to sexual gratification seeing me in such a condition.

"Well, lookie here," the giant thug cackled, "ol' Will looks like he tried to go one-on-one with a bulldozer! And just when our new client sends word he's ready for the deal to go down. Real shame we gotta miss all the action just because Capt'n Bucko went and got shitfaced on the local moonshine."

"Give me that," I groaned, reaching for the telex message held in his extended hand. The movement caused a power surge through my skull that can only be compared to being struck by lighting. I yelled out in pain as I collapsed back into my hammock, pinching my nostrils shut so my brains wouldn't leak out. For an instant the image of the decomposing RIHM head in the old Indian's shop flashed across my mind's eye, then it was gone. "Just read it to me," I pleaded. "And keep the wisecracks to yourself."

"It's enough to give a man religion, ain't it?"

"What's the telex say, Pugh, damn you."

"Says your old classmate is ready to begin accepting shipment. Says to bring the first lift in day after tomorrow. Says he'll mark the LZ with blue smoke."

"Great," I mumbled, "but does it give the coordinates where he wants us to go?"

"Ha!" Pugh bellowed. "Glad you asked, compadre. See, that's

the joke. Your pal was fuggin with us. We're going right on back to where we met him the first time."

"The Devil's Pass?"

"You get an 'A' for memory work."

"What an asshole. He could've told us that up front and saved a lot of time."

"He's an asshole all right," Pugh said. "But a crafty one. He got a full dress rehearsal of our methodology without us even realizing it; got a chance to look at our tactics without showing us doodily."

"What are you talking about, Gunny? We saw what he's got."

"Come on, Will. We saw three pseudomercs and an old TRAC-4. Listen, son, this Roast character ordered up one hundred tons of weapons and ammo. Take four men and a TRAC ten years to go through that much ordnance if they were fighting every day. No, that old school chum of yours has more going than a few private security jobs. I'd be willin to bet he's got a little army stashed away somewhere, just itchin to raise hell with the property lines. Hey! Where're you goin?"

While the Gunny had been rambling on, I'd summoned up what little willpower I could find and had finally managed to roll out of my hammock and lurch to my feet. I was in the process of staggering my way out the door and over towards the Shit House when Pugh realized he was lecturing an empty net.

"Gonna take some steam," I called back to him, most of the words catching in the web of cotton fibers in my mouth and throat. "Then I'm gonna plug the coordinates for Devil's Pass into the main frame and start figurin my lifts. Two days ain't much time."

"Damnation!" Pugh shouted. "You mean you still intend to go through with this fiasco? After what I just told you?"

"Nothing's changed, Gunny. Two million in gold is waiting out there. I could give a damn if that bastard has a little army hidden somewhere. He wants to take over a piece of Mexican desert and call it Roastland, more power to him. Hell, the Federales will wipe him out in a week if he tries to go conventional."

"That's not what worries me."

As a young man playing in the last days of the old National Basketball Association, Pugh had worshipped a legend of the game named Bill Russell. He still had a poster of the old B-Ball star, which he'd hung over the bar. At this moment, as I looked back into the Main House of the hacienda, I noticed for the first time how much Pugh had come to look like old Bill. His back slightly bent, his beard and hair flecked with gray, the lines in his long face all curved downward, he was the spitting image of his boyhood idol.

"It's a trap, Will," he said softly, reaching for his kneecaps, which he began to massage gently. "Sure as I'm standing here now, it's a trap. The bones never lie."

The bones never lie. The same words uttered by the old shaman. Any sane man would have started to listen at that point. Will Bucko just laughed and staggered off to his bath.

What a dickhead.

13

The billows of orange smoke marking the LZ were whipped away by the backwash of the Harrier's pusher nozzles as I set the bird down gently on the sunbaked earth and cut the throttle. Even before the engine had whined to a stop and I'd popped my harness release, the now familiar transport LAVs (Light Armored Vehicles) were churning out towards me. By the time I'd gotten the canopy open and propped myself up on the seat, Jerry's kids were already unloading the wing pods.

After nearly two weeks of making twice daily deliveries to the landing zone at Devil's Pass, events had gotten fairly predictable.

"Hey, Dung!" I called down to the guy supervising the unloading. "Give this to your boss." I tossed down the canister containing the latest spreadsheet printout from the P&B main frame. It indicated at least three more lifts would be necessary before the job was complete.

"I told you before, Bucko," the man shouted back angrily as he stooped to pick up the message tube, "the name is Marvin!"

Yes, he had told me before. From the first delivery day in fact I'd known that the blue-eyed Oriental in Roast's band of hired thugs went by the thoroughly Caucasian name of Marvin. Whether that was his first or last name, I never did find out. No matter, since he was in charge of the unloading team (Pugh had been correct—Roast did have a lot more men with him than he'd first let on), I saw him every time I hit the LZ, and had taken great delight in ragging his ass unmercifully about his heritage. He'd shrugged it off pretty well at first, but I could tell my barbs were beginning to get under his skin.

"Whatever you say, Wong," I shouted. "Or is Wong-wrong-Dong?"

Those watery blue eyes became mere slits of dark hatred. "How long do you intend to play this game, Bucko?" he hissed. "Until I kill you perhaps?"

Christ, the guy was really asking for it, but what else could I do? "How long is a *Chinaman,* fool!" I laughed. "You of all people should know that!"*

Marvin swept his AK-85 up to his shoulder and had me washed with his laser sight before I had a chance to react. For one brief instant I was sure I could see his finger squeezing down on the release mechanism that would instantaneously send seventy fléchettes of ultrasound tearing into my body.

The crisis passed. Slowly, his finger came off the release, and he lower the weapon back down to the ready. I could only surmise that at the moment of truth, Marv had caught a glimpse of himself impaled on a twelve-foot length of sharpened PVC pipe which, as both he and I were well aware, was Jerry Roast's preferred method of dealing with those who disobeyed his orders. One only had to look over at the fly-blackened body of the poor dumb sportsman who had failed to keep his shirttails tucked in to realize Roast was a harsh taskmaster. It had taken two days for the weight of the man's own body to work the sharpened pipe up through his bowels and vital organs and out through the back of the neck, and I sincerely doubted if one second of that experience had been very pleasant at all.

"One of these days, Bucko," Marvin snarled at me, pointing a finger instead of the AK, "one of these days I'm gonna make a meal of your guts."

"You want pint or quart?" I chortled back. "Tell you what— you promise not to eat me, and I'll promise not to tell your boss that you've been skimming ammo from my deliveries."

"THAT'S A GODDAMN LIE!"

"So? What's that got to do with the price of poontang in Paris? We both know who that racist pig will believe if push comes to shove. You'll have half a foot of plastic pipe up your ass before the sun goes down. So do me a favor, Bong. Get this aircraft unloaded and quit trying to be such a hard-ass, okay?"

"Some of my ancestors got straight A's at M.I.T.," Marv grumbled as he stormed off towards the TRAC-4 parked in defi-

* *Editor's Note:* Just for the record, we reminded Colonel Bucko that this "how long" joke was used in an earlier chapter and was an old and stale one even then. The author nonetheless refused to delete in spite of our objections.

lade on the far side of the LZ. "I shouldn't have to take this crap from some low-life Cauc."

In the TRAC, I knew, Marv would pass on the information provided by the spreadsheet I'd brought. Whether or not Jerry Roast was actually in the vehicle at the moment, I didn't have the foggiest.

The only time I'd actually seen the frigging berk who had once literally hazed my rear off, was back when I'd brought in the first lift two weeks before. The crazy bug-eyed sonuvabitch had come roaring up to the Harrier on a flat black four-wheel ATV, which had been modified extensively for his unique disability. He'd checked a few of the weapons I'd just delivered, and test-fired them on a couple of his boys (who were made to stand several hundred yards away with lit cigarettes dangling from their lips—the cigarettes were meant as targets I suppose although, predictably, set on full automatic the SPIKE III Assault Rifle took off their heads as well). Then, without so much as a word to me, Roast had roared back into his special TRAC-4.

The targets were left where they had fallen until the PA system on the TRAC resounded with Jerry's command. "Police up those butts," was all that he said.

I had not laid eyes on Jerry's obese ass again. Which didn't bother me a bit. Subsequent deliveries to Devil's Pass had become as routine as a South Florida weather forecast. Each day I brought in two lifts from Puta Madre. Each day four or five transport LAVs would be on the LZ to meet me. The weapons and munitions would be transferred, the loaded transports would form a convoy with the TRAC-4 and depart, and I would return home.

On one occasion—just out of curiosity—I'd planted an electronic homing device in a case of rocket-propelled grenades, hoping that I might be able to pinpoint just where all the shit was going. But the signal soon went dead, and the next day Marvin presented me with a mangled and flattened bit of metal and silicon chip, which I took to be a message from Jer that I should mind my own business.

Which I did, not only because of the several impalings visible around me, but because by this time I was going into the LZ bareback. Pugh had covered me again from the ridge line for the first few lifts, but when it appeared that Roast was on the level, he'd stayed at home and worked on his tan while I risked life and limb. Therefore, without someone covering my bundle, and with visions of the second two million in gold cavorting in front of my eyes, I complied with Jer's suggestion that I forget about finding the location of his home base and simply stick to delivering his guns.

As far as dogs were concerned (for those who need periodic plot updates), I hadn't seen a one. The old Indian shaman had obviously just been blowing steam.

"Hey, Bucko!"

Marvin's call interrupted what had become a fairly relaxing nose-picking session. He was standing on top of the TRAC-4 waving at me.

"What is it?" I gestured by cocking my head and cupping an ear.

"Boss wants to talk to you," Marv answered. "Come on up."

"Be right there," I hollered back as I slipped down from my perch on the top of the fuselage and into my seat. I reached for the radio.

"Pivotman, Pivotman, this is Foulshot, over." Pugh and I had agreed that in the event I was called away from the aircraft for any reason, I would contact him before vacating. Wasn't a damn thing he could do to help if I ran into trouble, of course, but I guess it made the old coot feel better knowing where I was.

"Foulshot, this is Pivotman," he answered a minute later. "Go."

"Leaving the bird for a few minutes, Pivotman. Mister Peepers wants to gab. If I'm not back by midnight, don't save supper."

It was the kind of thinly veiled code meant to be easily interpreted by someone monitoring our net. "Mister Peepers" obviously referred to Roast. "Midnight" meant the top of the hour. "Don't save supper" implied that we had some doomsday weapon rigged to blow everything and everybody away if the need arose.

We didn't, but as the Gunny always liked to say, "the tree of fear springs from the seed of doubt" . . . or jibberish to that effect.

The inside of the TRAC was like an oven on high-broil. How anybody in their right mind could sit in there day after day without sustaining serious brain damage boggled my imagination. By the time I'd clammered up into the Command bubble, I was dripping sweat like a Turkish wrestler pulling taffy.

"Bucko, Bucko," Roast greeted me from behind his apparatus, "whatever are we going to do with you?"

In the dim glow of the red battle lights, I could see that Jerry's immense body was stuffed into a scuba diver's rubber wet suit. I couldn't tell from his voice what kind of mood he was in, but I knew damn well it wouldn't do any good to beat around the bush.

"Damn, Jerry!" I immediately commented. "You can start by burying me in dry ice. Holy cripes! Is it hot enough for ya in here?"

"Sorry," he answered, not sounding that way at all, "I'm trying to lose a little weight. Doctor's orders."

"Hell, man, cut off a leg and be done with it! All you're taking off now is water bloat, and you're heating bill is going to be astronomical!"

"Yes, yes, perhaps you're right." Jerry leaned over to his console and pressed a microphone key. "Marvin, turn down the thermostat to one hundred and twelve. And have my doctor impaled. Thank you."

"A little harsh, Jer," I said, "even for you."

Roast waved a fat hand. "I realize now that the man is a charlatan. One fad diet after another. One week low carbohydrates, the next nothing but baking soda and bran. Oh, I'd drop a few hundred pounds—who wouldn't—but then I'd put it right back on. And then this," he gestured down at the wet suit. "I tell you, Bucko, if it wasn't for a rubber fetish I developed some years ago, I would take this thing off right now."

"Damn, Jer," I said. "Keep it on . . . please! I don't know what to tell ya. I guess if I was as fat as you I'd probably kill myself. Now what is it you wanted to see me about?"

There was a whir of machinery and suddenly Roast was holding my spreadsheet up in front of his vision device.

"According to this," he said, "there are three more lifts."

"That's right. My compliments to Doctor Fizz. You seem to be able to read as well as any eight-year-old."

"Three more lifts—the M2HB .50 caliber machine guns, ten thousand rounds of SLAP ammo, an 88mm antitank laser, a dozen cases of SMAWs, a few other miscellaneous items—then we're finished."

"Right again."

"That saddens me, Bucko, it truly does. Just when I was getting to know you again, we'll have to part."

"That's a fact, Jer."

"Why is it, do you think, that we professional warriors must always lose the ones we love?"

I found myself suddenly feeling extremely uncomfortable, and not solely because of the heat. "Ah, gee, Jer," I floundered, "what exactly are we talking about here—wife, girlfriend, family?"

"Yes, yes, yes, all of those, of course, but I was thinking more particularly of others of our same chosen vocation and gender, other warriors, other men of arms. You know, other GUYS! LOVE FOR OTHER GUYS!"

The sweat was pouring down into my eyes. Maybe that's why Roast had turned the TRAC into a sauna, I thought, so my eyes would burn a little bit like his when he got around to asking me out for a date.

"I think the word *love* is a little strong, don't you, Jer?"

"Oh, I don't know," the fat shit giggled. "Perhaps. On the other hand, it was good enough for the Spartans, and look what they accomplished. Hitler and Stalin were lovers, you know, as were Rambo and the Ayatollah Khomeini, Napoleon and Joseph Feen—the list is very nearly endless."

"I hadn't realized that," I coughed.

"Yes, it's true. So you see, what I'm about to say is not without precedent."

"Do you think I could get a glass of water?"

Roast chose not to hear my request. "Yes," he said dreamily, "love among warriors is as old as mankind himself. A love forged in fire, smeltered on the battlefield, hammered to perfection on the playing field of Eaton. When, for instance, you are roommates with someone through four years of a stressful situation like the Service Academy, a certain kind of unrequited love can develop. Would you disagree?"

Although I was relieved to hear that I was not the target of his amorous intent, I still got a sickening knot in my gut, for I suddenly had a hunch where he was going. "Listen, Jer," I said cautiously, "Kyle Befeeter died as he lived—by accident. Just because he fell out of my aircraft, I don't think that's any reason to blame me for his death. It could've happened to anyone."

"But you were charged by Federal authorities with his murder, were you not?" Roast asked, very quietly and very controlled.

"Murder is a pretty strong word, Jer. Let's face it. No corpse was ever recovered. How are we to know that Kyle's not still alive?"

As I recalled, some five or six years before when I had dropped the hog-tied Kyle Befeeter like a five hundred pound bomb from the center pylon of the Harrier, it had come at an altitude almost two miles above the Atlantic Ocean. Of course no corpse had been found, or would it ever be. Kyle Befeeter—Jerry Roast's sadistic roommate at the Academy—was by this time nothing but microscopic bits of fish shit.

Some would say, myself included, that fish shit was all he ever had been.

"He and I were very close," Roast said, tears straining his voice. "Did you know that?"

"Well, let's just say I suspected, Jer," I said, squirming to find a more comfortable position in my chair. "The way I remember it, you two were always holding hands and blowing kisses at each other in the mess hall and joining things like the Cork-Sniffers Club. And then—remember that time on a Come-Around to your room I caught you two in the shower? You told me you were just helping Kyle treat the acne on his back. Didn't fool me though." I began to guffaw like some backwoods hick about to deliver the punchline on a risqué joke. " 'Cause since when do ya treat acne with a big purple boner and a handful of K-Y Jelly, eh, Jer?"

"Exactly! So you can understand how devastated I was when word reached me that dearest Kyle had been lost at sea."

"Jerry," I said, getting serious for a moment, "I hope I don't have to remind you that my Harrier is rigged with a nuclear charge that will reduce several hundred square miles of surrounding mountains into glass if I don't return to base within a certain time frame. You'll never get away with it."

"Get away with what?" He sounded genuinely surprised.

"Murdering me in some silly attempt to avenge your sweetheart—whose death, I might add, I had nothing to do with."

Roast begin to laugh. "Murder you? Murder *you?* Do you think I'm mentally ill, Bucko? You're my golden goose! I'd never kill my golden goose!"

Truthfully, at that moment I didn't have an inkling of what he was blabbering about. Golden goose? How could I possibly be *his* golden goose. After all, I was the one making the big score, not him. It was all very puzzling.

"Then why this little chat?" I finally asked after the fat fiend had stopped wheezing. "Why all the true-confession shit? Do you think I give a rat's ass that you and Kyle Befeeter were cornholing each other on a regular basis? Live and let live has always been my motto, Jer."

"And a fine motto it is. Let's just say I wanted to clear the air, Bucko, since when we get down to final delivery day and payoffs, I'm sure things will be too fraught with distrust for the two of us to have any meaningful dialogue. You can understand. I just wanted you to be aware that I hold no personal grudge. Just because you were responsible for the loss of my eyelids, the failure of my career, the ostracism of my family, the demise of my mother, the overthrow of my Eskimo kingdom, and the violent death of the only man I've ever loved—well, as you so succinctly put it the first time we met: Business is business. Or, as my dear old dad liked to say whenever he fired someone: The Harvard Way is the only way. I hope we can both keep that in mind during these last few lifts."

"Well, Jer," I managed, still a little shocked that he blamed me for the Greenland Eskimo Revolt, "it takes a very big man to say that. A very big man indeed. I appreciate it. Hey, but listen," I pretended to check my wristwatch, "unless you want to get us both microwaved, I'd better be heading back to my bird. Sometimes those damn kitchen timers are real inaccurate, know what I mean?"

"Yes, of course. It's been a pleasure talking to you, Bucko. I hope it puts things into perspective for you."

"That it does, Jer, that it certainly does."

By the time I got back to the Harrier, the transport LAVs were all loaded and formed in a convoy, waiting only for my departure as their signal to move out. As my aircraft rose out of the LZ, I couldn't help grinning. I'd fudged the figures on the spreadsheet a little. The main frame had initially indicated that the deal could have been completed with only two lifts. I'd spread the final consignments over three to allow for the extra fuel I would carry on the last lift so I could finally follow the vehicles and find out once and for all where all the ordnance was being taken.

Roast had read over the doctored printout and hadn't blinked.

Tired but pleased with myself, I vectored for the coast, put the Harrier on autopilot, and turned up the volume on the stereo CD system. There was little chance of running into other aircraft: the Mexican Air Force ran most of their CAPs over Mexico City and other large metropolitan areas, and FAC never ran sorties this far south unless in hot pursuit. The only other possibilities would be one of the extremely few private aircraft belonging to the wealthy collectors, or some errant Piper Cub from the Belize Air National Guard whose compass was on the fritz. In any event, the Harrier's avionics would alert me to any problem.

Only one thing still troubled me: Why had Jerry Roast bothered to sit me down and give me all the reasons he had for killing me, then send me on my way with the equivalent of a pat on the back? Without a doubt, the man was a quarter short of two-bits.

Considering his reaction during our first meeting, I couldn't quite make myself believe he was really worried about the booby-trapped Harrier or being turned into fog by a nuclear device. Of the truly psycho people I've come in contact with over the years, I knew deep down that a crazy like Jerry would welcome the chance to be disintegrated if he thought—in the addled and confused toe-butter that was his mind—that he could benefit from it.

I decided once again to be extra wary during the last lift. It might be a good idea to bring Pugh along to cover me one more time.

The thought reminded me to check in with the hacienda. "Pivotman, this is Foulshot," I announced over the radio. "Coming into the barn with needles on empty. Light off the charcoal and break out the steaks. ETA one hour and twenty minutes. Do you copy, over?"

All I got back was a lot of atmospheric static. When I glanced over at the little digital alarm clock glued to the bulkhead, I realized why. Five after five. Every day at seventeen hundred Gunny Pugh pulled on a stinking set of sweats and his old Gyrene combat boots and took off on a three-mile run. In all the years that I'd known him, he'd never missed his daily run except when actually engaged with the enemy or boffing the hired help.

That the crusty old fart would abandon the radio while I was still off on a mission might seem a trifle cavalier to some, but considering the fact that the previous two weeks had gone so routinely, and that there was little he could do to help even if something had gone wrong, it was perfectly understandable that he'd decided to get his running in before supper.

Oh, well, I thought, maybe I'll just strafe his ass with the Harrier's cannon when I got home. If he wanted to run so bad, I'd give him a damn good reason to.

Forty-five minutes later I hit the coast and banked the aircraft for the final leg south. It was a slow and roundabout way of getting home, but without sophisticated navigation aids and with fuel at a critical level, it was the safest method.

The fact that I did not vector directly from the Devil's Pass to Puta Madre, thus cutting my flight time in half, would haunt me for the rest of my life.

I was still twenty miles out when I saw the smoke, the thick black acrid kind that makes you think of ten acres of old rubber tires going up in flames. At first I guessed it was only the villagers celebrating the feast of Saint Andy the Devine, the patron saint of food consumption and high-pitched shrieks. Why would my neighbors burn their town down, though, I wondered. Sure, every year on this particular feast day things always got a little wild, what with most of the adults getting liquored up on Agua Pendejo then running through the streets shouting "Hey, Wild Bill! Wait fer me!" but I could not recall anyone ever setting fire to anything.

It was a real puzzlement until I got close enough to see that it wasn't the town burning that had produced the huge cloud of smoke, it was the Hacienda del Placenta Negro.

My heart rate went from sixty to a hundred and twenty within seconds, and as I guided the Harrier upwind of our property and then in for a closer look, it doubled again. Immediately I could see the STOL ramp in the backyard had been destroyed, torn to shreds. All around it the lawn was littered with the contorted shapes of dead men, wrecked vehicles, and the still-smoldering craters and rubble left by high explosives. There was no doubt that a battle had been fought down there, a very recent battle. But who? And where was the Gunny?

Pounding a fist on my thigh for comfort, I pushed my fear back down my gullet and shook off the chilling effect of an adrenaline overload. I corkscrewed the Harrier into a tight downward spiral, alert to any movement that might signal an ambush while at the sametime trying to make my brain sift what I was seeing into important and unimportant facts.

It was the inflatable bulk synfuel tanks out back that were burning, not the hacienda itself, although even from altitude I could see where the walls of some of the buildings had been breached by small arms and rockets. Nothing was moving, not even the barnyard menagerie we kept in the front yard. As far as I could see, not a living thing remained.

There was not enough clear space around the hacienda to put the Harrier down, not even in the vertical mode, so I flew into Puta Madre and landed in the deserted plaza. The town, too, was empty I noticed as I fell from the cockpit, chambered a round into my bufgun, and began jogging back to the hacienda. Something extremely heavy had gone down, something real bad.

I found the first body out near the front gate. A heavy caliber bullet had taken out the guy's chest, but I could see all I needed to see in what was left. The bastard had been armed to the teeth; M-16A3, grenades, cavalry sword, stomping boots. He was dressed in a blood-soaked set of black Levi's jeans, a sleeveless denim jacket of the same color, and olive drab web gear that had U.S. stamped on it. High on a naked bicep, a crude homemade tattoo read simply "Elvis Lives."

For the second time in the history of Puta Madre, the Comancheros had come.

14

I found Gunny Pugh out by the swimming pool. The Comancheros had crucified him high on the trunk of a palm tree using a section of timber taken from the gutted hacienda as a crossbar. From the number of bullet holes visible in his brave old body, I figured he'd probably already been dead when the bastards nailed him up to their jury-rigged cross.

I had not wept openly since the day my father had died more than twenty years before, but without any hesitation, with the shock and the grief and the incredible sense of loss overwhelming any other emotion, I fell to my knees beneath my friend and let it all hang out. Black Pugh had been many things to me during life —a teacher, an uncle, a brother, a partner—but most of all he'd been the guy who'd always been there when things went to the redline, someone who could be counted on when the bad guys were on your six and your wing racks were empty, someone you could rely on without a second thought. And now he was gone.

There in the smoldering ruins of our home and business I suppose I cried for myself as much as I did for the old man, for with his death I was as alone as I had ever been. There could never be another like him, no one to fill the empty sleeve that now hung from my right shoulder, no one to kick my butt when I needed it, or laugh at my jokes, or bitch about my habits, or tell me stories of the Old Corps and what it was like to live in a world without RIHMs. With Pugh went a piece of me, to whatever lies in store for old warriors and dead heroes. One day I would get that piece of myself back when I stood next to him in heaven or in hell, but until then I knew there would always be an aching spot in the middle of my soul.

The long shadows of day's end gradually lengthened and when I could no longer wash away any more grief, I got up and started looking for a ladder. With the bulk synfuel tanks in flames out back, there was no way I could refuel the Harrier and go after the Comanchero raiding party. As much as the perpetrated outrage demanded swift justice and revenge, there was nothing immediately I could do except take care of the Gunny. My friend would not spend the night hanging from that tree, even if I ̤̣̤ the damn thing down with a pocketknife.

I built a bier for him out of empty wooden ammo crates down on a spit of land jutting out into the ocean, a place where the God of Battle would be sure to see the signal fire. The crates were doused with a little synfuel I'd found in the kitchen, and when the last pale streaks of daylight out on the far horizon snuffed out, I tossed a lighted match and stepped back. For one last time, Gunny Pugh lit up the zone.

Me and a bottle of Agua Pendejo spent the night guarding the flames. By morning what-had-been was only ash. A soft offshore breeze gently scattered the old man's remains over earth and waves. It was done.

As was my public grief. It was soon replaced by rage and guilt. A close inspection of the hacienda and the grounds told me without words what had happened. The Comancheros had attacked in strength across the back lawn, probably only a few minutes after my last radio contact with the Gunny. From the signs left I determined that Pugh had fought a retrograde operation, first pulling back from the ammo bunker and hangar (where our main comm center was located), to the hacienda's walls. From that position he'd gradually been forced to fight from room to room around the patio.

The old man had not gone lightly. I counted the remains of at least twenty-five dead Comancheros, most cut to ribbons with fifty cal, 7.62 NATO, and RPG shrapnel. From the amount of blood and other pieces and parts lying all over the property, I deduced that the scavengers had probably suffered at least double that number in wounded. In the smoke blackened Rec House I found an M-60 machine gun with two melted barrels surrounded by about a quarter ton of empty brass. Pugh's favorite 9mm automatic pistol, magazine empty, lay on the deck not far away. The bastards had only taken him because he'd run out of ammo.

How long had he held out? I could only guess. But there was no doubt in my mind that had I flown straight home from Devil's Pass I would have arrived in time to prevent the final outcome. Such a conclusion did not exactly cheer me up.

A certain madness took over at that point and I lost all sense of what I was about. I remember grabbing my bufgun and running from the hacienda, following the multiple sets of tire tracks lead-

.ng from the front gate towards town. Yes, I would chase down the Comancheros on foot even though they had at least a twelve hour headstart and were no doubt miles away. I would chase them down and slaughter them—no matter how many, no matter how well armed—with a bufgun and twelve rounds of AP Ball. So what that I hadn't eaten in twenty-four hours or that I'd drunk three quarters of a gallon of something akin to pure wood alcohol during the night, or that I didn't have the slightest idea where I was going? I was determined to avenge Pugh with blood, and lots of it.

And so it was perfectly understandable (at least in my mind) that by the time I'd sprinted the quarter mile from the hacienda to Puta Madre, I was a slobbering, puking, out-of-breath mess, staggering into the plaza barely able to hold the bufgun in my hand. Had the Comancheros left even one scout to cover their rear, I would have been skunk bait.

The plaza, still empty except for the Harrier, at once became a carnival ride, one of those monstrous mother-humpers that whip you around on three separate axes; the kind that shoves your stomach up into your sinuses while every ounce of blood collects in your left big toe. Such shenanigans, as we all know, can lead to only one thing. Dizzy, sick, and badly in need of a shave, I collapsed to my knees, then to all fours, and retched up a great splendid fountain of green bile and a bunch of sparrow bones, a process that took maybe five minutes to complete.

As the worst of my sudden illness passed, I became aware of a certain almost psychic message that I was no longer alone out there on that ancient cobblestoned plaza. Still coughing and gagging on a piece of something caught in my throat, and with my eyes watering like a couple of golf course spigots, I finally managed to fall back on my knees and look up.

I'd been right; I wasn't alone anymore. There to greet me, in all its horrid implication, was the great all-seeing lens of a hand-held minicam. The dark glass eye was only a few feet from my face, its little red monitor light blinking as brightly as a Dutchman's ass. As I wiped away a long tendril of sticky stuff dancing from my grizzled chin and felt my stomach begin to heave one more time, I realized that my whole act was being recorded for posterity . . . and I didn't even have rerun rights.

It was like being in one of those nightmares you have when

you're a kid; no matter how close the danger, your body refuses to function. For the longest time, I just sat there swaying on my knees, my mouth opening and closing without making a sound, my tongue furling and unfurling to some unheard distant bugle call, my eyes rolling, my brain paralyzed. At last, using what little strength I had left, I managed to raise an open hand and shove it in front of the lens. "No pictures," I gasped. "Please. No pictures."

Was I surprised as the minicam slowly lowered and the unmistakable equine face of Sandinista Riviero filled my vision, complete with horn-rimmed glasses and an evil catlike smile? Not really, for as I stated before, I for one know the full ramifications of revenge and the driving all-encompassing force behind it. I was only glad that the damn little red light was out.

It was about that time that the sun sent a thermal dagger deep into my skull and with only a scream as accompaniment, I took a half turn to the left, keeled over backwards, and blessedly passed into the great beyond.

I awoke to darkness and the faraway strains of soothing accordion music—"The Beer Barrel Polka," I think. Something cool and wet was caressing my forehead.

"Hello, Señor Will," someone said. "How you feelin?"

"Is that you, Rudy?" I asked the dark. I thought I recognized the sound of the real-estate agent's voice. It was my own—raspy and weak—that I had problems with.

"*Sí.* Can I get you something to eat? We got some pretty special chili pie left over from dinner."

"No, thanks." I reached up and felt the washcloth over my eyes. I pulled it away and immediately regretted it. "ODD DAMN!" I howled. "TURN OUT THAT LIGHT FOR GOD'S SAKES!"

"Easy, Señor Will," Rudy soothed as he expertly placed the wet rag back over my face and eased my head back on the pillow. "It is only the 'power-on' light from my portable radio. You must rest. Someday, you might even be able to walk again."

"Where am I? How did I get—"

"You are in the back room of my office—you remember, just off the plaza. I had them bring you here when you passed out."

"No, no," I whimpered, "I mean, what planet am I on?"

Rudy laughed heartily although I didn't understand the joke. "Very funny, Señor Will," he finally said. "It is good to see you have retained your sense of humor, even though poor Señor Pugh is dead and you are financially ruined."

The horror came rushing back. I groaned.

"It's okay though," Rudy continued. "You got a whole month's rent on the hacienda paid in advance. Lotta damage though. Lotta, lotta damage. But we can discuss that later."

"That last thing I remember," I said, "was having this bizarre nightmare about Harry Riviero's wife videotaping me. Then, hell, then I guess I just blacked out."

"Hey, that sounds pretty damn gruesome, Señor Will."

"Yeah."

"But it wasn't no nightmare."

"Don't dick with me, Rudy."

"Whatever you say. Harry and Sandinista, though, they put on the show anyways."

I don't think what Rudy said immediately sunk in. I was still kind of mentally wiped from all that had gone on. "Show?" I chuckled. "What show?"

The Gringo Hour White Paper Special. Harry and his old lady videotaped the whole battle over to the hacienda. The big fight, you know? I guess they figured that pictures of you cryin and pukin and spittin up your guts was good B-roll reaction material."

"They can't do that!" I bawled, reaching with a desperate clawlike hand to grab Rudy's sleeve. "Not without a signed release from me! They run that tape and I'll sue their asses!"

"Be calm, my friend. The Agua Pendejo is still eating away your brain. You must rest and regain your strength. Then you can present your case to the magistrate in Mexico City, although I'm afraid it will not do you too much good."

"What're you talking about?" I asked weakly. The awful throbbing pain was getting worse.

I heard him sigh. "Well, to tell you the truth, the program has already been aired. About an hour ago. Pretty damn graphic. After the first three or four dismemberments, I don't let my kids watch."

"Damn it to hell! I'll take those two for every centavo they ever earned!"

"Maybe. Maybe you get lucky. Maybe the courts decide something in forty, fifty years. On the other hand, we got a saying down here, Señor Will, when somebody does something that somebody else don't like too much but probably can't do too much about. That sayin is—loosely translated you understand—that sayin is 'Tough tamales.' I think that fits your situation pretty damn good. Now you get some sleep, okay? Maybe we start rehabilitation tomorrow sometime. Easy stuff, like chewin."

Gradually, over the next several days, I was able to shake off the aftereffects of the Gunny's murder and get back on my feet. From Rudy I learned that just as I had deduced, the Comanchero raid had been directed solely at the Hacienda del Placenta Negro. The marauders had bypassed the town entirely. Nevertheless, the citizens of Puta Madre, being neither particularly brave nor well-armed peasants, had fled to the hills at the first crack of automatic weapons fire coming from the ranch. According to the young women who worked at the hacienda, Pugh had ordered them all home and then covered their escape by single-handedly holding off the horde of bandits.

A horde, Rudy added, that seemed to know their way around pretty darn good for tourists.

After a long time, the shooting had stopped. A half hour later and the Comanchero rides were seen roaring up the coast highway, headed for who knows where. There were many blooded and bandaged visible among their number, many lying on makeshift stretchers. With some of their vehicles smoking badly, others coughing and sputtering, it appeared more as though the Comancheros were limping away from a defeat rather than speeding away from a victory.

"Clearly," Rudy concluded, smiling sadly, "Señor Pugh kicked some ass."

As much as it pained me, I finally summoned the courage to drop by the Puta Madre television studio and take a look at the documentary tape Harry and Sandinista had made.

Not all that bad for video-verité even though most of the footage had obviously been taken through a telephoto lens from well outside the hacienda grounds. The initial action scenes were extremely chaotic—more than once Harry or Sandinista had been

forced to dive for cover with the resultant confusing camera angle
—and there was too much noise and smoke to really be able to
tell what was going on. But there were a couple of real delightful
shots of Comancheros getting greased, and I saw one armored
buggy go spinning off in flames just like any of a hundred thousand Stephen J. Cannell TV shows popular during the last century.

On several occasions the camera was able to zoom in on the
faces of the attackers for tight close-ups. It was pretty damn plain
they'd already realized that they were up to their asses in carni-
vores, for I saw fear etched on those cruel ugly mugs, fear and a
reluctance to proceed any further against the old black man, the
old black man who was cutting their force to bloody ribbons.

Had I not already known the final outcome, I might have suspected that Pugh had a chance. Sadly, I knew better.

All at once, up on the screen, I detected a subtle difference in
the Comancheros tactics. Most casual observers would not have
noticed the change, but with my experience I was able to see that
someone had goosed the boys into action. Whatever threat or
reward had been offered, it worked. No longer content to hunker
down and wait things out, the Comancheros began to make sui-
cidal charges into the maw of Pugh's gun, which had been set up
in the Rec House.

Dead bandits (and parts of dead bandits) began piling up
around the Rec House door like so many artificial fireplace logs.
As soon as one team would fall, however, another group of
screaming maniacs, firing as they came, would continue the assault, climbing over around or through the slippery red goo that
had pooled in front of the tiled entrance way.

When I heard the last burst of M-60 fire, then twelve more
muffled shots coming from a pistol, I knew the end was near. An
assault squad of Comancheros bolted through the darkened doorway and for a good sixty seconds it sounded like a FAC firing
range, all weapons on automatic. Finally, after a short period of
complete silence, a figure appeared in the Rec House doorway
and waved to someone on the back wall. The Gunny had been
overrun.

Although I knew what was coming, I could not tear my eyes
from the screen as the tape continued to play. After the Rec
House had been secured, there were a number of jump cuts, first

of another squad of Comancheros rushing into the Rec House, then a scene of a group of men dragging Pugh's lifeless body out the door, then a whole series of shots taken of looting and senseless vandalism. Finally, I saw a shot of the swimming pool and what appeared to be a gathering of what was left of the Comanchero raiding party.

They had been summoned, obviously, to witness the ceremony.

The next jump cut, jerky and for a moment out of focus, showed the body of my friend being lifted on the crossbar to the trunk of the palm tree where a huge Comanchero on a ladder waited with hammer and nails. I watched, not out of morbidity or a desire to see this final outrage, but because I hoped to see as many faces as I could, to burn them into my memory, so that when the day of reckoning came—as it surely would—I would know exactly who to select for my own experiments in cruelty and violent death.

I was rewarded a thousand times more than I could've hoped. With the lens on full telephoto, either Harry or Sandinista lingered on Pugh's face for a moment, then made a jerky quick pan to a man who was obviously leading the group in some sort of pseudorcligious chant. I could not hear the words, but I recognized the face.

Who wouldn't? The man who called himself Ramases the Second, Supreme And Ever Shall Be Chief of the Comancheros, was as easily recognized as the only American president forced to resign from office, or the chump who used to play second banana to Johnny Carson before he was indicted for lottery fraud. Half naked under an old flac jacket and some Kelvar groin armor, the glistening oiled shape of Ramases was a remarkable example of the human body run amok on steroids and weightlifting machines. The greasy bastard was at least three hundred and fifty pounds of massed, well-defined, sculptured muscle.

Of course, body builders and iron pumpers with similar bodies were as common as field lice (sic) down on Miami's infamous Muscle Boardwalk; it was Ramases' face that set him apart from the hoi polloi. Framed by locks of long thick black hair preciously curled in permanent-wave ringlets, the man's face was a testament to the ancient industrial art of plastic surgery. Rumor had it that he'd been under the knife more than thirty times, and by God it looked it.

Not a line or crease or wrinkle marred one millimeter of almost translucent skin, even though conservative estimates placed his age at around fifty. His low forehead and almond-shaped eyes suggested more than the occasional facelift and tuck, and his chiseled up-turned nose looked like something shaped out of processed Plas-tex. The lips were extremely well shaped and effeminate, the effect heightened by the addition of black lipstick. The chin was jutting and square, and incongruously dimpled. All in all, to my eyes, Ramases II's face was abstract art taken to its logical conclusion—the real and surreal combined to form a steaming pile of spaniel shit.

I watched the sonuvabitch conduct his little ceremony of martial arts moves and twitching upper lip sneers with the certain knowledge that our paths would someday cross. On that day, I pledged to myself, he'd get his final facelift.

Before the last section of the tape came on, showing my less than heroic reaction to the attack, I turned off the machine. I had seen enough; the sight of my own vomit would not help matters at all. Vowing to begin my quest for revenge before another day passed, I hurriedly returned to Rudy's office.

"Rudy!" I hollered. "Where can I get some gas in a hurry?"

"I'd say the Taco Wagon is your best bet, Señor Will. Order the flautus platter with a side of beans and guacamole. Take about fifteen minutes."

"No, you cretin! I mean syngas, for my aircraft!"

"Why didn't you say so? Try the Texaco station out on Route 13!"

"THE TEXACO STATION! OF COURSE! HOW STUPID CAN I GET?"

"I really don't think you want an answer to that question, Señor Will. By the way . . ." Rudy shuffled some papers on his desk and held up a long pastel blue business envelope. "This mailgram arrived for you while you was away."

Hoping against hope that I'd finally won the Reader's Digest Sweepstakes after so many years of trying, I snatched the envelope out of Rudy's hand and tore it open.

"Sic transit meum et tuum," the message read.

I was momentarily dumbfounded, and I guess it showed on my face.

"Damn, Señor Will!" Rudy asked. "More bad news? Who's it from?"

I looked over at him and shrugged. "Hell if I know. Here, take a look for yourself. I can't read Polynesian, and there's no signature."

Rudy took the mailgram and studied it for a few seconds. "This ain't Polynesian, Señor Will," he finally said, "it's Catholic. You know, like Latin."

"Still Greek to me. Can you translate it?"

"*Sí,* but not too good. Literally, it means 'So passes mine and yours.' "

"What the hell does that mean?" I yelled.

"Beats me," Rudy admitted. "Maybe it's an advertising slogan from the Vatican."

"Fat chance," I said, taking back the message and reading it again. My mind went into high gear. Something was way out of line. "Hey, wait just a second!" I finally blurted. "There's no mail service to Puta Madre on Tuesdays, not even mailgrams. Where did you get this?"

"Special delivery. About an hour ago. Some Chinaman come by on a bike and dropped it off."

"Chinaman, eh? Did this Chinaman have strange blue eyes?"

"Now that you mention it, yeah. Kinda like that guy on the *Late Show* the other night—Cool Hand Luke."

Marvin. That meant Jerry Roast. In the confusion I'd completely forgotten about him and our deal. Now this message delivered by Marvin. What did it mean? Was he letting me know that he was welching on me? Clearing out without paying? Or was he trying to tell me something else?

Our last conversation together focused in my mind, and the horrible truth became clear. Somehow, someway, Roast had had a hand in Pugh's murder. *"So passes mine and yours."* My friend for his friend. If that was the case, then I was personally and directly responsible for Pugh's death. I had killed him, as surely as if I'd put a Blooper to his head and pulled the trigger. The initial guilt that I'd felt over his passing—that I'd been late returning to the hacienda—was suddenly compounded a thousand times over with the realization that Roast must have planned it that way all along, to get even with me for killing Kyle Befeeter.

How the Comancheros had gotten involved, though, I did not know. Unless . . .

Almost in a state of shock, I stumbled back down the road to the hacienda where the bloated and rotting bodies of the outlaws still lay as they had fallen nearly a week before. A few of them still had their weapons, mostly broken or otherwise unserviceable, but in good enough condition for me to be able to read and record their serial numbers.

Out near the remains of our offices, I uncovered the cement storage safe where we kept our backup computer discs. Although the P&B equipment had all been destroyed, Rudy had an IBM compatible in his office and I was able to boot up the records. Sure enough, the weapons carried by the dead Comancheros corresponded to weapons I had sold to Jerry Roast. The bastard had been reselling them (at a tidy profit I was sure) to Ramases.

No wonder he'd called me his *golden goose*. And I'd just supposed he'd been making a pass.

The idea was staggering, but I could see no other explanation. There was only one thing I did not understand: Why was I still alive? Nearly all of P&B's inventory—save the few odds and ends scheduled for the last few lifts—had been delivered. Since they didn't need me around any longer, why hadn't Roast and Ramases simply planned the attack to coincide to a time when I'd be at the hacienda? Then they could have nailed my ass along with Pugh's. (Sorry, Gunny, no pun intended.)

But no, I was still alive and kicking, so there was a good chance, I concluded, that Roast didn't have much control over the actions of Mr. Badass Ramases. Maybe the Supreme Chief of the Comancheros had jumped the reservation early, screwing up Jerry's plans.

On the other hand, Roast was pretty friggin nutzoid in his own right. Maybe he figured that my knowing I had caused the death of my best friend, and having to live with that knowledge, would be more agonizing and torturous than getting snuffed in a big fight.

If that was the case, then he was right. In the days, weeks, and months to come, not one sober minute went by when I did not think about how my own greed, stubbornness, and stupidity had cost Black Pugh his life.

I say sober because for the next six months—give or take a month—I tried to keep my mind fully occupied with emptying every bottle of Agua Pendejo in Puta Madre directly down my throat.

Oh sure, before I got completely shitfaced I made a few lame attempts to track down the Comancheros and/or Roast and his gang, but the trail was cold and Devil's Pass was empty, and after a while the Harrier began to have mechanical problems that I had neither the will nor wherewithal to fix. I parked the bird under some camouflage netting out back, drained the oil, unhooked the battery, and put her up on cinder blocks for the duration. After a couple of ridiculous tries at tracking Ramases on a little motor scooter Rudy loaned me, I gave up completely and crawled into the bottle for good.

I am told I became the town joke.

I am told that for a few centavos I would dance the old soft-shoe for hours.

I am told that I would do my Ed Sullivan impersonation continuously until someone either took a shot at me or bought me a drink.

I am told that for the price of a bottle I would draw wiring diagrams for top secret FAC weapon-systems or the chain of command in the U.S. Department of Commerce.

I am told that I never shaved or bathed or changed my clothes or underwear and that I soon smelled so bad that I was banned from the cantina as well as the cantina's outhouse.

Things got so bad, I am told, that I was at last carried to the hacienda by a band of masked vigilantes who warned me never to enter Puta Madre again upon pain of getting tossed in the water-waste-treatment plant. From then on food and booze were placed on my doorstep in the mornings before I rose and in the evenings before I rose. It made things much easier all around.

I guess you could say I became a lush.

On the first anniversary of the raid I passed the point of no return. That night, as a freak tropical storm raged outside, I "ate the sparrow" twice, and was well along towards the third when what was left of my mind imagined a visit by the Angel of Death.

I was lying in my hammock, staring out through the patio doors when a gigantic bolt of lightning illuminated the grounds outside. For a split second I thought I saw an apparition dressed in a dark, hooded cloak, an apparition peering in at me with eyes like aluminum pie plates.

Hey, I remember thinking, pretty damn nifty hallucination. Better have another drink. Goddamn Grim Reaper was right outside my door. Shit, it was like a Woody Allen flick.*

Suddenly, without warning, the patio doors crashed open and the Angel of Death floated in without an invitation, accompanied by a howling wind and pelting rain that quickly turned the floor to mud. For some macabre reason I thought this was the funniest thing I'd ever seen and began laughing.

Death, I quickly discovered, did not have a very good sense of humor. A skeletonlike arm appeared from under the Angel's cassock and with one motion dumped yours truly out of his hammock and onto the slippery deck. I recall looking up at the shadowy figure standing over me and wondering who was going to water the plants when I was gone.

As so often happens during freak tropical thunder storms occuring during the nighttime hours, a particularly close bolt of lightning struck the Power House and the lights of the hacienda flickered, then went out. Being already three sheets to the wind, I incorrectly interpreted this occurrence as being the final curtain, assuming that the darkness was the result of my life reaching the end of its third act.

What followed was a bit of nasty business, but I swear it's true. There in the dark I felt Death's powerful hands tear my clothes from my body until I lay naked on the cold mud. Then frozen fingers were grotesquely tinkering with my manhood, manipulating and fondling and generally bringing it to a state of tumescence that had not been experienced for many months. Despite the booze and the cold mud and the chilling fear of being so close to Death, "Old Saltpork the Sailor" totally ignored my misgivings and inebriated state and jumped to attention.

I think I heard the rustle of wet plastic, then a soft warm wetness replaced the Popsicle fingers and I felt myself being en-

---

* Woody Allen, a brooding philosophical genius of the late twentieth century who wasted most of his life making movies. It was Allen who once wrote: "What is it about death that bothers me so much? Probably the hours."

veloped by the long infinite night. Pretty damn kinky when you get right down to it, but I think most men pray they'll go out getting their ashes hauled. My only hope was that the Angel of Death didn't turn out to be some fucking guy or a barnyard animal.

The Act started slowly but quickly picked up speed. Before too long the Grim Reaper was bouncing around on my poor old part like some damn wild bronc rider determined to break "Ol' Blue" or die trying, all the while making little groaning sounds that became more and more pronounced as we sped towards the ultimate fulfillment. For my part, I simply lay back and tried to enjoy what I took to be my last date. True, the cold muddy floor under my back was a little disconcerting, and the open patio doors were allowing more and more wind-driven rain into the room—and me without a sump pump—but what the hell, I've had worst.

Or at least that's what I thought until, just seconds before the Act would have been culminated, a spectacular bolt of lightning lit up the room. Imagine my horror when my eyes discovered that my lover was not the Angel of Death at all. Instead, what I beheld in that moment, writhing on top of me like some well-paid porn queen wired to the gills, was none other than the wicked witch herself, Sandinista Riviero. With her bony hollow chest heaving, her eyes tightly shut behind her designer glasses, her mouth forming silent crudities, and her skin glowing with the pink luminescence of passion, she was every sexual nightmare I'd ever had, brought to life.

Sweet Jesse! Talk about your complete turnoff! The Angel of Death I could live with (?), but one look at Sandinista in the throes of orgasm was enough to turn Mighty Joe Whatshisname into limp doughnut dough. I began to scream, hoping against hope that I was having the DT's. With all the strength I could muster, I threw the naked mad woman off me and began pulling myself through the mud towards the door, whimpering and crying like someone who'd just been screwed by a truck.

She came after me. I felt her cold bony hands tugging at me, grabbing me by the leg, then slipping down to my ankle. Summoning one last surge of strength, I kicked her away and rolled through the thick mud out onto the patio.

The storm still raged. I managed to pull myself to my feet, then fell. The months of physical inactivity and abuse had weakened me more than I'd realized. Still screaming, I began to crawl towards the cliff, already knowing how things must end. Once more, the churning sea and the jagged rocks beneath La Hacienda del Placenta Negro would claim a cursed and tormented soul.

Turns out, you see, that the old Indian shaman who sold RIHM parts had been right after all when he'd told me to "Beware of the Dog."

PART THREE
Getting Even

15

"That's the most ridiculous story I've ever heard!" Melodie said from her hospital bed as I wearily drew near the end of my tale. "What happened then?"

"Eventually I reached the edge of the cliff and rolled myself off," I answered, trying to catch a bit of *The Flintstones* on Mel's vid-display while finishing my sordid confession. "Wasn't until late the next morning I discovered I'd lost my way in the storm and had mistaken the side of the swimming pool for the edge of the cliff. The pool had been drained some weeks before so all I got out of the deal was a cracked skull and a pretty severe cold from lying naked all night in a tropical rainstorm. Turned out to be my lucky day. When I finally got back to the Main House, the Angel of Death was gone. The only evidence left that she had been there at all were the fingernail scratches on my chest and the itching around my Main Man."

"Oh, Will!" Melodie gasped. "Don't tell me you—"

"Yup, you got it. Not only did Sandinista drive me to the brink of suicide, but she left me with a dose of the crabbies. Which, it turned out, probably saved my life."

"Crotch bugs saved you life? Why, that's preposterous!"

Melodie Lane's reaction was, to my mind, a sure sign she was getting better. Over the past few weeks, as I'd spilled my guts to her, she'd been a quiet and attentive listener. Seldom during my daily visits to her bedside had she interrupted or commented on my sad story. Now, with her sudden impolite outburst, I was sure she was well on the road to recovery.

"Hard to believe, I know," I said, "but it's true. That dose of crabs saved me. And I'll tell you why."

"Please do." She sounded a little skeptical.

"Apparently," I said somewhat pompously, "you've never been blessed with an infestation of *pediculosis pubis mexicanus.*"

"I should say not," Melodie snorted, "and if I had, I certainly wouldn't tell you."

"Roger that. Anyway, the Mexican variety of pubic lice is about as mean and virulent as you could imagine. The itch is indescribable; I mean there are times you want to go after them with a garden rake and napalm!"

"Ouch."

" 'Ouch' isn't even close, baby. Hell, pure hell. Itch got so bad I started looking for a loaded pistol."

"Oh, Will. Wasn't that a little bit of overkill for such tiny bugs?"

"The gun wasn't for the crabs, Melodie. The gun was for *me!* Would've done it, too, if I hadn't accidentally spilled some Agua Pendejo on my skivvies while I was working up the courage to blow my pecker off."

"You mean the local firewater you were telling me about?"

"That's right. Shit soaked right through my underpants to the source of the agony. Relief was instantaneous. Must've been a hundred thousand little dead bastards within seconds. I know, I made a body count. Only trouble was, even something as powerful as Agua Pendejo only knocked some of the little buggers out. As soon as they regained consciousness, they went right back to sucking and biting and procreating like mad. Sorta like native Parisians."

I looked over to where Melodie was propped up in bed and smiled weakly. Over the weeks the colonel's skin had healed to the point where she now looked like a large unidentifiable (aren't they all) piece of Kentucky Fried Chicken—original recipe. Only her face had been spared, and it was there that I detected a certain lack of understanding.

"So how did the bugs save your life?" she asked.

"Hell, Mel! It's simple. I had to pour so much booze on my crotch that I didn't have enough left over to stay drunk! Pretty soon I was so sober that I realized I didn't want to die until I'd gotten my revenge on Roast and Ramases, not to mention Frank Tibbs. I started working out again, eating the right foods, washing and shaving, brushing my teeth, cutting down on salt. Cleaned up the hacienda, made contact with a few of Pugh's middlemen, got enough hardware on consignment to keep me fed, and over time, make a small profit. Within the year, I was back on my feet, all thanks to those damn lice."

I grinned at her—one of those worldly grins that tells everyone how amazed you are with the strange unpredictability of fate. Saved by a dose of the crabs; perhaps he should pen a hymn or volunteer for the Salvation Army or at least donate his body parts to science.

"Gee, Will," Melodie commented a moment later, "how come you've always gotta be such a goddamn pig?"

"Come again?" I recognized the dissatisfaction in her voice, and I couldn't understand what it meant. Here I was, trying to explain exactly how and why I'd come north to save her butt, and she was already pulling my chain.

"Although I don't know why I should be so surprised," she muttered. "It's so typical of you. Giving credit to the crabbies when your real thanks should've gone to the woman who infected you with them."

A very long time had passed since I'd last been treated to the full benefit of Melodie Lane's wondrous logic. So long in fact, that this latest demonstration caught me like a wallop from the flat side of a shovel. I groped for some answer to her idiotic pronouncement but could find nothing that remotely came close.

Somehow it seemed totally in keeping with the moment that the hospital room's vid-display should at that time begin playing the theme song for *Mister Ed.*

The natural unquenchable curiosity so common with those who carry the X chromosome pair manifested itself at this point; Melodie chose to ignore my lack of response to her previous question and plowed ahead to new and more fertile fields.

"So what happened when you finally caught up to Jerry Roast?" she asked, reaching over to the bed table for the vid-display's remote control. I couldn't help thinking how much her arm resembled a fried chicken wing complete with a few horrible-looking golden bristles of hair. She zapped off *Mister Ed,* and I thought I knew why—professional jealousy.

"I didn't," I said. "By the time I was able to locate and buy the parts for the Harrier, all traces of Roast, Ramases, and the Co-mancheros were gone. It was as if they'd disappeared from the face of the earth. I checked, all over Mexico—no unexplained murders, no brutal attacks on unwary motorists, no reports of raids or attacks on innocent peasant populations, nothing."

"Nothing? Sounds hard to believe."

"Do you think I'm lying?" I was beginning to get a little pissed. "This was Mexico, remember? Not exactly a country wired for sound. And unfortunately, being a wanted criminal here in the States, I didn't have access to GANGFACS traffic either."*

"But surely you could've *bought* some information?"

"With what?"

"That first two million you got from Roast."

"Ramases took it when he raided the hacienda. No, at the time I was just making ends meet. As far as I could determine, the Comancheros had vanished from Mexico all together."

Melodie scowled. "All you had to do was give me a call, Will. I could've told you that Ramases led them back over the border and up into the Northwest where they pillaged, raped, and killed everything in their path. Thanks, I imagine, to all the weapons you sold them!"

Yes, I concluded, Colonel Lane was definitely getting better, or at least returning to her natural state. Only an ignorant field-grade split-tail FAC fighter-jock could've blamed Will Bucko for the rampage of the Comancheros. I chose to ignore her accusation and finish the goddamn story.

"Over the last five-six years I'd hear something—maybe that Comancheros had been spotted up around Spokane or one of them had been killed near Boise or a raiding party had been reported operating around Portland. As soon as I heard something like that, I'd pack up and fly north. And while I never had any success finding Roast or Ramases, there was always plenty of work for a hired TopGun up in those parts, plenty of outlaws and plenty of desperate citizens willing to pay for their extermination. On those jobs I had many adventures and many a close call, and many a pretty gal showed me her charms and affection, but I never found the bad guys I was really looking for."

"And you never settled down?" Mel asked, feigning innocence. "With one of those cute bimbettes who showed you her pretty pink ass?"

"No. Never had a chance. Sooner or later, after I'd cleaned out whatever nest of snakes I'd uncovered, the good citizens would get a little antsy about having a renegade jet jock in the chicken

---

* GANGFACS were periodic messages sent out from FAC Headquarters to all commands covering outlaw gang activities, locations, tendencies, and tactics as reported by operatives and moles buried in the enemy infrastructure.

house and I'd be asked to leave. Either that or Federal authorities would start poking around, or I'd catch wind of a FUC'er or a bounty hunter getting close. That's why I always returned to Puta Madre. That's where my home was, you see. That's where Pugh was scattered, and that's where my friends were."

"And it was also outside the jurisdiction of the United States."

"That too, I guess."

I thought how unfair it was that Melodie's incredibly voluptuous body had been so nastily treated by the RIHMs while her motorized mouth had been spared. If, say, they'd cut out her tongue and left her skin alone, I would've been a happy man and I'm not ashamed to admit it.

"In fact," I continued, "Puta Madre is where I'd be right now if Phil McBride hadn't shown up one day wearing too much Bronze-Tan and a sombrero. Told me about your predicament up here. Said the President herself had authorized him to offer me a full pardon and a commission as a brevet lieutenant colonel if I would lend my assistance."

"I wouldn't think a true patriot would've needed such incentives," Melodie grumbled.

"Get real!" I laughed. "And after the way our last commander-in-chief loused up my deal, this time I made damn sure I had everything in writing. Tell ya the truth"—I paused and winked at Melodie, a move I knew infuriated her—"the rank I could've survive without—it's only honorary and the pay sucks—but with that pardon I can go after Roast and Ramases here in the States without worrying about bounty hunters and FUC'ers breathing down my neck."

"Well," Melodie sort of snipped, "I'm so glad you didn't come all the way up here to Motown solely on my account."

"Don't lose any sleep worrying about that. Just figure you owe me one. Now," I said, pulling a Slim Jim sausage out of my jacket to snack on, "tell me what you've been doing for the past ten years besides getting that unattractive RIHM-job. I read about the shoot-out at Kahana Bay; what else have you been up to?"*

---

* For gallantry in action, then Lieutenant Colonel Melodie Lane was awarded the FAC Gold Cross with Almond Clusters when, during the days of June 25th through 28th, 2042, her Cutter command, FACFS-10

"Hell, Will," she sighed, "it's all old cheese. Why do you want—"

"Because," I interrupted, "I once had a hell of a crush on you. Still do, in fact, provided your skin clears up. I'm interested."

"There's not much to tell," she said, dismissing my romantic overtures as she always had, as if they were too bizarre to even acknowledge. "You knew that Hank and I were married soon after the Battle of Boca Grande."

"No," I admitted, "I didn't." Hank Manoosh had been my roommate at the Academy and we had been close friends before Melodie had turned him against me. I knew he'd been planking her, but the news that the two of them had gotten married was a bitter pill to swallow.

"Hank was killed, you know," Mel went on, "two years ago. Crashed and burned on a training flight out of Jacksonville."

"No, I didn't know that either. I'm sorry." And I truly was.

"We had a son. His name is Buck. He's six now. Living with his grandparents in Ohio."

An empty gesture, I thought, but a gesture just the same. "Thank you, Melodie," I whispered. "You guys didn't have to do that."

"Do what?"

"Name the boy after me," I mumbled softly, staring at my half-eaten sausage stick. Hell, it was embarrassing.

"HA! Whatever gave you that absurd idea?" Melodie laughed, for the first time in a long while. "We named him after Hank's grandfather. His name's Buck, not Bucko. Come on, Will, get serious!"

Melodie was saved from a painful rectal examination when a breathless orderly wearing the insignia of the General Staff came charging into the room just as I'd unwrapped another spiced sausage stick. He was looking for me.

"Colonel Bucko, sir! The commanding general sends his regards, sir. He'd like to see you immediately if not sooner in his office at the RenCen. Says he's got the information you've been waiting for."

"Thank you, Corporal," I answered, trying not to appear too

PitVipers, single-handedly held off the first, and only, appearance of RIHM contamination in the Hawaiian Island chain.

excited in front of enlisted personnel. "Please wait outside. I'll be with you in a moment."

When the orderly had left I moved closer to Melodie. "Well, old girl," I said, "if that's what I think it is, I guess this is good-bye."

"Don't bet on it," she said courageously, reaching for my hand. "I'll be good as new in a few months. The commandant has already promised me a command in FACWEST. Could be I'll be your new boss."

"Not fucking likely," I said in the friendliest way I could. The FAC doctors had told me that while Melodie would probably live, she would almost certainly be retired from the service for disability and probably spend the rest of her life posing for holograms in medical journals. That she would hold command or even fly again was impossible.

"What do you mean?" she asked, a note of fear in her voice.

"Nothing, nothing." Hell if I was going to break the bad news to her. "Only, well, I'm going to ask for independent duty. You know me, Mel. Orders make me nervous. Tell ya what, though, if I run into any trouble, I'll let you know."

"Promise?"

"Yeah, I promise." I lifted her crusted hand from mine and gently placed it down on the sheet. I suddenly got this horrible cold feeling of déjà vu. It had been a situation very similar to this many years ago when I'd said a final good-bye to the Wolf. "Gotta go. You sure there's nothing I can get for you? Candy, magazines, a year's supply of Clearasil?"

"No, nothing. Good-bye, Will. And thank you for saving my life. You're a good friend."

"Like I said, you owe me one. Good-bye, Melodie." I stepped back, gave her a little wave, then turned towards the door.

"Aren't you going to kiss me?" she called.

I turned back to her and forced a grin. "Like you said, Mel—get serious."

"Touché," "Turn about is fair play," "He who laughs last"—all that sort of heavy philosophical crap never made up for the fact that when I walked out of her hospital room that day so long ago, it marked the last time I was ever to see Melodie Lane alive.

Even if she did look like a gigantic cold sore, I should've kissed her good-bye.

"There's good news and bad news," General Skoff said as he watched his aide moved the cursor over the giant color-coded computer map of the North American continent, which dominated one whole wall of the office. "The good news is that Roast has been spotted in Denver. The bad news is that FAC Headquarters has him listed as a Code-7 undercover operant. You know what that means."

Yes, I knew. A Code-7 attached to an informant's file meant that the intelligence being provided was so good that any and all outstanding criminal charges against that person were considered null and void. Basically, a Code-7 was a license to break the law, if not kill.

"Hey, General," I said angrily, "you know what you and Headquarters can do with your Code-7. That bastard was directly responsible for the death of my best friend, not to mention several thousand innocent Americans caught in the Ramases Northwest Rampage. His ass is mine."

"At ease, Colonel!" the general growled, glaring at me like I'd just harked a big yellow goober on his dress jump boots. "Let me remind you, sir, that the State of Emergency declared by the President last fall still exists. Until she lifts it, you remain an active member of FAC. And as such, you will obey the orders of those above you in the chain of command, or by God, sir, I will have you court-martialed and lashed with the cat-o'-nines! Do I make myself clear?"

"Very clear, General," I fumed. "Very clear, indeed. Perhaps, however, if the general had a more *personal* stake in seeing Jerry Roast brought to justice, things might be a little less so. Maybe you should've been there when they crucified Gunnery Sergeant Pugh. Maybe then you'd understand where I'm coming from."

The general just stood there for a moment steaming. Then, slowly, he unclenched his tiny little fists and spoke in a quiet, controlled voice. "Bucko, you ignorant piece of mildew. For your information, my son and daughter-in-law and their three children were killed by Comancheros out in Oregon two years ago. I know Roast was involved. I'd like nothing better than to open him up with an E-tool and spike his guts to my tank turret. But it can't be. I've got orders. He's a Code-7. Now, Colonel, can you dig it or not? Because if you can't, just tell me now and I'll have you placed under arrest. Three days, four at the most, you'll be locked up in a nice cold cell down in Leavenworth while that bastard Roast collects hazardous duty pay. Do you copy, Colonel?"

"Yes, sir," I said, giving up, "I do."

"Good. Now, are you ready for your next assignment?"

"Yes, sir."

"Lights, Abner."

The general's aide hit the dimmer switch, and the office got dark except for the computer map on the wall. As the general briefed me on my new orders, the aide used an electronic pointer to keep track of his boss's comments.

"As you know, Colonel, for the past twenty-five years we've been fighting a stalemate out west. While the Western RIHM tribes control most of California, Nevada, Arizona, and parts of New Mexico, we've been able to hold the line, even push them back a little, especially in the areas of Colorado, Idaho, and Wyoming."

I watched the cursor dance around the western fourth of the United States where the high-water marks of RIHM infestation were marked in pink. After their initial successes earlier in the century, the Western RIHM tribes had been held in check fairly successfully by FAC so that their current lines, marked in red, were half again as penetrating as the earlier pink.

"Now," the general continued, "with our recent success here on the border against the Great Northern Horde, the United States of America is finally ready to take back what is rightfully ours. You heard it here first, Colonel Bucko . . . The great California invasion we've all been waiting for is about to become reality. Show us the game plan, Gary."

It was the fourth different first name the general had used for his aide since I'd arrived in the office, and I was sure the kid was as confused as I was. Nonetheless, he hit a switch which changed the huge screen to a large-scale map of the California coast. Some two hundred miles off shore of what had once been Los Angeles was a vast armada of naval vessels represented by computer-generated facsimiles.

"My God," I muttered in awe, "the First Fleet. I thought it was just a legend!"

"It was," the General answered, "until a few years ago when we took back the shipyards in Puget Sound. Combined with the rebuilt yards on the East Coast at Charleston and Newport News, we've been able to assemble a naval amphibious force this country has not seen since the days of the Second Great Pacific War. And you, sir, have been chosen to be the ember that ignites the flame destined to drive the Mutant and all he holds near and dear straight to hell in a handbasket! Let me hear you say A-MEN, COLONEL!"

"A-MEN COLONEL!" I bellowed.

"Good man. Harvey, the lights."

Dutifully, the general's aide (whatever his name) brought up the house lights. I turned to find the general holding out a thin oilskin packet to me.

"Colonel Bucko," he said very quietly, "these are the sealed orders from the President of the United States to the Commander in Chief of FAC Forces Pacific giving the exact time, date, and location for the D-Day invasion. No one but the President herself and the commandant knows what these orders say. It is one message, I shouldn't have to tell you, that we cannot risk sending over the air, much less through the mail. If it fell into the wrong hands the RIHMs will be waiting on the beach for our boys and the slaughter will be catastrophic. Therefore, the orders herein contained must be hand-delivered, by someone with the cunning and guile to make it through enemy territory safely. Someone with the intestinal fortitude to be skinned alive rather than lose them to the enemy. Someone with balls of iron, blood of steel. That man is you, Colonel Bucko, you and your marvelous flying machine! You are to deliver these orders in person to the CICFACPAC. So go my boy, go with my blessings. Go, go with the great Jehovah, Lord God of Hosts, and for the United States of America and all who sail her! Go, my boy! Go and do good!"

What had started as a very militarylike briefing had turned into a bawling shouting revival meeting straight out of the early days of TV evangelism. I was a little embarrassed and greatly confused, but I accepted the orders and the embrace of the general without any fuss. I probably would've been able to get away scot-free if that damn aide hadn't whispered something in the general's ear just before I reached the doorway.

"Oh yes! Colonel Bucko!" the general called. "Robert here has reminded me of something. On your way out, pick up that damn Canadian troublemaker you brought back with you from across the river."

"Aw, come on, General," I whined, "Chandelier's just trying to keep morale at a fever pitch. Good Godfrey, man! Your troops have never been happier!"

It always galls the hell out of me when some Holy Roller high up in the military denies his hot-blooded young troops the chance to sample the pleasures of Venus simply because he's too old to get his own musket primed. I knew from firsthand knowledge that the group of refugee nude dancers from Windsor had been organized by Chandelier into a troop of performers that had the FAC rank-and-file lined up for hours outside an old motel over on East Jefferson. She'd even managed to come up with a few stud males for the distaff side of General Skoff's command.

"Suck lemons, ya old prude!" I barked, almost totally out of control. "You want to ruin morale by harassing that brave woman just because she's trying to make a buck, you go right ahead. But leave me out of it!"

"At ease, Bucko!" Skoff answered. "I wasn't referring to that delightful and courageous lady. A lady, I might add, whom I've asked to be the third Mrs. Cy Skoff. Yes yes, it's true," he blurted happily, probably in reaction to my expression of horrid disbelief. "And by God she's accepted! I'll tell you, Colonel, makes a man feel twenty years younger and as virile as a pedigree bull to have a thing like that performing the Dance of the Seven Veils for him in private. Ahh, booty fit for a king, if I do say so myself!"

While I just stood there with my mouth catching flies, the dreamy faraway look in the lewd old ram's eyes slowly returned to normal. "No, Bucko," he said, pivoting sharply and returning to the mass of paperwork on his desk, "I was talking about that young troublemaker Doone. The lad is totally incorrigible. Get rid of him."

I took a couple of steps back into the office. "General, Johnny's just a boy," I said, unsure as to why I was defending the kid except for the fact he'd saved my life a couple of times. "A teenager. High spirits, tons of energy, hormone hysteria. Just the natural exuberance of youth. Come on, you were a teenager once, right? Try to remember what—"

"You brought him here, Bucko, now you get rid of him. Read the charges, Arnold."

The general's aide (who—shades of Paul-John Fritz—I was beginning to dislike more and more) held up a computer printout and began to read.

"Misappropriation of FAC weapons, petty larceny, threatening a commissioned officer, assault and battery on a commission officer, breaking and entering, failure to maintain radio silence, failure to maintain blackout security, failure to carry an ID card, failure to change underwear on a regular basis, failure to *wear* underwear on a regular basis, carrying chow out of the mess hall, failure—"

"That's enough, Ted," the general cut in, silencing his aide and pointing his finger at me. "Take care of him, Bucko. Otherwise I'll be forced to shoot him at dawn. That is all."

Looking back on it, sometimes I wish I'd taken Skoff up on his threat. The world, I think, would be a safer place now if I had.

16

"Oh, Will!" Chandelier whimpered, wiping the whipped cream from her lips. "I never knew it could be like this!"

"You mean you've never tried it with real pie before?"

"Never! *Mon Dieu! C'est très bien!* Give me more!"

"You've gotta be kidding," I teased. "You want more?"

"Yes, yes. Harder harder!"

"Okay." I smiled ruthlessly. "If that's what you want . . . 'Who starred as Pa Cartwright in the hit series *Bonanza*?' "

"That's not harder!" she chirped, clapping her hands in joyous anticipation. "That's easy! Pa Cartwright was played by the late Lorne Green!"

"Absolutely correct," I sighed, pretending to be awed by her knowledge of Canadian TV stars. "Damn, another piece of the pie. What flavor is it this time?"

"Ah, strawberry, I think," she moaned. Once again I found myself transfixed by the sight of her erect nipples protruding from the thin T-shirt she'd had on when I'd appeared at her apartment door a few hours earlier, game board in hand. "No," she continued after some hesitation, "I've already had strawberry. What's the flavor for Westerns? Key Lime? *Oui,* Key Lime. Hand it over, *ma petite chose.*"*

I dug into the assortment of pies I'd brought to her crib for this last game of Trivial Pursuit (Canadian film and TV version). So far, she'd guessed and eaten her way through five flavors. What a pig.

"One more and you win," I reminded her. "Then you promised to give me a French lesson."

"I most certainly did not!" Chandelier exclaimed, her pretty dark eyes shining with either anger or lust as she rolled the game dice.

---

* "My little thing"—Chandelier's pet name for me back then. I'm still not sure why she called me that, although I'm positive it was not a reference to my "love" equipment.

"Whoa!" I said. "Can't blame a guy for trying. Do you want your last question or not?"

"Go ahead. What's the category?"

"Game show hosts."

"Merde! My worst subject."

"What late 1950s game show host was famous for raping his executive producer with a curling broom?"

Chandelier cocked her head for a moment, as though deep in thought, then she reached out and swatted my face. "Very sneaky of you, Will. You made that up. Ask me the correct question."

"All right already!" I laughed. "Geez! You sure take this game seriously, don't ya. The real question is, What game show host made his living giving contestants the answers?"

"Alex Trebek."

"You got it. Game, set, match, and a slice of apple."

I watched the lovely creature nearly inhale her sixth chunk of pie and wondered once again how she kept her weight down. Just another of her little secrets, I concluded, little secrets that I had gradually discovered since our safe return from the Windsor mission.

She was, for instance, almost as big a fanatic of Pre-Blast television and movies as I was, and we had spent many romantic hours discussing the social symbolism in Eddie Murphy films or whether *Lifestyles of the Rich and Famous* was a true representation of late twentieth-century value systems. When she wasn't tied up organizing her girls, and I wasn't keeping Melodie Lane's spirits up over at the hospital, we would meet in her quarters in the old Fisher Building for pizza and reruns of *Leave It to Beaver* or *The Man from U.N.C.L.E.,* both high on our list of favorites. Conversely, we both despised Sylvester Stallone movies and any spin-off from *The Cosby Show.*

With such strong feelings in common, I found myself getting emotionally attached to someone for the first time in a very long while.

"You know, Chandelier," I said cheerfully as she gulped down the last bites of her reward, "this is our last night together. I leave tomorrow at dawn."

"Mais oui, Will," she answered, brushing the crumbs from the front of her T-shirt and the electric-blue bikini briefs she was

wearing. "You have mentioned that fact quite often over the last few hours. What is the point?"

"The point is . . . I may not be coming back."

I thought I saw moisture glistening in her eyes. She squirmed towards me across the bed knocking the assortment of pies all over the deck and placed her head on my chest. "Do not talk that way, Will. It makes me very sad. Of course you will come back."

"Maybe. Maybe not. I only want you to know that . . . that these last few weeks with you have been the happiest of my life."

"I know," she murmured. "I have never seen such a wonderful collection of vid-tapes. We are *très* lucky that FAC has such an extensive library. All the good shows, the ones my *grandmère* used to tell me about—*Happy Days, Laverne and Shirley, The Brady Bunch, Charlie's*—"

I silenced her tearful babbling by gently placing an index finger over her lips. "No, Chandelier," I said, "I don't mean the videos. I mean being with you. Talking to you and sharing your dreams and watching the funny way your boobs jiggle when you run to answer the phone. Just being next to you, like this, feeling the warmth of your loins, smelling your perfume, imagining what— OUCH!"

She had bitten my finger—pretty damn painfully.

"Will," she said, as I cussed and examined the wound, "do you want to sleep with me? Is that what all this nonsense is about?"

"Well," I stammered, "now that you bring it up—"

She pushed herself away from me and got to her knees. "But I thought you and Colonel Lane—how do you say—were an item?"

I reached out and gently caressed a smooth thigh. "That was a long time ago. Now we're just friends."

Her face took on a perplexed expression, as though she was dealing with life and death instead of a proposition for a roll in the hay. "But how can I believe that?" she finally asked. "How do I know you will not go back to her as soon as she recovers?"

"That's over. I promise."

"Ah, Will. I care for you deeply—I will tell you that. But men have made promises to me before. Usually they end up broken."

"Who? The men?"

"The promises."

"Yeah, sure. And what about Cy Skoff? He says you agreed to marry him."

She smiled. "Mad Dog is a nice guy, but he is too old for me. Right now, however, I must be kind to him. After all, I'm making some good bucks keeping his troops lean and mean. The last thing in the world I need is to anger him and wind up getting deported. Try to understand."

"Okay," I said, "but what's that got to do with you and me jumping in the sack right now? Like I said, you may never get this chance again."

"Listen, Will," she sighed, "I will make a deal with you. When you return from your next mission, if you still feel the same way, then I will open my precious thighs for you and give you what is mine to give. Until then . . ."

She rolled off the bed, walked over to the stereo, and turned it on, then returned and stood at the foot of the bed. Slowly, sensuously, as she had danced so many times before in the clubs of Windsor, she began to dance for me, peeling away what little clothing she had on until she was clad only in a pair of high heels and a smile.

"Worth coming back to, don't you think?" she panted from luscious wet lips as she trailed a long painted fingernail down between her breasts and across her flat stomach.

I could only nod, wipe the drool from my chin, and whimper.

The next morning, with a heavy heart and aching nuts, I completed my preflight checklist and eased the Harrier out onto the runway. I was in no mood for the idle banter of Johnny Doone, who had been placed in the backseat of the TAV-8B after being escorted from the Grand River stockade by six armed FAC guards.

"Jack it up, old chub," I heard him say over the intercom. "Let's see what this little zoomie'll do in the quarter, eh?"

"Put a lid on it, Doone," I growled into my mask, "or you'll be punchin out at 30-K without benefit of silk."

"I'm sweatin it, Uncle Snit." The teenage hoodlum laughed. "I really am. Anything to munch on back here?"

My hand was only inches from the rear-seat EJECT lever when my attention was diverted by a radio call from the tower giving me final clearance. After one last check of the controls, I eased the power up, and slowly the Harrier began to roll down the runway.

By the time we were airborne and gear-up, I'd forgotten about Doone, Chandelier, Melodie Lane, or anything else that did not have something to do with flying. Ask any jet jock, and he'll tell you the same—there is nothing quite like lifting off at dawn with full tanks of syngas, bound on a mission upon which the entire country is relying. It tends to blot out everyone and everything not directly related to flying. Hell, Doone could've been back there eating his instrument panel for all I cared. I was doing what I had been born to do, experiencing the only thing that had ever given me true happiness. I savored it like a man dying of thirst might savor a cold brew.

My filed flight plan (as devised by FAC OPS) was a fairly routine route across the northern tier of CONUS with stops in Duluth, Minot, and Helena before hitting Seattle for rendezvous instructions with the First Fleet.

That was the plan that had been filed; it wasn't the one I flew. The country could wait—I had more important things to do . . .

"So this is Denver," Doone said as he dropped off the Harrier's wing onto the Tarmac of Stapleton. "We gonna be here long, ol' Varnish? 'Cause I gotta pee something fierce."

"Yeah, we'll be here awhile, son," I answered, looking around for a budget Rent-A-Ride sign. "Like I told you—I've got to look up an old school chum. You can come with me and see what the real world is like or stay here and play vid-games in the arcade till your miniscule brain rots. Take your pick, but don't get in my way."

"Miniscule? Am I suppose ta know what that means?"

"Think of a grain of sand, John, then divide by seventy-two." Without waiting for a response, I headed off towards the blinking lights of a rental stand. "Come on, kid. You can go potty later. Follow me and I'll show you what a real adventure is all about."

An hour and a half later we were passing out of Denver's Outer Defense Zone in an old 4×4 Chrysler Stamper—the one with the chrome clenched fist as a hood ornament. It wasn't much for speed, but in a crunch it could take an unpaved forty-degree grade without spewing its guts, and it had been specially prepped for local conditions by the rental people.

FAC had declared the greater Denver area RIHM-free a few years before, but there were still sightings of a few rogue males that made occasional raids on unsuspecting farmers or miners in the area. Since there were always a few eastern pukes who liked to mix a little hunting with their ski trips, the Stamper had been equipped with a roof-mounted Mark 19 40mm machine gun with an ancient but serviceable AN/TVS-5 night sight.

I wasn't after RIHMs though. And the cheap skis we'd rented from a sporting goods store in downtown and had lashed to the Stamper's roof rack were just for show. I hadn't come to schuss downhill or whatever else idiots do on the snow-covered slopes of Colorado in late March. I was looking for bear.

"I don't get it," Doone complained, as he ground down to second gear and turned off on a snow-covered single-lane highway that led, inexorably, farther up into the mountains. "How do ya know this guy Roast is up here?"

"I told you, kid," I answered, glancing up from the road map, "I've got a friend back in Washington high up in FAC Intelligence circles who owes me one. Or at least he did. Now he doesn't. That's how I know."

"And this glit we're going to see, he's a FUCer, eh?"

"The biggest . . . in more ways than one."

"How come we're bustin our buns in this vehicle when we could be flyin your bird?"

"Look around you, kid. Mountains on all sides. Altitude, terrain, fuel consumption—all too risky. Besides, I want this to be a surprise. Damn Harrier makes too much noise."

The road curved sharply as it followed the contours of a steep canyon. Doone panicked and down-shifted directly from fourth to first; the Stamper sounded like its transmission had been hit with a HEAT round.

"This beast we're driving now ain't exactly what you would call silent as a dead kitten," the boy muttered as the truck's rear end slewed back and forth across the icy pavement. He regained control, and we continued to climb.

"Yeah," I said, once my stomach had settled, "I was thinking maybe I'd walk the last few klics. Just keep it on the road, okay,

Johnny? And by the way, I didn't sign up for any insurance. Any accidents go straight on your record, pal."

The threat had no appreciable effect on his lunatic driving habits, and by the time we passed through the little town of Buffalo Creek I was beginning to suspect that Doone had been lying when he told me he knew how to drive a stick.

"There should be an old mine access road coming up on your left," I said as I checked the map in my lap. It wasn't the map that the Rent-A-Ride had provided, but a high-resolution aerial-recon photo I'd lifted from the FAC files back in Motown as soon as McBride had clued me in on Roast's exact location.

We almost missed the turnoff. The access road hadn't been used in many years, and it was overgrown with brush, so it wasn't until we were almost past it that I saw it.

"Hang a right!" I screamed. "I mean LEFT!"

Too late. Doone was doing fifty-eight when my command(s) caught him by surprise. One of the reasons the Stamper never really caught on with the American public, despite its power and leather seats, was a center-of-gravity so high that something like fourteen million drivers rolled the sonuvabitch in its first five years of operation. Too much speed in a tight turn and you were likely to be watching the world go round from a completely new perspective.

We tumbled for about a quarter mile until finally coming to rest right-side up. Thankfully, due to the high-impact harness straps we were wearing, and a rollbar made of solid molybdenum steel that had been installed during some previous recall, the driver and I were each in one piece.

"Well, that was interesting," I commented, trying to pry my white-knuckled fingers away from the door's armrest. "Maybe I'd better drive the rest of the way. What do you say, kid?"

That face! Jesus! I looked over, and the idiot was just grinning at me, with that Alfred E. smile of his that reminded me of REM hollies taken during bad drug trips. His mouth was leaking bright red blood by the bucket full.

"Damn, John!" I groaned. "Are you all right?"

The boy slowly turned away from me and spit out his window. It looked like the parting of the Red Sea. "Sure, just bit my tongue off is all," he said, wiping his mouth with the back of his hand and then cranking the indestructible Stamper back to life.

"Hey, next time, Old Knarl, give me a little warning when you want me to turn, what say?"

Unbelievably, the vehicle was still functional. In spite of my protests, Doone turned around and drove us back to the access road turnoff.

Twenty minutes later, after a few more hair-raising moments, which included riding to the top of a steep ridge line on a road only two inches wider than our wheelbase, we arrived at a spot high above a small cluster of shacks and cinderblock buildings that had once been a mountain community called Greenhorn Gulch. From my spot on the ridge, I could look right down into Jerry Roast's camp without worrying about being seen.

"Are you sure that's them?" Doone asked after he'd rigged some camouflage netting over the Stamper. I was studying the layout in detail with binoculars when he crawled up beside me.

"Yeah. No doubt about it," I said, handing the glasses to the boy. "About three fingers inboard from the large red pine on the left. That's his TRAC-4. He's painted it white to blend with the snow, but you can see it if you know what you're looking for."

"I got it, Old Scout." Johnny shifted his elbows so the binos were trained in a slightly different direction. "Your buddy's got a big family, boss. I count twenty or so vehicles parked around the burg. They all look serviceable. Hey! Lookie that! Bunch of guys outside that big white building. Shit! They're roastin weenies! What say we join 'em?"

Doone was almost to his feet when I grabbed the seat of his pants and roughly pulled him back down beside me.

"Listen carefully, Johnny. We go down there now and there will be two more weenies added to that fire in less time than it takes you to bathe."

"But hey, Big Buck, I thought we were here to see your old pal?"

"When the time comes, I will. Until then, we will stay out of sight and try to keep warm. Any questions?" He smiled and shook his head. I think he was beginning to get the picture that this wasn't exactly the social occasion I had at first let on. I grinned back at him. "Good. Now go rustle us up some grub. I packed some Cee's under the backseat—Ham and Muthas for me, Pork Loaf and peanut butter for you. And no fires. We eat 'em cold."

"Wouldn't have it no other way, Old Scout," the boy said evilly. "Wouldn't have it no other way."

We waited there on the ridge above the old town of Greenhorn Gulch for three days—freezing our wangs off and being bored silly. Slowly, and by the numbers, I spelled out my plan to Doone, the whys and wherefores and likely outcomes. He didn't have much problem understanding any of it, except the part about betraying the United States of America. I told him not to lose any sleep over it. Being a Canadian citizen, he didn't.

"It's *your* country, Old Sly," he said. "You wanna screw-over the land of yer forefathers, that's your business."

On the morning of our fourth day on the ridge, just when I was beginning to doubt if Phil McBride really was the officer in charge of all FAC Counterintelligence or just some stupid bird-colonel who'd been dicking me around, I heard the unmistakable womp of a CH-92 chopper echoing off the surrounding mountainsides. I turned the binos to a western gap where I was sure the bird would have to come. Sure enough, within a couple of minutes the fat grasshopper-shaped body of the Nightlifter helicopter appeared, speeding towards us like a huge black bug.

I reached over and shook Doone awake. "Time to tighten your pucker-string, kid. Rock 'n' roll is here to stay."

As Johnny happily climbed out of his warm sleeping bag, I watched the big Nightlifter circle Greenhorn Gulch, then settle down into a snow-plowed LZ in back of the building that had once been Ed's Community Market but now apparently served as Roast's headquarters.

I dialed the binos to *Extreme Close-up* and did a slow pan of the area. Bingo. Out on the edge LZ to greet the chopper was none other than my old pal, Marvin the blue-eyed Oriental. He waited until the chopper revved down and the twin rotars had almost stopped before charging through the still swirling snow to take a position just aft of the aircraft. A few seconds later, the big rear door ramp of the Nightlifter opened and a squad of Comancheros came rushing out on armed motorcyles and ATVs. They rushed out to the perimeter of the LZ and set up a hasty defense.

It wasn't until the leader of this group signaled the chopper that the LZ was secure that Ramases II, dressed to kill in synthetic bearskin, black denim, and engineer boots, came stomping down the Nightlifter's ramp.

Didn't surprise me a bit that Marvin was down on one knee bowing to the sonuvabitch.

17

I waited until most of Roast's men were preoccupied loading the Nightlifter with a store of wooden crates that had been hidden under camouflage tarps near the LZ. Dressed in a set of salty-looking black denims I'd brought along for just such a purpose, I made my way down from the ridge into Greenhorn Gulch itself.

Walked right in, bold as you please, armed only with my bufgun in a backsling holster and a couple of ASPs (9mm Automatic Assault Pistols) slung crossdraw low on my hips. Since I looked pretty much like one of the newly arrived Comancheros, none of Roast's undisciplined sentries even bothered to ask for ID. Wasn't until I got all the way to the steps of Ed's Community Market that someone finally inquired about the orange fright wig I was wearing under the Kelvar Nazi helmet.

"Where you think you're goin, Bozo," a huge black dude wearing the forehead tattoo of a Comanchero palace guard growled at me.

"Well," I said in a friendly manner, "I was hoping I'd be able to get a minute with Ramases."

He looked me up and down. "I am not familiar with you, Bozo. You are not one of my men. Those who wear Comanchero Colors without being Comancheros pretty much die young."

I pulled the helmet and wig from my head and tossed them at the guy's gut. "Tell Ramases Will Bucko wants to see him."

The Comanchero looked startled for an instant, then made a quick move for the .45 stashed in a holster under his armpit. He hadn't even begun to clear leather when he discovered the muzzle of an ASP digging into his groin.

"Or maybe I'll just tell him myself," I hissed, my face only inches from his.

He showed no fear, only resignation, and as he turned and led me back through the building—the ASP at the base of his spine —I knew that this was one of the ones who only understood strength, one of the ones who would never listen to reason or logic, only the simple declarative sentence delivered by a bullet to the brain. Because of what I'd already done to him, I would either have to kill him or spend the rest of my life making sure I'd locked the bathroom door behind me.

Ramases and Roast were in Ed's back office, toasting each other with bottles of cheap Beaujolais, when the captain of the guards and I slammed through the door and announced ourselves, he with a howl of rage and a full spinning backkick that would've made any karate instructor proud, me with a quick six-shot burst from the ASP that took the fool's foot off and silenced his Bruce Lee imitation in mid-whoop as 9mm hollowpoints stitched their way across his chest. The poor dumb cluck was probably dead before he hit the deck.

"BUCKO!" I heard Roast exclaim.

I caught sight of him madly clicking through various lens settings, adjusting his vision apparatus from close-up to wide-angle. Meanwhile, Ramases had kicked backed from the desk and pulled out his own personal side arm, a .357 Magnum with a twelve-inch chrome-plated barrel. He was about to hammer down on me with it when I imagine he caught sight of the still-smoking ASP, now aimed in the general direction of his head, and slowly let the huge weapon rotate by its trigger guard into the muzzle-down attitude of surrender.

"Let it drop, Ramases," I said casually while poking the riddled body on the floor with the toe of my boot to see if there was any glimmer of life left. "Then grab a chair. I figure you've gotta be smarter than your private secretary here."

"Jumbo never did score very high on his College Boards," the humongous muscle-bound bastard said in a quiet, almost feminine voice. "So, Bucko, we finally meet."

Out of the corner of my eye I caught Roast reaching inside his robes for something. With the ASP still pointed at Ramases' head, I kicked at the desk and sent it crashing into Jerry's huge belly. He made a sound like overripe fruit hitting pavement and a fancy-looking little double-barrel derringer went clattering across the floor.

"That's a no-no, Jer," I cautioned him. "Now put your hands on the desk where I can see them. . . . That's a boy."

"I should've killed you when I had the chance," Jerry spat, the innumerable jowls hanging from his chin already dripping sweat.

I moved a couple of steps closer to him, then picked up a

pneumatic staple gun that had caught my eye. "Jerry," I said, "if you scream I'll kill you right now. Do you understand?"

Without waiting for an answer, I stapled his lips shut.

Jerry called my bluff, however, and began to scream blue murder, but all that came out were the muffled cries of a hog with its throat slit.

"Pain and suffering—music to my ears," I said to Ramases, gesturing at the squirming blob behind Doctor Fizz's marvelous vision contraption, "but hard on conversation."

"Guy's a pussy." Ramases grinned. "What else is new?"

Up close, the ruler of all the Comanchero tribes looked even weirder than I remembered from Harry Riviero's video documentary. There's something about too much cosmetic surgery during advanced age that throws everything out of kilter. Underneath all the mascara and eyeliner and goo, Ramases' much altered face had a shiny, tightened, inhuman look of a puppet molded from Plas-tex.

"Good Christ, you're ugly!" I whispered to him.

"And you're a dead man," he answered evenly, flexing a gigantic bicep and studying the definition as if growing bored with me already. "By now my guard will have this place surrounded. Anything happens to me, they'll put you on a spit and bar-b-que your ass. Then they'll make you watch while they eat you, one joint at a time."

"Ooooh," I moaned, "how very picturesque. And what happens if I don't kill you?"

"You're still dead, only they'll probably let you die in a day instead of a week."

"Hell." I grinned. "Doesn't seem to be any way out of this mess. How about we try to work out a deal?"

"I'm listening. You're still a dead man, but I'm listening."

Under the heavy makeup—the pancake, the black lipstick, the blush—I saw a shadow of a deathmask, the outline of a skull. It was like looking into a coffin, two years after burial. A cold chill ran up my spine, and I shuddered.

"I came for him," I said, nodding towards the muffled Roast, who was trying—unsuccessfully—to pry his lips apart. "I've got no quarrel with you. I just want him."

Ramases blinked a couple of times with his big curly lashes, then arched an obviously synthetic eyebrow. "Then why didn't you just wait until I'd gone?" he asked. "We could've avoided all this unpleasantness."

"Because," I said, "I didn't want to spend the rest of my life worrying about Comancheros being after my butt for killing this shit without your permission. I've got enough trouble."

"Oh yes," Ramases said softly, "I heard. Murdered a FAC major a few years back?"

"Yeah, whatever. Thing is, I want Roast . . . And I also want the two million he owes me."

Ramases got a real chuckle out of that. His face was so tight, though, that when he tried to smile all he could manage was to bare his teeth.

"Bucko, you are amazing," he said once he stopped wheezing. "You call that a deal? My boy, there's absolutely nothing in it for *me!* I make a deal like that, I'd be laughed out of town. Go ahead and kill me, I could give a fuck."

The way he said it—offhand and with a nonchalant wave of his hand—I knew he meant what he'd just said. Life, even his own, meant absolutely nothing to him.

I sat down on the edge of the desk and rested the ASP on my thigh. It was time to lay things on the line. "Oh, there's plenty in this for you, Ramases. First off—and this is just to whet your appetite so to speak—you might be interested to know that Jerry Roast here is a FUCer. FAC undercover. A Code-7 no less, license to cheat, lie, steal, and fornicate with foreign governments. And he's been playing you for a sucker."

For the first time since I'd come into the office, I think I surprised the mutilated bastard.

"I don't believe you," he said.

"Is that right. Think about it, Ram. Last five or six years— Washington, Oregon, Idaho—every time you and your tribes were about to take over an uninfected piece of real estate, along comes FAC to drive you back into the deserts. Ever wonder how they were always able to be there in the nick of time? Okay. I see I've got your interest. Now ask yourself this—how did Bucko find this place? How did he know Roast was using an old ghost town called Greenhorn Gulch as a staging area for the seven tons of ordnance he and his gang took out of the Rocky Mountain Arsenal last week?" I reached into my black denim jacket and pulled out the aerial recon-photo, then tossed it at Ramases. "There's your answer, pal."

He studied the recon-photo for a minute or so, then tossed it on the floor at his feet. "So? FAC's got a picture of this place. So what?"

I was relieved to discover the guy wasn't the superman everybody said he was. Muscles, yeah, but his brain was just ordinary.

"Come on, big guy," I said, "use your head for something besides facial implants and fat-reduction tubes. You know the FAC Intelligence boys can resolute down to serial numbers and fingerprints with flics like that. You think they couldn't see the TRACs and ammo crates marked Rocky Mountain Arsenal stacked up out back? So ask yourself—if FAC knows then how come FAC hasn't hit this place with everything its got? Damn, Ram, you know as well as I do that there's a whole squadron of A-38s stationed in Denver. So how come this place is still open for business? I'll tell ya. It's because that blob of polysaturate over there is *a code-7 fucer and can do anything he damn well pleases as long as he keeps FAC informed! and that included murdering my partner!*"

I realized I was finally getting through when Ramases tried to scowl. All he managed however was a narrowing of the eyes and a curling of the upper lip; it was physically impossible for him to put creases in his forehead.

He shifted his weight in the chair so that he was facing Roast. "Makes sense," he said. He reached over and ripped the staples out of Jerry's mouth. "What've you got to say for yourself, Roasty?"

Roast had continued to rant and rave despite having his lips sealed with the heavy steel staples. The noise he'd been making had so far been muffled enough to allow for conversation. As soon as Ramases took out the staples, however, Jerry proceeded to go bat-shit. I guess he sensed that his big butt was in a peck of trouble.

"LIES!" he roared, "ALL LIES! HE'S THE ONE WITH FAC, RAMASES! THAT'S HOW HE GOT THAT PHOTO! THAT'S HOW HE KNEW WE WERE HERE! IT'S A SETUP!"

Calmly, Ramases took the pneumatic staple gun and resealed

Jerry's mouth. He looked over at me again. "What's your answer to that, Bucko?"

I laughed. "Sure. A setup. If that's true then ask yourself this, Ramases. How come I'm not up on a ridge line vectoring that attack squadron down on this place right now? You think FAC would pass up an opportunity to cream the great Ramases? Give me a break."

"If what you say is true," Ramases ruminated verbally, "then why didn't Roast give me to FAC during all these years he's supposedly been their narc?"

"Because you were his meal ticket, his number one customer. I bet he's made millions playing both sides against the middle."

Ramases gave the struggling Roast a long hard look. "You know, I've always had my suspicions about this fellow—something, I dunno, something just wasn't right. I think you're telling the truth Bucko, I really do. Only . . ." He turned again to face me. "I'll kill him myself. You still die."

"No," I said, drawing my final ace from an inside pocket. "I want him." I held up the thin oil-skin packet so Ramases could see the unbroken Presidential Seal. "This is the battle plan for the invasion of Southern California," I said very matter-of-factly. "FAC made a big mistake assigning me the mission of seeing it was delivered. Way I see it—more than you, more than even Roast—FAC is responsible for the death of my partner. This country has dorked around with me my whole life. Now it's going to make me rich. Two million in gold, Ramases, and carte blanche with the big-eyed butter-butt here. In exchange, not only do you get to climb on that chopper of yours alive, but I'll hand over these battle plans, which you can sell to your RIHM buddies for all the loot you could possible ever want. That's the deal."

"Oh." Ramases seemed surprised again. "You know about the RIHM-Comanchero treaty?"

"I told ya, Jerry's a FUCer. And I've got an old buddy high up in FAC Intelligence who owed me one. I've seen the file, Ram. It's as thick as the yellow pages."

He stared at me for a long time, with black eyes of cold death. "What's to stop me from saying yes and then blowing you to hell when I get outside this room?"

"I'm glad you asked," I said, turning over the collar of my flac jacket to reveal the miniature microphone pinned there. "Show 'em what we got, Johnny."

Thirteen seconds later and the office was rocked by the concussion of a hundred 40mm grenades raining down in rapid fire on one of the town's abandoned buildings. The ground shook, and plaster came falling from the ceiling over our heads. Impressive as hell if I do say so myself.

I let the demonstration go on only long enough to establish my point. "Thanks, John," I shouted into the mike. The explosions stopped and I looked over at Ramases who appeared convinced. "MK-19 automatic grenade launcher," I said. "My men have this whole area zeroed in. If I eat it, O Great One, you eat it. It's that simple."

Slowly, reluctantly almost, Ramases pushed his massive muscular self out of the chair and stretched. He adjusted the imitation bearskin that had bunched up around his crotch, let out a deep belch, and brushed away a lock of curly black hair that had fallen across his parchmentlike face.

"Deal," he said.

"Well, I guess this is *adiós* for a while, Jer," I said, hefting the seabag full of gold credits to my shoulder. "But don't you fret. I'll be back in the fall and we can talk about old times . . . if you still feel up to it."

Dawn was only a few minutes away. Ramases and his boys, along with Marvin the blue-eyed Oriental and the rest of Roast's gang of thugs, had verticaled out of Greenhorn Gulch in the Nightlifter just after midnight. I'd kept my part of the bargain, and Ramases had kept his; Roast was mine.

"Please, Bucko, for the love of God, don't leave me."

All the screaming, begging, pleading, and weeping of the last six hours had reduced Jerry's voice to a scratchy, blubbery rasp. Sometime in the wee hours of morning—when he finally figured out what was in store for him—he had begun to lose his mind . . .

Doone and I had had some trouble digging the pit, not only because the ground was frozen but because of the tremendous amount of earth that had to be removed to allow room for Jerry's bulk. It had taken sixty pounds of high explosive and a mechanical back-hoe to dig the correct size hole. And once we'd rolled his body into the abyss, it had taken another hour and forty-five minutes to fill the son of a gun back in again.

Out of pure sadism, I punched on the flashlight and let the beam pass quickly over Roast's face. He screamed in agony. Without his vision device, even the low candlepower of the flashlight hitting his lidless eyes was enough to cause pain.

We had buried him to his neck in the cold ground, facing the east. When the sun came up, Jerry would be the first to know.

"BUCKO, PLEASE!" he screamed at my fading footsteps. "MY GOD! THIS IS INHUMAN!"

I stopped. He was right, it was inhuman to leave him like that. Better to put a bullet between those bulging eyes, I thought, and be done with it. My hand was already reaching for the butt of the bufgun when I remembered all those mornings so long ago at the Academy—the leeches attached to my chest and groin, the shove-outs and green-benches and electroshock, the push-ups over beds of sharpened nails, the beatings and torture, the daily agony, misery, and fear. Then I remembered what they—Roast and Befeeter—had done to Melodie Lane's sweet body under the guise of the plebe indoctrination system. Finally, as Jerry continued to whimper, I saw the body of Black Pugh being nailed to a palm tree. A shadow fell across my soul.

Yes, it *was* inhuman to leave Jerry Roast like that . . . but it was just what the bug-eyed fuck deserved.

"MAY YOU ROT IN HELL, BUCKO!" Roast yelled as he saw me turn to walk away. "May you rot in hell . . . alongside that black whore-son that you once called friend! I only wish he could've suffered just a little bit more!"

Oh, Jerry, you poor poor chucklehead. His words stopped me in midstride. I was thinking about working on my field-goal kicking technique when I spotted a twig from an aspen branch on the ground nearby, a twig already sprouting with the first indications of spring.

I bent down and picked it up, then made an about-face and went back to where Jerry's huge bald head, as smooth and white as a cue ball, jutted out from clods of still-frozen earth. The sky had begun to display the faintest traces of light, enough of it for me to see him fairly clearly. I squatted down next to him, the twig in my hand.

When he saw what I had in mind, Roast went totally mad,

screaming and bellowing and slobbering like a great white cow being led to slaughter. I paid no attention to him. Instead, I reached out, and with just the very tip of the twig, where the new growth had already begun to form, began to gently trace the letters of Black Pugh's name on the surface of Jerry Roast's eyeballs . . .

"Here ya go, Jer," I whispered. "This bud's for you."

When I finally got back to the ridge line where Doone and the 4×4 Stamper were waiting, the sun had already broken over the peaks to the east, and the echo of Roast's screams reverberating off the mountainsides had become a constant animal wail of despair, pain, and utter terror.

Doone was studying the area of Greenhorn Gulch through the binos as I headed for the Stamper. "Hey, Buck," I heard him call out, "you ain't going to leave him like that, are ya, eh? Like, his eyes are startin to cook like a couple of fried eggs!"

"Come on, kid," I said, just before jumping behind the wheel and slamming the hatch behind me. "We've gotta get back to Denver." I jacked the ignition and revved the engine and waited for the boy to join me.

"This ain't too pleasant, old coot," he said, eventually falling into the seat beside me. "I'm all for righteous revenge but . . . damn, Colonel, this is downright savage!"

I turned and glared at his zit-encrusted face. "Keep your trap shut, boy," I growled. "There's more here than meets the eye."

"Ha, ha, very humorous, old Duff. But I ain't shittin ya none, eh? I sure as hell ain't gonna go to sleep for the rest of my life hearing *that* in my dreams." Doone jerked a thumb in the general direction of the faint, but still audible, cries from Jerry Roast.

"Then maybe you'd better cram something in your ears, John," I snarled, shifting the Stamper into gear and popping the clutch. We pulled out in a shower of dirt clods and slush.

"Not very likely, by Jesus," I heard him say over the roar of the engine.

By the time I saw what he was up to, it was too late. With one hand I reached over and tried to pull him back down, but he'd already climbed behind the MK-19 mount. He fired off a full belt of grenades before I could slam on the brakes. The Stamper's engine stalled, and I jacked the wheel to keep us on the narrow trail.

We slid to a stop. There was a moment of silence, then we heard the faraway popping sounds as the grenades started to hit the LZ where the MK-19's firing computer had been locked on since the night before.

It was about that time that Jerry Roast stopped screaming.

18

"You haven't changed much, Will—except for that gut I mean. Still the same irreverent comic book character you always were. Personally I believe you, but what the admiral will make of your story, I couldn't tell."

Commodore Jumpin Jack Fry FAC-NF (Naval Forces), an old pal and the commanding officer of the USS *Walter Payton*, adjusted his cap and motioned me to follow him through his sea cabin door and out to the bridge. On the way, he dismissed the two FAC sentries who'd been dogging my footsteps ever since I'd put the Harrier down on the *Payton's* bucking flight deck a few hours before.

Jumpin Jack hadn't changed much either. A few gray hairs perhaps, and the makings of some nice deep crow's-feet at the corners of his eyes, but he was still the tall chiseled naval officer I'd met ten years before when he'd commanded the only antisubmarine destroyer left in the then woefully depleted FAC naval arsenal.* Jack and I had been coconspirators back then, in a FAC covert operation that had not worked as well as we would've liked. The final results of that action had nonetheless been spectacularly successful: the end of Carlos Membranous and the destruction of the Shrimper Fleet. Now Jumpin Jack was in command of the *Payton*, a brand-new Halas-Class hydrofoil landing-platform battlewagon (LPBB) that was also serving as flagship for the First Fleet.

We passed onto the *Payton's* super hi-tech bridge where large vid-font display screens with computer-generated graphics gave the captain an instantaneous picture of all necessary data.

"Captain is on the bridge," the quartermaster called out as Jumpin Jack and I moved out into central conn.

"As you were, gentlemen," Jack announced. "Anything on Sea Search, Jim?" he asked the OOD as he made a quick scan of the display screens and then the real horizon. (My old friend began

---

* The USS *Duke Wayne*.

hopping up and down in place, and I suddenly understood how he'd come by his nickname.)

"Nothing, Skipper," the Officer of the Deck answered. "Task Force remains disbursed as per admiral's orders."

"Very well. I'll be up in Flag," Jack said.

"Aye aye, sir."

We went out onto the flying bridge where a gentle Pacific breeze blew steadily from the east. I followed Jumpin Jack up a metal stairway and past another sentry in FAC dress blues. After checking with the admiral's aide, we found her taking some sun out on the port wing of the Flag bridge.

"Excuse me, ma'am," Jumpin Jack said as we approached her. "You said you wanted to meet the crazy wildman who landed that Harrier without clearance this morning. Well, here he is. The famous Brevet Lieutenant Colonel William T. Bucko. Will, snap off a salute to Admiral Martha Jean Jascoolie, Commander in Chief, FAC-PAC."

"Ma'am," I responded, tightening my buttocks and clicking my heels and generally acting like a limey subaltern reporting in for duty on the Indian frontier. "My pleasure, I can assure you."

"At ease, Colonel Bucko," the admiral said with a smile. "Nobody likes an ass-kisser."

She was, to put it bluntly, a mere wisp of a woman. No more than four foot ten, glasses, snow-white hair cut conservatively, maybe ninety pounds soaking wet, Admiral Jascoolie looked like everybody's dear old grannie. Yet anyone who'd not had their head buried in compost over the last twenty-five years knew that Martha Jean Jascoolie was just about as tough as they come. Although she only wore her silver FAC wings, I knew she'd been awarded nearly every medal for gallantry and heroism in the book and had worked her way up the ladder to become FAC's first female combat officer of flag rank. Approaching sixty years of age, her handshake still left my knuckles full of bone splinters.[*]

"I met your father once," she said, craning her head back so she could look me in the kisser, "when I was an ensign. He was

[*] For more on this remarkable woman and her astonishing career, see H. M. Semple's work, *Paint and Powder: The Story of Fleet Admiral M. J. Jascoolie* (Oldbat, Kentucky: Randi Publications, 2058).

somewhat of a turd, but a hell of a pilot. We owe a lot to old bushwhackers like your dad, you know. They held this country together in the dark days after the Big Blast. Wasn't for him and other crazies like him, we'd all probably have gills by now and be eating pond scum through our nostrils. Speaking of lunch, have you eaten yet?"

"No, ma'am," I said, somewhat mesmerized by her rapid-fire verbiage and the fact that she'd so precisely described my father.

"Then let's adjourn to my cabin, shall we? You can tell me your story over some bouillon and crackers. Oh, and where's his friend, Captain Fry? I understood he landed the TAV-8 with a passenger onboard."

"Ah, yes, ma'am, that's true," Jack said. "Canadian civilian. Teenager. He's down in the galley eating his way through a month's worth of stores. We may all be on bread and water by the time he's finished."

"Oh, I shouldn't worry about that, Jack," the admiral said sadly, "for I believe that very shortly we'll be engaged in mortal combat. And unless we are very very lucky, there will soon be a whole lot fewer mouths to feed around here." She looked up at me. "Sorry, lad," she said as she took my arm and steered me back towards her quarters, "but I call 'em like I see 'em. Now, let's hear your story . . ."

". . . And so, admiral," I concluded, reaching for my eighth cup of coffee, "the boy and I gased up the Harrier, flew west over the Rockies, and then punched right through RIHM air defenses by flying all the way to the coast at fifty feet. Once we were over the water, I elevated to forty-five thousand and started looking for you."

"But, Bucko," the admiral asked, sipping a cup of tea, "how did you know where we would be?"

"General Skoff gave me your general location, Admiral. I figured I wouldn't have much trouble spotting four hundred and twenty or so ships. And I was right. Once I found the Fleet, I only had to look for the largest ship ever built. Here I am."

Ms. Martha Jean (as I had come to think of her) put down her teacup on the coffee table and promptly got lost in thought. Since Jumpin Jack had departed sometime earlier to check on his ship, she and I had been alone in her cabin through most of lunch. She had listened to my story—by necessity starting with my Mexican adventures—without interruption.

"Do you mean to tell me, Colonel," she finally said, somewhat hesitantly, "that these girls actually dance *completely* naked in public on one's table?"

I was a little surprised at her question, but answered it nonetheless. "Yes, ma'am," I said, "except for high heels and maybe a birthmark or two."

The admiral yawned. "How incredibly boring. But never mind that—please tell me why I shouldn't have you hung from the main yard for turning the President's battle order over to Ramases."

"Admiral." I chuckled. "I was wondering when you'd get around to that. Quite frankly, it's rather an intricate plan. I don't know whether a woman could be expected to—"

"I'm sure you're trying to be funny, Colonel," the admiral interrupted in a voice that could've baked paint, "but I must tell you, we are not amused. Get to the gaw-damn point or you'll be shark bait before eight bells."

Martha Jean had the makings of a smile on her face, but her eyes told me that she was dead serious. I decided to dispense with the opening joke and get right to the meat of my speech.

According to FAC Intelligence (Phil McBride, in particular) the Western RIHMs had been anticipating an invasion of Southern California from the sea for almost a decade and had geared themselves for its defense. One of the primary reasons the rest of the west had not had a serious RIHM problem was due to this preoccupation with defending the southland.

Even so, the RIHMs had been faced with a tough strategical decision: Whether to stretch their forces to defend the entire shoreline from south of San Diego to the San Francisco Bay or concentrate their forces farther inland where they could respond en masse when the actual invasion beaches were identified. From what FAC had been able to gather from aerial recon, the RIHMs had chosen the latter choice; most of their armies were currently massed inland but close enough to the coast so they could respond quickly to any FAC landing force.

"So this was my thinking, Admiral," I said. "I figured that if the RIHMs believed they knew where and when the invasion would come, they would marshal their forces in that area, ready to push us back into the sea with the advantage of overwhelming numbers and concentration of fire. But they had to believe that such information was completely reliable. If it had leaked out of FAC, they would never have taken the bait. The information had to come from a human that they trusted to be crass and evil enough to betray his own kind."

"Meaning you, Colonel Bucko?" Martha Jean asked.

"No, ma'am, meaning Ramases. But I had to convince him so he could convince the RIHMs. Therefore, it was necessary for me to execute Jerry Roast."

The admiral held up her hand. "I don't want to hear any more about *that* part of your trip. It sounds like cold-blooded murder to me, but that's neither here nor there. What I want to know, Colonel, is what were the instructions contained in that Presidential order? Otherwise, even if your harebrained plan works, it's possible we might land the invasion force on the very beaches those mutants are defending in strength."

"I'm one step ahead of you, Admiral. As my old English teacher in high school used to say: 'Never give Will Bucko a sealed envelope for delivery—might as well order a sailor not to dip his wick on libs while you hand him a six-pack of condoms.' Excuse me, ma'am, no offense."

"Please, Colonel, I know what a condom is," Martha Jean said. "I used to own one in Aspen. Continue."

Aspen? I didn't know what the hell she was talking about, but I plowed ahead anyway. "Using a special steam-technique developed by an old friend of mine, I was able to get into the envelope without breaking the seal. Admiral, the President wanted you to hit the Monterey Bay on the sixth of April."

"The sixth, eh?" Admiral Jascoolie rubbed her chin and for the first time I noticed she had a number of gray whiskers growing there. "That's four days from now. If the RIHMs take your bait, then we must go ashore on or prior to that date, otherwise they will know they've been duped."

"Boy!" I applauded. "They don't call you the Micro-Processor of the High Seas for nothing, do they?"

"Young man," the admiral said in a steady unrevealing voice, "my old friend and mentor, General Scotty Pottabomb—God rest his soul—once told me about you. He mentioned a sense of humor that few could understand. I'm beginning to see what he meant. Please watch what you are saying or I will be forced to have you clapped in irons. Do I make myself clear?"

"Yes, ma'am, extremely clear." (She was also known throughout the Fleet as the Terror of the Bounding Main, but you can damn well bet I wasn't going to mention it.)

"Good. I must say you've painted me into a rather tight corner, Will. For your information, my last briefing with the President indicated that in fact the Monterey area would most probably be our objective and I've had my staff working on the plan ever since. Now . . . well, even with the high-speed main-frame computers this ship is equipped with, one does not simply crank off a new invasion plan of such magnitude overnight. There are close to a million details that have to be considered and promulgated. So if you will excuse me, I must pass the word to my staff immediately."

"Why, yes, ma'am, of course," I said, putting down my coffee mug and standing to attention. "And thank you for the chow."

"Oh, did you like those cucumber sandwiches?" She seemed pleased.

"Delicious, ma'am."

"I made them myself. Take a few with you when you leave."

"No, thank you, Admiral, I'm stuffed."

Martha Jean gave me a crooked smile. "That, judging by your belt size, is fairly obvious, Colonel. On the other hand, it could get worse."

"Ma'am?" I questioned, sucking in my stomach as far as it would go.

"If this little ruse of yours doesn't work, you'll be stuffed a little bit more—with a twenty-four pound cannonball, which I will personally shove up your ass an ounce at a time. Good afternoon, Colonel. On your way out, ask my aide to come in. That is all."

Just my luck, I thought, as I ducked through the hatch door into the outer office. I fly two thousand miles and risk life and limb only to be castigated by an admiral who was apparently suffering through delayed menopause and who made sandwiches that tasted like stamp paste. Well, I'd damn well done my patriotic duty. It was time to start thinking about the *personal* business still ahead of me.

* * *

"The admiral wants to know if you have a steady girl or not, Will," Jumpin Jack Fry asked me four days later on the eve of battle as I joined him and his officers in the *Payton*'s wardroom for evening meal.

"One in every port," I quipped. "Pass some more of those flapjacks down here, would you please, Skipper?"

"By heavens!" Jack laughed. "Where do you put it? You've had six helpings of those sourdough beauties already, Will. What the hell are you trying to do—outweigh the ship's anchor?"

It was a typical Naval Force's wardroom kind of joke—friendly, benign, and imbecilic. Just as typical, the officers sitting around the table liked to kill themselves pretending to crack up over their CO's splendid bit of improv (although I'd lay ten-to-one that he had made the same silly crack a thousand times before). I answered the only way I knew how.

"Blow it out your fanny pack, Jack. If I'm gonna get my dick handed to me tomorrow, I'll do it with a full belly, thank you very much."

The officers around the table figuratively split a gut over my response, and I began to suspect that their boisterous laughter and camaraderie was fueled not by an appreciation of the manly art of repartee, but was instead a result of the numerous rounds of grog Jumpin Jack had authorized for all hands.*

"Gentlemen," Jack bellowed, staggering to his feet, "a toast. On the morrow, the manifest destiny of our nation will once again become a reality. To victory . . . from sea to shining sea!"

"TO VICTORY!" the rest of the wardroom responded as they shoved back their chairs and got to their feet, grog tankards in hand.

From experience I knew this to be the signal for the start of a seemingly endless round of other toasts ranging from salutes to

---

* By an Act of Congress in 2038, members of FAC Naval Forces were allowed a "ration of grog" whenever the captain saw fit to issue it. The grog was limited to a brew with not more than three-point-two percent alcohol content, better known as near beer. It is estimated that in order to be legally drunk from such a drink, one would have to consume forty gallons of the stuff in less than an hour. To which I can only add—it has been done.

the President of the United States to congratulations over some department onboard having the most fully charged fire extinguishers for the last quarter. It was the diversion I'd been waiting for. After grabbing a couple of quarts of grog from the cooler, I slipped out of the wardroom and headed topside . . .

Only two years old, the *Walter Payton* was a marvel of rediscovered American industrial might. She was six football fields long with two separate flight decks for both fixed-wing and rotar aircraft. Capable of speeds up to sixty knots, she was armed with the very latest in laser and particle-beam weaponry as well as the standard thirty-inch guns, which could fire a projectile the size of a medium tank up to a range of forty miles. Her crew numbered four thousand; her complement of aircraft was an entire FAC Wing; she berthed a Division of FAC ground troops. Even with such a load, when she stood on her hydrofoils, she was said to display all the speed, grace, and power of her athletic namesake. What made the ship truly remarkable, however, was the fact that she was powered almost entirely by solar fuel cells buried under the transparent plas-steel of her flight decks. Despite being the size of a small city, the *Walter Payton* could steam for days on only a few barrels of synfuel.

Her crew called her *Sweetness.*

In the last purple haze of sunset I stood on the *Payton*'s fantail and looked toward the dark eastern horizon. Out there, somewhere, was the ancient site of L.A., once a great megalopolis but for almost forty years only miles of ash and rubble. Tomorrow the men and women of FAC would storm ashore at beaches called Redondo, Santa Monica, Huntington, and Newport. They would, I knew, be in for the fight of their lives, for while the latest intelligence indicated that the RIHMs had gone for my trick and had marched many of their southern legions north to reinforce armies already in place around Monterey Bay, resistance on the L.A. beaches would undoubtedly still be quite stiff. The enemy, after all, had had ten years to prepare his defenses.

Those beaches, I knew, would be a living hell of pillboxes, dragon's teeth, tank trenches, land mines, sink holes, and mutated creatures that would defy all imagination or reason. A soldier could handle laser blasts and machine-gun nests, but try dealing with a six-year-old human child with the head of a bat coming at you carrying a satchel charge, or maybe a bulldozer chugging after you with fully functional human arms and legs grafted to the controls. I knew what the RIHMs were capable of —I had never forgotten the sight of Paul-John Fritz's head grafted onto a giant chickenhawk—and I shuddered to think what some fuzz-faced corporal would do when confronted by an enemy with the body of a woman and the head(s) of a Labrador retriever. Personally, I'd shit.

No, even with most of the RIHMs on a wild-goose chase up the coast, tomorrow would be a bloody day of trial by fire for the troops of FAC, and not everyone would come out of it alive or sane. Still facing the east, I raised the quart container of grog to the darkness.

"To victory," I said, then drank long and deep.

"Hey, old Scroat, save some of that for me!"

The teenage hoodlum had snuck up on me, and the sound of his voice caused some of the grog to go down the wrong pipe. I spent the next five minutes trying to clear a passage to my lungs. He spent the entire time pounding on my back while making comments about my inability to, quote—handle the hard stuff—unquote.

Providentially, I hadn't seen much of Doone since coming aboard. Security had whisked him away when I first landed the Harrier, and we'd been kept separated until I was able to tell my story. Jumpin Jack had informed me that since there had been no available space in Officer's Country, Johnny had been given a berth with the Black Gang—those crew members assigned to the Engineering Spaces. Doone had been there one day when a contingent of engineering chief petty officers had petitioned the *Payton*'s executive officer to either move the Canadian lad or face a mutiny.

Young John had subsequently gone through the other departments aboard the huge ship with like results until finally a private berth had been found for him in a paint locker about as far forward as one could get. I had been hoping against hope that he'd been washed overboard.

"How'd you find me?" I was finally able to choke.

"Hell, Colonel," the boy said cheerfully, "I only gotta look for that bird of yours back there when I want to trace your wax."

He gestured back down the flight deck where the shape of the

Harrier loomed out of the night. With the other quart of grog I'd filched from the wardroom, I'd bribed one of the crew-chiefs down on the 0-1 level to bring her on up on the aft elevator, telling him I wanted to be off early in the AM to lead the charge against the beaches. She now sat off to the far starboard side of the helo flight deck, out of the way and pretty much invisible in the darkness.

"Maybe it'd be a good idea if you unfound me, kid," I muttered. "I've got work to do, and it doesn't include you."

Doone made a snorting sound that was part laugh, part expectoration. "Anything's got ta do with cracklin RIHMs includes me, old Stuff, and that's a damn fact."

For once my temper got the best of me. I reached out and grabbed him by the front of his flight fatigues and drew him in close.

"Get this straight, Doone," I snarled. "You and me are no longer a team, do you understand? From now on I work alone. You want to waste RIHMs so bad? Then you go ashore in a Mike boat tomorrow morning with the landing force. Believe me, you'll get all the mutants you can handle on Malibu Beach."

"Oh yeah? And where will you be, Colonel?" Doone asked, apparently not the least bit impressed with my demonstration of Basic Hard-ass.

"That's none of your business. I've got some personal scores to settle in this thing, Doone. They don't concern you—at all. So scram, kid, before I toss you overboard."

I pushed the boy away, hard enough to make him lose his balance. He stumbled backwards, then regained his footing.

"Don't piss me off, old Muff," he said. "I made a promise before we left Motown. I promised Chandelier I'd look out for ya, and that's what I'm gonna do whether you like it or not. Far as I'm wired, you're a loonie that oughta be scrapped for salvage. But Chandelier, she thinks different. And what Chandelier thinks is what I'm goin on here. You and me is glued, old Elf. You gotta kill me to make it diff."

"Easy enough!" I shouted.

"Make yer play!" he answered.

I reached for the handgun in my shoulder holster, then thought better of it. Any commotion like the sound of a shot would alert someone on the *Payton*'s bridge to what I was about before I was ready. There was no alternative except to try to string him along.

"Aw, don't waste my time, John," I said as disgustedly as I could. "To Chandelier, I'm just another customer. A few drinks, a few laughs, a nude dance or two, then it's good-bye Plas-tex siding contractor from Columbus, hello toothpaste tube manufacturer from Peoria."

"You're wrong about that," Doone said. "She told me she's givin up the profession . . . just as soon as she earns enough to get you and her started in another life. Look, Colonel, I don't care all that much what happens to you myself, but Chandelier, she's like a big sister to me. She asked me ta look after ya, and that's what I gotta do. You can stand here and flap your chin till ya lose fifty-sixty pounds of flab and I'll still be in your pudding. So why don't ya save your breath and get to the—"

The handle of my 9mm pistol interrupted his speech as it came in contact with the side of his head. By the sound of the crack I figured he'd be out for the rest of the night at least.

But I had failed to take into account that not only did teenagers have skulls as hard and as thick as a bank vault, but that my trusty handgun was made almost entirely of plastic. I heard Doone groan, realized my hand was full of broken pieces of weapon, then felt a battering ram slamming into my belly. The air went out of me with an audible woosh and I suddenly found myself on my backside trying to get my lungs to work again. From far away, I thought I heard Doone talking to someone.

"Ding dong dammit!" he fumed. "That hurt, old Mung! You Evil Dunk, I think ya drew blood!" Suddenly, the voice was very close to my ear. "Listen to me, Colonel. Don't try no more of this monkey business, eh? I don't want ta hurt ya none. So do us a favor, what-say? You just let old Doone tag along with ya. That way Chandelier will be happy, I'll be happy, and you'll have somebody ta bitch at when you step on yer own cranker again. Ya see, old Skiff, I got the feelin that you're about to be flappin on out of here shortly. You can take me with ya, or have me report to the Flight Boss that an enemy agent is highjackin one of the *Payton*'s birds. All the firepower the *Sweetness* has, they'll blow you outta the sky in about half a sec."

The boy's sucker punch to my midsection had paralyzed my diaphragm. There are few things as scary as being unable to breath for periods over ten minutes so it was in a state of shock that I nodded to his request that he be allowed to once again tag along.

A few hours later, when I'd regained my breath and the night had descended with its full black shroud of concealment, Johnny Doone and I climbed aboard the Harrier and quietly went about our preflight. When the time seemed right, I juiced up the bird, flipped on IFF so the *Payton* would know we were a "friendly," then lifted off in the vertical mode.

I left the radios off. There was nothing anyone could say now to change things. Titanic forces had been put in motion, and there was far too much momentum already built up for anything to be slowed or stopped merely by the issuance of an order. The admiral and Jumpin Jack had only two choices: To shoot me down, or let me go. If they allowed me to fly away, they risked nothing. Even if I was a traitor, any information I might have would come too late to do the RIHMs any good. Considering the fact that any surface-to-air fireworks would most probably be spotted ashore by the enemy, I was pretty sure that Martha Jean and Jack would just decide to let me be.

And for once I was right.

When it felt as though we were at about five thousand feet, I eased the stick and rudder into a right turn and let the compass roll by until we were headed in a southeasterly direction that would take me to the cliffs of La Jolla.

19

The morning progressed like slow death. A dense blanket of fog, trapped by the high cliffs along the shore, refused to burn off. This stagnant bank of dull gray cotton stretched as far up and down the coast as we could see, and I knew that I'd soon have to make a decision about putting the Harrier down through it—a thought which had about as much appeal as neurosurgery performed with an ice ax. Still, there was nothing else for it. We were low on synfuel and had already waited almost four hours for a break.

Why "Mom" had picked the cliffs of La Jolla for her golden years, I didn't have the slightest idea; it certainly couldn't have been the morning view.

As Doone and I circled, our radios crackled with the sounds of the battle being fought one hundred and twenty miles to the north where the First Fleet's invasion force had hit the L.A. beaches an hour before dawn. The battle had begun while we were flying down from our overnight pit stop on San Clemente Island and continued as we circled the fog-bound cliffs just up the coast from San Diego. With nothing much else to do except dodge seagulls and wait for a break in the soup, Johnny and I monitored the fight on the TAC-1 and TAC-2 freqs. And as we listened, the genius of Martha Jean Jascoolie began unfolding like a tabloid Sunday supplement featuring women with giant breasts.

After a small diversionary fleet had hit Monterey Bay far up the coast, the first waves of the landing force had come skimming across the L.A. beaches in big ALHCs (Armored Landing Hover Craft) followed by a thousand AMTRACs, and before the RIHM defenders could wipe the sleep-slime from their eye stalks, a hundred thousand angry Americans were onshore, backed by a full complement of supporting arms, naval gunfire, and close air support.

The fighting was fierce, and the casualties were appalling but we were firmly established on dry ground.

Once it was clear to the RIHMs that the invasion was coming across the beaches of L.A., they committed the few remaining inland reserves that had not been sent north to Monterey Bay, rushing them to the front to deaden FAC's ever-building momentum. It was exactly the move Admiral Jascoolie had been waiting for. With the enemy's rear cleared out and reserves committed, she launched every helicopter in the Fleet in a classic vertical envelopment maneuver. Three motorized divisions of FAC commandos were thus deposited behind the RIHM lines and the enemy found themselves caught between the proverbial rock and a hard place.

Doone started getting real surly and cranky in the Harrier's backseat when he realized the significance of what he was hearing, upset I suppose because he was missing out on all the killing. I told him to hold his water, that there would be plenty of fighting left for all since it would take months to clear out the pockets of RIHM resistance in the L.A. basin alone, much less the entire state.*

Meanwhile, with the main-tank fuel gauge indicating Fumes Only and my kidneys about to explode from all the Nehi Orange I'd guzzled for breakfast, I made the decision to land. It would have been suicide to drop straight down through the fog bank laying over the cliffs, so I flew inland a few miles until the gray curtain broke just enough for me to spot a nice flat man-made plateau which, according to my Rand-McNally, had once been the site of a housing project called Strawberry Woods.†

"Sorry, Johnny," I said after putting the Harrier safely down, "this is where we part company."

"No way, Boss," he began to argue over the intercom. "Only way you can—"

"Shut up, boy, and listen. Even though we came in pretty damn low, there's still a chance the mutes spotted us on radar. Could be they'll send a patrol out looking for us. It's not likely, since the fucks are spread thin around these parts, but they still

---

* As I would personally discover almost a year later when I got smoked while leading a Cutter strike over Beverly Hills.

† In typical California fashion there were no strawberries, no woods, and no houses for that matter, just mile after mile of slag and rock and scorched earth. The Big Blast had pretty much made the California truth-in-place-naming law a moot one.

might get curious or lucky or both. I need you to stay here and guard the bird."

"Dammit, Colonel," the boy fumed, "I told ya I promised Chandelier I'd—"

"John, when the time comes, there's enough fuel in the reserve tanks to get us out of here free and clear. . . . But if anything happens to this aircraft, we'll both be dead men because there's no way we'll be able to fight our way through to our lines on foot. The RIHMs aren't likely to be looking for FAC action this far south, but like I said, if we were blipped, they might send out a small patrol just to be nosy. I'm trusting you to make sure if they do come sniffing they don't find anything but hot lead. Besides, I told you before . . . my business down here is personal." As if to emphasize what I'd said, I slipped the K-17 fighting knife out of its sheath on my calf and held it up for him to see.

"Aw shit, old Sock," the boy started to whine, "you got me totally confused! I thought you told me last night we were comin down here ta see your ma. What's the deal now with the blade? You fixin to open her can?"

Exactly. But I wasn't going to tell Johnny the truth, because for all his macho and bravado he was still a kid, a kid who would not understand why a man might find it necessary to gut his own mother—IF SHE REALLY WAS MY MOTHER—even if she was a RIHM.

"Hell no, kid!" I answered. "My God, that's the sickest thing I ever heard! No, see, the knife is for mutant parakeets—ugly disgusting things with the attached heads of small preschoolers! Horrible. Really horrible. Especially when they start singing the alphabet song!"

He thought I was crazy, I'm sure. Maybe I was, but there wasn't time to discuss it. Without any further explanation I jumped down from the aircraft and got my bufgun and a translation helmet out of the Harrier's small storage bay. Tight-lipped, I helped John rig the cammie net over the bird, made sure he was checked out on the M-249 SAW (Squad Automatic Weapon), and showed him where I kept all the junk food and extra pop. Finally, with the fog beginning to lift, I gave him his final instructions.

"Okay, John, I'm gonna tell you this once, and that's it. If I'm not back by nightfall, put the barrel of your pistol in your mouth and blow your head off. I've seen what these Western mutes can do with a prisoner. You think the Northern Horde was bad? Believe me, you don't want to be taken alive by these bastards, no way. They'll have you decked out in turkey wings and chicken thighs before you can fart the 'Tennessee Waltz.' Any questions?"

"Yeah," he said, pausing in midbite, "anymore Fritos?"

Lord help me, there was something I liked about that boy despite his crudeness, bad complexion, and arrogance. I guess he reminded me of myself at that age. Instead of slapping him silly, I grinned, gave him a thumbs-up signal, and stalked off towards La Jolla.

As I had suspected, the RIHM lines were very thin around the La Jolla–Mission Bay–Torrey Pines area, the rugged coastline there unsuitable for even the most daring amphibious assault and therefore not requiring a strong defensive force to protect it. Heading due west from where I'd landed the Harrier, I saw none of the enemy until I reached old Interstate 5 at which point I was forced to wait for a convoy of troops to pass. Obviously the news of the battle up north had reached the San Diego garrison, and they were on the way to aid their genetic siblings in L.A.

While I waited for the convoy to pass, I noticed something strange. Every once in a while a RIHM would come tumbling out of the cargo hold of one of the speeding vehicles, hit the pavement and bounce a few times until the body either reached the side of the highway or was creamed by the next vehicle in line. It was, I concluded, a weird way to be treating your troops on a day that'd you need every swinging reproductive part to fight. But hell, they were mutants, right? What did they know about the sanctity of life?

The long convoy of vehicles (which, I might add, were made from old scavenged MotorCraft parts, Firestone Steel-Belted radials, and living animal tissue) finally passed out of sight. I was about to slide down the canyon wall and cross the highway when another vehicle, this one as large as anything I had ever seen on tracs and resembling a cross between a front-end loader and a cement mixer, rumbled into view. Slowly and deliberately, the huge machine drove along and scooped up the RIHM carcasses that only moments before had fallen from the troop convoy. The poor wretches (some still alive) were then lifted and dropped into the huge revolving mixing element.

It wasn't until the machine passed me that I caught a glimpse of the inside of this crucible and saw it to be nothing more than a cauldron, a blast furnace full of fire and flame and an eerie orange-red glow of intense heat.

The RIHMs did not mess around with their war dead, I concluded. No warrior's grave in Arlington for them. No, sir. Just a quick trip to the communal oven. Slam-bam thank-you ma'am. Christ, based on what I was seeing, RIHMs didn't even wait until you were dead to fry your bod. Must've been great for morale. Still didn't explain why the unfortunate few had been tossed from the vehicles in the first place though. Probably caught porking the general's wife, how the hell should I know.

When the RIHM's Graves Registration Vehicle (as I had come to think of it) at last passed around a bend, I slid down the canyon wall and got across the highway as fast as I could. Before long I was climbing the steep grade on the other side, struggling against the knee-deep slag and waste. Like the rest of Southern California, nothing grew here, nothing lived except the RIHMs. It was moonscape, and I wondered again why FAC and the United States government wanted it back so badly. Sure, beachfront property might someday be worth something again, but it would be a cold day in hell before you could get a decent price for anything inland.

For just a moment I wondered why we just didn't let the RIHMs have it and be satisfied containing the bastards west of the Rockies as we had been doing since the late thirties. But I knew the answer. This was part of CONUS, part of the original fifty-five. No President, Congress, or Commandment of FAC was crazy enough to commit political suicide by writing off Southern California. No, we would retake our property with steel and blood because it was ours, and always had been.*

It must've been close to two in the afternoon when I finally reached the top of the coastal bluff overlooking La Jolla. By then the fog had burned off, and I got a breathtaking view of the Pacific as well as a glimpse of what a RIHM retirement community was all about.

* *Editor's Note:* Although a helluva lot of long-dead Indians and Mexicans might argue with the colonel on this point.

The dome-shaped huts, most made of organic waste bricks and
a translucent skinlike membrane, were scattered all over the
steeply sloping hillside, some attached to boulders and rock out-
croppings with strands of synthetic ligament and cartilage, others
clumped together in rough circles, which brought to mind holo-
graphs of ringworm I'd seen in a *Better Homes and Garden* medical reference book.

And everywhere were the totems, the horrid totems of the
Western RIHMs. If ever the human race needed an excuse to war
against the mutants, it was those abominations with their array of
artifacts dangling from the crossbars, artifacts like headless
Barbie dolls and yellowing denture plates and bones of men and
women just like you and me. Along with the gutted Sony
Walkmen and empty canisters of Comet cleanser and windblown
copies of *Photography Today,* were the dried scalps of human
beings and the shrunken heads of their pets. Skulls and ribcages,
picked so clean as to look like plastic, hung next to pieces of junk
mail and the hood ornaments of pre-Blast luxury cars. On one
pole I spotted the complete skeleton of a human infant hanging
next to an empty 2-liter bottle of Coke. Suspended from the very
top of this totem was a scalp that might've belonged to any one of
a hundred thousand tall blue-eyed blond fashion models. The
golden strands of hair drifted lazily in the gentle breeze, a breeze
that also rattled the bones like some macabre set of wind chimes.

I shuddered at the sound. Anger, revulsion, fear—all played
their part in how I felt at that moment as I checked one last time
to ensure the bufgun was locked and loaded. I adjusted the volume control on the translation helmet, and then, without too
much worry about if and how I might ever get out of what I was
getting into, I began a hut-to-hut search-and-destroy mission.

At least that's what I had in mind when I started. After about
six huts, I came to the conclusion that someone had beaten me to
the punch. All I found were dead RIHMs.

What had killed them was not visibly apparent; perhaps it was
some sort of strokelike reaction to the bad news coming from up
north. A few of the creatures were sprawled across their floors as
if stricken suddenly without warning, yet most were lying balled-
up on their mattresses as though death had come as no surprise.
While there is no way to "read" the expression of a RIHM, I got

the impression from the contorted shapes and gapping mouth holes that they'd all died in agony.

I was halfway through the village when I spotted my first live one, a big sucker exiting a hut while carrying a speargun and an old TV set. When he saw me, he dropped the tube and began fumbling with the rubber bands on the speargun. I waited patiently until he'd loaded and cocked the thing before I leveled the bufgun and blew his bowels to Escondido.

It was a good clean kill and it renewed my flagging spirits. Maybe the RIHM claiming to be my mother was still alive after all. Quickly but carefully, I worked my way down the slope towards the beach, growing more and more sure that I would find her living close to the water's edge. She was, after all, an Island RIHM and not as apt to opt for the high ground as her avian-oriented cousins.

I found her in a small structure made of sea-tortoise shells and old beer bottles and what appeared to be the same kind of sticky shit I'd found in the Northern Horde headquarters back in Windsor. She was administering to another RIHM at the time, a Western version layed out on a cot. By the sounds of hacking and gurgling, I had to figure the patient was fast approaching check-out time.

I stood in the doorway for a second, surprised a little that this last part of my mission had been so easy. There was little doubt that this was the RIHM who claimed to be my ma, for she had that gray-green reptilian skin of the Island RIHMs as well as the telltale tentacles bunched around her shoulders. Still, I could've been wrong since they all look the same to me. Only one way to find out.

"Darvon?" I called out softly.

She turned her head—or at least turned the part that I assumed was her head—and I was sure I heard a little cry or gasp. "Oh my," the translation helmet deciphered. "Will? Is that you, Will Bucko?"

"Yes, that's right," I answered. "There's a nasty rumor going around that you claim to be my mother."

"Yes, I'm afraid that's true," Darvon gurgled and grunted. "Only it isn't a rumor. Far from it. I'm sorry, son, but it was time you knew."

"Well, pardon the hell out of me if I say I don't believe a

goddamn word of it," I said smoothly. "Not that it matters much. One way or the other, you're puppy chow, lady."

I brought the bufgun up so the muzzle lined up with her midsection. There was no missing my intention, yet the one called Darvon didn't make a move to escape. Instead, she wheezed something the translation helmet didn't immediately pick up.

"What was that?" I asked, not really interested but enjoying the opportunity to prolong her torture.

"I said why do you hate me so much?"

"Hate you?" I chuckled snidely. "Lady, I don't even fuckin *know* you! But if there is the slightest chance that you and I are somehow related then I'm duty bound to end this little tragedy with a bufgun slug to your main-housing."

"My God," she snapped, "like father, like son. I should have known."

"What kind of crack is that?" I kind of exploded. "Don't be bad-mouthing Wolf Bucko in front of me, you slime-shute. *You* were the one who walked out on us, remember?"

"And what choice did I have?" For some mutant about to eat lead, Darvon was showing no signs of begging for mercy. Far from it. "For your information, young man, your father was a foul-mouthed drunken bigot who used to knock the both of us around pretty good if I recall correctly. Sure, I walked out on the creep, and I tried to take you with me, but he got a court order and came and got you. There wasn't anything I could do! The judge did not take kindly disposition towards a woman trying to make it as a street mime in New York City!"

I shook my head in amazement. "Ya know, you ought to write all this down. This is real top-notch tear-jerker stuff. You could probably sell it to ABC as a movie of the week."

"Don't be such a putz," she said weakly. "Oh, well . . . it really doesn't matter anyway. If you've come all this way to kill me, go ahead, get it over with."

Sound advice, but I wasn't about to let her go that easily. "Wolf Bucko had his faults," I said, "but he was the greatest jet-jock that FAC ever had. A lot of people have told me so."

One of her tentacles uncurled, and she waved it at me as though delivering a lecture. "Just because he could fly a high-performance aircraft by the seat of his pants doesn't mean he was a good human being, Will. In the air he was a god. On the ground he was a nasty, vile, self-centered chauvinist who was addicted to booze and speed and a few other chemicals you've probably never heard of. I understand he once shot your dog's leg off."

I was stunned. I had been almost thirteen when Pop blew Tripod's paw away with a .38 Special for peeing on his dress shoes. That was a good ten years after my real ma had boogied out on us. "How the hell did you know that?" I blurted.

In the back of my mind I had never really wanted to believe Frank Tibbs's accusation that my ma had become Darvon the RIHM, figuring it was most likely some scheme hatched to coerce me into throwing in with the enemies of mankind. But the more I talked with this creature, the more my doubts mounted. Maybe—God help me—maybe she really was my mother.

"Oh, even after I went through the changes, I kept in touch with old friends," she said, almost—but not quite—happily. "Frank Tibbs mostly. After your father died I wanted to get in touch with you, but it looked as though you were going to make a career in FAC and we decided that the last thing a FAC officer needed in his promotion file was the fact that his mother was a RIHM."

"So why tell me now?" I gulped. "I know I could've gone to my grave happy without knowing. Why now?"

"Selfishness, I guess. I just wanted you to know that I loved you. I'm dying, you see."

"You got that right," I said, once again pulling a bead with the buf. I felt no guilt. The least a son could do, I thought, was put his ma out of her misery. I would've done the same for a wounded hound so why not render the same humane service to something that had once been my own flesh and blood. My finger tightened on the trigger, but I did not pull. A few things were still nagging at me.

"Let me ask you this," I said, lowering the bufgun's muzzle, "before I end your misery. Were you and Uncle Frank getting it on behind my father's back? Was that the reason Tibbs became a traitor?"

Darvon made a strange honking sound that the translation helmet had trouble with—it came out something like "Please die a horrible death with seaweed plugging your colon."

"Now you listen to me, Will Bucko," she bristled. "I'm really disappointed that you would even suggest such a thing, but I guess that's so typically human, and so typically 'Bucko.' You know nothing about Frank Tibbs so you have no right to call him a traitor."

It was my turn to get a little hot under the collar. "Bull-loney! He was Pap's wingman, but he hung the Wolf out to dry over San Jose! He went over to the enemy and took his Cutter with him! He led the massacre at Scottsbluff! He tried to help Carlos Membranous take over the Gulf! Hell, he was up north just a few months ago assisting the invasion of Motown! Hey, lady, if that ain't being a traitor, I like to know what is!"

"He saved your life more than once" was her predictable response.

"I never asked him to," I said as calmly as I could.

Darvon seemed to wrap her tentacles more tightly to her body as if holding herself down. When she spoke, the tone suggested the same. "Frank Tibbs was forced to make a choice that I hope you will never have to make," she said. "Did you know he had a family?"

"Who? Uncle Frank? Come on, he was a bachelor."

"You're wrong. Before the Big Blast, he had a wife and three children. They were visiting relatives in Los Angeles when the missiles came."

"So were forty million other tourists," I said, truthfully but facetiously.

"My word," Darvon gargled, "you still don't get it, do you? You know nothing of our kind. Yes, forty million were killed, just on this coast. But others who were not at ground-zero survived, and their molecules, their DNA, their very structural being was irreversibly altered by the radiation storm and the chemical elements already polluting the air. These survivors became the first members of—"

And here she made some sound that translated badly into *"the ones who were reformed."*

"It took years," she continued, "but when Frank finally got the proof that his wife and children still lived—albeit in a different form—he was faced with the choice: to stay in FAC and perhaps kill his own family, or come over and fight to protect them against a world gone mad. He made the only decision a sane being could; he chose family over country."

"Aw, save your Robert E. Lee stories for bedtime, Ma. The fact remains, Tibbs was responsible for Pop's death."

"That's not true, boy," a gargling, gasping rasp came from the cot where the ill RIHM lay. It took a second for me to realize that the words had come through the helmet without translation. "I told the Wolf what I was up to before we launched that day," the RIHM went on. "It was his own decision to go into San Jose bareback."

The thing on the cot then proceeded to go into a coughing fit that was sure to result in bronchial cells being spewed on the ceiling. Darvon rushed to administer to him, and I was left standing like the often-mentioned chicken by the side of the road.

I'm not sure when it finally dawned on me that the babbling RIHM in the hut with us was none other than Major Frank Tibbs. His metamorphosis from human to mute was nearly complete, and the final bit of restructuring was obviously tearing him a new asshole. From where I stood, I could see the gaping cavity of what had once been his chest, now an open runny sore full of blue-green organ meat and purple tubing and putrid flesh dripping with an oily brown goop that reminded me of FAC mess hall gravy. His head had taken the general shape of a pup tent and the numerous eye stalks, jutting up at all angles and heights, appeared to be fully developed.

Frank screamed then, a horrible wailing scream of agony. His spine bowed and for a moment I thought he would actually break himself in two. Daryon wrapped two of her tentacles around him and held him down until the spasm passed.

"Yes, it's me, Will," he croaked. "I guess to human eyes it's pretty awful, huh? The conversion is more difficult for some than for others. It has taken me more than twenty years and I'm still not there."

By this time I'd managed to accept the reality of this unfolding nightmare, but the idea was still staggering: Mom a RIHM, Frank a RIHM, who the hell would be next?

"Even going into San Jose alone your pa would've been all right," Tibbs whistled, "if he hadn't burned up most of his ordnance trying to nail my butt. I tell you now, I was sorely sorry to hear he'd bought the ranch. He and I were like brothers."

"Kiss my ass, Frank," I said. "You knew the kind of jock Wolf was better than anybody, so you knew damn well that nothing would keep him from his mission, not even being out of ammo."

"That's just not—"

I cut him off. "No no no. I don't wanna hear it. Hey, listen, I can understand family loyalty. If Darvon is telling the truth, then I can understand you going over and joining your wife and family. But you've gotta understand—the both of you—that family loyalty works both ways."

With that I took three fast strides across the tiny room and stood over the abomination that had once been Frank Tibbs. I raised the bufgun, hit the charging rod, then jammed the barrel into the creature's feeding hole.

"Will!" I heard Darvon shriek. "What are you doing? Are you insane?"

"No, Ma," I said, "but Pap's dying wish was that someday I would splatter Uncle Frank's brain matter over hell and creation. Nothing personal, you understand, Major, just family loyalty."

I felt Darvon's tentacles reaching out and grasping me, trying to pull me away. But it was too late. I pulled the buf's trigger, and Wolf Bucko was finally and forever avenged. If you expected anything less, then you haven't understood a single thing I've written.

20

I kinda expected Mom to get a little more upset. Not only had I murdered Uncle Frank in cold blood, but had pretty well screwed up the entire interior of her home. I mean, the hollowpoint bufgun round had spread Frank Tibbs around six ways from Tuesday and if there was one square foot of that hut not decorated with RIHM slime after the big chunks had come to rest I'll eat my FAC piss-cutter.

I waited outside for Darvon to complete her cleanup as well as work her way through the traditional RIHM death wail. Ideally, the whole community would have gathered for the ceremony, but today no one showed up. I figured it was because they were all either dead in their homes or off playing golf.

Yeah, okay, I'll admit it: while I waited for her to finish knashing her beak and gashing her leg-pods with dull oyster shell and crushing tentacle tips between stones of pumice, I began to feel a little guilty. In truth, Frank Tibbs had saved my life at least twice that I was sure of: once at Yaki Point (see Volume One), once at the sinking of Paradise Cove (see Volume Two). Maybe I'd been a little too quick on the trigger.

On the other hand, not only had he selfishly converted to RIHMdom for personal reasons, but he'd messed Melodie Lane up pretty bad and had been less than a sweetheart to me during our last meeting in Windsor.

No, I finally concluded, he'd jolly well gotten what he had coming to him, and that was that. He'd made the choice to become a mutant of his own free will, just as I'd made the choice to blow his fucking head off. And I ask you—what are we fighting for if it isn't the right of free will?

Besides, no matter how he'd tried to reshape the truth, Frank Tibbs had been directly responsible for my father's death. Even with only RIHM sludge running through his veins, Frank should've known blood was thicker than water . . .

At last, after the most god-awful racket I think I'd ever heard, Mother finished her song to the dead and came out of the hut, her tentacle tips all bandaged and the pod gashes all stitched up. I was ready for a real chewing-out (figuratively and literally), but got one hell of a surprise instead.

"Thank you, son," she said, her grunts sounding hoarse from all the death-wailing she'd been through. "I don't think I could've taken much more."

I was absolutely dumbfounded. "Wha-wha-what?" I stammered. Was she actually *thanking* me for waxing Tibbs? "Excuse my ignorance, Ma, but it seems I recall you doing your damndest to stop me!"

"Well, of course!" she answered as if the whole thing was obvious. "I couldn't very well appear to be *encouraging* you, now could I? Frank was a dear dear friend. What would he have thought of me if he heard me telling you to blow his tootle off? Just would not have been proper."

For a moment I was sure the only act left remaining to me was to turn the buf on myself and get it over with. Obviously there was no way I was ever going to catch up to all the crazy absurdity constantly hatching around me.

"Damn it, Ma!" I finally blurted. "Are you saying you *wanted* Uncle Frank dead?"

"Now I didn't say that," she seemed to scold. "If there had been any other way, I would have welcomed it. But . . ." She paused and turned her large lumpy body to face the slope behind us. "Did you see them in their huts when you came down?" she asked.

"The dead ones?"

"Yes."

"I was meaning to ask you about that."

Sluggishly, Darvon began moving towards the trail leading back up the bluff. "Come on," she said. "I'll escort you out of here. There might be a few troops left around. I thought I heard a shot. Just before you arrived."

"Yeah," I said, "I had to plug a live one that drew down on me."

"A looter probably," Darvon said. "The security troops travel in squads, so it was probably a looter. They show up every once in a while. Their greed is more powerful than their fear of the Fever."

"Fever?"

"Technically speaking—psittacosis. Also known as parrot fever, a virus disease of parrots and related birds communicable to man. Unfortunately, it is also communicable to the Ones Who Were Reformed . . ." Darvon paused. When she spoke again there was a discernible anger in her voice. "Especially those who continued to worship and experiment with birds even after the disease and its cause became known to us. Now, as you can see, their religious fanaticism is killing us off wholesale! There is no cure, Will. The People Who Were Reformed are doomed!"

"Hey, that's a tough break, Ma," I said, trying to control the desire to break out in song. "That explains Uncle Frank's condition then. Parrot fever. Who would have ever thought he'd come to such an end."

Darvon had continued lumbering up the trail. "Oh no," she said. "Frank didn't have the Fever. He had syphilis. Syphilis killed him. We get that too. From infected toilet seats."

The laughter bubbling in my gut was almost impossible to contain as I recalled an old joke. When I spoke I could hardly keep a straight face.

"Syphilis huh? Wait a minute, Ma. Technically speaking—wasn't Frank Tibbs a major?"

"That's right."

"Well hell! He couldn't have died of syphilis!"

"Why not?"

" 'Cause, the way I heard it, syphilis is a disease of the *privates!*"

At which point I completely lost it. I fell down and began pounding the slag with my fists, laughing as hard as I ever had in my whole life. I laughed until my belly muscles cramped and my face was wet with tears and my jaw felt as though it was in a vice.

Finally, when I could stand the pain no more, I gave one last chuckle and rolled over on my back. Darvon, who hadn't made a sound since I delivered the punchline to the oldest joke in FAC, stood over me. As might be expected from a creature that was a cross between a squid and the Creature from the Black Lagoon, there was no way to read her expression, but from the tone of her gurgles I determined she was a little disgusted.

"By the sacred water snakes," the helmet translated, "are YOU a chip off the old block!" One of her great tentacles uncurled and lifted me to my feet. "Come on," she said, "before I forget I'm your mother and extract all your vital body fluids."

She continued to trudge up the hill and I followed.

So, I thought, parrot fever was killing off the RIHMs. It explained the dead ones in the huts, and it also explained the RIHM soldiers I'd seen being dumped off the troop transports. Damn! They were fighting a war against the human race while at the same time being slaughtered by a bird disease. Such irony. Paul-John Fritz would've loved it.

And talk about life imitating art! I was pretty sure H. G. Wells had used a similar plot gimmick in *War of the Worlds*. But hell, that was just a story! This was the real thing!

I heard Darvon speaking again through my earphones. "I know Frank tried to get you to take the cure," she said. "To become one of us. I'm so glad—the way things turned out—that you decided not to."

"Yeah, you and me both," I gasped. The climb was kicking my tail.

"I mean," Darvon continued, "it would have been nice. You and Melodie could've come here for visits. We could've gotten to know one another again. Yet I suppose it just wasn't meant to be. You have your own life to live."

The climb was definitely taking its toll on me. I was huffing and puffing and sucking wind like a heart-lung transplant candidate so I was not really listening to her. Suddenly an awful thought struck me.

"Hey, Ma. This fever . . . do you . . . are you . . ."

"Do I have it? Yes, I'm afraid so," she answered without breaking stride. "It takes longer with my tribe—the Ones Who Are Like Octopus—but I've already got a dose. The medicos give me a month, maybe two, then . . . well, it'll be time for the great aquarium in the sky."

"I'm sorry to hear that," I said.

It seemed like the right thing to say, although I wasn't sure if it was true. Let's face it, even if she was my mother, there really hadn't been much time for any significant bonding. On the other hand, I was beginning to like this creature. Probably because of her dry sense of humor and wit which seemed so much like mine. And I'd always imagined I'd gotten it from Pa.

"Don't worry, Will," she said. "When the time comes, I've got some pills I can take. Then I'll just go to sleep. None of the macho crap Frank insisted on. He said he wanted to be clear-headed and alert when he died. Well, he got his wish, I guess."

We continued to climb and before too long I could barely breath so I left all the talking to Darvon. She told me stories about her early years with Dad, about her days in New York City trying to get into show business, and how she'd gone to Cuba just before the Big Blast and how distressed and angry she was when the Limited Nuclear Exchange caused the cancellation of her first dramatic role, that being "Woman—the Oppressed Figurehead of War Mongering Capitalism" in Juanita Jumbulya's scathing musical *Cuban Holiday.*

I'd seen the PBS version of the play on vid-tape. It was pure propaganda horseshit—almost as bad as a Red Chinese ballet—but I didn't tell Darvon that. Come on, she had enough problems for pete's sakes!

And then, as though some short circuit in the house lights had finally been fixed, something Darvon had said earlier finally flick-ered and then came on with an almost blinding flash. If I'd heard what I thought I'd heard, the possibilities were bone-chilling. Right there, three quarters of the way up the trail, I stopped in my tracks.

"Yo, Ma," I called out. "What exactly did you mean when you said *Melodie* and I could've come to visit? Why'd you include her?"

Darvon ground to a halt and slowly turned. She seemed to study me for a few moments, and I suppose my concern was pretty apparent. "My dear boy," she said kindly, "I thought you knew."

"Knew what?" I could feel my heart trying to break out of my chest like that nasty little creature in *Alien.*

"That Melodie Lane is one of us, One Who Was Reformed. Didn't Frank tell you? He administered the cure while she was staying with us in Windsor."

Well, cut my legs off at the knees and kick me in the head! Mom's news knocked me flat on my keister, and I thought for a second that I would be physically sick. Visions of Melodie in that cocoon back in Frank's room at Northern RIHM Headquarters —all the slime and sticky goop and stink—streamed through my mind, and I had no problem at all believing what Ma had just

told me was true. Yes, Melodie too was a RIHM, or would be
shortly. Good grief. This story had to end soon, I decided, or I
was going to end up like a box of No-Salt Saltines—completely
crackers.

"Don't take it so hard," Ma soothed, sensing my anguish.
"There are worse things that could've happened to her. Would
you have rathered they skinned her out and hung her from one of
our totems? Would you have preferred that her living body was
used as a nesting place for our young larvae? No, of course not.
Besides, what's done is done. There's nothing you can do."

Even though the term *young larvae* was probably redundant,
overall she was absolutely correct, and I realized that. Still, the
news shook me pretty badly, and I guess I sorta broke down. For
twenty years I'd harbored a secret belief that one day Melodie
and I would get together and begin producing offspring the likes
of which the world had never seen. With the bad news delivered
by Darvon, that cherished dream suddenly loomed as almost a
nightmarish certainty.

I think my subsequent ranting and raving and railing to the
heavens were more in frustration than anything else. Maybe I
was a little heartbroken—sure, who wouldn't be when the love of
one's life is declared to be a mutant? On the other hand, I still
had Chandelier waiting in the wings, and even before this bad
news from Mom the lady with the ta-ta's of steel had begun to
look a whole lot better to me than poor old battered and bruised
Melodie Lane. Yeah, now that I think back on it, I was simply
showing my frustration over the loss of another old friend when I
began beating my helmeted head against that boulder next to the
trail leading out of La Jolla. Anybody thinks different has got this
tall tale confused with some goddamn pulp romance novel.

Speaking of pulp, despite the plastic of the translation helmet
I'd fairly well done a serious number on my forehead when I felt
Darvon's tentacles wrap around my body and gently pull me
away from the blood-splattered stone. Through my sobs I could
hear her soothing voice as she drew me away from my pain and
into her bosom.

"There there, my son," she said, "everything is going to be all
right. Believe your old Mum who knows from personal experience—there's more than one fish in the sea. You'll find someone
else . . . eventually."

Funny, even though I felt a little awkward at first wrapped in the tentacles of an Island RIHM, and even though up close Ma smelled like several tons of heated fish fertilizer, there was something very comforting in her embrace. For just a moment I felt as though all my troubles and pain were being transferred, as though a heavy field transport pack filled with forty-odd years of excess baggage was being lifted from my shoulders, to be toted awhile by someone else. It was a good feeling, a feeling of safety and comfort. Maybe even love, who the hell knows.

Not me. Discoveries like that take time, and time was something that I was not going to get. Still tightly held in her motherly embrace, I stiffled my blubbering and looked up at her.

"Thanks, Ma," I said.

A split second later I watched the top of her head explode in a mist of gray-green gore. I remember she groaned—it sounded almost human—then crumpled, taking me with her beneath her bulk. And that was it. Mercifully, she never knew what hit her; she was dead before her bottom touched the ground.

Shoot—I remember thinking—orphaned again.

No doubt about it, Darvon was dee-dee. And I would've shared the same fate if the boy hadn't managed to hack his way through to me before I suffocated. In the last throes of her life, Darvon's tentacles had involuntarily contracted, squeezing me to her body protectively with bands of steel cable. I'd have been a goner for sure if Johnny hadn't chopped through to me with such speed and determination. Of course, he made a hell of a mess in the process which only added to my ever-increasing sense of loss.

"Hey, there you are, Old Lug!" he shouted excitedly when he'd at last axed his way through to me. "Figured you was tinned meat, eh? Old Johnny came through for ya though, eh? Skunked this 'un with one shot from the blooper a hundred yards up the trail! Seen ya was in trouble so I let her rip. Damn fine shot, if I do say so myself."

I couldn't speak. He managed to tug me out from beneath what was left of my mother and then pulled me over into some shade. I was covered with gore and RIHM snot and a lot of stuff that was totally unidentifiable, but it didn't seem to bother the kid. He pulled my helmet off and held a small flask up to my lips while he lifted my head with his other hand. I drank.

"BLOODY HELL!" I sputtered, spitting the revolting stuff on the ground. "WHAT IN THE—WHAT IS THAT STUFF?"

"Bubblegum Schnapps," he answered, apparently mystified as well as angered by my reaction. "And you won't be getting anymore of it, ya ungrateful twit. Stuff costs six credits a gallon, even at the FAC Package Store."

"Damn it, boy," I fumed, "I thought I ordered you to stay with the Harrier."

"Yeah, mebbe you did, old Dump, but I ran out of chow and came out lookin for a refill."

"By God, Doone, you've gone too far this time! If you can't obey the orders of your elders then you can damn well find some other poor bastard to plague with your company! I'll have no more of it!"

Admittedly, I was upset. Quite a bit of real bad shit had gone down over the last few hours, and I was sensitive to most of it, perhaps overly so. Still, the boy had willfully disobeyed my orders. I looked around for my bufgun.

"Jeez, Colonel," the boy complained, "you sure are a two-faced sumbitch, ya know that? Here I go and save your tail from a RIHM about to snuff your act, and all you can do is wrankle about some friggin order. You can kiss my richard, old Tuck, and I mean that sincerely."*

I was about to yell at him that rather than saving my life he'd murdered my mother. Then I thought better of it. The fewer number of people who knew my family history, the better. Never knew when I'd decide I might like to run for high public office. Better Ma's skeleton remained in the closet—locked and bolted from the inside.

"And anyways," Doone went on, a real disgusted look on his always sour teenage face, "I came after ya because I got a message over the squawker, not because I was hungry—though I am. It was from FAC—your pal the admiral, in fact. She said for me to come find you and tell you to get your butt up north ASAP. Place called Anaheim."

"Anaheim? What the hell is so important about Anaheim? It doesn't even have a beach."

---

* As Doone used to tell me with a leer and a *Monty Python*-style wink-wink, "richard" was long for "dick."

"That I don't know, Colonel, not being in charge of the overall invasion. I was monitoring the radio all afternoon and it sure sounded to me like FAC was going through the RIHMs like an acetylene torch through butter substitute. Then all of a sudden they stopped. About a half hour later, they were puttin in the long-distance call to you. Sounded impatient when they got through. Admiral said something about it being your chance to save the human race."

"Damn!" I groaned. "Again?"

The boy just looked at me and grinned.

"Oh well," I said, drawing in a deep breath, "let's get to it then. Help me up, will ya, kid?"

With Johnny's help I got to my feet and shook out the cobwebs. There was no necessity for any real hurry. I knew FAC could wait—the parrot fever would be more effective than any ten FAC divisions at rolling back the enemy, and once Admiral Jascoolie heard about the plague infecting the RIHMs I was sure she would break off contact and just let what was left of the mutants' army rot on the vine. No more fine young men and women in FAC blue and gray would have to die; all they had to do to win was sit back and let nature take its course.

In the meantime, I had one last chore to perform.

"Look around in these huts and see if you can find a couple of shovels, kid," I said to Doone.

"Shovels?" The boy sounded as though I'd just asked him to jam a Plas-tex straw up his peter. "What do we need shovels for? Is this another one of your—"

"Johnny," I said as gently as I could, "please do what I ask without a lot of your usual crap, okay? Otherwise, son, so help me, I'll cave in your skull and have your brains for breakfast. Am I coming through loud and clear?"

"Yeah, Colonel," he said slowly, "five-by-five." I think he could read me well enough by then to know I meant business.

We buried my mother a little farther up the slope, where the view was better. I suspected it was what she would've wanted, being a creature of the sea and all. We stacked rocks over the grave and I fashioned a cross out of some cardboard and Elmer's glue I found in one of the huts. It would undoubtedly be destroyed the first time the rains came, but that didn't bother me much. It was the gesture itself which counted, just like everything else in life.

Doone thought I was loony-tunes of course—burying a RIHM under the symbol of Christianity like that, and then observing a moment of silence. It could very well be that he was right, yet looking back on it today, to my mind it remains one of the few decent things I've ever done.

"Good-bye, Ma," I whispered just before I followed Johnny up the trail. "It was nice knowing ya."

21

Using what little synfuel the Harrier had in reserve, and throttling down almost to stall speed, the boy and I made Anaheim in about an hour. A FAC air controller vectored us in on top of the invasion force's headquarters and even before the turbine had whined down Doone and I were out of the cockpit.

While John wandered off in search of some chow, I was escorted to the fly tent where Admiral Jascoolie and General Throckmorton "Blue Thunder" Bottomly were in conversation. The fact that the admiral was ashore alerted me that something fairly heavy was going down.

"Here he is now," I heard Martha Jean say as she glanced up and spotted me. "Come right over here, Colonel Bucko," she called out over the hubbub and controlled confusion common to any field headquarters in the midst of battle. "Have you met the Commander of Ground Forces?" she asked as I approached. "General Bottomly this is Will Bucko."

"Blue Thunder" and I had never met yet I knew his reputation. He was one tough hard-nosed sonuvabitch, as the empty right sleeve attested. The missing arm—so the legend went—had been torn from his body by a RIHM many years before during a night assault on his laser battery's position in the Cascades. Legend further had it that the then Sergeant Bottomly took one look at the blood spurting from his shoulder, ordered up a flame thrower, used it to cauterize his wound, then led the successful counterattack that wiped out a whole battalion of RIHMs.

Total bullshit of course, but what legend isn't?

The troops called him "Blue Thunder" because of his dark complexion. It was said that when he got angry his face actually got darker, going from ebony to blue-black, the same color as the sky during a serious midsummer boomer.

"General," I said, shaking his hand, "I think I've got some good news for you. You too, Admiral."

Quickly and succinctly, I briefed them on what I had learned about the RIHM plague and its devastating effect on the enemy. "From what I saw earlier today," I said, "they're dropping like household pests in an Orkin commercial. All you've got to do is sit tight. In a few days, a week, all you'll have left is a little mopping up, maybe some raking and shoveling, at the very most a little spade work. No offense, General."

Bottomly scowled and glanced over at the admiral. "That's good news, Colonel," he said, not sounding quite as thrilled as I would have expected, "only that's not our problem at the moment. We've got the enemy well under control."

"You see, Will, it's not because of the RIHMs that I ordered you forward," the admiral jumped in. "Throckmorton's forces have already driven the survivors deep into the Hollywood Hills where they will be easy pickins for us when we get a firmer foothold ashore."

"What about all those divisions of mutes you tricked into moving up to Monterey Bay?" I asked. "They must've heard by now that we're ashore in strength down here. Aren't you concerned that they'll mount a counterattack? Like I said, this parrot fever shit has so far only infected a small percentage. They can still mount a stiff offensive."

Behind her strong corrective lenses, the admiral's lovely gray eyes seemed to sparkle. "Tut tut, one step ahead of you, Colonel," she bragged. "Even as we speak, every available aircraft in General Cy Skoff's Central Command is in the process of slaughtering those RIHMs we lured up to Monterey. Caught them by total surprise, strung out on the Pacific coast highway trying to get back down to L.A. Southern California is ours!"

I could tell by the tone of her voice that she was as pleased as polecat piss with the way her plan had been going. And I couldn't blame her. If she pulled it off she'd be placed right up there with other military geniuses in American history like Stonewall Jackson, Douglas MacArthur, Chester Nimitz, and Wonton Phelps.

"No, our problem is not with the mutants, Colonel Bucko," the admiral went on, suddenly arching her plucked eyebrows to a more worried position. "It's with Ramases."

For a moment the name startled me. In all that had gone on over the last few days, I'd almost forgotten that evil scuzz-sucker. Suddenly, however, my body and brain were jangled with a not unfamiliar surge of pure adrenaline. Ramases. He was the last brush stroke in the portrait of revenge I'd been painting since the

Comancheros had nailed Black Pugh to the palm tree in Puta
Madre.

"So the bastard finally surfaced," I muttered. "Where is he?"

"He and about three hundred of his closest friends are holed
up on the grounds of an old amusement park," Blue Thunder
answered. "We've got him surrounded."

"Then I'd suggest taking him the easy way," I said. "Vector a
flight of B-1C's over his ass. Vaporize him with a few ten-thou-
sand pounders. No fuss, no muss, no bother."

"My sentiments exactly," the general agreed. "Only, we've got
a situation. Major Hogg," he called across the busy tent to a
muscle-bound woman with an FP brassard who looked like she
lifted trunk engines in her spare time, "bring in the prisoner."

They must have kept the guy stashed just outside the tent,
waiting for his big entrance, because after only a few moments
Major Hogg returned dragging my old pal Marvin the blue-eyed
Oriental by his stacking swivel. The muscular major deposited
him in front of the general and without prompting tore the swath
of gaffer's tape from Marvin's mouth. Judging by the pieces of
flesh and lip that came off with the tape, I suspected it was as
painful as a sulfuric acid douche.

"Tell us again, you mange maggot," the general snapped.
"Quickly and truthfully if you value your life."

Marvin had been glaring at me ever since he'd been brought in.
He smiled a nasty little smile. "I need a butt," he said.

Blue Thunder reached in his pocket, pulled out a pack of
Kools, extracted a cigarette, then jammed it as far up Marvin's
left nostril as it would go. Needless to say, Marvin screamed
bloody murder, but he got the picture and soon was spilling his
guts.

"Ramases, he's got a major nuke warhead. Ten megaton job.
Had it for years. Got it out of a MX silo out in Nebraska. He's
got the serial number if you wanna run a computer check. Says
unless his conditions are met, he's gonna let it off and start this
whole damn thing all over again."

I knew immediately what Marvin meant. A nuclear explosion
of that magnitude would undoubtedly result not only in thou-
sands of FAC casualties, but the possible creation of another line
of RIHMs, a line unsusceptible to bird diseases, maybe a line
unsusceptible to anything. Just as the original RIHMs had come

out of the various and distinct radioactive soups of the Big Blast, so too might a new line of creatures develop if another nuclear weapon was detonated. And, as Marvin had so aptly put it, the whole damn thing—the battles, the fights for survival, the wars between mute and man—would start over again.

Neither Admiral Jascoolie nor General Bottomly said anything, so I knew they'd already heard the punch line to Ramases' message. I had a sneaking suspicion what it might be, but I had to go and ask anyway.

"So what's the deal, Marvin?"

He really gave me the once over then, with his evil hate-filled eyes that reminded me of YMCA swimming pools just before the tiny tots were allowed to jump in for their morning swim and ablution.

"Ramases wants an escort to the Mexican border," Marvin said, "for him and his boys, otherwise he blows up the world. But before that, he wants Will Bucko to come and see him. Says he wants to talk about a deal that went sour. Says to send Will Bucko to him—alone—or he blows up the world."

Yup. Just about what I was expecting. Christ, what a shitty day. I let my breath escape in a long hissing exhalation, then glanced over at Blue Thunder. Once again, I didn't have to ask.

"We checked," the general said. "Warhead and detonator are on the missing nuke list—a MIRV that got misplaced back when the collection was conducted. I'm afraid we have to go under the assumption that Ramases is telling the truth."

"Will," the admiral said, putting a kind wrinkled hand on my shoulder. "Even though you are still a breveted FAC lieutenant colonel and subject to your oath of office, I cannot order you to go in there. Cannot and will not. To comply with Ramases' demand would quite probably mean certain death for you, and I will not have that on my conscience. But my, oh my, Will! Think of the time you would buy us! Time, my boy! A precious commodity! Time to evacuate, pull our forces far enough back so that even if that psycho *does* detonate, we'll be able to deal with the fallout, keep contamination to a minimum. So what do you say, Will? You got any balls or what?"

I didn't answer. The wheels and gears were clinking in my brain. Was there any way I could worm my way out of this predicament, I wondered?

"Come on, Bucko," Blue Thunder snapped, "it's not like you've got a choice. You're going to die one way or the other; we all are sooner or later. Why not go out a national hero instead of just another bit of atomized meat?"

That did it. I looked the man straight in the eye. "Well, hell, Gen'rl," I cawed in my best southern-cracker-stoned-out-of-his-gourd-on-Wild Turkey-voice. "If'n ya put it that way, wha' the hay! Lits git on ta et!"

Yeah, I was out of my mind, but it had been one of those days, and all I wanted to do was get the damn thing over with. Tell you the God's honest truth, the Long Sleep just didn't look all that bad at that stage of the game. Fact was, I would welcome the opportunity to get some shut-eye.

At about quarter to six, Major Hogg dropped me off at the amusement park in a LAV displaying a white flag. It was one of those early evenings that Southern California was famous for before most of the radioactive dust settled—chartreuse sky highlighted with brilliant little explosions of light produced as bits and pieces of space debris more than a half century old burned up on contact with the atmosphere. The sun, all burnt orange and purple and shimmering through the haze and smoke of battle, was a couple of hours from setting. Plenty of daylight left for what had to be done.

Out of choice, as well as in compliance with Ramases' instruction, I was alone. The admiral had been forced to order Doone placed in a straitjacket when he'd heard what my plans were, and under armed guard he was at the moment being choppered back to the *Payton.* I missed him, but after taking one look at the man-made mountain rising out of the oily billows of ground smoke some half a mile away, I knew this would be no place for a kid . . .

On the day of the Big Blast, Anaheim had been far enough away from any of the various ground-zeros so that it and the amusement park for which it had once been famous had not been turned into powdered atoms. There were enough skeletons of buildings, rides, and attractions left standing so I could imagine what the place had looked like before the missiles struck. The mountain, with its painted-snow peak, still stood over the heart of this once-upon-a-time world of my grandparents' generation,

luring me on like some gigantic sweet as it had done to so many
millions before. I knew, instinctively almost, that whatever
destiny awaited me was somehow connected with that mountain,
a mountain that looked so lifelike, yet also so incongruous, so
make-believe.*

Without much further thought, I checked over my equipment
and weapons one last time, then climbed over a barrier of several
hundred rusty and bent turnstiles, which I assumed had once
guarded the park's main entrance. I had come to fulfill Ramases'
demand, but I had not come unarmed or unprepared. Admiral
Jascoolie had made sure that I had everything my heart desired
in the way of toys including a new multishot BUF-A3, a cranial
mounted infrared night vision device with heat imagery capabilities, an AT-16 LAW with a six rocket magazine, and the very
latest in FAC personal battle armor. If Ramases wanted my ass,
he'd have to dig for it.

The way I figured things, there were only two possible scener-
ios for this little encounter. One, Ramases would just send all his
boys at once in one big mob to stomp me into a puddle of
phlegm. Second—and the one break I was hoping for—was that
the idiot would want to play games with me before he personally
greased my hams.

As a consequence, rather than being frightened or alarmed, I
was kind of heartened when the lone Comanchero wearing the
huge plastic head of some fucking cartoon duck stepped out onto
Main Street and leveled a Thompson submachine gun at me.
Before he got off a shot, I aimed from the hip and put a bufgun
round right square in the middle of his beak, then watched in
amusement as the top third of his body went south for the winter.

Obviously Ramases wanted to play games. Relieved, I continued to walk towards the mountain, jacking another round into
the modified buf.

I'd only covered another hundred yards or so when I was as-
saulted by the amplified sound of an old-fashioned calliope play-

---

* *Editor's Note:* Upon the advice of our legal department, we cannot
divulge the name of either this mountain or the amusement park over
which it stood. All we can say is that its rodentlike corporate logo is still
world-famous, especially in France.

ing "It's a Small World After All," followed by a grenade rolling towards me down the absolutely spotless street.

There really wasn't time to react. The grenade exploded a few feet in front of me, sending a blast of hot shrapnel in my direction. Most of it clattered off the battle armor but a few birdshot-sized particles punctured the Plas-tex joints in the suit and penetrated my body.

Dismissing the pain and the blood, I immediately hit the deck and rolled out of the street, scrambling into a gutted ice-cream parlor once sponsored by Carnation. Peeking over the frame of a glassless window, I spotted three more ducks scurrying towards me, hell bent, I presumed, on avenging their uncle's death. One of them was carrying a loaded RPG launcher and I knew I had to get him first. The other two only held automatic rifles.

Patiently, I waited until the Comanchero with the rocket launcher stopped to take a bead on the ice cream parlor. Hugging the deck, I rolled into the open doorway, cranked off a lucky (admittedly) buf round that not only hit the X-ring, but found the dude's stash of extra RPG rounds as well, causing a sympatetic detonation that left only a scorched beenie-hat and a pair of smoking combat boots standing in the street.

The other two Comancheros, their costumes splattered with catsup-substitute and precooked brain matter, were on Queer Street thanks to the concussion of the blast. I easily stood and pumped a half a dozen forty-five caliber wad-cutters into each of their plump duck bodies. (As Black Pugh used to emphasize in his personal combat lectures—always use a handgun when you've got a sure thing; save your heavy ammo for the serious stuff.)

Hugh, Dew, and Lou were a cinch; the mouse's moll wasn't. She was waiting for me on a parapet of the castle, a fact I discovered only a few seconds before an energy beam from a particle weapon zapped my battle armor at groin level and knocked me into the cheap seats.

Typical broad, I recall thinking, always going for the nuts first.

I was flat on my back, and could smell the stench of burning Plas-tex and fiber steel, but my wanger was still there, which meant the beam had not penerated. Recalling that the recharge time for a particle weapon of that period was on the order of fifteen minutes, I was fairly confident that I was going to bag me a mouse when I rolled over and popped the clear plastic sight on my AT-16.

Sure enough, using the heat-seeking imagery scope over my left eye, I found the silhouette of the distaff member of the famous mouse duo cowering in one of the castle's steeples. While she desperately worked on the recharger, I sent the LAW round on its way with a quick depression of the firing key. A second later and the world was rid of another man-sized rat.

As pieces of mouse costume and castle steeple drifted down on my head, I made a quick heat-image scan for the Mick, but he was not in range, and I had no time to fart around due to the conflagration started by my rocket round. The whole damn castle was ablaze and I was forced to detour around the area in order to continue towards the mountain.

At a large man-made lagoon filled scummy black water and the broken parts of minisubmarines, I was pleased to dispatch a strange goofy creature that was, to my judgment, part dog and part horse, although to this day I can't be sure. The life-sized cartoon character of whatever-it-was came at me with twin Uzi submachine guns blazing, but I guess wearing such a large and deformed plastic head was detrimental to forming a good sight-picture because the Uzi slugs fell harmlessly to my rear. To steady my aim I propped the buf on a large sign that read Line Forms to the Right—Waiting Time One Hour and Forty-Five Minutes, dialed up the special *Grape* round on the bufgun's ammunition selector, then transformed the Comanchero bearing down on me into hamburger with a thousand tiny tacks traveling at 1,200 feet per second.

"I hope you didn't leave a deposit on that costume, pal," I roared, finally getting into the swing of things.

It was then that I noticed that one of the Uzi rounds had hit my right foot. Hurt like hell. The wounds from the grenade were starting to sting a little too, and it was getting a bit sticky inside the armor. Sticky, wet, and warm. I'd been holed a lot more seriously than I'd at first thought.

Wasn't much time for church services though. The huge castle fire and a shifting wind were blowing thick clouds of smoke in my path so I had no alternative except to take another detour. A few minutes later, as I limped past a collection of gigantic cups and saucers (yeah, sounds like pure foolishness, but I'm not kidding), things took a turn for the worse.

Hey, maybe if it hadn't been my own life on the line I would've found it all quite amusing, for there, suddenly blocking my path, was a particular hairy and ugly Comanchero all dressed up in drag, his over-and-under sawed-off twelve gauge trained on my navel. At first, I wasn't sure who this rump-ranger was suppose to be, what with his lady's bouffant wig of dark black hair, long dress with puffy sleeves and conservatively cut bodice, and heavy white pancake makeup on his face that only began to cover up the telltale signs of five o'clock shadow. Christ, I thought, what kind of kinky transvestite shit were my grandparents exposed to when they were kids? No wonder they'd grown up to be such slack-jawed cretins.

Then, as the weirdo with the black hair and ruby lips was joined by seven other park characters, each dressed as some sort of whimsical (if well-armed) dwarf, I suddenly knew who I was dealing with.

"Well, if it ain't Sleepin Beauty," I scoffed. "By the looks of it, honey, your wake-up call came a little too late."

Of course, I knew the character wasn't suppose to be Sleeping Beauty, but I figured it this way: obviously the dickhead in drag had spent a lot of time in preparation for this act. By pretending not to be able to ID him, I knew I would piss him off, maybe enough for me to get the drop on him.

It worked. As I stealthfully slipped a thermite grenade off my utility belt, I heard the numbskull say,

"Sleepin Beauty, your ass, man! Don't ya recognize Sno—"

I didn't give him the chance to finish his lines. The thermite grenade rolled under his skirt and went off.

"Baked beaver, anyone?" I shouted, as I methodically hosed down the startled dwarfs with one of the Uzis I'd taken off the dead goofball back at the sub pen. Large wet chunks of Sleepy, Bashful, Grumpy, and the rest of that motely crew went spinning off into the ether *(and no, I don't give a runny fart what the rest of their names were)*. By the time the Uzi clicked on empty, the whole "Whistle While You Work" bunch was history.

Bad luck. A couple of the miserable pint-sized losers had gotten off a few shots in my direction before they ate lead. As I once again took a bearing on that mountain, a white-hot shaft of pain nearly doubled me over.

When I stopped howling, I discovered a barbed spear round had taken me under the left arm where the battle armor was weak. Felt like the thing had gotten into a lung. I tried to tug it out, but the barb caught on a rib and I decided to leave it alone until I could get some sound professional advice from a FAC surgeon, not to mention a megadose of painkiller.

Breathing was going to be a problem. This heartening bit of information became abundantly clear before I'd taken a half a dozen steps. Just couldn't seem to get enough air, almost as if I had one of those plastic dry cleaner's bags wrapped over my head. As I staggered over to a convenient park bench and grabbed a seat, my vision blurred and I felt cold and clammy, nauseous. After coughing up about a tablespoon of pink-tinted fluid, I knew for certain that I wasn't operating at a hundred and ten percent anymore.

Hell, you've gotta lose some weight, Will, I remember scolding myself. Buy an exercise bike or start jogging or get a membership in a health club—something. You're a fat out-of-shape pig, man! Face it!

Wait a minute, pal, I admonished myself. Self-pity was not going to help. Too late for crash dieting or laying on the guilt. One quick way to lose forty pounds though—get rid of the battle armor.

Painfully and awkwardly, I shed myself of the cumbersome armor as well as all nonessential equipment and weaponry. By the time I finished, all I was left with was my blood-soaked long underwear, boots, and loaded bufgun.

Better, but I was still feeling a little queasy when I finally summoned the strength to get moving again. I had no other choice, however. The sun was about to set; long shadows had fallen across the park, the longest being thrown by that man-made mountain. In any other circumstance, darkness would have been my ally. In my present physical condition, though, I wasn't so sure I could make it through the night. I would either bleed to death, or pass out and then likely be discovered by the roving bands of costumed Comancheros. No, I had to get this absurd thing over and done with while there was still light to see.

Frankly, I just didn't want to die in the dark . . .

* * *

Evil incarnate was waiting for me, as it had been all my life.
When I at last dragged myself to the base of the mountain and
into the open-air structure where so many had once waited patiently for their E-ride thrill, he was waiting for me, standing in a
bobsled that sat at rest on a set of small-gauge railroad tracks.

Because of my sweat and pain, I could barely see him—a
blurry image of mankind's deepest and darkest fear—and for just
a moment I thought I was hallucinating. Ludicrously, he wore
the costumed head of The Mick, King of the Rats.

It was Ramases all right, though; there was no missing that
oiled muscle-bound body. With all the strength and rage I had
left, I tried to raise the bufgun and send him on a one-way ticket
to Haiti (sic). Yet even with the surge of adrenaline that accompanied the recognition of that monster, my body finally let me
down. The buf slipped out of my numbed fingers and clattered
uselessly to the deck. I fell to my knees and groped for it. It was
no use.

He was laughing. A high-pitched feminine laugh that cut
through me like slivers of glass. I felt a new flow of hot blood
gush from my chest as I tried unsuccessfully to stand. A weari-
ness I'd never experienced before overwhelmed me. Sleep, I
thought. Soon to sleep.

"Welcome to fantasyland, Bucko," I heard him say. "I've been
waiting to take you on a ride. Never thought you'd make it
through; you're tougher than I would've guessed."

"Eat fuck," I gasped.

"We'll see. In the meantime, I'm gonna enjoy watching you
pay the freight." I heard rather than saw him step out of the
bobsled. He walked over to where I lay and squatted down next
to my head. "Feeling a little fatigued are we, Bucko?" he asked in
that lispy fruity voice of his. "Plenty of time for beddy-by later. I
want you awake now, wide awake."

I summoned up one last ounce of strength and lunged for the
buf. My hand came up short. Ramases reached for something in
his belt, shifted his weight, then drove a mountain climber's piton
through my outstretched palm, pinning me to the deck.

My scream came from somewhere deep in the secret recesses of
my soul.

"Yes," he cackled, "that's what I like. I want to hear you

scream, my man. Want to hear you scream like I screamed when the RIHMs found out the information about the invasion you sold me was wrong. I could've ruled the world, Bucko, could've ruled the world. I knew they were all dying of the virus, that's why I threw in with them. They were going to destroy FAC, and I was going to step into the void when they were gone. Ramases, ruler of the planet. Nice ring to it, don't you think?"

"Bite my ass," I whispered.

"Hmmmm. Not a bad idea."

All I could do was watch as he slipped a huge fighting knife out of his belt and calmly cut a large slice from my buttock.

"Guests," he said, jamming the dripping piece of flesh into my face, "should be served first."

I spat at him, a pink-tinted mouthful. He laughed and tossed the morsel of meat away. "Maybe you're right," he said. "Probably tastes like shit. Let's get down to business, shall we? You're most likely wondering why I called this meeting—are you listening to me, Bucko?" He reached out and slapped my face. "Don't die on me now. I've got things to show you, things to tell you. For instance—do you have any idea what the RIHMs do to humans that betray them?"

He paused to lift the cartoon head from his shoulders. Even in a state of shock, I was incredulous. Far from the face of the aged pretty boy I'd seen in the Colorado camp, Ramases visage had been replaced by a big blotched purple and black bulb, all swollen and misshapen and oozing fluid. Nose, ears, lips, scalp—all were gone, hacked away by some chisellike instrument. At a few points glistening white bone had actually been exposed. Real real nasty-looking.

"Like it?" he asked.

"Hell, Ram," I managed, "I've never seen you without your makeup before. Must be hard getting dates."

He hissed and drove his knife blade deep into my thigh. I screamed again. Things were beginning to get repetitive.

"They flayed every inch of skin from my face, you FAC bastard!" Ramases screamed, the exposed muscles of his face twitching in tempo with his words. *"Every inch! With a dirty carpenter's plane."*

"Don't know what you're complaining about," I whimpered

from between gritted teeth. "Looks like you finally found a plastic surgeon who knew what he was doing."

Ramases twisted the blade in my leg, tearing and ripping. If he hit an artery it would be fade to black.

When I stopped screaming and opened my eyes, his big bruised turnip of a face was only inches from mine. He seemed pleased; at least he was grinning. Of course, maybe not having any lips made him look more amused than he really was.

"Don't worry, Bucko," he said. "I'm not going to let you die. Not yet. No way. I want you alive. To witness the end of the world!"

"Who are you trying to bullshit, Ram? You hit the button now and your own ass gets fried."

"Look at me, Bucko. There's no use going on looking like this."

"You've got a point. But listen, don't you think detonating a 10-megaton nuke is a little much for a simple suicide? Hell, hand me the buf and I'll do it for ya with about half a credit's worth of lead."

"No no no, Bucko," he said, shaking that horrible purple head of his that looked like an Anatomy-I handout on facial muscle structure. "I've got it all planned. Why do you think I waited for you? You and I are going out together, at the center of the fire storm, a fire storm which will undoubtedly produce another batch of RIHMs. *And maybe this time they'll win, Bucky-boy!*"

"Come on, you asshole," I argued. "You're still a human, no matter how awful you look. Haven't you got any loyalty to your own kind?"

He pulled the knife out of my leg and wiped the bloody blade on my longjohns. A sound that could've been a laugh came from somewhere inside him as he got to his feet.

"So naive, Bucko, so naive. It is because I am one of you that I wish to destroy you. How else does one become a god?"

Well, that did it. Another crackpot philosophy had been hatched in the land of La La. No use trying to talk him out of it. He was wacko. "Totally and fer sure," I think the correct terminology goes.

I watched him check the delicate-looking lady's Longines on his wrist, then look towards the west.

"Time I got going, Bucko," he said. "Sorry, but I'll have to leave you here. Only enough juice available to take one of us to the top of the mountain. So, choke on your own blood, as we used to say in the early days. And try to remember—in the last few minutes left to you—that you are responsible for all this."

"Oh sure," I answered with a phony sob, "and blame me for the *Challenger* disaster, the sinking of the *Lusitania,* and the Chicago Fire while you're at it. No way you're laying this on me, pal, no way."

My last-ever wise-ass remark got no response. He'd already turned and walked over to the control panel where I watched him throw a switch. A low electrical hum ensued, and I heard the clank of the bobsled's wheels on the track as the surge of power caused it to jump. Ramases climbed into the cockpit, pulled down the roll bar, then shouted in my direction.

"Bye-bye, Bucky-boy! I'll be on top of my mountain here if you need me for anything. Just remember, when the sun goes down, the dial lights up!"

"Roast in hell, you maniac," I gasped, but I'm sure he couldn't hear me because he'd released the brake on the ride and was already clattering off up the inclined track . . .

While the sounds of the bobsled faded, I tried to make my mind function. Was there anyway I could stop Ramases? I doubted it. Certainly couldn't follow him up the mountain. Still, if I could somehow get word to FAC, they might be able to hit the park with conventional weapons before he got to wherever he'd stashed the detonating device for his bomb.

With some vague illogical notion about dragging my disfigured butt out of the park to warn the admiral of the doublecross, I began to crawl, leaking blood with every move, creating more pain than I really had any way of handling. But I gave it a try. Inch by inch, I hauled my aching wounded body away from the mountain and back towards the main entrance of the park, hoping that the Comancheros had gotten wind of their boss's plan and had already beat feet out of there. If any of them were left, and caught me in the open, I'd be fileted like a piece of well-marbled tenderloin before Ramases had a chance to turn me into cosmic stuff.

I think I might've gotten about two hundred yards before I pooped out. Just couldn't move. Out of gas. Mind in a fog. Pain gone, replaced by a warm numbness that all but paralyzed my limbs. Good try, Bucko, I told myself, but it's time to let things ride. Maybe you'll come back in your next life as something safe and sane like a pinball mechanic, live a long and useful life, die of natural causes. This one, though, was pretty much *fini.*

Strange. Once I'd figured that this was all she wrote, a peaceful calm came over me. As I drifted gently towards death I couldn't help think back on my life and wonder how the balance sheet would look to the Big Guy at the home office. Probably the figures would be a tad in the red, but maybe he'd give me a break and let me off with time served.

It started getting cold. Wasn't that the usual sign? (Hell, I don't know. Maybe it had something to do with the sun setting.) From far away I heard the sound that had been music to my ears since the day I was born—the low throaty harsh roar of jet engines thrusting man and machine through the air faster than either had any right to go. The sound grew louder, coming my way it was, and I managed to roll over and look up into the darkening sky.

And then I saw it (as the late great Mike Nelson used to say), coming in low over the park, an F-1020 Cutter with the Day-Glo orange death-head painted on the tri-tail. The Death-Head Squadron, FACFS-6, Wolf Bucko's outfit. Suddenly I sensed that my old man had come to take me home.

"Yeah, well hell, Pop," I whispered, "what kept ya?"

He must've heard me because he dipped his wings as he passed directly overhead, a jet-jock's salute to a comrade. I tried to return the gesture, but nothing worked.

The phantom Cutter pulled into a tight, almost vertical climb and cut in afterburners. Straight up she flew, higher and higher into the purple sky. I watched in awe as the aircraft became only a faint glimmer far overhead, then disappeared entirely. The roar of its engines faded to a dull, faraway sound. My God, I thought, he's taking that bird right on up to the stars! Go for it, Pop! I closed my eyes and tried to imagine how good an electric blanket would feel.

Then, strangely, the song of the engines began to grow again. Reluctantly, I opened my eyes and was sure I could see Wolf Bucko's aircraft again, a pinpoint of reflected light that I might've been confusing with the Evening Star.

No. Moving too fast for that. The Wolf had put the Cutter into a dive. Straight goddamn vertical dive. He dropped like a bullet, coming right down on top of me. Hot shit, Pop, you gotta be pulling a negative ten g's. But come on, pedal to the metal, your boy is waiting. Been a lot of adventures since you left. I'll enjoy filling you in.

He hit Mach One when he was still at twenty grand, the subsequent sonic boom joyously rattling my teeth and breaking my eardrums. Hot damn! He was still in the dive! He'd have that bird cranked up to three thousand knots by the time he got to me! That's the way a real jet-jock goes out, I told myself, faster than he's ever gone before.

Closer and closer came my final vision, the roar growing louder and louder in my head, even though I was deaf. It wasn't until the last possible second that I saw—somewhat confusingly —that Wolf had overshot me and instead was heading straight for—

The explosion was more realistic than I would've supposed for a dream. I remember seeing the silver blur of the Cutter going into the mountain, then a gigantic ball of fire filled my sight, followed by a blast of heat so intense that only the gutter I was lying in saved me from being immediately turned into one big cinder. As it was, as I felt my hair melt and smelled the unmistakable stench of human flesh being broiled, I mercifully slipped across the river and called it a day . . .

Epilogue

It wasn't until some weeks later, when I was finally released from the Intensive Care Unit and put on the ward with the other casualties of the Battle of the L.A. Basin, that I learned the truth of what happened. Jumpin Jack Fry told me, on one of his infrequent but short visits to my bedside.

After the explosion (nonnuclear), a FAC Commando unit had rushed the burning park. Through some stroke of incredible luck, they'd found me—more dead than alive—and within minutes had me on a MEDIVAC chopper headed for the medical facilities aboard the *Payton*. Burned, holed, and otherwise maimed, the surgeons didn't give me much chance of surviving, but I fooled 'em all. I'd never tap dance again, and would need a number of skin grafts and a new method of taking a crap, but I was going to make it.

The Cutter I'd seen augering into the fake mountain had been real. Wasn't the ghost of Wolf Bucko at the stick, though, but Lieutenant Colonel Melodie Lane . . .

Jumpin Jack played me the black-box cockpit tape recording, but it didn't mean much to me, mainly because Mel was so far gone that about all you could hear was a confusion of spits and gurgles and gargles. FAC translation teams worked long and hard, however, and eventually they determined that she had kamikazied into the mountaintop singing an old Kenny Rogers tune called "Let's Go Out in a Blaze of Glory."

The story of Melodie's last mission, as it was pieced together by others for the citation awarding her a posthumous Medal of Honor, went something like this: After being released from the hospital in Detroit, she had requested and been given command of FAC Fighter Squadron Six, even though most medical experts gave her, at the most, six months to live. She had led the Death-Head Squadron against the RIHMs at Monterey Bay, but in the midst of the battle, for reasons no one could immediately explain, she had broken from contact and turned the command over to her XO with orders to her wingman not to follow. She had last been seen on radar headed south.

Headed south to Anaheim, it turned out.

Apparently Mel had monitored the Invasion Force's Command frequency and had heard about Ramases and his extortion scheme, and the fact that FAC was pulling back to prevent the bastard from setting the nuke off. According to recordings of all radio transmissions at that time, however, there was no way for her to know I was involved; my name was never mentioned.

She must have known of her genetic infection by then of course, even if her doctors didn't—known that she was transforming into a RIHM. Unlike Darvon and Frank Tibbs, I believe, she did not welcome or accept this as her fate, choosing instead to take her own life rather than become one of the enemy. Understandable. She'd spent nearly her whole career fighting the mutants; to become one of them must have seemed like the lowest form of treason to her. So she went out with all the blaze of glory sixteen tons of napalm hanging on her wing pylons could produce.

How did she know Ramases would be on the mountain? I don't know, although given his psychological profile rap sheet it was a pretty good guess that's where he'd be. Guy was a megalomaniac. Where else would he be except a place symbolic of domination?

Another question. How did Melodie know she wouldn't set off the nuke herself? Actually, she was taking a fairly safe risk since a fusion weapon comparable to the one Ramases had requires the equivalent of an atom bomb to set it off. I suppose Mel was gambling that Ramases couldn't get to the detonator in time once he realized that she was going to crash his party.

So everything associated with her final flight—obtained from available facts or logical deduction—was explainable. Well, almost everything. A couple of questions still haunt my mind. For instance, if Mel didn't know I was down there, how could you explain the waggle of wings when she flew over me? And how about the precise timing which brought her in at the very moment I'd pulled myself away from danger and then could go no farther—was that pure chance too?

Perhaps. But to my dying day, I will believe she knew I was there, that there was—and always had been—a place in her soul for Will Bucko. On the transcript of the black-box recording, her very last words were officially listed as "garbled." Over the years, I've listened to that tape a million times and you will never convince me that she was not calling my name . . .

And so it is time to bring my tale to an end. There were other adventures, both past and future, but they had no bearing on the main thread of this story. Besides, after what had happened during those few days on the Coast, life kind of lost its luster for me. No longer would danger and intrigue get the juices flowing or the sap rising or the blood burning or any one of another hundred or so cliches common to stories such as mine.

Maybe Doone was right, maybe I was just getting old, but maybe I'd just seen one too many friends of my childhood pass away. Maybe I was seeing, for the first time, a true picture of my own mortality, I don't know. Things are never as clear as they were when you were seventeen. Good and evil, friend and foe, pain and pleasure, love and hate—they all seem to mush together over the decades until they all look the same, bland and gray and without much heat. And I suppose that's good, for too easily the passions of youth can break the heart and soften the brain. Be advised . . .

Good-bye and God bless.

Canker Bay, Maine
1 March 2068

Editor's Note

On October 5th, 2046, Brevet Lieutenant Colonel William Thomas Bucko, Commanding Officer of FACFS-8, was awarded the Congressional Medal of Honor for actions above and beyond the call of duty during the Battle of the L.A. Basin; in particular, the events at the Anaheim Amusement Park. The medal was conferred on him by the President of the United States on the steps of the United States Service Academy at Quantico. The event marked the third time the nation's highest award for heroism had been presented to Colonel Bucko, making him the only person in the history of the United States to be so honored . . .

On February 28th, 2082, Colonel William Bucko, USFAC (ret.), passed away in his sleep at his home in Canker Bay, Maine. He was seventy-eight years old. He is survived by his wife, Chandelier, three children, and fourteen grandchildren.

The guy was a real piece of work.

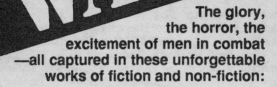

WAR

The glory,
the horror, the
excitement of men in combat
—all captured in these unforgettable
works of fiction and non-fiction:

☐ **BATTLE FOR HUE, TET,** 1968 (NF)
by Keith William Nolan 10407-6 $4.95

☐ **BODY COUNT** (F)
by William Turner Huggett 20093-8 $4.95

☐ **DELTA FORCE** (NF)
by Col. Charlie A. Beckwith
and Donald Knox 11886-7 $3.95

☐ **MISSION M.I.A.** (F)
by J.C. Pollock 15819-2 $3.95

☐ **WAR STORY** (NF)
by Jim Morris 19362-1 $4.50

At your local bookstore or use this handy coupon for ordering:

DELL READERS SERVICE, DEPT. DW1
P.O. Box 5057, Des Plaines, IL. 60017-5057

Please send me the above title(s). I am enclosing $_____.
(Please add $2.00 per order to cover shipping and handling.) Send
check or money order—no cash or C.O.D.s please.

Ms./Mrs./Mr._____

Address_____

City/State _____ Zip _____

DW1–2/89

Prices and availability subject to change without notice. Please allow four to six
weeks for delivery. This offer expires 8/89.